Shirley Phillips

THE BIG SPENDER

Limited Special Edition. No. 4 of 25 Paperbacks

Through her existence as an army officer's wife and a long career as a professional nurse, the author had many events to put into words. Writing has always been a hobby, with no consideration for her work to be published. The quality of her work being recognised by Austin Macauley changed her life.

Shirley Phillips

THE BIG SPENDER

AUSTIN MACAULEY PUBLISHERS™

LONDON • CAMBRIDGE • NEW YORK • SHARJAH

A CIP catalogue record for this title is available from the British Library.

ISBN 9781528917254 (Paperback)
ISBN 9781528961837 (ePub e-book)

www.austinmacauley.com

First Published (2019)
Austin Macauley Publishers Ltd
25 Canada Square
Canary Wharf
London
E14 5LQ

Thanks to my son, who encouraged me to continue writing after the death of his father—my husband.

Table of Contents

Chapter 1
Lottery Night

The two lounges of The Sunshine Mount Nursing Home were snug and warm. The yellow-curtained windows glowed golden from the outside; attractive to visitors and possible future residents. The damp, cold autumn air of late October 1998 held a promise of an early winter. Winter was always early in Pendarren. Each day at the home was barely different from the one before. When someone died, the atmosphere was gloomier, but a little interest was roused when a day or two later the residency welcomed someone new.

Saturday was different. It was the night of The National Lottery Draw and most of the twenty elderly residents of Willow Unit lounge were with avid interest on the big television screen in the corner of the spacious room. They waited for the programme to start.

Crippled Bronwen Dew, one of the residents, had twice won ten pounds. It gave hope to every lottery player in Willow Lounge for winning ten pounds. Possibly more; perhaps millions. That would certainly cause a stir at the home. It would cause a stir throughout the town, come to that.

Just before the programme started, the buzz of excitement would reach its crescendo, and then abate when the numbers were being called.

The carers had not long cleared the tables after supper. Some of the residents were still at the tables; their lottery tickets in front of them. Usually everyone moved into the lounge area to watch the television. The view of the big screen wasn't good from the dining tables, but the sound could be clearly heard, and that was the more important.

Those few who hadn't bought tickets to play knew better than to interrupt the quietude needed to hear the numbers being called, but there was still a little time before the programme began. It was a quarter to eight o'clock, so the bustle of excitement hadn't yet turned to silence.

As well as the possibility of winning, Bronwen enjoyed The National Lottery Draw programme. Listening to the banter of what her companions would do if they won millions of pounds amused her.

A voice was heard. 'What would you do with your millions if you win, Arthur?'

'I'd buy a' aeroplane and fly. Never been up in a 'plane. Always wanted to.'

A longing voice broke in. 'I'd go to one of those lovely islands with palm trees, and where it's always warm and sunny, and where the women dance in grass skirts.'

'But who would wash you and take you to the lav, Brynly?'

'I would pay a hundred pounds to anyone who took me,' Brynly laughed at himself, irritating his miners' coal-dust lungs, which brought on a bout of coughing.

'Your winnings wouldn't last long then, Brynly,' cackled Tilley Tittle-tattle, so called because of her interested in other people's affairs and her enjoyment of gossip.

'What would you do then, Tilley?' someone asked.

Tilley frowned. 'Nothing. What the hell good would a load of money do me? No amount of money would change this.' She referred to the paralysed left side of her body; the result of a stroke.

'What are you doing the lottery for then, Tilley?'

'Give to my kids. They'd soon make short change of it.'

Jack Sharp, also a victim of a stroke in his seventies, voiced his plan if he won. 'I'd get one of them funny scooter bikes I see people riding when I'm took to town. I see fellers older than me driving 'em.'

'Them's mobility scooters,' Beryl Thomas said. 'Women drive them as well. If I won a million, I'd buy one and go hell for leather on it till I got home.'

Beryl often talked about going home, though she knew it had been sold to pay for her residency at The Sunshine Mount Nursing Home. She liked to pretend she would be going home one day. No one spoiled her dream by reminding her of the bitter truth.

Beryl went on. 'If I win, I'd have a lovely new kitchen put in,' She sighed, perhaps realising the impotence of that dream.

'Bronwen, what would you do if you won millions of pounds?' a voice called across the room.

The victim of poliomyelitis as a child, disabled Bronwen Dew had to twist her head around to face her questioner. It was legless diabetic Tom Daly; two lower limbs amputated in his fifties.

'Give half to you, Tom, if I won a million. But I'd be satisfied with another ten pounds. I've had two ten-pound wins with three numbers up and they say third time lucky, don't they? But I suppose it would go where any extra cash I do have goes; into my Mary's purse.' Mary, Bronwen's daughter, always cadged money from the small weekly amount her mother received.

'Well if I win,' Tom replied, 'you and I would travel the world before either of us leaves it.'

Bronwen grinned. 'How would we do that, Tom, when we haven't a good leg between us?'

'He'd pay someone to carry the two of you,' someone suggested. 'In a wheelbarrow, I expect.'

That remark was followed by a loud burst of laughter.

'Shut up, the lot of you,' someone else shouted. 'If we don't have a bit of hush, we won't even hear the numbers, let alone win.'

'How much must be won to buy a miracle?' Blind, paraplegic, seventy-two-year-old Harry Bright thought he spoke to himself, but he was heard by those around him. No one replied.

The time was getting near to the big draw and the residents started chatting quietly between themselves, telling each other what they would do if they won a million.

Bronwen spoke to Tilley, sitting opposite her in an upright chair, her paralysed arm supported by pillows.

'You know, Tilley, if I won a few thousand, I would fly to America. To New York. Me and Lewis often talked about it, especially after we'd been to the pictures. That's what I'd do; go to America.' She sighed before flattening the pages of her notepad and poising her pen to take down the numbers. 'Right then, eyes down. The run-up is about to start. Funny my Mary hasn't come yet, though.'

'Don't worry,' Tilley responded, 'she'll come waddling in, in a minute. And I think you'd have to win more than a few thousand to go to America, 'cause you'd have to take her with you.'

Bronwen didn't like the way Tilley described her daughter's way of walking, so said nothing. It hurt because it wasn't far from the truth.

As she scurried up to the main entrance, thirty-one-year-old Mary Dew gasped. The hill approaching The Sunshine Mount Nursing Home was steep and she was late. It was ten minutes to eight o'clock, and she was usually there before half-past seven.

The nursing home looked cheerful and welcoming. The curtains of the ground floor windows had been drawn and beamed warmth and comfort to the outside cold mist of approaching night.

Mary was worn out after her scurry up the hill. She was unused to bursts of energy.

The more she avoided energetic movements the slower and tardier she became, not realising she wasn't doing the best for herself.

Her partially paralysed mother, Bronwen Dew, was wondering why she was late; what had happened to her. Not that anything other than the mundane ever happened to Mary. Being more than three stones overweight didn't help grace her movements or add interest to her ordinary, everyday life.

Having inherited the unflattering features of her father's face didn't help. She considered Mother Nature to have been unfair. She had his wide nose and heavy jaw-line, yet she wasn't blessed with his dark, almost black, thick curling hair. However, she did have his wide, brown eyes, even, strong, white teeth and an appealing smile. But Mary rarely smiled. She rarely laughed, either. When hearing a joke, she had to have the punch line explained. By then the humour was lost.

Bronwen, her mother, was beautiful. Her fine features and wide, long-lashed grey eyes were often admired. Though paralysed from groins to ankles, she had fine bearing. Her stance was graceful and her head held high, even when she manoeuvred her wheelchair to wherever she wished it to go.

Mary had her mother's tawny-coloured, straight lustrous tresses. It was elegant the way she wore it, but Mary considered it old-fashioned.

Mary, all too often, put her hair into the hands of the hairdressers in the town to practise their skills. Consequently, her hair had been over-permed, over-bleached, highlighted and dyed into every available shade. The trauma her hair had endured left it lustreless, dry and without style of any description.

Bronwen guessed why Mary was late visiting her that night—she'd had a hairdressing appointment. She looked forward to seeing her daughter but despaired of seeing what might have been done to her hair. There was no telling what to expect when she turned up at the nursing home on a Saturday evening.

'Thank goodness there are only three hairdressers in town she can go to,' Bronwen said to Tilley.

'Yes,' Tilley agreed, 'she'll turn up here bald one day if you don't put a stop to it.'

Mary always thought her hair looked lovely after letting a hairdresser try out a new style on her. She was blind to the reason for the stares of others. She was deaf to spiteful remarks and giggles.

Mary tried too hard to improve her appearance and the result was usually an unsightly mess. Her dress-sense made her mother cringe when she turned up in clothes meant for an elegant eighteen-year-old. Bronwen was too kind to pass disparaging remarks. She loved her daughter as any mother loved her child. She wouldn't deliberately hurt Mary or disillusion her. She tried to protect her from the hurtfulness of others. They wouldn't understand that Mary's immature behaviour was the result of being born deprived of intellectual development.

Bronwen realised that Mary, at the age of thirty-one, shouldn't have to be protected, but she couldn't cope without advice and support. The concern of how her daughter would manage after her death was a blight on Bronwen's existence.

It saddened her to know Mary wasn't likely to have the joy of being married and being a mother herself. She knew Mary dreamed of being married and having babies. It seemed she was doomed to spinsterhood, unless a poor, boring man, no other woman wanted, happened along and asked for her hand in marriage. If that happened and Mary accepted, it would be her misfortune to discover, too late, that he was a blackguard, or of some such character.

Mary didn't attract males and she had few female friends, apart from her neighbours and the carers at the home. Bronwen was grateful to her close friend, Stella Vaughan, a senior carer at the home, for her endeavours to improve Mary's life-style. Stella felt partly responsible for Mary's well-being. This was not only because of her love for Bronwen, but because of the strong feelings she had in her heart for Mary; much like that for a young sister.

Stella was thirty-four and lived with her unmarried brother, Colin Pritchard, since her divorce from Steven Vaughan. They lived in King Street, the next street of terraced houses parallel with Queen Street, where Mary lived.

Bronwen was also grateful for the support of some of Mary's close neighbours when Bronwen left to go into a nursing home. They helped by keeping an eye on her, in case she became ill or had an accident. She was prone to switching things on when they should be off and vice versa.

There were some who had given up on her. To them she was simply lazy and uncaring.

She lived on her own in the house which both she and Bronwen were born. It had become increasingly neglected with Mary's lack of enthusiasm and coping ability. She didn't possess the scintillating personality of her mother which, perhaps, would have made up for her shortcomings.

Bronwen and her late husband, Lewis Dew, were blessed with Mary when Bronwen was in her late thirties. Because of Bronwen's physical disability, they didn't expect to become parents.

As a child Bronwen had contracted poliomyelitis. She was six when the devil disease took her. It was thought she wouldn't survive the severe affliction. She did, but was paralysed. Her parents, John and Dilys Pugh, considered that God had been kind to them when all He did to Bronwen was disfigure and paralyse her legs. They thanked Him for allowing them to keep her, even though she would never live a normal life. They certainly didn't expect her to marry and bear a child.

The birth of Mary was long and difficult, the trauma of which was to the detriment of the child's subsequent development. She had a learning difficulty and her doting parents realised she wouldn't thrive without constant supervision. They accepted that her abilities wouldn't reach to an acceptance into a college to pave the way for an academic and professional future, as they had hoped. She could barely read and write. However, they loved her dearly.

Bronwen met Lewis Dew when she was twenty-four and he ten years older. She had resigned herself to her wheelchair and to being an "old maid", until one Saturday night when her father brought Lewis home to share their supper.

John, Bronwen's father, and Lewis had been drinking together at the Colliers' Arms. Lewis became a regular Saturday night visitor to the Pughs' home after that.

Lewis wasn't handsome, but he was strong, tall and broad-shouldered. He had a thick thatch of dark brown, curling hair; his crowning glory. His voice matched his size yet was that of a kind and gentle man. He had wide, soft brown eyes, a quick wit and an easy sense of humour. To Bronwen, he was as entertaining as Charlie Chaplin and as handsome as Lesley Howard, the famous film star. She fell in love with Lewis, but never did she think he could have the same feeling for her. She was a cripple; lifeless from her thighs to her ankles. With the aid of ugly boots attached to metal bars which, she thought, resembled scaffolding on a collapsing building, she was able to stand for just a few minutes on her legs—bones covered with skin.

As a result of circumstances which increased with the time spent together, the relationship between Bronwen and Lewis became a mutually loving one.

It began because of a yearning Bronwen's mother, Dilys, had for a glass and brick lean-to to be built between the scullery of their terrace house and the wall of the adjoining one. In the terrace of forty houses where they lived, she had seen several of her neighbours built-on structures and wondered if it were possible for them, the Pughs, to have one.

'It would be nice to have a glasshouse built onto the scullery, like the Joneses and Philpins, John. It would be handy to keep things tidy.'

'Yes, love, let's think about it,' John had replied. 'With sculleries being added to every other house in the street, I can't see why we can't have one. I'm not sure we can afford it, though.'

Unnoticed by Dilys, John kept back a few shillings from his pay packet until he had enough cash to buy the building materials from a hardware shop in the town.

The building would cover the outside lavatory and coal-hatch and provide space to store buckets, bowls and the tin bathtub.

John asked his good friend, Lewis Dew, for his help and advice. They were both miners with skill for hewing coal and erecting pit-props. They had little knowledge of building structures, other than knowing it involved bricks and mortar, and in this case, large panes of glass.

Lewis agreed to help John to build the extension. It took more time than expected; allowing time for Lewis to fall in love with Bronwen.

Dilys was delighted with the glass and brick extension. She thought it the best in the street. It didn't matter to her that on wet, windy days the roof leaked, and rain ran down its walls.

Lewis was sorry when the extension was completed because then he had no excuse to go to the Pughs' home to be near Bronwen.

He confessed his feeling for her and asked John and Dilys for permission to ask Bronwen to marry him.

Lewis didn't see Bronwen as a cripple. He saw her as the sensitive and beautiful woman that she was; long lashed, soft grey eyes, big in her flawless face of peaches and cream and a sunny smile which always played about her pretty lips.

She was gentle and kind. This was evidenced by the many friends who called to see her to share joys and sorrows. She had a compassionate nature and a striking personality; no one became bored in Bronwen's company.

John and Dilys were apprehensive about how Lewis would cope with Bronwen's disability. They wondered how he'd feel when he saw Bronwen's wasted legs. Bronwen did, too. She made a point of removing the shawl which covered them so that he could see their unsightliness. Her intention was to give him the opportunity to change his mind about wanting to marry her, if he so wished.

'Look, Lewis, they're like sawn off broom-handles. Are you sure you want to marry them?' Bronwen expected to see shock on Lewis's face.

He went on his knees, leant forward and kissed both her legs.

'To me they are beautiful. Everything about you is beautiful. I love you more than I thought I could love anyone. Please, marry me, Bronwen. But before you say yes, I'd better tell you, my legs wouldn't win any prizes either. Legs don't matter. I love you, and always will.'

Bronwen laughed as much with happiness of him still wanting her, as with his humour.

They had a simple wedding and afterwards made their home with John and Dilys at 22, Queen Street, Pendarren. Bronwen and Lewis had a blissfully happy marriage. 22, Queen Street was a home of love and laughter.

As it happened, Lewis managed Bronwen's incapacity better than John and Dilys had. He was strong and for the first time in her life Bronwen saw a little of what went on beyond Queen Street.

When he wasn't at work, Lewis took her shopping to the nearby town, to the open market. There were day-outings to the seaside and on Sunday evenings to chapel.

He was proud to push her wheelchair to wherever they went. He would cradle-lift her as if she were featherweight, before settling her safely seated on a normal chair. He parked her wheelchair in a place out of everyone's way, until it was time to lift her onto it to go home.

When they were blessed with Mary, named after Lewis's mother, she was looked upon as a gift from Heaven; a miracle.

They had little money, though considered themselves wealthy, having each other and Mary. It ended after thirty years, when a massive heart attack took Lewis.

Bronwen was devastated. When he was taken, a piece of her went with him. She would have lost the will to live were it not for having Mary to care for, and her parents to comfort her.

Mary was fifteen when her father died. He had thought her beautiful and repeatedly told her so. No one flattered Mary again, except her mother and grandparents.

It was ironic that both Bronwen's parents outlived Lewis; but not for long. First her father, then months later her mother passed away. Bronwen and Mary found themselves on their own.

Without her parents, and especially without Lewis's love and physical care, Bronwen found it impossible to run the household. Being wheelchair-bound, she wasn't able to care for herself and Mary, as well as maintaining the home. She had to increasingly depend on Mary, who'd had nothing to do with her care when her father and grandparents were alive.

Mary was out of her depth when it came to helping her mother or managing the home. She couldn't, adequately, care for herself.

For the first time in her life and to the detriment of her health, Bronwen had to take the helm of running the household. Trying to keep things ticking over after the terrible loss of Lewis and then her parents, proved too much for handicapped, broken-hearted Bronwen.

The home became neglected. She was ashamed when people called. It was malodorous and disorderly. The contents of the shelves of the pantry diminished. Even when she made out a clear, itemised shopping list for Mary, she proved incapable of replenishing the small stock of food that was essential. Invariably, she bought the wrong items and ate out in the town's cafes to satisfy her ravenous appetite, rather than go home to prepare a meal to share with her mother.

Bronwen budgeted carefully to ensure all the bills could be paid, but she failed. Their weekly financial allowances didn't stretch to Mary's irresponsible spending.

'I'd have to be a millionaire to pay these bills and keep up with your spending, Mary,' Bronwen had once told her.

'I wish you were a millionaire,' Mary had replied. 'You could pay someone to do all the washin' and cleanin'.' She giggled. 'An' empty your commode,' Mary was inarticulate, however much her mother attempted to correct her.

Mary's irresponsible behaviour depressed Bronwen. She carried on as best she could, for as long as she could. She was able to set the table, clean vegetables and wash up afterwards. Being in a wheelchair made it difficult to reach the cupboard shelves in the living room-cum-kitchen, or the rings of the gas cooker in the scullery. For her, the handling of hot pots and pans was unsafe.

To prepare wholesome meals, she had to rely on Mary, who had little idea of how to cook, despite her mother's teaching and supervising. Mary became fat as Bronwen became thin. She didn't seem to notice her mother having to survive on bread and butter, cakes and biscuits. Mary would eat those, then go out and gorge herself at the corner fish-and-chip shop. When she brought some home for Bronwen, they were cold and inedible.

Bronwen's near neighbour, Dulcie Curtis, could see what was happening, so when putting out the family's meals, she would set an extra plate for Bronwen—but only for her, not Mary. Mrs Curtis considered her big and old enough to cater for herself. This embarrassed Bronwen, resulting in her keeping the meals warm for Mary. Mary ate and enjoyed Dulcie's meals and told her so. The meals stopped coming.

Since the house became disorganised and unclean, the many people who used to call on Bronwen stopped doing so. The shame of that and Mary's lack of ability to manage, also deterred Bronwen from having community carers in.

She'd had to try to stop using the commode at night because Mary wouldn't empty and clean it when necessary. It didn't matter during the day when Bronwen was able to wheel herself to the outside toilet, but during the cold winter nights that was difficult and dangerous.

Consequently, she decided their lives had to change.

'I have to go away, Mary. We can't manage here,' Bronwen spoke with tears in her eyes.

Mary looked surprised. 'Go away, Mammy? Why? We'll manage here. I'll try harder. Anyway, where will you go?'

'Into the nursing home, my lovely. It's not far, so you can visit me when you want to.'

That seemed to appeal to Mary. 'That'll be all right. It's like a posh hotel. I'll visit you every day.'

Bronwen asked her social worker, who called from time to time, to arrange her admission to a nursing home; The Sunshine Mount Nursing Home. It was a walking distance from Queen Street.

'I've been expecting you to make that decision, Mrs Dew. To be honest, you've taken longer than I expected, but I had to let the decision come from you,' Miss Ellis, the social worker, spoke with sadness in her eyes. 'After all, you're just in your fifties. That's too young for going into a nursing home for the elderly. But you can always come home if you change your mind.'

'We both know there'll be no turning back,' Bronwen replied.

The social worker's eyes welled with tears. 'I'm so sorry you have to leave your home, which holds many happy memories.'

'Come now, Miss Ellis, no need for you to get upset. As you said, I can always come back. Perhaps I have a rich relative in Australia, or somewhere, who will die and leave me a million pounds. I'll come back then. I'll be able to have ten carers to look after me.' Bronwen wiped away her tears and tried to put on a bright smile; but she didn't feel like smiling.

Miss Ellis had recognised that Mary didn't have the inclination or the ability to help her mother. It was mutually agreed that Bronwen's decision was best and Mary should live on in the home and learn to look after herself. But she didn't learn; it was beyond her capabilities.

Not long before he died, Lewis had purchased their house for a reasonable price as a sitting tenant. His life's savings paid for it; a nest egg for himself and Bronwen, for when in their dotage. He and Bronwen had decided it would be a good investment for Mary's future and they would start saving again for their old age. Of course, at that time they didn't realise fate was about to change their lives.

The house was now Mary's. Initially, she was pleased with the arrangement of her mother moving into a nursing home. She wouldn't have to concern herself about her mother's disablement. She wouldn't have her mother continually chastising her for not keeping the house clean, for not doing the laundry or for lying abed until mid-day. She wouldn't be obliged to prepare food; she would buy food which didn't need preparing and cooking, or go to the fish-and-chip shop. As well as this, she would visit her mother at the nursing home every day and meet more people.

Mary gave no thought to her mother being wrenched away from the home in which she had been born and where she had enjoyed many happy years. Also, she didn't realise her mother was young to reside at a nursing home with all others who were much older than she. Bronwen did, but the companionship she would gain would be better than the imprisonment and loneliness she suffered in the home which was once her paradise.

Though handicapped by partial immobility, Bronwen had a keen, sharp mind and kept herself as active as her paralysis would allow. Her arms had become strong, having to do the job of her legs. They were her hoist between chair and bed, to and from chair and toilet or commode.

Miss Ellis helped Bronwen to pack her cases for moving into The Sunshine Mount Nursing Home. Tears misted their eyes, but not Mary's. She looked on with a lugubrious expression, not fully understanding the heartbreak of her mother. She thought she should be glad to have a nice warm room without having to worry about the cost of the gas, the electricity bills, the food bills, or her commode not being emptied and cleaned.

However, it didn't take long for Mary to discover that her mother's move to the nursing home didn't make life as carefree as she had expected. She missed her and realised how much she had done in the home despite her handicap.

Mary didn't know when to change the sheets on her bed or how to wash and iron them. She ran out of her unemployment benefit before she was due for more, so she wheedled money from her mother's purse. Mary was always running out of money.

Bronwen had spent all the money she and Morgan had saved for that rainy day. In the nursing home Bronwen worried about how to finance Mary. She couldn't manage on her income.

Bronwen had a weekly allowance which was ample for her needs, so what she didn't spend went to Mary or into the home's collection box. She often wished for a little fortune to be thrown into her lap, or that Mary would get work somewhere, to earn just a little money. However, that was never to be.

Since Mary left school she'd had a number of positions, but none seemed to be within her abilities to meet the expectancies.

Eventually, after long periods between employments, she became permanently unemployable. It was recognised that she was unable to overcome her learning difficulty.

She didn't like early rising and her parents and grandparents had spoilt her—little Mary needed her sleep. They allowed her to stay in bed until she felt like getting up. Consequently, she thought that was the norm.

When first her father died and then her grandparents, she found her days of staying in bed until she felt like getting up were over, until her mother was admitted to The Sunshine Mount Nursing Home.

Thereafter, Bronwen did her best to organise Mary's life from her chair in the lounge of the nursing home. She wished she had enough money to employ someone to look after her daughter, but that was a pipe dream. Mary was a constant worry. She was blind to her mother's concern and it wasn't revealed.

Bronwen's friends, the other residents and carers at the home, clearly saw the position. There were times when hints were dropped to Mary in attempts to stop her causing her mother's discontent.

'Why don't you pull yourself together, Mary? Your mother gives you all she can, but look at you—you look a sight.' Dora, a senior carer, considered she knew Bronwen and Mary well enough to speak her mind.

Dora wasn't the only one who told Mary to pull herself together. The younger carers did too. Mary was indifferent to the remarks, but when Bronwen was near enough to hear them, she gave hard looks—the limit of her threatening nature. It was, temporarily, enough to put a stop to the interference.

Mary's existence seemed to be restricted to daily visits to the nursing home, but it was a duty she, unnecessarily, inflicted upon herself. Bronwen hadn't planned it that way. She would have liked to see Mary with some specific interest of her own and living a normal life. However, she needed to see her luckless daughter often to ensure she was coping all right on her own. Bronwen, herself, couldn't have done much about it if she weren't, except to involve friends and neighbours. She did that only as a last resort. She was too sensitive to give others the responsibility, unless it was necessary.

People knew that Bronwen wouldn't use them unnecessarily. She was well thought of by all who knew her and they, more often than not, took their troubles to her. She was a good listener and always gave comfort and reassurance.

Her good friend and carer, Stella, was a godsend. She would burst in on Mary at home when she least expected it.

'Good god. This house is like the tip. Come on, Mary, move yourself. Let's get some shape here. Your mother would blow her top if she saw this.'

Mary knew her mother wouldn't "blow her top". Bronwen wouldn't lose her temper, however riled. Stella helped Mary to change her bed-sheets, helped her to clean up and wash piles of dishes and pots and pans that had gathered about the scullery sink. They would be covering the tables and usually scattered on and under chairs throughout the house.

Mary was glad of the help. She loved Stella and since she lived in the next street, it was easy to get to when she needed help. Mary often needed help. Luckily, her house in Queen's Street was a short walk away from where Stella lived.

In the beginning of Bronwen's residence at the home, hardly a day went by when one of her neighbours or friends from the nearby streets didn't call to chat and to ensure she was well. As time passed, the visits decreased and eventually they became months apart. Only her good friend, Dulcie Curtis, living just a few doors away from Mary, at 16, Queen Street, and Bronwen's two cousins, Ruth and Edna, continued to visit her regularly. Mary, however, visited her mother every evening. It was the main event of her social life.

Chapter 2
Awful Lot of Money

After her energetic dash up the hill, Mary leant against the stout wall of the main entrance to The Home. She pressed the prominent brass bell in the panel at the side of the heavy, locked door.

The door was always locked to keep people in, rather than to keep people out. It was a safety measure, to prevent the elderly-confused letting themselves out to make their way home. Sometimes their confusion refused to let them admit that their real homes had been sold to pay for their present existence. Their predicament saddened Bronwen. However, she felt confident that her home; hers, Lewis's and Mary's, would not be sold to pay for her care. The house was legally Mary's and had been for long enough not to be taken from her.

Mary hadn't caught her breath when a uniformed carer opened the door before the clang of the bell had faded away. After dark, the door was locked to late visitors.

'Oh, that was quick,' Mary said with surprise. 'It was as if you was standing in the 'all waitin' for me.' The staff and residents had become used to Mary's lugubrious tone and slow perception.

'Come on in quick, Mary,' the carer snapped. She was in a hurry. 'I was just passing through the hall on my way to Willow Lounge to take the lottery numbers. It'll be starting any minute.' She ran off.

Of course, Mary remembered. It was Saturday night. National Lottery night. She rummaged in her handbag for her lottery ticket. She couldn't find it, but it was there somewhere, unless it had dropped out of her purse when she was in town that afternoon.

She'd had two pounds' worth this week. Two lines; not much, but only one line of the right numbers she needed. Her mother spent five pounds every week. It was Bronwen's only luxury, though Mary would have preferred the five pounds to be given to her. She couldn't understand why her mother bothered to play the lottery. She would never win. And what if she did? How could she spend it?

Bronwen spent her money only on the National Lottery and a daily newspaper. The daily newspaper was a necessity, not a luxury, as was playing the lottery. What was left of Bronwen's state allowance was usually given to Mary. However, little by little over the years, Bronwen had managed to accumulate almost two hundred pounds in an account at The Midland Bank. It would be left to her daughter when she passed on or used for a possible emergency.

Bronwen acquired most of the money by selling some of her clothes when she left home. Also, from the reluctant sale of Lewis's and her parents' clothes, which she hadn't had the heart to part with before. She had tended them as if they were still in use, but when she went to The Sunshine Mount Nursing Home, she emptied the wardrobes to give Mary more room. Mary wondered why her mother cried as she handed them over to a woman who bought and sold second-hand clothes.

Mary thought her mother would have given the money she'd had for the clothes to her, to buy new clothes for herself. It rankled that she didn't. Often since, she had tried to make her mother withdraw the money from the bank so that it could be spent. Bronwen was adamant that the money would remain where it was, and she added one or two pounds to it whenever she could. Rarely, she plopped a few pence into the residents' savings box to pay for summer outings.

Mary often thought of what she would do if her lottery numbers came up and she won thousands of pounds. She would buy lots of lovely new clothes and take a cruise around the world on a luxury liner.

She walked down the corridor of Willow Unit on the right of the building, where the more able and compos mentis residents spent their daytime hours in the lounge area.

Laburnum Unit, on the left, was where those residents who needed constant observation spent their day. Mary didn't look in that direction and held her breath because sometimes an acrid waft of incontinence left the lounge area. It faded as she walked further up the corridor towards Willow Lounge. This time she cringed. She didn't hold her breath long enough. She had no understanding of the exigencies of the aged.

She reached the lounge area of Willow Unit, stealthily pushed one of the heavy double-doors ajar and sidled into the room. She then tiptoed to where her mother always sat in a wide, comfortable armchair. Her wheelchair, however, was always beside her, within reach, in case she needed to go to the lavatory or to her room.

No words passed between mother and daughter. The lottery programme had started. The exciting run-up to the numbers being drawn was flashing on the wide television screen and all eyes were on it. Even those of the few residents in the room who hadn't participated looked and listened. A few of them, who thought they couldn't spare the money, avoided being called "mean" or "stingy" by openly decrying gambling as being a fool game. Not Bronwen Dew, or most of the twenty residents in that lounge.

She sat with her Bic ballpoint poised over a blank sheet of her writing-pad. When Mary arrived, she raised the pen in a wave and beckoned her to sit in the wheelchair, which she did. Mary knew better than to speak or move in any way that would interfere with the lottery numbers being copied.

She hadn't found her own ticket but decided to take another look in her handbag when the programme was over and use her mother's numbers to check her own. She was sure her tickets were somewhere in her bag; not that she expected to win anything. She'd never managed to get more than two numbers. Rarely, she had one.

Her mother didn't fare much better. When she had twice won ten pounds it had been picked up from the lottery point by Bronwen's closest friend, Stella Vaughan. Stella had been Bronwen's main carer since the day she was admitted to The Sunshine Mount Nursing Home. Bronwen loved Stella as she did Mary. Bronwen had befriended all the nurse-carers but the relationship between herself and Stella was special.

On her way from the home, after she'd been on a morning duty shift, Stella got a number of lottery tickets for Bronwen and those other residents who wanted to try their luck. She collected their pound coins when she went off duty and handed them in at the betting shop.

It was the twice winning of ten pounds that motivated Bronwen to go on playing the lottery. As well as that, she enjoyed sharing the excitement of possibly winning with her companions at the home.

During the time her mother was taking the lottery numbers, Mary slumped in her wheelchair, pleased with the time to recover from her sprint up the steep approach to the home. She didn't bother to look at the television or listen for the lottery winning numbers.

Bronwen did and gasped with excitement at what she saw and heard. She gave Mary a hard elbow dig, making her jump. She had forgotten she was on the wheelchair and hadn't thought to engage the brakes. Her heavy bulk set the wheelchair running backwards towards the other side of the room; the dining area of the unit. Some residents were sitting at the tables, finding it easier to check the numbers there rather than balancing their sheets of paper on their knees.

'Mary, Mary! I can't look!' Bronwen shouted. 'I've got five numbers! Quick, listen for the bonus number!'

As she spoke, the bonus number was announced but Mary was too intent in trying to stop the wheelchair. A carer standing by pushed the wheelchair carrying the dazed Mary back to beside her mother's lounge chair, from where it had come, and snapped on its brake. The wheelchair had been designed for an average sized person. Mary had difficulty tugging herself out of its seat.

The carer tutted. 'Watch out, Mary. Wake up. You could have bumped into somebody.'

Mary ignored the carer's rebuke to try to do as her mother told her, but she had missed the drawing and calling out of the bonus number.

Her mother was behaving out of character. It wasn't like Bronwen to be anything but calm, yet she seemed to be struggling to keep control of her excitement after hearing the clear, silken voice of the female announcer. Bronwen heard the bonus number herself; twenty-two, one of her lucky numbers, and wrote it on her pad,

'There is one lucky jackpot winner, to receive twenty point five million pounds.'

'Oh, my God!' Bronwen held her hand to her chest to steady her fluttering heart. 'Oh, my God. I think I've got all the numbers. Here, check these numbers, Mary.' She pushed her ticket and pad to her daughter who stood in stunned silence beside her mother's chair.

She dragged up a lounge chair and sat beside her mother. She began by staring at the numbers. Mary was too slow for Bronwen, who sat stiffly in her chair, eyes closed tightly and hands over her ears. 'Call out the numbers and check my ticket, quick, Mary, quick! I think I've got all the numbers!'

'Take your 'ands from your ears then, Mammy!' Mary shouted.

'What?' Bronwen shouted back.

Mary removed her mother's hands and directed her to look at her ticket whilst she called out the numbers. 'Two, seven, seventeen, forty-eight, forty-nine and the bonus number is twenty-two.' Mary had to concentrate hard on the task of checking the numbers; the significance of the possibility of getting all the numbers was lost to her.

'Number twenty-two is the bonus number, Mammy. Same number as our 'ouse.'

'Yeeeeeh!' Bronwen screamed.

Everyone's attention was already on her, waiting to hear the result. Some jaws dropped, some eyebrows raised, some gasped. Some didn't know what was happening and were digging those sitting next to them to explain the reason for Bronwen Dew's unusual burst of excitement.

'Mammy, shut up your screamin'. Everybody'll think you're mad or something.' Mary looked about her, feeling embarrassment at her mother's outburst.

'Can't you understand? I've won the lottery. We're going to be rich,' Bronwen was frustrated at her daughter's lack of enthusiasm.

'Geraint!' Bronwen called out. 'Where are you? Come and check these numbers for me.'

Eighty-year-old resident, Geraint Lloyd-Davies, had missed the calling of the lottery draw numbers. His prostate gland let him down at the least bit of excitement; he'd had to go to the lavatory.

'Geraint!' Bronwen called out again, 'come here quick!'

They had always been on first name terms, but many others felt more comfortable addressing him formally. He would recognise Bronwen calling him from a mile away. He recognised, from the tone of her voice this time, she needed him urgently.

'All right, all right, I'm coming as fast as I can. Wait, will you?'

Geraint tottered along the aisle; the middle of the residents' dining and sitting areas, carrying his Zimmer-frame walking aid.

'Do you think I've got a jet engine up my bum?'

'Not yet, you haven't, but I'll buy one for you. You can tie it to that Zimmer, not that it will help you move faster, because you only carry it.'

Mary moved out of her chair to another one nearby so that Geraint could sit next to her mother. He dropped onto the seat and looked at the lottery numbers as he groped in his pockets for his own ticket and his spectacles. Bronwen bounced with impatience; she knew he wouldn't be hurried. She waited until he was ready. He was an expert mathematician. Before retirement, he had been a successful accountant.

'Well, I'll be jiggered,' he muttered, moving his spectacles up and down on his face to get the clearest view of his own lottery ticket, 'I've won ten pounds. I've got three numbers up.'

'Geraint, for God's sake, will you shut up and look at my numbers.' Bronwen was becoming increasingly frustrated.

'All right, all right, Bronwen Dew. Calm down, will you? All in good time I'll tell you how many numbers you have.' He turned to Mary who sat motionless with a sheet of paper in her hand. She had scribbled down the bonus number which everyone was calling out to her.

Geraint took it from her. 'Here, give it to me, Mary, and you, Bronwen, give me the numbers you took from the announcer.' He wrote the numbers on Mary's sheet except for the bonus number, which was twenty-two.

He flattened the two pieces of paper on his knee with the palm of his hand and studied them. 'Right, call out the numbers on your lottery ticket now, Bronwen.'

She did so, slowly and clearly. Geraint's eyes widened.

'No, it can't be right,' he said, shaking his head. 'Read them out again, Bronwen.'

Bronwen struggled to contain her impatience. Her eyes closed before opening them and raising them to the ceiling. She called out the numbers again.

'My goodness, Bronwen, if I'm not mistaken, you have all the right numbers. I wonder how much you've won.' He hadn't heard the announcer's last call.

A voice from across the room answered his question. 'Twenty point five million pounds!'

The voice confirming the fortune that had been won came from diabetic, legless Tom Daly.

Tom had been taken into The Sunshine Mount Nursing Home fifteen years before. Bronwen remembered him from when she was a little girl, sitting in her wheelchair at the front of her home on warm sunny days. Then, he had a thick mop of ginger hair and a beard and moustache to match. Now it was almost white, but with fine pink, streaks; remnants of its past redness.

Tom had deliberately happened by 22, Queen Street to talk to her. She was nice to him and enticed her mother to bring out a plate of food for him as well as for herself. They had often dined *al fresco* on the pavement outside Bronwen's home.

Tom left home when his widowed mother married again to a man he despised, and the feeling was mutual. Tom became a tramp, roaming the streets, begging for scraps; a dangerous existence for one with diabetes.

It was a happy day for Tom when Bronwen arrived at Willow Unit of The Sunshine Mount Nursing Home. Her admission was helpful for the matron because Tom wasn't a popular resident. He smoked and went into rages when his cigarettes were taken from him. They were withheld until it was convenient for someone to supervise him as he smoked. Bronwen was the only one who could calm him when he was in one of those rages. His red hair had paled but his temper hadn't.

A number of lounge chairs were marked with Tom's cigarette burns. More than once he had caused havoc when scorched blankets filled his room with acrid smoke, and the corridor outside it. He was inclined to fall asleep with a lit cigarette between his nicotine-stained fingers.

Every week, since the National Lottery started, he had at least five pounds' worth of lines and every week he promised to take Bronwen on a world cruise if he won. Every week she agreed to go with him—if he won.

Now, as he stretched his neck and body as high as he could over the heads of those in front of him to see Bronwen, he called out to her. 'I knew one of us would win one day, Bron. Shall I make the phone call for you? That's the first thing you have to do.' Tom didn't attempt to disguise his excitement. He bounced on his wheelchair like a cat on a hot, ash hearth. If he'd had legs, he would surely have jumped and fallen off his chair. He did that sometimes, with excitement or anger.

He was the only resident who possessed a mobile phone and had taught himself how to use its several functions. Mobile phones were rare in those days.

Bronwen called back to Tom, 'Yes, Tom. Make the call.' Bronwen assumed he knew the number to call. 'And after that, call Stella and tell her to come in straight away. Tell her why. Though she won't believe you.'

Cautious, Mr Geraint Lloyd-Davies put his hand on Bronwen's shoulder. He and Bronwen had been companions for many years. Their relationship was such that each knew all about the other's life, past and present. They sometimes argued, disagreed and bickered, yet remained endeared to each other.

'Now, don't hurry things, Bronwen. Let's do a bit of thinking. We mustn't let things get out of hand.' He wriggled in his chair with excitement. 'We don't want one of us to have a stroke before some of the twenty and a half million pounds has been spent.'

Mary began to stir out of confusion and appeared thoughtful. 'How much is twenty an' a 'alf million pounds, Mr Lloyd-Davies? Is it more'n twenty thousand? 'Cause tha's awful lot of money.'

Geraint, Bronwen and those residents close enough to hear and see all looked at Mary with dropped jaws of exasperation.

Tilley Tittle-tattle, sitting close by, broke the pregnant pause. 'Lord God, Bronwen,' she said, 'how could a scholar like you have such a dunce of a daughter? My lot are no brains of Britain, but your Mary takes the biscuit.'

Bronwen sprang to Mary's defence, her mind taken off her lottery win.

'We can't all be clever, like you and me, Tilley. I haven't been able to give my Mary experience of large sums of money. But at this very minute, my lottery numbers must be flashing on the big computers of Camelot, who as you know, runs the lottery, so I soon will be. And as you said, there's not one of your lot has a brain worth bragging about.'

Tilley didn't know who organised the National Lottery. It was of no interest to her. She apologised. 'Sorry, Bron. Sorry, Mary. That was a spiteful thing to say but I couldn't help it.' Tilley wouldn't deliberately hurt Bronwen. She was one of the few residents to whom she looked as a confidante. Bronwen always listened to her family problems.

No one else dared pass any further disparaging remark. Their thoughts went back to the possibility of Bronwen becoming a millionaire.

Mr Geraint Lloyd-Davies was as amazed at Mary's innocence and the ignorance of her question as everyone else, but he wouldn't insult her. Hurting her would be hurting Bronwen and he wouldn't do that. Anyway, he understood Mary's problem. He was tolerant of it and tried to help.

'Mary, my dear,' he said, 'even one million pounds is far, far more than twenty thousand pounds. It's much more, and it seems your mother might have won more than that.'

He wrote the two sums on the back of the piece of paper on which he had his lottery numbers written. 'Look here at the difference,' he said, as he beckoned Mary to study the figures.

'How can all those six nothin's on tha' line be more than them nothin's on tha' one?' Mary's confusion was increasing by the second.

'Never mind, now,' Bronwen interrupted to prevent Mary further embarrassment in front of the other residents. 'Let's wait until Tom's made that phone call to the lottery people. Perhaps it will all come to nothing; a mistake.'

The news about Bronwen's win soon reached the office where Matron Helen Phillips was writing her daily report. She was the nurse in charge of The Sunshine Mount Nursing Home.

'Bronwen Dew's won the lottery,' old Evan Thomas gabbled. On his feet he was the fastest resident. Well into his eighties, he could jog, and he did so everywhere. He was often asked if he could walk. He thought he always did.

'Oh, good,' Matron responded with little interest, assuming Bronwen had won another ten pounds.

'She's won millions and millions of pounds.' Evan's arms lifted to the air in amazement. 'She's had all the numbers and the jackpot.'

That made Matron sit up. She couldn't resist checking. She went to the lounge of Willow Unit. She didn't believe Evan was right, but then it was possible, she supposed. Large amounts were won every week.

The big room was noisy; buzzing with excitement. She turned off the television.

The room became as still and silent as an empty chapel.

Everyone's eyes and ears went to Tom. He was dialling a phone call to Camelot. After a few minutes, he got through. He told them who the lucky lottery winner was and that he was calling for her. He began nodding his head in reply to whatever was being said on the other side of his phone.

'Yes, that's right,' he eventually said. 'Mrs Bronwen Dew is living here in The Sunshine Mount Nursing Home. I'm her friend. She said I should phone you and she told me to tell you she will wait to hear from you.'

There was another pause when Tom was listening at his earpiece. He covered the mouthpiece and shouted across the room. 'Geraint, quick! Bring me Bronwen's ticket with the winning numbers on. They want to check.'

Geraint forgot his Zimmer-frame. He snatched Bronwen's winning ticket from her and dashed across the room as fast as Jogger Evan Thomas would have, dodging other residents until he plunged the ticket into Tom's left hand.

Tom read out the winning numbers.

'Yes!' he yelled. 'Thank you, thank you! Bronwen is rich! Mr Lloyd-Davies, take my phone to Bronwen, they want to speak to her.'

Geraint grabbed Tom's phone, shuffled back to Bronwen and thrust it into her hand. She held it in the air. 'What do I say?'

'Put it to your ear and answer their questions, Bronwen,' Tom urged.

'Hello!' Bronwen shouted. 'My name is Bronwen Dew and here are my numbers.' Geraint had taken the piece of paper on which were written all the numbers and thrust it into Bronwen's hand. She read out the numbers.

'Yes, thank you. We'll talk to you tomorrow, then.' Bronwen, as if in a trance, handed the phone back to Geraint. 'Yes,' she said looking around the sea of expectant expressions. 'It looks as though I've won the lottery.'

A loud cheer from the residents filled the room, including that from Matron Phillips and the carers.

'Congratulations, Mrs Dew!' Matron shouted as she clapped her hands. 'The future is going to be very special for you. You'll have to learn how to spend money.'

'We're going to be in the papers and on the news,' someone called out.

Mary sat in stunned silence. She couldn't understand the significance of what was happening. She picked up her pink shower-proof jacket and put it on in preparation to escape the scene when Stella ran into the room.

She lived nearby. She had leapt into her ten-year-old Austin mini car, dressed as she was in a shabby leisure suit. She had already heard the news by phone from Tom, and then from a couple of people she met in the corridor on their way to the toilets.

'I couldn't believe it was true,' Stella gasped. 'I got here as soon as Tom told me. Is it true, Bronwen? Is it true Mr Lloyd-Davies?'

'It looks like it. Indeed, it does,' Geraint replied. He looked dazed.

She roughly embraced Bronwen. 'My lovely girl. Now, if all this is true, you'll be able to live a little before you die.'

Stella looked up at Mary, standing mesmerised beside the two women.

'Don't go for a minute, Mary. You and I are going to The Colliers for a few drinks, paid for from your mother's purse. We'll celebrate.'

Bronwen laughed. 'I could be rich, but my purse is empty.'

'Hang on a minute,' Geraint interrupted. 'Bronwen hasn't received a penny yet. Give her a chance to see what is going to happen.'

Stella recognised that Bronwen didn't look well, which was unusual. She was emotionally overcome by the events of the evening. Apart from her paralysed legs and simple hypertension, Bronwen enjoyed good health. Stella decided to calm the atmosphere. The best way to do that was to leave and take Mary with her.

'I'll be here to see you first thing in the morning. I'm not taking my Sunday off. Matron is a carer short, so I've volunteered to do an early shift for her.' She looked at Matron as she spoke.

Matron nodded. 'Yes, thank you, Stella.'

'Yes, all right, my lovely,' Bronwen sensed Stella's understanding.

Stella turned to Geraint. 'You give us a couple of quid for a few drinks then, Mr Lloyd-Davies. You'll give it back to him, won't you, Bronwen?'

'Yes, love, I will. Give it to them, Geraint. It can come out of that ten pounds you've won. There'll be plenty more where that comes from, unless I'm dreaming.'

Bronwen sounded weary. A wave of fatigue flowed over her and she needed to rest. She hoisted herself from her lounge chair into her wheelchair and made for the exit. Geraint, also, recognised her deflated enthusiasm and gave Stella a five-pound note for her to leave. He frowned. 'And don't spend it all on drink.'

Matron had been standing beside Bronwen, enjoying the atmosphere which seldom changed from one day to the next.

'I'll wheel you to your room, Bronwen. Save the little bit of energy you have left to get to bed.'

'Thank you, Matron. I need to think and sleep on what's happened or going to happen. If it's true, how on earth do I begin spending all that money?'

'Well, it will have to be on earth, Bronwen. No pockets in shrouds, as they say. And I don't think you need worry, because no doubt, you'll have plenty to help you. Before I take you to your room, I expect you'll want to go to the toilet, will you? Even millionaires go there.'

Bronwen chuckled at Matron's facetious remark. 'Do they? Then I don't suppose I should change that habit. And talking about change, Helen, you and I must talk in the morning. I think things might have to change, just a bit in my life before I pass on, as you so tactfully put it. That is, if all my numbers have come up right and there's no catch.'

When inside Bronwen's room, Helen gathered her nightdress from a chest of drawers against the wall, before closing the pretty chintz curtains.

'Pity to shut the world out, isn't it? And it's not as if someone's going to be looking in at you. Not up here, but they might downstairs since you've become a millionaire overnight.'

'I hope not,' Bronwen's eyes widened. 'I don't want to feel like I'm in a circus. It's a good thing you gave me this room if that will be the case. I'll have somewhere to hide. Anyway, I like this room better than the one downstairs. The view is beautiful. Much nicer looking over the fields and mountains than the concrete courtyard at the front of the home and the chimney-tops of the town.'

'You didn't mention the cemetery you overlook, as well,' Matron said. 'It obviously doesn't bother you.'

'No, of course not. It's where I'll be going someday. I'll be joining my loved ones. Lewis is down there, waiting for me, so I like it being part of my outlook.'

'I'm grateful to you for giving up your ground-floor room without a fuss. As you know, those other two rooms were occupied at the time. With your state of mobility, you should be on the ground floor, but I needed your room when Martha Tate took bad. She's ninety-four and when God is calling, it's easier for my carers and myself to keep an eye out when our dying dear ones are nursed on the ground floor.'

Thirty-eight-year-old Helen Phillips was a born nurse. She was a widow; her husband having been killed in the Falkland war. She had two sons in their late teens. Of average height, she was spruce from the tip of her sensible black shoes to the top of her well-groomed, brown hair. Silver-buckled at her trim waistline, she was an epitome of professionalism. Beneath that was compassion, kindness and sensitivity. A stern front allowed her the weakness to shed tears in private. Bronwen knew she often did.

'No need for gratitude,' Bronwen yawned.

'Thank you, Bronwen. And don't go to sleep worrying about nosy parkers. There are plenty here who will look out for you. Anyway, you must be absolutely exhausted now, and things always seem more complicated when we're tired.

'You don't win millions of pounds every day. I think you ought to take the sedation tonight or you won't sleep after what's happened to you this evening. I'll bring it up when I bring Mr Lloyd-Davies's medication and for my other residents in your neighbouring rooms.'

Helen moved Bronwen's commode close to the side of her bed. 'I know you can manage and like to be independent, but you call if you need help. Goodnight, now.' She almost closed the door after her. She knew Bronwen liked a slit of light from the corridor during the night.

Matron was about to leave but turned to add a last-minute thought.

'Something has occurred to me, Bronwen. You mightn't be needing this room for much longer, will you?'

Bronwen hadn't had time to think of that issue. 'Not need the room? Of course, I will. Can't see how having plenty of money should change that. Anyway, let's see what tomorrow brings.'

Bronwen could not imagine living in a salubrious home of her own. At least, not at that time. She was overtired. It was hours before she dropped off to sleep, even after taking night sedation. Thoughts of getting all the numbers of the National Lottery went around and around in her head.

Her mind couldn't accommodate to the fact that a fortune would be put at her disposal. She was troubled by the thought of all the fuss that went on during the evening. If a mistake had been made, she would feel foolish if there was no lottery money coming to her. And what if she has won the National Lottery, what would she do with all that money? She didn't have enough time left on Earth to spend it, even if she lived to be a hundred, and that was unlikely. Perhaps she should try to break the habit of a lifetime and become a spendthrift. It would be difficult. She could never spend for the sake of spending and certainly not before looking at the price tag and wondering if the amount on it could be afforded. Were those days over?

She would certainly donate to charities but not millions of pounds. She was not a rich millionaire; there were those who gave millions to the poor of the developing countries, but she understood they had billions of pounds in their banks. It comforted Bronwen to think she could give to those close to her; make life easier for them and solve financial problems. But how should she go about it? She couldn't very well give the same amount to everyone. How could she decide?

Certainly, she knew Mary would be there with both hands out and Bronwen would fill them. Mary would spend for the sake of spending and would probably be wasteful. Bronwen would not allow that. Mary was thirty-one years of age and had a great deal to learn; certainly, about money, of which she knew nothing. She couldn't manage her small weekly allowance. How would she fare with large amounts? She simply couldn't, and that was that.

Bronwen became more disillusioned with every sleepless minute. What was she to do? The answer was to ask Geraint. She knew she could depend on him. There was nothing about money Accountant Geraint Lloyd-Davies didn't know. He took the *Financial Times* and studied every column. He had a computer in his room on which he spent hours studying the stock markets and countries' economies. He had spent the last of his savings on the purchase of a computer. Yes, Bronwen thought; Geraint would know what to do and it would enrich his existence to manage her affairs. That was a comforting thought.

She dropped off to sleep after she heard the cock crow at the nearby Duffy's farmyard. Her last thought was not of being rich, but of Lewis. She wished he were with her. Not that he would know how to spend millions of pounds, but he would share her problem.

She remembered one of his often-spoken clichés: a problem shared is a problem halved. Equally, a joy shared is a joy doubled. Which one of those sayings was appropriate to the present situation, she wondered?

Time would tell. Bronwen hoped it would say what she wanted to hear.

Chapter 3
How to Be a Millionaire

The chime of church bells dominated Bronwen's dream. Her eyelids flicked open to find her room filling with daylight. Someone was opening the curtains. The bells weren't a dream; they were real. They and Stella had awakened her.

'Wakey, wakey! Good morning, your ladyship. You're starting your life of luxury right—staying in bed until you feel like getting up.'

Bronwen was startled into lifting herself up from the pillows. She noticed immediately that her commode had been moved from the side of the bed and put in a far corner of the room, where it stood during the day.

'Stella! It's your turn for a Sunday off. What are you doing here?'

'I told you last night I would work an early shift today. You weren't thinking straight, or didn't hear, because there was so much going on. I told Matron I would work an extra shift because I wanted to be here to help you deal with being made one of the *nouveau riche*. Everyone's going to be at you with questions about what you're going to spend your millions on. Matron is glad I agreed to do this shift. She hasn't left the office because of phone calls. She hasn't been able to be hands-on, as she usually likes to be, bless her. An extra pair of hands was needed and mine happened to be available. You know, Bronwen, it's incredible how…'

'Shut up and draw breath, Stella. Let me come to myself before you make a speech.' Bronwen yawned. She scratched her head with one hand and removed the bedcovers with the other before lifting her lifeless legs over the side of the bed. She turned and glanced casually at her precious, ornate bedside clock; a present from Lewis for her thirtieth birthday.

She expected the hour-hand to be somewhere between seven and eight, where it usually was when she awoke of a morning.

'Good Heavens,' she gasped. 'I thought I was dreaming the church bells were calling us, but I wasn't. They're ringing like mad. Surely it's not ten o'clock.'

She reached out, picked up her spectacles from her bedside table, put them on and cast the neat chain they were attached to around her neck. Stella had attached a fancy chain to Bronwen's spectacles because she was always forgetting where she'd put them. Bronwen stared at her clock, expecting herself to be wrong about the time. She wasn't.

'It's gone ten.' She was in awe. 'Hand me my denture pot, Stella. I don't want to be seen without my teeth. Why didn't someone wake me—I've missed breakfast and I should have been up to try Martha Tate with a cup of Complan. Oh, dear, and I should have taken my blood pressure tablet.'

'You can take it with your breakfast,' Stella said. 'Stop moithering and take your time.'

Bronwen spent many hours beside Martha Tate's bedside; she was living her last days and being nursed in a room reserved for the terminally ill. No one knew exactly when God would take her, except that it would be soon.

Although it wasn't known whether Martha could hear what was going on around her, Bronwen talked to her as if she could.

'I gave Martha as much fluid as she could manage to get down this morning,' Stella reassured Bronwen. 'She seems to be deteriorating by the day now, and her skin is beginning to break down. I wish the owners had coughed up and let us buy that special bed and mattress we wanted for her. Anyway, never you mind about Martha now. Have this bit of breakfast and take your tablet. It's not much because the lunches will be served soon.'

Stella set the breakfast tray on the bed-table before giving Bronwen a glass of orange juice and a small pot containing her medication.

'Most important first,' she said.

Bronwen went silent. She was deep in thought. 'Stella, I'll ask Matron to order one of those special beds tomorrow,' She hesitated. 'Nothing can be done today; it's Sunday. If it's right that I have a lot of money coming, it will be a good way of spending some. And if it's wrong about the money, the company will have to wait for it. We'll risk it.'

'Bronwen, that would be such a good thing to do. When poor Martha is not with us, there'll always be someone to use it. And you can afford one—you'll be having a very big cheque slapped into your hand any day now. You've won the lottery whether you like it or not, and from the number of times the phone has rung already this morning, asking about it, you won't be able to keep it to yourself.'

'That's what you were going to say when I shut you up, wasn't it? You were going to say how incredible it is that people outside get to know what goes on here. I'm not so worried about that. A nine days' wonder is soon over.'

'This one won't be, my lovely. You will live with this wonder until the end of your natural. And what I was going to say was, it's incredible how relatives turn up who you never knew you had. Mary mouthed about your win in the pub last night. I don't think she realises the significance of what's happened, and to tell you the truth, neither do I. I hope you do.'

Bronwen paled and held her head in her hands. 'Stella, of course I don't. I'm relying on you, Geraint and Tom to help. We'll just wait until we hear how I'll get the money and how much. Then the five of us must get together and sort things out. Mary'll have to be in on it whether she understands or not; you'll have to help her. And when we do have a meeting about it, for goodness sake, don't swear. You know Mr Lloyd-Davies doesn't like it.'

Stella laughed. She knew her weakness. 'I'll try,' she said, 'but they are only words, aren't they?'

'Well, use clean ones,' Bronwen was now smiling herself. 'Don't use the B or F words.'

'As I said, I'll try, but I forget myself when I feel mad about something. Colin doesn't like it either, but he gets it something rotten whether he likes it or not—when he deserves it. Not often, bless him. He's as good as gold.'

Stella referred to her bachelor brother, Colin Pritchard, who doted on his sister, six years younger than himself. He had always disliked Steven Vaughan, her ex-husband, and was glad when they divorced, and she came home.

Bronwen felt relief that Stella and Colin kept a watch on Mary. Being an adult, she shouldn't have needed watching, but she lacked the ability to be in control of her life and always would.

Stella constantly chastised, corrected and quarrelled with Mary, but she had a will of her own. She would allow Stella to interfere with the way she lived only when in the right mood, or when she was out of her depth. She had a learning difficulty which didn't preclude a stubborn streak.

On Bronwen's advice, Stella once slackened the reigns of Mary's supervision.

'Leave her be to get on with it until she shouts for help. See how she makes out,' Bronwen had said to Stella. Stella frowned, obviously having doubts about the outcome.

However, Stella did as Bronwen bid, but she found it hard not to call on Mary. Mary was hurt, thinking Stella didn't care for her anymore; like so many others, had given up on her. She was wrong; Stella cared very much. There was a strong sense of belonging between the two young women. Bronwen was the link.

When Bronwen became a resident of The Sunshine Mount Home twelve years before, Stella was already a carer there. She was in her late twenties then and going through a bad patch in her marriage.

She had been told by spiteful gossipers that her husband was having an affair with a woman who worked for the same pharmaceutical company as he did. It had deeply humiliated and hurt Stella. Her suspicions were confirmed.

She left their home and went to live with her parents and bachelor brother, Colin. She had often bent Bronwen's ear and cried on her shoulder.

Bronwen couldn't understand why a man could treat a lovely woman so cruelly. Stella turned many an admiring eye to her shapely form, dark brown, curling hair and flawless complexion. She was warm-hearted and gentle, yet strongly assertive when necessary. Bronwen loved Stella as she did Mary, her daughter, though they were as alike as chalk and cheese.

Stella thought her husband had thwarted her because after two years of marriage, she hadn't produced a baby. Bronwen and Mary helped Stella to overcome the trauma of divorce.

When Stella's father died and not long afterwards, her mother, the house became hers and Colin's.

Though in his thirties, he was still a bachelor. He'd had girlfriends but not one he could have lived with for the rest of his life. He was satisfied with his life at 10, King Street with Stella and his work as a master builder. He was his own boss with a business ticking over well enough to give him a satisfactory living.

To please Stella, Colin called at Mary's house from time to time to ensure there were no structural defects to correct and to ensure the electricity and plumbing were functioning safely. On one visit, he teased Mary and asked her if she would notice if the roof fell in. She took him to be serious.

'Don't be daft. 'Course I would,' she had replied.

Colin had teased. 'Well, I'm not sure you would, Mary.' She had given him a doubtful look.

He had ranted on at Mary as Stella often did. 'Mary, you need to get a grip on yourself,' he said in a threatening tone. 'Get off your fat arse and do some clearing up here. What if your mother has to come back? She could never come into this.'

Mary took no offence; neither did she ever heed his advice. 'Oh, shurrup, Colin. You know tha's not goin' to 'appen, don' you?'

Mary was wrong. Bronwen had won the National Lottery and was now rich. The house was an end of row dwelling, so with planning permission

it could be extended, renovated and constructed to suit her needs and she would come home. Where else could she go?

As Stella helped Bronwen to dress and talk over the clanging chimes of the church bells, neither of them thought about returning to Queen Street. They were more concerned with dealing with the publicity which winning twenty point five million pounds would bring.

Stella left Bronwen alone to take her breakfast and for her to put the finishing touches to her grooming.

'I have to sort out the linen up here, and then I'll see you downstairs,' Stella told her.

Bronwen wouldn't enter Willow Lounge until she was satisfied with the way she looked. She dressed well and although her emaciated legs made her feet look big, they were a normal, adult size. She always wore attractive shoes. She hadn't until she married Lewis. Before then she had worn only huge, ugly, heavy boots attached to leg irons. No one explained why; they didn't help.

However, she had only three smart pairs of shoes; one pair for daywear, one for eveningwear and one pair for special occasions. She promised herself that if, by some miracle, she became rich, she would buy three pairs of shoes for every day of the week. She would send Stella to get them. She knew what Bronwen liked. Or she would choose them out of a catalogue. Anything to avoid exposing her legs. In a shoe shop, her ankles or above, might be seen.

No one in the nursing home had seen Bronwen's legs, except those few who physically cared for her. They were Matron Phillips, Stella and the resident doctor who visited Bronwen from time to time. She was always conscious of the abnormality of her legs. Wherever she sat, she always wore trousers or a long skirt and covered her lap with a pretty, coloured shawl. She had gathered a change of shawls over the years. They were an important item of her wardrobe.

The only resident who had seen Bronwen's legs was her friend, Tom Daly. He had seen them when she was a little girl. To him, her wasted legs looked as good as anyone's.

Bronwen took a last look at herself in the wardrobe-door mirror to be sure she was ready to appear in the lounge before leaving the covertness of her room. She propelled herself to the lift which was between the ground and first floor. She pressed the button and the lift appeared almost immediately.

Bronwen wished Stella could have stayed with her to face all the other residents, after their excited reaction of the evening before. She guessed they would have been talking about her lottery win all morning. They'd be wondering when the Camelot people would be coming to give her the cheque.

Since each day in the home was much the same as any other to the residents, they wouldn't want to miss anything different; certainly, something that was rarely, if ever, seen in a nursing home.

Stella deliberately let Bronwen go down to face her companions on her own, as she always did. It was best to keep things as normal.

'They never will be again, though,' Stella muttered to herself as she walked down the corridor to the linen room. She had a headache thinking about it and Bronwen hadn't yet received the cheque. Goodness knows how she must be feeling, Stella thought: strange and confused, to say the least.

Stella decided it was a good thing Bronwen was strong-minded.

Bronwen manoeuvred her wheelchair towards Willow Unit lounge and dining room. The nearer she got, the louder the voices within became. The different tones reached her: the sounds of the television, the loud chat and the clatter of crockery and cutlery as the tables were being laid for lunch. The double doors at the entrance were wide open, as they always were at that time of the day. It allowed residents with a mobility problem, whether walking, wheel-chairing or Zimmering, to move in and out independently. It was also more convenient for the meal trolleys to be pushed and pulled in and out.

The instant Bronwen passed over the threshold, the din dropped to an uncanny silence. Someone had switched off the television and the two carers stiffened to stillness in laying the green and white checked tablecloths. All sights turned towards Bronwen. For a few moments, it was as if time stood still.

Tom Daly broke the silence.

'Bronwen! Bronwen! I've been waiting for you to come down. You're late. Aren't you well or something?' He wheeled himself to be beside her, into the space of room between the sitting and dining areas.

'It's the "or something", Tom, and perhaps you can tell me what it is. I have the distinct feeling that I was being talked about when I came into this room. I could have cut the air with a knife.'

The television was switched on again, the carers continued with the laying of the tables and several peopled called out to Bronwen at the same time.

'It's because you've won the lottery, Mrs Dew!' Megan, the outspoken, sixteen-year-old carer shouted across the room. 'The Camelot people rang Tom with a message for you. He put on his posh voice. He was ever so good. And no, nobody's been saying bad of you.'

'That's right, honest-to-god, Bron,' Tilley Tittle-tattle added. 'It's marvellous. And you still young enough to enjoy it. Not on your last legs, like most of us.' She tutted and pinked as she realised the insensitivity of her choice of words. She attempted to correct herself. 'Well, you can get about all right in your chair, can't you?'

'Yes, Bronwen, you can pay somebody a hundred pounds an hour to push you now,' someone called out. Everyone except a few, sitting at the back of the room, laughed. The stiff atmosphere dissipated and was replaced with the usual camaraderie. She couldn't stop herself feeling guilty, seeing the frowns of those who felt envious. Geraint had warned her there would be some and she hadn't believed him, until now.

'Tell us what you're going to do with all that money, Bronwen. You can buy a house like Buckingham Palace and have a dozen nurses to look after you.'

Humorous comments reached Bronwen from all directions. She held her hands to her ears. 'Shut up, all of you. I haven't had the blooming cheque yet and I'm already hoping I won't.'

'Well, you can hope all you like.' Tom spoke quietly to her, though everyone who wasn't deaf heard him. 'Those from Camelot rang me on my mobile just an hour ago and told me to tell you to call them back. I gave them my number last night, remember? They want to come here on Wednesday to give you the big cheque. If it's one of those huge six foot by four things, Bronwen, like we've seen on the telly, you'll never get it into your purse.'

'Oh, my God,' Bronwen gasped. 'I hope not.'

Tom laughed. 'Don't be daft, Bronwen. You know I'm only joking.'

'Tom Daly, I don't feel like joking,' Bronwen looked peeved. 'Have you mentioned about them coming on Wednesday to Matron?'

'No. I thought I'd better tell you first. They said they'd speak to her after they've spoken to you. They asked her name, so I had to tell them, didn't I?'

Tom frowned. He felt guilty as he looked around a room of, what he thought to be, threatening expressions.

'Yes, yes, of course you did, Tom. And we mustn't use your phone to ring them back; it costs too much.' Bronwen turned her wheelchair around to leave the room. 'I'll go straight to the office now and see if I can phone from there. I want to see Matron, anyway.'

'Wait a minute,' Tom called after her. 'You can't call them if you don't know the number. Here it is.' He handed her a flattened piece of an Embassy cigarette packet, on the back of which was written a long string of digits.

Bronwen grinned. 'Oh, yes. That would help, wouldn't it? Thank you, Tom,' She looked around the room. 'Where's Mr Lloyd-Davies?'

'Here I am, Bronwen. I've been to the lav. Shall I come with you to see Matron Phillips?' He tottered towards her carrying his Zimmer. 'I'll only speak when called upon to, though.'

Tom answered. 'Yes, yes. Go with her, Mr Lloyd-Davies. Just in case they ask something awkward.'

'Yes, you better had, Geraint,' Bronwen agreed.

Helen Phillips, the Matron, was sitting in her office writing the morning's report. Bronwen knocked the open door and Helen looked up.

'Come in, both of you,' she said, standing behind her desk, beckoning them to chairs in front of her. 'I hope you feel better after your little lie-on, Bronwen. All the excitement of yesterday evening was too much; you looked all in.'

'Yes, thank you, Helen. It did take a bit out of me, to say the least. The whole thing is beginning to get me down already. I hope this money, which is not yet in my hands, won't change things for me in a way which won't be welcome.'

'It won't, Bronwen, it won't,' Geraint reassured. 'I'll help you to enjoy it as much as you should. Now I'll just sit here and say nothing.' He sat back in the chair, crossed his legs and folded his arms in a gesture of being an onlooker.

'Mr Lloyd-Davies is right,' Helen said, before responding to Bronwen's lament. 'And to tell you the truth, I was a bit shattered myself by the time I got home last night, but couldn't sleep for hours thinking of the amazing thing that's happened to you. Your life will change—and for the better. You're in your sixties; young enough to enjoy your good fortune in whatever way you wish.'

Bronwen tutted and shook her head. 'You couldn't sleep either, could you? And yet you were up not long after the crack of dawn to come here. You put me to shame.'

'My choice. It's my life's work and in my time I've experienced many strange and new situations, but none as unique as this. God is smiling upon you, Bronwen. We won't let Him down. Tell me, though, where do we go from here?'

'They rang Tom and asked him to tell me to ring them this afternoon. I wonder if you would allow me to ring from here, your office, because I think it might be a lengthy call. I'll pay for the call, of course. And you and Geraint are here to help me. Tom said they want to speak to you after I've spoken to them. He said they want to come on Wednesday to present me with the cheque; my tummy is doing somersaults just thinking about it. I hope they don't want to make a big thing of it, Helen.'

'From the little I know, they usually like to. But this being a nursing home for elderly and infirm people, they won't understand the drawbacks. I'll explain it to them as best I can. 'If the handover of the cheque will be here, we can make a little celebration of it, in our own way, and let all our residents enjoy seeing you become rich. They all think highly of you and they wish the best for you. Another thing is, your winning will give them hope. I can't see anyone else at Sunshine Mount winning the big money, but it will add excitement to their attempts. If anyone else does win, I hope it will be me.' Helen chuckled at the possibility of her winning the National Lottery.

'You never know,' Bronwen replied, then hesitated before she went on. 'Now, before I ring, I want to ask you to do something for me tomorrow morning. That is to contact Gordon Williams, that appliance rep who comes here, and order a special bed and mattress for Martha Tate. I was in her room yesterday when Tonia and Gillian came to turn her, and they mentioned that her skin was beginning to break down and they wished they had the special bed and mattress that you wanted for her. The girls forgot I was there, so they didn't think about the confidentiality of the matter. They were too involved in making Martha comfortable.'

Bronwen didn't tell Helen that Stella had, also, told her something similar about a special bed and mattress. She didn't want to get Stella into trouble for discussing matters which didn't concern other residents or anyone else.

'I would like you to order that special bed and mattress you had in mind and I'll pay for it. It had better come quick for Martha to have the benefit of it. And when she's gone, you'll always have use for it. Can't get away from seeing people die here, can we?'

Helen gasped. 'Bronwen, it's a four-figure sum. I think, in the region of well over a thousand pounds. Are you sure you want to do that? You realise you're spending your winnings before you've received them, don't you?'

'Yes, and if it wasn't Sunday, I'd ask you to ring today, just in case this winning the lottery business is all pie in the sky. Please do that for me. Tell them to bring it tomorrow. They won't mind waiting a few days for the money. And if all this is a sham and there is no big money coming to me, they'll just have to wait a bit longer to be paid.'

'That's very good of you. I'll ring first thing in the morning. They're in Cardiff, so there'll be no reason for them not to deliver tomorrow afternoon or certainly early evening. You're right about Martha; there's no time to wish and wonder. She's ninety-eight and weakening by the day. Nothing we can do about that, but I want her to go in peace and comfort. I'd never forgive myself if she has a pressure sore.'

Matron tried not to be morbid. 'Come on, let's ring Camelot now. I think Tom ought to be here. I'll go and get him. He's already spoken to them, so it might be a good idea for him to be here. He seems to know all about it.'

Bronwen didn't think Tom would like to be in the office. He considered it above his station, but Helen returned within minutes, pushing Tom in his wheelchair. Bronwen had rummaged in her handbag until she found the winning ticket. She reckoned they'd want to hear the winning numbers again, coming from her.

The all-important telephone call was made and Bronwen confirmed that she would be available on Wednesday afternoon. With a trembling hand, she handed the phone to Helen.

'Good morning. This is Matron Phillips speaking. Where do we go from here?'

Tom's beady eyes gleamed from under a bush of gun-grey eyebrows. He nodded and shook his head as every word registered in his sharp mind. When the call was over, Helen too, sat in silence to recover from the strange ordeal before relating the plan for the coming Wednesday.

'Two people, a man and a woman, from Camelot will be here by tea time on Wednesday afternoon,' she said. 'I was speaking to a man. He wanted the presentation to be at some special hall and would have arranged transport to take all who wanted to go, residents and their relatives. He didn't take into consideration that some of our residents, who will want to be in at the presentation, are unable to travel in a bus to some place miles away without special facilities and extra staff to look after them. He suggested getting more staff in and they would finance the occasion. You heard me tell him that it wasn't that easy. He didn't understand the staff simply weren't available or that there were residents here with special physical needs.

'A key figure in this, for instance, is you, Mr Lloyd-Davies. You need convenient toilet facilities. He apologised for the lack of understanding. He asked me to arrange a buffet tea here and they would pay the caterers.'

Geraint looked to his feet to hide his embarrassment. 'Yes, I know it's a bit of a nuisance. I'm on the hospital list to be put right, but the list seems to be very long.'

'You're not a nuisance at all, Geraint, and I don't want you thinking that way. Your knowledge is essential to me. If it weren't for you being able to manage things, I don't know what I'd do.' Bronwen's words salved Geraint's conscience. 'Thank you,' he nodded.

Bronwen went on. 'Can something be arranged here, Matron? Would it be a terrible inconvenience?' She felt she was adding to the matron's commitments.

'Not at all. Our kitchen staff will be in their element. They'll be the caterers and Camelot can pay them through me. So, all I have to do is to let our kitchen staff prepare a buffet, as they always do on special occasions, and we'll go from there. We'll make a profit for the residents' fund, but we'll keep that under our hats.'

As she spoke, Bronwen's anxiety increased. She was at a loss for words. But Tom wasn't, and what he said didn't reduce the stress.

'I'll bet they'll have a cameraman with them,' he said. 'The fact that someone from a nursing home for the elderly has won over twenty million pounds is going to make big news. I'll bet it's never happened before. It'll be encouragement for all elderly people to keep trying the lottery. It will me, anyway.'

'Yes,' Helen agreed, 'but I'm going to keep things very low profile. We'll be as helpful as we can with as little disruption as possible.' She paused and looked directly into Bronwen's eyes.

'Bronwen,' she said, 'come out of your trance and shake yourself back to normal. Everything's going to be all right.'

Bronwen appeared mesmerized. She blinked hard and shook her head. 'Yes, Matron, I'm back with you now and trying to get what is happening straight in my head.'

The small office became loud with sounds of laughter. Nervous laughter.

'Go and get your lunches, now.' Helen sounded like a matron again, 'And, Mrs Dew, you should spend some time with Mr Lloyd-Davies between now and Wednesday. Regarding those two coming on Wednesday, a man and a woman; I was given their names but have forgotten. They will want to give you advice about how to manage your fortune, but if I were you, I'd tell them you already have a first-class accountant. Geraint Lloyd-Davies is an expert and he'll be your adviser.'

Five feet six inches in height, Geraint Lloyd-Davies felt ten feet tall. His nonchalant expression disguised his true feeling.

'Yes, Matron, he's already offered, thank goodness.' Bronwen recognised his pride.

She and Tom wheel-chaired themselves back to Willow Unit lounge. Geraint trailed behind carrying his Zimmer-frame.

'Dear God, in Heaven,' Helen heard Bronwen mutter, 'what have I got myself into?'

Bronwen sat at her usual table for four with Tom, Geraint and Tilley. She couldn't eat her lunch. She toyed with the roast lamb and three veg and got no further than smearing her knife and fork. She managed a few mouthfuls of her dessert. She noticed Tom didn't seem to have an appetite, either, but Geraint and Tilley cleared their plates.

Geraint was excited about his future involvement in high finance. He'd spent most of that morning in his room in front of his computer, researching the money markets, banks and building societies. Between mouthfuls, he talked about his findings. No one understood.

Bronwen noticed Tom's unusual silence; his spirit seemed to have slumped. She didn't comment, but Stella did when she approached their table with the drinks trolley. She didn't have to ask what anyone wanted; tea for Bronwen and Tilley, coffee for Geraint, though she did confirm Tom's drink.

'Tea without sugar, Tom? You've got your sweetener in your pocket? What's the matter, my lovely, you look down in the mouth? You'd like three spoons of sugar in your tea, would you? Fed up with that old sweetener. It's not the same as a couple of spoons of sugar, is it? I don't think I could cope with being diabetic.'

'No, I'm all right, Stella. Diabetic I am and diabetic I'll stay. I know that. It's just that with Bronwen being rich now, I don't expect she'll stay here. Bronwen and I have known each other since time immemorial.'

Bronwen became morose. She felt herself becoming depressed. 'And we'll always go on knowing each other, Tom. You know those three rooms down the corridor as well as I do. Well, I'm going to end up in one of those the same as you will. And we'll have a fancy bed and mattress too, because I've ordered one for Martha Tate.'

Bronwen referred to the three rooms on the ground floor of Willow Unit, in which those residents who were living their last days were allowed the dignity of dying in peace and comfort. Just the one was occupied at the time but sometimes all three were. They were there when Martha moved in, but since then several companions had passed away.

'For Christ sake, Tom,' Stella tutted. 'Anyone would think you'd lost a pound and found a bloody penny instead of never again having to worry about the price of fags going up.'

She deliberately clattered the cups and saucers and spoke quietly not to be overhead by those on the next table.

Geraint frowned at Stella as he stirred his coffee. 'No need for the coarseness, if you don't mind Nurse Vaughan. And I'll remind you it's the Sabbath.'

'Oh, sorry, Mr Lloyd-Davies; I know you don't like me swearing. If you like I'll go to Chapel when I go off duty, if Chapel is open.'

Stella was being facetious. They all knew the chapel opened only for funeral services. Its congregation of the locals had diminished to nothing over the years.

Geraint's dining companions tried to stifle sniggers of amusement behind hands, though they didn't succeed. He gave each a look of disdain.

'That'll be the day,' Tom chuckled, 'Stella Vaughan going to Chapel. I expect it would open up just for you, Stella, if you'd give notice.'

'Tom Daly, shut your mouth before I come and shut it for you,' Stella snapped, her face like thunder. Tom laughed all the more.

'That's more like it,' Stella said complacently. She completed serving everyone their chosen beverage before clattering huffily out of the room. She felt embarrassed at having let her tongue run away with her, but she felt a few hard words were needed. She was satisfied that they seemed to have had the right effect. They were more cheerful, except for Mr Geraint Lloyd-Davies; he continued to scowl.

She looked back before pushing the trolley through the double doors. 'I'm going to Laburnum Unit now, to help with the toileting and settling everyone down for the afternoon. I'll pop in and see you before I go off duty, Mrs Dew.'

Stella could be heard trolley-clattering down the corridor towards the kitchens. The use of Bronwen's surname told her Stella was not in good humour. She was used to her being unable to hide her emotions. The effect of Bronwen having the winning numbers of the National Lottery was to put everyone's nerves on edge. Something was about to drastically change, and no one knew what to expect.

Bronwen hoped things would get back to normal after Wednesday's presentation of the cheque, though something in the crevices of her mind told her they wouldn't.

After lunch in Willow Lounge, everybody turned to their comfortable chairs or to their rooms for an afternoon nap. Bronwen went into Martha Tate's room and held her hand for a while. She told Martha what she thought was about to happen as a result of her getting all the numbers of the National Lottery. She wasn't sure whether Martha could hear what she was saying, but she did open her eyes and look intently onto Bronwen's face from time to time. Bronwen thought she saw the hint of a smile once or twice. Anyway, she felt surprisingly better having put the events of the previous evening and morning to Martha.

Chapter 4

The Scroungers

The remainder of that Sunday afternoon passed as every other did. The normality, however, didn't last. It ended during the evening, when Mary visited her mother.

She was earlier than usual, and she wasn't alone. A middle-aged couple trailed behind her who were vaguely familiar to Bronwen.

The woman had jaw-length, bleached, black-rooted, platinum, blonde hair with a fringe to her pencilled eyebrows. She had too much make-up on her chubby face. She wore a stylish, long, expensive-looking winter coat and tan-coloured calf-length boots up to the hemline of a brown, modern-style, slightly-flared skirt.

The man looked younger than his wife and was dwarfed by her. Bronwen assumed they were husband and wife. She was tall and, at least, as many stones overweight as Mary. The man was short and beneath his loose attire, couldn't have weighed more than Bronwen.

He was dressed as if he were on his way to a gymnasium to "work out", but his physique indicated that he never did. He wore a pair of bulbous, pale blue jogger bottoms and matching sweatshirt, both which looked too big for him. On his feet was a pair of elaborate trainers with huge tongues sticking out beyond the laces. His hair was cropped close to his skull and he had an earring in his left earlobe: one of Bronwen's pet hates—middle-aged men wearing earrings.

Mary's hair, which had been washed, set and styled by a hairdresser in the town to something which resembled a multi-coloured bird's nest the afternoon before, was now flat and scraggy. Mary had wasted her money yet again on trying to look attractive. Her face wasn't heavy with make-up as it usually was; she looked washed out.

'Mary, my lovely, you're early today and you don't look well. What's the matter?' Bronwen became immediately worried that Mary was going down with some illness. One of her nightmares was of Mary getting poliomyelitis, as she herself did as a child, which had destroyed the muscles of her legs.

'I'm all right, Mammy. Me and Stella went to The Colliers' last night after leaving here. Loads o' people bought me and Stella drinks when I told 'em you'd won the lottery and I fink someone mus' 'ave put somethin' in my drink to make me bad. She 'ad to drag me 'ome and she give me awful row when we got in. She said I shouldna' drunk all them drinks.'

'Never mind about what happened when you and Stella got home, love. Tell me about that afterwards. Now, introduce me to your company.'

The woman barged in. 'Well, Bronwen, darlin', don't you remember us? I'm Rodney's wife Bessie and this is Rodney, the youngest of your cousins. Your mother's youngest sister's boy. We're the Duncans from Sesame Street. You must remember us.'

Bronwen put on her spectacles to have a sharper sight of them. 'Oh, good Heavens, of course.'

Bessie had changed; got older and fatter. Rodney, older and thinner.

'What are you doing up here?' Bronwen asked, thinking they had come to the home to visit an elderly friend.

'We've come to see you, of course,' Bessie said, looking surprised that Bronwen didn't realise that. 'We called in for Mary to give her a lift up. We thought she'd be coming to see you.'

'I come to see my mam every day,' Mary said, looking put out. 'It's no' only on a Sunday I come.'

'No, of course not, darlin'. I know that. I thought we'd come with you this afternoon to congratulate your mother on her big win. We only heard this afternoon.'

'She only knew herself yesterday evening.' It was Geraint. He'd seen the couple coming in with Mary. He guessed they were the first of many scroungers Bronwen would have to deal with. He intended to help to protect her from them. He was sitting in a lounge chair opposite Bronwen, his Zimmer frame in front of him with a hand on its crossbar.

Bessie's nose and mouth puckered. She raised them to the air as if Geraint were a foul smell. She looked at him, up and down with disdain. 'Yes, we know, thank you,' she sniffed, as she turned her back on him.

She went on to talk about their family as if she couldn't stop; mentioning the names of people Bronwen hadn't heard of for years. Bessie included Rodney in the conversation, mentioning his mother's name frequently. Bronwen realised it was intended to remind her of the family relationship. Rodney dutifully nodded or shook his head as he thought timely, but sometimes nodding when he should have been shaking.

Bronwen was angered by Bessie's belittling attitude towards Geraint, but her kind temperament prevented her from saying anything discourteous to her. She could see Mary getting more agitated by the second and decided to say something to end the visit before she did.

'Well now, Bessie. Just what brought you here to see me today when I've only seen either of you no more than once or twice in the last twenty years? Rodney's mother didn't speak to my mother for years after my grandmother gave my mother a set of old jugs that his mother Elsie wanted.'

'We just came to congratulate you and to see you are well. We didn't come for a handout, if that's what you're thinking. We came to offer help. As you know Rodney had his own business for years and handled his own accounts. We wondered if you would like him to help handle your business.'

Bronwen stifled a gasp. For a few moments she was at a loss for words. Mary spoke for her.

'Yeh', an' he went bangcrupp, di'n't he?'

Bessie's hackles rose. 'Wasn't his fault. People didn't pay their bills.'

Geraint rose from his chair and walked around to face her. 'He went bankrupt because he's a nincompoop and couldn't run a business to save his life.'

Bessie opened her mouth to say something, but Geraint cut her short. 'Bronwen is too nice to tell you that she thinks you're here to scrounge because she's come into money.'

Bronwen cringed, but she knew Geraint was right. 'Thank you, Bessie, thank you, Rodney, but I will manage quite well. The management of whatever money is coming to me has already been arranged.'

Breathing heavily with disgust, Bessie rose from her chair, protruding her plenteous bosom. 'If that's your attitude, we'll be off. But I think you might regret leaving us out.' She turned on her high heels and beckoned Rodney to follow.

The room had become quiet. Bessie didn't realise that everyone was listening. Some of them laughed as the odd couple left the room. Some scoffed.

'My God,' one of them said, 'it's amazing how the worms crawl out of the shit when there's a bit of money about.'

Bronwen was upset. She couldn't cope well with confrontation, however slight. Geraint put his hand on her shoulder. 'You'd better get used to that sort of thing, my dear,' he said, sounding sad. 'You'll have a lot of hands out and begging letters. Let me, Tom and Stella deal with that sort of thing, will you?'

'And me,' Mary piped up. 'I won' 'ave noffin' to say to strangers who come knockin' at my door again.'

Bronwen wasn't sure Mary would be able to live up to her decision, but she said nothing to discourage her. She wanted the matter closed. She changed the subject.

'Yes, you're right, my lovely. Forget Bessie and Rodney now. Tell me what happened to you and Stella last night? And why do you look so untidy today?' Bronwen didn't risk hurting her daughter by asking why she looked untidier than usual, as someone else might have.

'Well, I've been clearing up most of the day. Stella made me, in case you'll want to come home, now you've go' a lot o' money. Stella gave me awful row for sayin' in the pub that you won the lottery and was a millionaire. When Aunty Bessie came and wha's 'is name, I was sleeping. I 'ad a 'eadache. Still got it.'

'Well, love, even if you hadn't announced my business in the pub, it seems it won't be long before the world and his wife will know. Especially after Wednesday, when two people are coming to hand me the cheque. My stomach churns every time I think about it.'

Tom had wheeled himself across and braked his wheelchair besides Bronwen.

'I know those two parasites, Bronwen. The Duncans from Sesame Street. They've been in the debtors' court more than once. They owe money to a lot of people who are worse off than themselves.'

Bronwen didn't tell Tom they were related. She was ashamed of them.

Tom nearly forgot himself in front of Mr Lloyd-Davies. 'If I ever find the likes of that sort of scrounging bas...' He stopped himself in time. Geraint, sitting opposite, raised his eyebrows to let Tom know he was listening.

'I'm off to my room to do a bit of searching of the Internet before I turn in,' Geraint said. 'There's something of interest I'm anxious to study.' He rose from his chair and walked away carrying his Zimmer frame. 'Good evening, Bronwen. I hope you get a better night. There's nothing to be said or done until after Wednesday afternoon.' The time and day were obviously engraved on his mind, too. 'Good evening, Tom. Good evening, Mary dear, and good luck with the clearing up of your house. It will have to be done, you know, but we'll help you.' He was almost through the heavy double doors before he shouted a good evening to everyone else.

Geraint looked younger than his eighty years though his face was creased with wrinkles. He had sharp eyes and a bright smile. He wasn't liked by everyone but respected for his integrity and wisdom.

Bronwen yawned. 'I'm tired, Mary, love, and you are as well. We'd best call it a day. You go home now, get yourself washed and get an early night.'

'Yes, all right, Mammy,' She pecked her mother's cheek and walked out of the room with Tom following her. He saw her to the exit.

He watched Mary waddle ungracefully down the hill as he muttered to himself. 'You're going to have to change, Mary, or you will fall by the wayside, no matter how your mam will try to hold you up.'

Mary did eventually change, but not a lot. It would take more than money to solve her problem.

Chapter 5
Martha Tate's Deathbed

The next day being Monday, the matron contacted Gordon Williams, the representative for the Cardiff company which supplied aids for the disabled. He knew the type of bed and mattress the matron was interested in, because on his last visit he had shown pictures of it and they had discussed its benefits. She was impressed and subsequently contacted the management to suggest that one of the beds be purchased. They had to refuse because of its high cost and a decline in profits over the year. People had died at The Sunshine Mount Nursing Home and their residencies hadn't been replaced.

Gordon Williams was delighted to hear from Matron Phillips; he had made a sale. He arranged for immediate delivery of the special bed and mattress to the home.

During the late afternoon, Bronwen's thoughts were deviated from her lottery win. The special bed and mattress arrived, and she spent a few interesting hours watching it being unwrapped, sanitised and made up in readiness for the transfer of Martha onto it from the well-worn, tired mattress.

The new bed was bigger than Bronwen had expected, having been shown a picture of a similar one by Helen. The real thing amazed her. The base could be raised or lowered, tilted to the right or left and the mattress could be raised at the top or bottom by pressing levers. Although it weighed heavily, it could be moved when brakes were released by being pushed or pulled with a light hand or foot.

Kindly, dependable Dora, a senior carer, treated the bed as if it were a toy, trying out all the gadgets. She bounced on the mattress, ignoring her undignified stance when her skirt rose above the knees of her splayed legs. There were screeches of laughter. Not from Mr Lloyd Davies. He decided he needed the lavatory.

Dora wasn't in the least embarrassed. 'Thank you, Mrs Dew, thank you, Matron, this bed is lovely. Best to try it out before we put Miss Tate in it, isn't it?'

Matron laughed. 'The bed isn't yours, Dora. At least, not yet.'

'Crikey, not for a long time, I hope,' Dora frowned.

The carers had fun trying out the bed to make sure it was safe before transferring Martha onto it. A representative of the company which supplied it was present to demonstrate all its uses.

Bronwen was allowed to be there to hold Martha's hand and explain to her what was happening, though she showed no response.

Martha was carefully transferred onto the new mattress. The result was her appearing comfortable and everyone delighted with the new, hi-tech piece of equipment.

The invoice was on Matron's desk. It was to be settled as soon as possible, after the day she was told to expect the big cheque. She couldn't bring herself to think she would. Things like that didn't happen to the likes of her, and she began to worry about how the new mattress and bed would be paid for. She felt sure there would be some catch, even though she had selected all the numbers of the lottery.

She need not have worried; there was no catch. The settlement of payment for the new bed would be paid forthwith.

The day of celebration of receiving a cheque for twenty point five million pounds was to be the following Wednesday. For Bronwen, it didn't dawn quickly enough. She wanted whatever was to happen, to be over and done with. However, the event was surprisingly easy, and more than that, she enjoyed it.

On that big day, shortly after two o'clock, a chauffeur-driven limousine drew up onto the courtyard of The Sunshine Mount Nursing Home. All those residents who could walk or steer their wheelchair themselves to the windows, had stretched the curtains far back to have a good view. There were gasps of wonder.

'Wooo, there's posh for you,' someone said.

Another added, 'I expect Bronwen will soon have a car like that.'

No further audible comment was made as interest turned to two elegant people getting out of the back seat of the car, after their uniformed chauffeur opened the door for them.

One was a handsome man, probably in his sixties, wearing a superior, grey suit. He had well-groomed, grey hair and a neat, matching moustache and beard. He carried an important-looking briefcase.

The other person who alighted form the ostentatious vehicle was a graceful, young woman in her early thirties. She wore a light blue matching coat, dress and accessories. Her hair was raven black, and her dark, creamy facial colouring indicated she was of Asian origin.

She saw staring faces at the windows and waved to them. One or two waved back but most were too much in awe of the refinement.

The chauffeur smiled at the faces of those at the windows. One of the faces belonged to Marlene, one of the carers.

'Cor, in 'e smashin'? I wouldn't say no to him.'

She was nudged by a colleague standing next to her. 'Shut up. Don't be common. You wouldn't say no to anybody.'

Matron was standing on the threshold of The Home to greet the two VIPs. She introduced herself and beckoned them to enter. Matron Phillips looked immaculate, not having been hands-on with the routine work of the units that morning. She had spent her time checking that every inch of the home was spotless, that the residents were comfortable, and she hoped upon hope that there was no aroma of bleach and disinfectant, or even worse, excreta. Matron was fastidious about that, but in a nursing home for the elderly, "accidents" were inevitable. The fact that some people considered that one could get used to the smells was against her principles.

She had checked with the kitchen staff that everything was in order for a teatime buffet to be taken at around four o'clock. The kitchen buzzed with excitement, and Matron was confident that Hettie, the kitchen manageress and her team, would excel.

'We won't let you and Bronwen down, Matron,' Hettie reassured her. They had previously organised Ivor, the maintenance man, to erect the long, rough wooden, trestle tables that were used on special occasions. The roughness of the wood was hidden by being covered with pristine, white tablecloths.

Matron led the two smart Camelot VIPs, followed by the chauffeur, into the hall, where, in the centre, Bronwen sat erect in her wheelchair with Tom in his wheelchair on one side, Geraint on the other. For the time being, his pride of being able to walk without his Zimmer frame took precedence over his dependence on it.

Stella stood behind Bronwen, nervous knuckle-white hands on the handles of her wheelchair. Bronwen looked her best; hair, make-up and dress. Stella had taken time to ensure she looked her most beautiful.

The man slowly approached Bronwen. 'Hello, Mrs Bronwen Dew. I'm delighted to meet you.' They shook hands.

'Thank you. And I'm pleased to meet you. Please call me Bronwen, Mr...'

'My name is Richard Mannering. My colleague is Miss Sara Malik.'

Sara shook hands with Bronwen. 'My name is Sara,' she said and smiled a smile which could have melted ice. 'Richard and I are happy to be here. We've delivered to many lucky winners, but this is quite different.'

'Yes,' Richard agreed, 'quite different, and we hope it will give encouragement to others like yourself, Bronwen, to enjoy playing the lottery. Lady Luck smiling on someone in your position lets others know that winning a fortune isn't confined to those who are fully able.' He looked down at the soft, flannel shawl that was spread across Bronwen's lap. Beneath, her deformed legs were covered with a fine wool trousers of a suit that Stella had chosen. It was worn in case the shawl accidentally slipped down, though that was unlikely.

'I'm sure you will enjoy being wealthy. And from what I know of you, you deserve to.'

'Thank you, Mr Mannering, I will, and so will my daughter and companions.' She, knowingly, turned to Geraint. They both realised that Richard Mannering must have made enquiries about Bronwen's past. Her personal data would now be on Camelot's computers. And no doubt would Geraint's.

Bronwen introduced her companions to Richard and Sara. 'This is Mr Geraint Lloyd-Davies, my accountant, this is Tom Daly and Stella, my dear friends. And over there,' she said, as she pointed to Mary, trying to be invisible as she sat on a stool by the lifts, 'that is my daughter, Mary. She is very shy.'

Mary's face flared to a bright rosy, pink; she lowered her head. She blushed easily when being introduced to someone. At that moment, Bronwen thought she hadn't looked so smart since—she couldn't remember when. Stella had chosen her clothes, dyed her hair back to near its natural colour and styled it. She also ensured that Mary's face was just touched with a light make-up and not plastered thickly, as she would have done herself.

'I look like a' old maid,' Mary had said when she was dressed.

'And that's what you'll become if you go on wearing the ridiculous garb that you do.' Stella had bullied. Mary was glad she had listened to Stella; she felt smart.

She looked up and smiled at Richard Mannering and Bronwen thought she looked attractive in spite of being overweight. She'd lost a few pounds since Stella insisted on her following a low-calorie diet. Stella was determined that Mary would go on losing until most of the excess blubber had been shed. The fish-and-chips shop was out of bounds.

The chauffeur, who had been standing near the door with a camera, interrupted and spoke to the matron. 'Would it be all right for me to take a few photographs?'

Matron didn't answer until she looked at Bronwen for agreement. Bronwen nodded.

'There's your answer, then,' Matron replied, 'but when we're in the lounge having tea with our more infirm residents, I must ask you to remember that they might be disturbed by a bright flashing light.'

'Yes, of course,' he agreed. 'My name, by the way, is Tony.'

'Right then, Tony. Let's all move on to our visitors' room. It allows more privacy when the need arises. I think this is one of those times.'

Matron Phillips led the VIPs, Bronwen and her company into the visitors' room on Willow Unit and shut the door after everyone was seated.

There was much small talk and the atmosphere became more relaxed. Tom was glad that he allowed Stella to cut his shoulder-length hair and regretted not letting her trim his unruly moustache and beard to make them neater. He became conscious of it when the lovely Sara talked to him and Geraint. Bronwen talked to Richard, Stella talked to the smart chauffeur. Mary moved and sat near her mother in silence since Stella had told her to speak only when spoken to. She enjoyed listening to Stella sweet-talking the handsome Tony.

Matron poured white wine into the home's best glasses and handed them around on a neatly set tray. The driver would have liked to accept a glass of wine, but he looked at his boss's expression and refused. He took a glass of fruit juice.

When everyone had a glass in hand, Matron proposed a toast to Bronwen. She waved her glass around before taking a gulp. She hoped it would steady her nerves. 'Good luck, Bronwen,' was choroused.

The small talk ended when Richard Mannering opened his brief case and took out an envelope. He handed it to Bronwen, who looked at it and pondered. She seemed reluctant to open it, as if she were meant not to.

She opened it with shaking fingers, withdrew the cheque and stared at it. It was computer-printed. She had expected it to be made out in handwriting; in the same way as she had, on rare occasions, seen cheques.

'Twenty million, five hundred thousand pounds,' She read what it said slowly and quietly, as if to herself. 'It won't sink into my numb brain,' she said, shaking her head. 'It's hard to believe that this little slip of paper can change my world.' She looked around the room at the faces of her silent companions. The expressions were blank. 'And all yours, too.'

She returned the cheque to the envelope with shaking hands. 'Yes,' she said, 'thank you. Do I keep it now?'

No one spoke; they looked and wondered what the next move or word would be.

Richard Mannering broke the silence. 'It's yours, Bronwen. I take it you have an account at your local bank?'

Mary, now sitting on the carpet at her mother's feet, made a quick response.

'Yes, she can't touch tha'. I's for 'mergencies.' Everyone looked surprised. There was determination in her voice. For some reason, known only to Mary, she was afraid her mother would be asked to dig into her precious savings. 'She mustn't use tha',' she insisted.

Stella cringed with embarrassment. Tom and Geraint looked at each other and shook their heads in disbelief of Mary's naivety.

Bronwen stroked the top of Mary head. 'No, my lovely, we won't touch that.'

She looked at everyone, her expression apologising for Mary's ignorance.

'Mary, like myself, is having difficulty grasping the reality of the situation. She'll learn; given time.'

The lovely Sara crossed the room and sat on the carpet opposite Mary.

'Of course, she hasn't. What's happened to Bronwen is rare, indeed. Virtually overnight she has become rich beyond her wildest dreams.' She took Bronwen's hand. 'I am an accountant, as your friend, Mr Lloyd-Davies is. But he has years more experience than I have, and I assume he will be advising you, as well as taking care of your financial matters. That's good. However, I'd like you to take my card,' She rummaged in her fine, blue leather handbag and withdrew a business card. 'And Richard's, too.' She turned around to face Richard and held out her hand for his personal card which he took from his jacket breast-pocket. He had been watching and listening intently to what was being said at that side of the room. He, dutifully, gave it to Sara and she put the two cards into the palm of Bronwen's hand. Bronwen put them into her new handbag; small and neat, again of Stella's choosing.

'If you have any problem or need advice, you mustn't hesitate but to call me on that number,' she pointed to Camelot's number. 'Or that long figure there, which is my personal phone number. I should always be available to you but if, by any chance, I am not, you have Mr Mannering's card. That's right, isn't it, Richard?'

'It is, indeed,' he replied. 'Now I have to ask you to do something for me. Would you all bunch closely together for Tony to take more photographs? And when we are taking tea in your dining room, would you mind him taking photographs there? One with myself handing the cheque to you, Bronwen, although I've already given it to you. Perhaps I can borrow it back for a few minutes. The photographs are not for the world to view but for our own records. Tony, I know, will be discrete to avoid upsetting anyone.'

Richard Mannering looked at Helen who was still sipping her wine. 'Is that all right with you, Matron?'

She smiled as she tipped her lips from her glass. 'Yes, of course, and I'd be grateful of copies of the photographs for our own records.'

Tony replied. 'I'll get them to you as soon as possible.'

They all moved into a huddle around Bronwen and three photographs were snapped with a break between each one when Tony reminded everyone to smile.

'Now,' Matron said, 'we must go in to tea. The residents are wanting theirs, but more than that, they are waiting to be involved in the proceedings. You must understand, Mr Mannering, that some of them are quite elderly and have trouble accepting experiences which interfere with the security of their routine.

'Then, there are those you might think are oblivious to what's going on but, I assure you, their minds are as sharp as mine. They are delighted for Bronwen.'

With her hand in her pocket, Matron Helen Phillips crossed her fingers that no one would come out with some embarrassing remark. Sara nor Richard, as far as she knew, were familiar with the care of the elderly and infirm.

Matron led, with Bronwen's wheelchair close on her heels being pushed by Stella. Then came Tom, being pushed by Mary. Geraint was some time following; he had to go to the lavatory. His prostate was playing up as it was apt to do when he was stressed or excited.

An unusual loudness came from the lounge of Laburnum Lounge as the attendant company walked down the corridor towards it. Bronwen wondered why it was so noisy until she got there. She gasped with surprise when she found the combined lounge and dining room areas were more crowded than she'd ever seen them.

Fifteen residents of Laburnum and twenty of Willow Units and relatives and friends from both, had turned up in droves for the special occasion. Some would-be interested viewers had to be refused entry and were outside, peering through the windows. A cheer, loud enough to raise the roof, was given when Bronwen entered the room.

'Good God alive,' Stella gasped. 'Where the hell have they all come from?' She couldn't understand how the news of Bronwen's lottery win had spread so far and so quickly.

The head cook and her assistants were scattered around the room busily removing cling-film from the dozens of plates of food. A table had been prepared for Bronwen and her company in a position where everybody could see them.

The lounge chairs of the totally dependent residents were in a half circle near the double doors, so that if anyone of them shouted for the toilet the carers could discretely take them there.

The tension of the moment was sensed by one of those residents who loudly shouted his need.

'Somebody take me to the lav,' he shouted. 'I want to shit. And be quick.'

The lovely Sara's eyes popped. Matron smiled. Stella cringed. Bronwen and Richard pretended they hadn't heard.

Hettie, the cook, sidled her way to Matron. 'Matron, there's never enough food for all these. I didn't expect so many.'

'Neither did I,' Matron replied, still smiling. 'But don't worry, Hettie, things will work out all right. And if they don't, it's not the end of the world. Bronwen's getting the big cheque and that's the most important.'

'Ay, I suppose so,' Hettie tutted as she waddled towards the kitchen area.

Bronwen sat at the top table with Richard Mannering next to her. Stella had arranged their plates neatly with a few sandwiches and *vol au vents* but neither, it seemed, felt like eating.

Richard Mannering gave a short speech of congratulations to Bronwen and handed her the precious envelope with one hand whilst shaking her free hand with other. A number of photographs were taken and there was loud cheering.

With so many people in the room, it became hot and stuffy. The residents began to get increasingly agitated and restless. More requests for the toilet were heard during Mr Mannering's speech. One elderly lady continually shouted, 'What's going on! What's going on! What's going on?'

She got on the nerves of the old man sitting next to her. 'Will you shut your bloody mouth,' he shouted. But she didn't oblige.

A carer tried to calm the noisy, elderly lady by explaining to her what was going on. 'Shush, Nell, it'll soon be over,' the anxious carer said in a hush, as she took the agitated lady by the hand and led her out of the room.

And it was soon over. Richard Mannering made excuses for himself and Sara for having to leave; they had a long journey back and a seasonal mist hovered outside. In autumn, there was always a mist greying the top of the hill where The Sunshine Mount Nursing Home stood. It would have dispersed by the time they had descended to the main road.

They bid Bronwen and her close companions farewell before returning to their magnificent limousine.

Among Richard's last words to Bronwen were, 'I think you will travel the world now you have the wherewithal to do so, Bronwen. You will take your daughter and close companions. You have my business card; I would like to get postcards from you. And I know Camelot would like to get postcards from you. It's good publicity to encourage people to play the National Lottery.'

Bronwen had sensed that Richard was advising her to get away from life within the home. She also sensed that he was rich and couldn't contemplate that he, one day, might end up in a nursing home. That was, if he lived long enough. He, nor Sara, would realise that nursing homes were an essential part of society.

Bronwen, had sensed that Sara, also was impatient to leave Laburnum Lounge. Seeing people with severe Parkinson's disease, the confusion of Alzheimer's disease and, what she considered to be indignities of life, clearly disturbed her. Like many young people, Sara hadn't given consideration to the fact that one day she, too, would be old—God willing.

Matron guided Richard and Sara out of the building. Bronwen, Tom, Stella and Mary waved them off as well as a crowd that had gathered inside and outside the home entrance hall. But not Geraint; he had gone to the lavatory.

As the big, black car purred down the hill, away from The Sunshine Mount Nursing Home, Bronwen patted her handbag.

'Right,' she said, 'now for part two of Bronwen Dew's life. Stella, push my wagon back to the table in top lounge. I'm starving.' She often referred to her wheelchair as a wagon. It was what Lewis had called it.

'Me, too,' Stella said 'My nerves have been too screwed up to eat for days. I'm going to dive into those chicken pieces and salmon sandwiches. And there's a lovely looking sherry trifle waiting for us.'

Stella was wrong about that. When she and Bronwen got through the door and made their way to the buffet table, they were disappointed. The long table was bare. It was as if a plague of locusts had passed over it.

Hangers-on of relatives and friends occupied every free chair in the room and were in groups, munching at what was on their tea-plates and happily chatting between themselves.

The carers sat beside the residents. They had been placed back at their original places and were helped to take their tea and sandwiches, which had been reserved for them.

Peace reigned.

Matron noticed the disappointment on Bronwen's and Stella's face. She went across to them. 'Don't worry; I'll arrange something for the starving few when I've got rid of this lot.' She referred to the hangers-on. 'The ceremony is over; all over, Bronwen, and it wasn't as painful as we thought, was it?'

'No,' Bronwen agreed and again patted her handbag. 'Those two VIPs were lovely. But it's far from over, Matron. In fact, I think that was the beginning of the beginning—far from over.'

Most of the carers on duty at that time were busy with those residents who needed help to take tea, then to the toilet before settling for the evening. They were tired and confused by the unusual event of the day. Some of them understood fully what had gone on, but were unable to express themselves. It seemed that being verbally aggressive eased their frustration. Those whose incapacity didn't allow them to partake fully in the celebration were more contented when the surroundings were back to normal. The carers, too, were tired after the excitement of the afternoon. If the inquisitive visitors left, would have helped, but Matron remained professional and lied when telling them they were welcome to stay for as long as they wished. Maintaining the good name of The Sunshine Mount Nursing Home was imperative to its future.

Inevitably, feeling that they had outstayed their welcome, the visitors got bored, and gradually dwindled away, satisfied having seen Bronwen Dew being presented with her fortune. Some had wondered what she looked like.

'I expect one or two thought it a waste for an old cripple like me to have won all this money,' Bronwen said to Stella.

'You're not an old cripple, and let them think what they like,' Stella replied. 'You look better than some of them who are half your age.'

'And what about all those who said well done?' Tom reminded Bronwen. She hadn't forgotten. In fact, she was surprised at the number of people who wished her well.

When all the residents were comfortable, the staff sat around a table in Laburnum Lounge, discussing Bronwen's day. They enjoyed warm cups of chocolate and food that Hettie and her assistants had freshly prepared for them.

By the time the night staff came on duty, the atmosphere had returned to normal. The handover took place and both teams helped to take those who wished to rest early to their rooms. Others were made comfortable in their usual chairs to watch the television.

The day staff donned their warm winter coats and left. It wouldn't be too long before they'd be on duty again.

Most of those who had taken part in the exciting and unique celebration of the afternoon would have an early night—but not eighty-year-old Mr Geraint Lloyd-Davies. He worked into the small hours, searching the Internet. It was always the same; whenever he started on his computer with the intention of having a short browse, he would be there for hours. The wonders of the computer, e-mail, and especially the Internet, were like magnets to him. The matron had advised him many times that to sit too long wasn't good for his circulation, especially since he had a renal problem. He was inclined to forget her good advice.

Before Bronwen won the lottery, he spent time in front of his computer researching as a result of what he'd heard on the radio or read in the newspapers. Now it was different. He was especially excited, having something positive to work on—Bronwen's fortune.

Initially, he needed to know how to deal with a vast sum of money. Was it any different from many years ago, when he practiced his profession? From what he discovered, financial jiggery-pokery hadn't changed much, except that the sums dealt with were larger.

He decided how he would advise Bronwen. It would be to take small steps, one at a time. He thought it would be unwise to discuss investments and accumulation of interest with her. He would arrange his advice in a way which would be suitable for her. Her considered her to be highly intelligent and would be quick to understand, so he would be careful not to be patronising.

At first, he would advise her to travel, but not far and not for long. She had mentioned to him during one of their casual chats that she'd like to go to America. Geraint considered a trip to America too ambitious, as yet. She wasn't used to being away for long periods. One thing for sure, he would advise her to retain her room at The Sunshine Mount Nursing Home. One could never tell how things would turn out. He decided to advise Bronwen to keep her old home, 22, Queen Street, as a base, but to get it renovated and made suitable for her to live in comfort. Stella's brother, Colin Pritchard, was a master builder and would be the man to do that.

Of course, Geraint would retain his room at The Sunshine Mount Nursing Home, even though he guessed Bronwen would expect him to move out when she did. They would live at her old home which could be made luxurious with no expense spared. He decided he would like that. Stella would live there. Bronwen wouldn't leave her behind, and she needed Stella's practical caring skill to continue. The whole arrangement would be better for Mary. Bronwen's fortune, Geraint thought, had come just in time to prevent her daughter sinking into an abysmal rut.

His head was buzzing with ideas, but first, he must put them to Bronwen. She was the deciding force. He was tempted to tap on her room door there and then to ask her if she felt like talking, but he resisted. It was past two o'clock in the morning. She wouldn't be pleased. She might even be frightened. Yes, he thought, things will have to move slowly. He decided to suggest a meeting to mull over ideas, and initial measures which should be taken.

First thing in the morning he planned to ask to speak to Matron Phillips in private. He would request a loan of the home's mini-bus. He and Bronwen and possibly Tom and Stella would go to Bronwen's bank in town and deposit the big cheque. The home's transport was designed for people with wheelchairs, so it was essential that they have use of it until Bronwen had her own suitably designed vehicle. She wouldn't yet have thought of getting one.

Geraint was grinning as he lay on his bed wondering how the staff of the bank would react and indeed, the manager, when twenty and a half million pounds was deposited into Bronwen's account.

Geraint felt rejuvenated with the challenge of helping Bronwen. He fell asleep with a smile on his aged face, after using his urinal for the umpteenth time. His dreams were filled with columns of numbers of pounds which he added up over and over and couldn't get them to balance. He was relieved when his prostate awakened him to use a urinal yet again.

He was on a hospital list to receive specialist advice and treatment for the prostate gland problem. The sooner that was attended to, the better.

Chapter 6
Millions in the Bank

The morning following the presentation of the winning lottery cheque began as all days did in The Sunshine Mount Nursing Home, except that Geraint Lloyd-Davies didn't appear for breakfast. That was unusual. When Dora, the carer,
knocked on his door and had no reply, she opened it slightly and called out to him.

'Are you awake, Mr Lloyd-Davies? Can I help you to wash and dress?'

No reply; she became alarmed. She entered the room to check that he wasn't ill, or worse. To find someone had died during the night was not an uncommon event at the home.

Geraint awoke with a start when Dora shook him. 'It's all right, Dora,' he muttered sleepily, 'I don't think I'm dead.' She laughed with relief at his careless humour.

'I feel a bit tired this morning, Dora. I'll just take my pills and lie on for a bit. I've missed breakfast, but that won't hurt.'

'Well, all right, Mr Lloyd-Davies, but you know Matron doesn't like that. She will want you to keep mobile and it's not like you to want to lie on.'

'Tell her I was working half the night on Mrs Dew's affairs. She'll understand. And if you don't mind, tell Mrs Dew that I'll see her in a couple of hours.'

'One of the girls from the kitchen will bring you up a cup of tea and a couple pieces of toast. You know you can't take your pills on an empty stomach.'

Geraint wished Dora would stop fussing. As soon as she'd gone, he used his urinal before falling back into bed and cocooning himself in the warm duvet. He'd have to get up when he wanted to pass urine again as his urinal was now full. What a nuisance! He hoped his prostate would stay calm for a few hours.

It did; he fell asleep.

When he awoke, he saw a tray of cold toast and tea on his bedside table. He remembered Dora bringing it in. He had stirred and taken his medication before falling asleep again. Now he felt hungry. He was glad it was nearly lunchtime.

He dressed himself as tidily as he could before going down to lunch. Without having one of the carers to help him to dress he looked bedraggled.

He remembered to take out his dentures from the pot where they'd been soaking overnight. He rinsed them under the running tap water before putting them into his mouth, but he didn't comb his hair or tidy himself up.

He went into Willow Lounge and sat next to Bronwen and Tom. Tom usually sat in another part of the room with old acquaintances. They were the smokers who commiserated with each other for being denied overseeing their own packets of cigarettes and matches.

Today he sat next to Bronwen, waiting for Mr Lloyd-Davies to join them.

'Mr Lloyd-Davies,' Tom spoke surreptitiously. 'I hope you don't mind me saying, but your fly is not done up. And you haven't done up your shoelaces. Watch you don't trip on them; we don't want you falling on your face.'

Mr Lloyd-Davies appeared agitated. He looked down and immediately did up his fly. 'Thank you, Tom. I must look a mess. I stayed up too long last night, playing at my computer and tired myself. I'll be all right once I've had a bit of lunch, though,' he looked at Bronwen.

'Bronwen, dear,' he said, 'I intend asking Matron if we can borrow the mini-bus this afternoon to take your cheque to the bank, as it's doing nothing in your handbag. You must put it into your account straight away. The sooner it's in, the sooner it will gain interest. We'll speak to the bank manager and explain how we intend to manage it at present.' He looked about him furtively, as if he were about to divulge a state secret. He hoped others weren't close enough to hear what he had said. He leant over the table and whispered to Bronwen. 'It might be a good idea to put it into four different bank accounts for a while.'

'Yes, pity to lose a couple of quid interest that could be added to your millions, Bron,' Tom smirked. Geraint recognised Tom's facetiousness and gave him a dirty look.

Bronwen nodded her head in agreement. 'Yes, of course, Geraint. We'll do that.' She would have agreed with whatever he had planned.

'Yes, that is a good idea, Bronwen,' Tom emphasised. 'If I were you, I'd do whatever Mr Lloyd-Davies says. He's an accountant; he knows exactly what to do.'

'Yes, Tom, I will. And I'm sure Matron will let us have a loan of the bus. Stella is on the late shift. She'll drive us if Matron can spare her off the team. We'll go when everybody is having their afternoon rest, shall we? You can come for the ride, if you like, Tom, and listen to what's going on. Will you ring and make an appointment? Mr Clapworthy is the bank manager's name. Geraint is right, the sooner this cheque is out of my bag, the better.'

She looked at her handbag which she'd hitched over the arm of her chair. It was old and shabby but of precious sentimental value. She removed it, put it onto her lap and smiled. 'Lewis gave me this bag years ago. Who would have thought that one day it would hold millions of pounds?' Her smile became a chuckle before she continued her instructions to Tom.

'And will you ring the house and tell Mary to be up here by two o'clock? She'll have to know what's going on. I'll pay your telephone bill; you've used it a lot on my behalf.'

'Are you sure you can afford it, Bron?' Tom laughed at his own joke.

'She can,' Geraint said. 'In fact, Bronwen, if I may suggest something else, you must get a mobile phone for yourself and one each for Mary and Stella before we start going places. Because, travel we will, and we'll need to keep in touch with one another.'

'What about a phone for you, then?' Bronwen asked Geraint.

'Well, I'll buy my own. I don't want to depend on you for that.'

She and Tom were exasperated and raised eyes to the ceiling with frustration. 'For goodness sake, Geraint. I've got millions to spend. Every penny any of you spend from now on, and I'm referring to Stella and Mary as well as you, Tom, you'll be doing me a favour by letting me do it. This money must be spent and I don't know how I'm to do it. And if you know of anyone in this home who is in need of something, that will be up to me as well.'

'Thank you. That's very kind of you, Mrs Dew.' Bronwen hadn't heard Matron Helen Phillips approaching. 'At the moment we're all right. You've already got us an enormously expensive bed and mattress. The management will appreciate that, and the fact that you've made this home famous.

'Someone from The Chronicle contacted me this morning and asked if your story could be put in the local newspaper. I hope you don't mind, but I agreed. They want a photo of you and your group of close companions. I made them promise not to make too much fuss. I think when people hear about your good fortune our empty residencies will soon be filled. You see, empty beds mean loss of income and that could lead to me having to lay off some of my carers. I don't want to do that.'

'All right,' Bronwen agreed apprehensively. 'As long as they'll come and go without, as you said, any fuss,' she paused. 'I have to ask you a favour now.'

'If it's to ask me if you can use the minibus, the answer is yes, of course.'

'There's something else, Matron. Could you spare Stella to drive us?' Bronwen felt humble. She knew that just one carer off the team increased the workload of the others.

Matron nodded. 'How could I refuse? You'll need to go to the bank in Pendarren, won't you? You're known there, Bronwen.'

'Yes,' Geraint interrupted. 'We have to get things moving. There's a lot to do.' He heard the lunch trolleys coming up the corridor and his hunger became the more important. 'Good, the food is coming. I'm hungry.'

Before Tom moved to the dining table, he dialled Mary's home. It rang and rang and rang. 'There's no reply,' Tom said.

'She's most probably still in bed,' Bronwen tutted. 'Keep ringing until she hears, Tom. We'd better get you a new phone as well, because that one must be nearly worn out.'

Eventually, Mary answered. 'Hello,' she was barely able to open her tardy mouth.

'Mary, this is Tom. Your mother said for you to be here by two o'clock.'

'Two o'clock?' She was beginning to rouse. 'I only just go' up. Wha' she wan' me by two for?'

'Never mind what for. Just shift your arse and get here by two o'clock.' Tom switched off and snapped his phone closed.

'No need to be rude to the girl,' Geraint frowned.

'Sorry, Mr Lloyd-Davies.' Even Tom tried never to be course in Mr Lloyd-Davies's company.

An appointment was made with the manager of the H.S.B.C. Bank, Mr Clapworthy, for half-past two. Since Geraint was the accountant, Tom had suggested he used his phone to make the appointment.

'You speak to the bank manager, Mr Lloyd-Davies. It's best you do all that sort of business. You're more used to it than I am,' Tom spoke as he handed across the mobile phone.

'Yes, all right, Tom. Thank you.' Tom had made Geraint feel important.

Stella, still wearing her spruce uniform, brought the minibus close to the entrance of the nursing home, to make it easier for everyone to get on. Bronwen and Tom were pushed up the ramp at the rear, designed to get wheelchairs aboard. Geraint and Mary sat on the scuffed, vinyl-covered seats. Geraint's two hands grabbed a tattered briefcase on his knees. Stella sat, looking pleased with herself, with hands on the steering wheel.

Bronwen's win on the National Lottery had become known to the few people working at the small-town branch of H.S.B.C., known to Bronwen as The Midland Bank, so she guessed they wouldn't be surprised at the large amount she was about to deposit. The cheque felt like a coal fire burning in her old leather handbag.

'You've got that cheque safe, Bronwen?' Geraint asked as Stella took a right turn into the town. He was nervous. He hadn't practiced his profession for many years but having scanned the Internet, he was reasonably confident that it would soon come back to him.

'Well, blow me,' Bronwen replied. 'I must have left it on the toilet shelf when I went, just before we came out.'

'You what!' Geraint yelled. 'Surely, you never did?'

She put her hand into her handbag and her fingers went directly onto the envelope which held the cheque. She withdrew it and waved it in the air.

Bronwen's joke was good incentive to cheer the air, but not for Mr Geraint Lloyd-Davies. He was not amused, and his expression said so as the others laughed.

Stella stopped the minibus at the corner of the main street, directly outside the H.S.B.C. Bank. There were two sets of disabled cards displayed on the front of the minibus dashboard, so she didn't expect trouble from a traffic warden, even if Pendarren had one, which it didn't. It was considered by the authorities not busy enough for a traffic warden—or affluent enough.

Stella manoeuvred Tom and Bronwen's wheelchairs out of the back of the van and helped Mr Lloyd-Davies down the steps of the minibus before handing to him his Zimmer frame.

'I'll leave that behind, Stella. I don't want them here to think I need help to walk.' Geraint returned the frame to the back of the minibus.

'You don't need help,' Bronwen reminded him, as she had many times. 'I don't know why you carry it, because carry it you do.'

'If it gives him confidence, there's no reason why he can't carry it, Bronwen,' Tom said as he turned to Mary. 'Now, Mary, you push me. Stella can't push me and your mother into the bank.'

Mary looked surprised to be entrusted with a responsibility but did as she was told. She looked untidy, having got out of bed before she wanted to. She had hurriedly dressed and had left the house before she was fully awake. She hadn't locked the front door of the house. She had often forgotten to do so. It didn't matter anymore; she couldn't remember where she'd hidden the key.

There were no other clients in the bank and the young lady who approached the odd group appeared to have expected them. She let the manager know they had arrived, and he appeared at the door of his office to show them in. Tom, Stella and Mary sat in the reception area. Mr Clapworthy invited only Bronwen and Geraint into his office.

Tom, Stella and Mary were offered cups of tea or coffee, but they all refused. Mary was about to accept but Stella gave her an elbow-nudge and sealed her lips. She was tired, hungry and thirsty and the half-hour wait felt like an age. It wouldn't have been so long had not Mr Lloyd-Davies need the lavatory. He was guided to the staff toilet by one of the clerks.

When he and Bronwen finally emerged from Mr Clapworthy's office, they were smiling. He looked quite pleased with himself, since Geraint had arranged to leave a large sum of money for Bronwen's immediate use with his branch; two million in her current account and the remainder in a deposit account. Mr Clapworthy bounced with nervousness; he hadn't dealt with such a large amount before.

'Two million in a current account!' he said with astonishment. 'That's not a good investment. The interest is quite low, you know?'

'We're not interested in gaining interest at this early stage, Mr Clapworthy,' Bronwen replied. 'We'll be travelling, so I'll need immediate access.'

Geraint nodded and looked at Bronwen. 'That's right. And you'll be buying some form of transport, won't you?'

Bronwen looked surprised. 'Oh, yes, of course.' Her eyebrows raised; she hadn't thought that far ahead.

The remainder of the millions were put in separate accounts; divided between four different establishments, until Bronwen and Mr Lloyd-Davies had more time to decide what was the best and easiest way to deal with it for the immediate and long-term use.

Bronwen was given a leather wallet embossed with the bank's name, containing a new chequebook, a debit card, and a gold credit card for an indefinite amount. Mr Clapworthy explained the benefits of it. Geraint confirmed the fact that the cards would be insured against loss or theft and repeated that the arrangement with Mr Clapworthy would be temporary. This was accepted, and Mr Clapworthy enforced the availability of his services.

Bronwen surprised the bank manager when she insisted that the same cards and terms be made available to Mary, Stella, Geraint and Tom and they should each have, as she had, a smart, leather wallet.

'You may charge me for them, Mr Clapworthy,' she said as she rubbed her fingers over the fine leather. 'I can tell they are quality.'

'Yes, but I think H.S.B.C. can stretch to one each for you,' Mr Clapworthy grinned.

Geraint wore a stern expression. 'Bronwen, are you sure of what you are suggesting?'

'Absolutely,' Bronwen spoke with determination. 'I know exactly what I am suggesting. And, from now, I want five thousand pounds to be put in an account for each of you.' She looked at Mr Clapworthy for his response. He nodded and made a note of her instructions.

'There'll be the signing to be done. I'll get our clerk to arrange the documents. We must arrange another meeting.'

Bronwen went on, 'We'll travel until my house, 22, Queen Street, has been renovated and made ready for us to live in comfort. We will travel together; go together as a group as any family would. And although I intend moving out of The Sunshine Mount Nursing Home to live in the community, I will retain my room because it's inevitable that I will end up there one day. But, God willing, not for a while. And the same applies to you, Geraint.' She looked again at Mr Clapworthy. 'The rooms will be paid for by monthly direct debit, please.'

Mr Clapworthy and Mr Lloyd-Davies nodded. It went through Mr Clapworthy's mind that Bronwen Dew knew what she was about. Her gentle manner and modesty disguised wisdom and a sharp mind.

She underestimated her ability. She was an avid reader of newspapers and magazines and had gathered a lot of interesting information that she thought would never apply to her. Now, she was finding that it did. Bronwen was a knowledgeable woman, though she would never have considered herself to be so.

When all were aboard the minibus, on the way back to the home, Tom, Stella and Mary said nothing. They waited for Geraint and Bronwen to tell them what went on when the big cheque was handed over. Geraint patted his briefcase.

'All is in order, my friends,' he said. 'Our finances have changed—mustn't make too much of it, though. Mustn't let a bank balance change what we are.'

Bronwen gave a loud, 'Yipeeee! And now, my lovelies, we spend, spend, spend!'

Chapter 7
Spend, Spend, Spend

After suppertime at the Willow Unit lounge that evening, Bronwen sat in her usual chair. Mary sat on her left and Stella on her right. Tom and Geraint, close by, were in chairs facing her. Though the afternoon's appointment at the bank had gone smoothly, and they had rested afterwards, there was tension in the air.

Bronwen's euphoria on leaving the bank had passed and now her mind was in a turmoil. What will happen next? She wondered. She sounded full of confidence when they were driven by Stella from the bank. Spend, spend, spend, she had said. But how? What do they spend the money on? What did she need?

She found herself in a new and rare situation. She knew Mary had dreamed of being rich but expected it to always remain a dream. She was the least equipped to be involved with millions of pounds. Bronwen realised Stella and Geraint would understand. She didn't think Tom would. He couldn't accommodate to the fact that he had five thousand pounds in his own bank account. Bronwen didn't know if he'd had a bank account. She knew Mary hadn't. Geraint might have to arrange that with the bank. More signatures would be asked for.

The planned meeting had to be short. Stella would be needed to help the carers in the Laburnum Lounge, preparing the residents for settling down for the night.

They gathered in a huddle to discuss their next moves. The sound of the big screen television was turned down so that those of the other residents had a choice of hearing what was going on within the group or take in the programme.

Tom, Stella and Mary were told earlier, in private, of their involvement in Bronwen's fortune. Mary especially, didn't understand the significance of five thousand pounds having been put into an account for each of them.

Stella gasped; Mary's expression remained unchanged.

'How much is that, Stella,' she asked.

'A lot,' Stella replied. 'I'll explain when I have more time. Shut up and listen for now.'

Tom shouted, 'Five thousand pounds! Five thousand, did you say, Bronwen? What the hell am I going to do with five thousand pounds?'

'It'll buy plenty of fags and matches,' Mary said as a comfort to Tom. She had recovered from being forced out of bed that afternoon and was excited about having plenty of money to spend.

'Can I go to the hairdressers and have a perm tomorrow, Mammy? A perm costs a lot, mind.'

'Doesn't matter about the cost, my lovely, but I don't think your hair would survive another perming. You don't want to be bald when we go on our trip, do you? Let Stella do your hair from now on. Look how lovely hers is.'

'Yes, I'll do your hair, Mary. No more messing about with it. Don't you ever dare step into another hairdresser's unless I'm with you. And while your house is being cleared out, you will live with me and Colin and I won't put up with any argument. You'll eat proper meals with us and hopefully lose some of the ton of blubber you're carrying.'

Mary pouted. 'A ton is a lot, i'n't it?' Her ridiculous statement was ignored.

Geraint gave the impression he hadn't heard. 'Let's get on. We haven't much time. If we can decide on just one or two points this evening, it will help.'

'Yes. For a start you'll need some suitable form of transport,' Tom proposed. 'Can't go on borrowing the home's minibus. You'll need something like a people-carrier, Bronwen. Or one of those stretch limousines that are on hire in the town for weddings and special parties. You can go a lot better than the home's minibus. That looks more like a prison van.'

'That's right,' Geraint said, 'but that's where I must take a back seat, so to speak. You'll know more about that, Stella. And your brother knows more than you. Could you ask his advice?'

'Yes, of course I can, but even Colin doesn't know all that much about cars. He's a builder. Can't you and Tom look on the Internet? Not one of those long ugly cars that look like train carriages, Tom. Something stylish that can fit into a parking space anywhere,' Stella sounded disgruntled.

'Yes, Stella, I see what you mean. But it will have to be bigger than the usual family saloon if you intend going places in it,' Tom responded.

'Yes, Tom, I do. I think I'll leave it to you men. You pick out something you think is suitable; write down a few details for me to give to Colin. And I'll ask my friend, Kevin. He knows about cars.

'We'll have to order it, won't we? It normally takes only a couple of days, but this will have to be specially designed for wheelchairs. I think we'll have to tread careful not to make mistakes. No spending for spending sake, or Bronwen will be broke again before she knows it.'

'That's right, Stella. Mistakes cost money,' Geraint said, shaking his head.

'One thing is for sure,' Bronwen interrupted, 'we don't have to be worried about cost. I have more than I will ever spend, but I still don't want to be cheated. Because I'm in a wheelchair, people sometimes seem to think my brains are in my no-good legs. We're none of us fools so we are not going to be taken for such.'

She looked doubtfully at Mary. 'Of course, Mary doesn't have the experience the rest of us do, so we'll just have to keep an eye on her.'

'And as I've told you so often,' Stella responded, looking at Mary, 'just speak when you are spoken to, unless you know what you are talking about.'

Mary took no offence at Stella's critical tone and Bronwen knew that she meant no hurt to her daughter. Bronwen knew Stella was protective of Mary. She had noticed it getting stronger over the years, as Mary's need for supervision increased.

'All right, Stella,' she said meekly. Then to her mother, 'Mammy, can we go on a world cruise on Queen Mary or one of the other big boats?'

Geraint intruded. 'Bit by bit,' he said, shaking his head. 'A trip round the world will take months. We need to start small, like a short cruise on one of the smaller P&O liners. I see offers being illustrated frequently on the Internet; just for about two weeks. Get the feel of things first, I say.'

'That's right, Geraint, but I'll say again, we needn't look out for cheap offers. Wherever we go, we can afford to go first class, can't we?' Bronwen asked.

'We certainly can, Bronwen. I understand. I'll see to it.'

'That's it. If you've got it, flaunt it,' Stella grinned as she rose from her chair. 'I wish I could stay but I must get back to the grindstone. 'The carers in bottom lounge will be needing my help. But before I go, there's another important consideration to be made.'

All eyes were on her as she paused, waiting for someone to ask what she was referring to. 'If, or rather when, we go off for a short time, I'm concerned about the times there'll be no arrangement for the disabled. You'll have to be carried, Bronwen.

'We both know that whenever we've gone away on the few day outings from here, there have always been times when you've had to be bodily moved. It's never been a problem because we've always had plenty of carers to help. But if we went on a short cruise, we won't know the facilities until we get there. No matter how much they promise that the disabled will be catered for, I will not be convinced that we'll not come across problems, no matter how many millions you have in the bank.'

Bronwen's expression of delight became deflated. She felt a nuisance; an encumbrance that would spoil everything. 'You're right, Stella,' she said sadly. She immediately brightened, 'But you lot can go.'

'Oh, no,' Geraint disagreed. 'We go nowhere without you and no mention of that again, if you don't mind,' He frowned at Stella, but what she said had to be said, no matter how much it would offend.

Stella looked prepared to dash away. 'I must go, or Matron will be after me. But before I go, Bronwen, I'll ask you to think of Kevin Grant.'

'Kevin Grant, that giant of a boy from Union Street? Why?' Bronwen knew the family.

'He's your boyfriend,' Mary said. 'You wan' my mam to give money to your boyfriend?'

'He's not my boyfriend,' Stella snapped, 'so you shut up about that. I think he could be the solving of our only problem,' she hurried away. 'I'll see you before I go off duty, Bronwen.'

Most of the residents who had been listening lost interest and someone switched up the tone of the television.

Tilley, who had been sitting closest to the group, mentioned an issue which would have troubled her. 'You'll have to be a good swimmer to go on a big boat. What if it sinks?'

Old George Payne, a companion of Bronwen, called out, 'Why don't you all go to America in an aeroplane, Bronwen?'

Bronwen looked across to him and smiled. 'I expect that's what you've always wanted to do, is it, George? Well, if you can get a couple of people to go with you; I'll pay. Trip's on me.' She wouldn't have pointed out that George was far too debilitated to travel to the next town, let alone to an airport and then to another continent, but she was of the belief that hope was good medicine.

Tilley Tittle-tattle, who was more incapacitated than George, shouted across to him. 'I'll come with you, George. I'll look after you. But if the plane has trouble, we'd have to fly, and that's harder than swimming.'

Everyone but Bronwen laughed. She thought that Tilley really felt she could have gone on a long trip and be able to look after George. She had looked after others all her life. Though she was partially paralysed as a result of a stroke and had chronic arthritis, inside her bent body there was a spirit which made her feel she could do the things she did when she was forty.

Geraint drew Bronwen, Tom and Mary back to the discussion of travelling.

'When Tom and I make bookings for a short cruise, Bronwen, we'll make sure you won't have to stand on your legs at all. We'll be going first class and if we come up against difficulties, they'll have me to deal with.'

Bronwen wondered how a wizened, little old man would "deal" with matters, but felt that he could. In his time he had been a hard, strong businessman. She was grateful to him. She wanted no one else to deal with all the money she had. She was glad that he, too, like Tilley, had a young spirit.

'Yes, I know, Geraint. I'm not worried at all about a thing now you are chief cook and bottle washer with Tom to help.' Bronwen deliberately brought Tom into her statement. He had been unusually quiet until that moment.

'I wonder what Stella meant when she said to give Kevin Grant a thought?' He spoke as if to himself, but he meant the question to be for everyone.

'I'll let you know in the morning, Tom, if I know myself.' Bronwen yawned. 'I'm off to bed; it's been a funny old day. Different, to say the least. I wonder how many more different days we'll have.'

'I'm going now then, Mammy,' Mary also yawned. 'Can you give me money for some fish and ships?'

Bronwen went to her handbag, took out her purse and peered into it. It was empty.

'No, I can't, Mary. Look.' She turned her purse upside down. Pieces of dust fluttered out. The situation made Tom laugh.

He could barely speak for laughter. 'She's a millionaire and she can't afford a bag of fish and chips!'

Geraint saw the funny side of the matter and he laughed, too. He was about to give Mary money from his pocket when Bronwen stopped him.

'My Mary's forgotten she's to go to Stella's house until our house is ready. She'll have something to eat there.' She turned to Mary, 'Wait until Stella comes off duty and you will leave together. She shouldn't be long. I have a feeling that your days of filling yourself up with rubbish food are over.'

The look of disappointment on Mary's face brought more laughter from Tom and Geraint. They were happy. So far, things had gone well.

However, Bronwen thought, this was just the beginning. She felt that things could go very wrong. She shuddered, and it wasn't from being cold. Willow Lounge was warm and cosy.

Later that evening, Bronwen sat in her room waiting for Stella to call before she went off duty. Bronwen was partly undressed and was washing at the sink in the corner of the room when Stella knocked the door. She pranced straight in. She didn't have to wait to be invited in.

Bronwen had taken out her dentures and had put them to soak in a weak solution of Steredent. Stella was one of the few who Bronwen didn't care about being seen seeing her without her false teeth.

'What did you mean when you told me to think about Kevin Grant?' Bronwen asked. 'Are you and he becoming an item? Mary put the thought into my mind because I know you've been out with him, on and off, for a long time.'

'Don't be daft. Of course, we're not.' Stella tutted. 'I'd have told you if there was anything in it, wouldn't I? I was thinking that he could come with us when we go away and be sort of a bodyguard. I know that sounds unusual, but if you need to be picked up from your wheelchair and carried up steps, or something, he's the one to do it. And there'll be a load of cases to handle. Mary and I have already made a list of what we'll be taking, and you can bet a pound to a penny her things alone will fill a couple of chests.

'Now, let me tell you. Kevin is six foot five in his socks, a yard wide, has muscles like an ox and is as strong as one. All he thinks about is working out, weight-lifting and cars. He's always tinkering about with that old banger he has, and he'll be able to share the driving with me when we've got a little minibus or something, for when we go long distances. And he'll know what sort of car will be suitable for you—for us. He knows more than my Colin.

'He's asked me out often, but I'm a few years older than he is and it doesn't seem right, somehow. I don't know why he sticks to me when he could get a pretty young thing. We get on well, though. He's nice; a giant on the outside but a pussycat on the inside. Think about it, Bron, and we'll discuss it with Geraint and Tom tomorrow. Paying for him to come with us is no problem, is it?'

'My God,' Bronwen gasped. 'I thought you'd never shut up. You've got my mind turning somersaults. No, I don't need time to think about it, but perhaps he won't want to be part of us. He's living with his family, isn't he, and a miner working at Tower Colliery? '

Stella looked surprised. 'Yes, that's right, Bronwen. How do you know that, then?'

'I knew his mother, Annie Grant, quite well. She had Kevin late in life as I did Mary. She's about my age.'

Stella began, 'She's passed on, and his dad. He's living with his sister and brother-in-law. They get on fine, but Cathy, his sister, is having a baby and Kevin is beginning to feel the odd one out. He's not happy in his job and he can see an end of Tower Colliery, though it mightn't be in the near future. Kevin says he can't go on for years there. He's always looking for another opening.

'Bronwen, I think he'd give his right arm for the chance to come away with us and do the heavy fetching and carrying. Give it a thought, will you? And we'll talk about it with Tom and Mr Lloyd-Davies.'

Bronwen looked sad; her mind wasn't fully on what Stella was suggesting. 'Sad, Hilda and Ted gone. Kevin and Cathie stayed in the house, then. They must have been quite young when their mam and dad went. See if you can get Kevin to come up for us to have a look at him. I'll ask Tom and Geraint what they think.

'Go home now, my lovely. You look tired and I'm not surprised. Don't forget to take Mary with you. I warn you, she's starving hungry. She'll eat you out of house and home. You must let me pay her way.'

Stella seemed to go off in a huff. 'For God's sake, Bronwen. I know you've got plenty, but do you think I'm going to ask you to pay for Mary staying with us?'

Before she closed the door after her, she turned and said, 'Remind me tomorrow to tell you how Colin is getting on with number 22. You'd die of shock if you saw it. He said he can't see it being ready for months unless he gets help, but employing someone skilled will put the cost up. He's had planning permission and he's building a two-story extension on the back which will be more than double the size of the house. And inside he's knocking walls down right, left and centre. He'll have an enormous bill for you, but I guarantee it will be fair.'

At the breakfast table the following morning with Geraint, Tom and Tilley, Bronwen discussed the possibility of Kevin Grant travelling with them as a sort of bodyguard and to help with the luggage.

Tilley knew Kevin Grant. 'Duw,' she gasped. 'He's a giant. Hands like shovels, feet like canal barges. Nose like a bent old carrot; broken from boxing. Don't know how anyone could have reached it, though, unless standing on a chair.'

The other three laughed, assuming Tilley had exaggerated, as she always did.

Tom knew Kevin, too. 'Tilley's right,' he said. 'And I think that's a great idea. Kevin is a smashing chap; very big man but not blustery in any way. Doesn't have much to say for himself but I wouldn't like to cross him. The size and look of him would frighten off any would-be robbers or muggers. It's bound to get known that you've got plenty of money, Bron, and someone like him might well be needed. You never know.'

Geraint looked peeved. 'Well, I can do that. I know I look not much bigger than a garden gnome but there's still plenty of fight in me.' He bent his arm and flexed his deltoids.

Tom blurted out words without thinking. 'Mr Lloyd-Davies, when push comes to shove, you've not much more strength in you than a bottle of pop.' Immediately, he resented his words. He felt like choking on them.

Bronwen nor Tom wanted to offend their friend but Bronwen had to say something near the truth. 'Geraint, you forget how old you are. You might feel like an eighteen-year-old, but you know very well you're no superman. You'll need protecting as much as any of us.'

Geraint frowned but he accepted the truth. 'Yes, I suppose so. I'll stick to the all-important accountancy and dealing with the masses of correspondence we'll be getting. It's beginning to trickle in already. It'll soon be flooding in, you see.'

He picked up a large, black refuse bag he had dropped on the floor when he sat down to breakfast. It was packed with envelops of all shapes, sizes and colours.

'Good God. It looks more than a trickle to me,' Tom stared with astonishment.

'Yes, Tom,' Geraint responded before addressing Bronwen. 'Would you mind if I asked Tom to call Mary on his mobile and ask her to come early today, to help us sort out this lot?' I know she'll be a bit slow at first, but it will be good practice for her. You're going to have to give her more responsibility, you know, Bronwen. We must try to build up her confidence,' He sounded humble; he was reluctant to ask her for Mary's help.

'Yes, of course, if he won't mind using his phone again. As I said, Tom, I'll pay all the phone bills from now on. We'll all have phones soon, as Geraint suggested. You'll know the ones to get. The hard bit will be teaching us how to use them.'

Bronwen knew Tom wouldn't mind. One of his pleasures in life was using his phone and having conversations with people to whom he thought worth talking to. He didn't think there were many. Another of his pleasures was doing something for Bronwen.

She went on with a more serious look about her. 'And one last thing before I go across to see Martha Tate—you don't have to ask me to give permission for every move you make. Whatever you do or think of doing, will help.'

'Right,' Geraint saluted. 'Now I'm going back to my computer to look at what short cruises are going within the next few months. But after Christmas and New Year. We must welcome the new year in with people we know, mustn't we? After you've had your smoke in the front hall, will you come up, Tom? We'll have another look at those people-carriers. From what I've seen, these stretch limousines are the ones which might suit us. But my goodness, they're costly. I'm out of touch with the reality of big money.'

'I won't be out of touch for long,' Bronwen said, shaking her head. 'I'm going to get used to it. I'm determined; I'm never again going to be bothered about cost. And if you know of anyone in this home who needs something and cannot afford it, you must let me know, please.'

Chapter 8
The Needy, Not the Greedy

That afternoon, Bronwen would have liked to sleep for an hour or so, as she usually did. She didn't have the opportunity; she was besieged by visitors who claimed, either to be related to her side of the family, or Lewis's.

Three couples were taken, two by two, to where Bronwen sat in the lounge. It began after she had transferred herself from her wheelchair onto one of the comfortable armchairs. After a few seconds of closing her eyes she felt a tap on her shoulder. It was by the hand of a woman of a couple who had been shown in by one of the carers.

'Hello, Bronwen,' the woman said. Bronwen was startled.

'Hello,' she replied, quietly but cheerfully. 'Who is it you've come to see? Some of the residents have gone to their rooms for an afternoon rest.'

The man spoke. 'It's you we've come to see, Bronwen. You don't remember me. I'm Clive and this is Agnes, my good wife. I'm a twice-removed nephew of Lewis's, if you see what I mean. You haven't seen me since I was a little boy.' He seemed amused by his description of being related to Lewis.

The couple were both well into middle age. Certainly, at least forty years since, whoever he was, was a little boy.

Without being invited, the woman sat beside Bronwen and began rummaging in a large, pseudo-leather handbag. She withdrew a photograph. 'Look,' she said, 'here's a family photograph with Lewis standing behind Clive. We'd just got married. We had a lovely do. We thought of inviting you, but it might have been too much for you, you like you are.' She glanced down at Bronwen's shawl-covered legs.

Agnes thrust the photograph into Bronwen's hand. She didn't have her spectacles on, so the photograph was a blur of a group of, at least, a dozen grinning faces. Before looking at the photograph again, she slowly took up her spectacles attached to the fine chain around her neck, which prevented her from losing them. She didn't recognise any of the faces.

'I'm sorry, I don't remember you, and Lewis never mentioned you. What is it you want?' Bronwen knew well what they wanted.

'Well, we've heard of you winning millions of pounds and thought since we were family we should let ourselves be known to you,' Clive declared.

'Why?' Bronwen was being deliberately obtuse.

Neither Clive nor Agnes could think of words that wouldn't make it obvious they weren't interested in money. Agnes shuffled uncomfortably in her chair as she thought of a suitable answer. She was saved the embarrassment of having to be truthful by the second couple joining them.

'Hello, Bronwen. We're Sam and Ethel. Bronwen recognised they were known to Clive and Agnes, but not to her. There was a distinct nastiness in the air as she sensed hackles rising.

'You've been here long enough,' Ethel snapped at Agnes. 'You'll tire Bronwen. You should know she's not a well woman.'

'I'm perfectly well, thank you,' Bronwen put in. 'Should I know you? And why have you come here?' She continued to be obtuse and enjoyed it. The arousal of adrenaline diminished her weariness. Geraint had warned her about such people, so she was prepared to deal with them.

'Who are you supposed to be related to, Sam and Ethel? My side of the family or Lewis's?'

Ethel went into her handbag and withdrew some old photographs, as Agnes had done. 'You'll see your side of the family and mine in these photos,' she said as she glanced at Agnes and Clive with a smug look on her over-painted face.

'We're distant relatives of your father's,' was the reply, 'and we're not here for a handout of your lottery winnings, like these two,' she nodded in the direction of Agnes. 'We just thought you might need help in getting about. We didn't think you'd want to stay here, in an old people's home. We've just bought a nice Mercedes and thought we could take you places.' Ethel looked as if she'd taken a mouthful of sour milk when mentioning 'old people's home'.

That attitude got Bronwen's back up, but she held her dignity. 'No thank you,' she smiled sweetly. 'That's very thoughtful of you. I have my own transport and good friends to accompany me, as well as my daughter.'

'You have a daughter?' Ethel said with surprise, looking hard at Bronwen's covered paralysis. 'I didn't know. What's her name?'

'Her name is Mary,' Clive spoke for the first time. He had been busy throwing threatening looks at Sam. 'You must be very distant relatives if you didn't know that.'

Bronwen felt a nasty atmosphere brewing between the two couples when a third couple joined them. The scraping of chairs and mutterings became loud enough to disturb the few residents in the room, who were trying to take their afternoon nap before tea.

'Tell them to piss off, Bronwen,' one of the female residents shouted across the room. She was none too pleased with having the afternoon's quietude interrupted, but more than that, she was concerned about them approaching Bronwen. It wasn't difficult to guess the motive of the intruders.

The visitors looked in the direction of the outspoken woman but pretended not to have heard her.

'Bronwen, I'm Mary Ellen, and I'm an old friend of your mam's and this is my son, Peter. It was Peter who said I ought to come and see you. You've won millions of pounds, haven't you?'

Bronwen remembered Mary Ellen who used to call on her mother from time to time, years ago, before she and Lewis were married. Mary Ellen and Dilys were acquaintances, not friends. Bronwen remembered her mother being nice to her and giving her tea but always admitted to being pleased when she went. Bronwen's mother had said she was a scrounger and a gossiper.

Bronwen felt she was being bombarded and felt a confrontation approaching between the six unexpected visitors. She didn't like the noise or the atmosphere and was about to scream out at them to be quiet when Stella appeared. It was her off-duty day, so she wasn't in uniform. She was smartly dressed, as always. Her tall frame, neat hairstyle, flashing brown eyes and a fine-featured complexion made her look special.

'Having trouble, are you, Bronwen?' she asked quietly and simply, peering from face to face of the people that were bombarding her.

'I think you should all leave. You seem to be forgetting where you are; in the home of elderly, vulnerable people. You are causing an unpleasant disturbance.'

'Who the hell do you think you are?' Ethel snapped.

'We've been given permission to visit Bronwen, you know,' Agnes added. 'We didn't just barge in.'

Mary Ellen sniffed. 'I thought Peter and I were doing a good thing by coming to see you, Bronwen.'

'I'm sorry I haven't given you a good welcome, Mary Ellen, but where have you been for the last ten years?' Bronwen asked.

'I've been bad. Bad heart and chest. Haven't been going out much,' Mary Ellen wailed, wrapping her coat tightly about her.

Stella went to the double doors of the lounge and stood with them wide open as she beckoned the visitors through.

When out in the corridor, she closed the doors and walked a few steps behind the gabbling group.

'Don't come here bothering Bronwen again,' Stella said in a threatening tone.

'If we want to come again, we won't ask your permission, whoever you are,' Clive snapped.

'If you want a hand-out from Bronwen, you won't get it. She's generous with her money. She's already given a lot away. But she's giving to the needy, not the greedy. Now, piss off, the lot of you, before I call security.'

'Don't talk to us like that,' Sam snorted, making for the exit. 'We're good Chapel people and you haven't heard the last of this. I'll find out who you are.'

'I'm Stella Vaughan, Senior Carer here and Bronwen's my closest friend. You are a hypocritical bastard; as are all of you.'

They left with tut-tuts and muttered words of, 'Disgraceful. I'm going to report that woman.'

Mary Ellen stalked to the office-cum-duty room where Matron Helen Phillip's deputy, Nurse Edna Banding, was sitting at the desk. She had watched Stella ushering them away with a smirk on her face.

'Did you hear the way that nurse talked to us?' Mary Ellen huffed. 'That sort shouldn't be looking after elderly people.'

'I didn't hear how she talked to you, madam? However, you are quite free to make a formal complaint.' She picked up a form from her desk and handed it to Mary Ellen. 'Here, you'll have to do so on this form.' Mary Ellen didn't accept the form. She cocked a snook and waddled away.

Nurse Banding went on, 'When I write my report, I'll mention the fact that you were asked to leave because you were all causing a disturbance. You only came hoping Bronwen would be generous with her recent lottery win.'

Edna and Stella watched the six people go to their family saloon cars; Sam and Ethel to their old Mercedes.

'Good riddance to bad rubbish,' Nurse Banding said. 'I shouldn't have let them in. We must be careful in future, Stella. Bronwen can well do without that sort of problem. Anyway, what are you doing here on your day off? Can't keep away, can you?'

'Something like that,' Stella said, 'and please don't scold me, but I've come to see Bronwen as well, but not to ask for a hand-out. She's already given me one. I want to ask if I can bring a friend of mine to see her later. I'll let her have a couple of hours rest first.'

The financial arrangement Bronwen had made for her close companions and the agreement that they will be going on a trip together was well known throughout the home. It was going to be more widely known after the weekly Chronicle came on the following Thursday. The newspaper's photographer had already visited, taken a photograph of Bronwen, Geraint, Tom, Stella and Mary in the front hall and a man had asked Bronwen to say a few words. She obliged.

'Just to say that elderly people should go on doing the lottery and not to give up the possibility of winning. Just because they might be a bit slower than they were a few years ago, doesn't mean that life can't be good. It is for me, as it was before I had all the winning numbers of the Lottery. But now I can do things and go places that me and my late husband used to talk about.'

Stella discussed the problem with Geraint. 'When Bronwen's business is broadcast in the local paper, me and Matron Phillips are really going to have to watch that she's not bombarded again. Those supposed relatives have upset her. Knowing her, she's most probably feeling mean for not giving in to them.'

She approached Bronwen. She had her eyes closed but wasn't asleep, though deep in thought. She was wondering about the people who visited, claiming they were relatives of either herself or Lewis. Bronwen considered that if they were true relatives, she would like to know them. The only relatives she was fond of and had contact with, were her two cousins, daughters of her mother's sister. They were Joan and Ruth, who were married and had families. Ruth sometimes had Daniel, her grandson, with her when she visited. She looked after him during school holidays to allow her daughter to keep her job in the town. They needed the extra wage. Joan, Ruth and Bronwen were close and she enjoyed their visits.

They were good to Mary and had often taken her into their homes. They used to visit her at home and took bits for her fridge and pantry shelf to help her. They had stopped when they found the house being neglected. They didn't admit this to Bronwen; they were afraid of her being hurt. The commitment was getting too much for them. They, too, were getting older.

On Ruth's last visit she told Bronwen that Joan's granddaughter, Hannah, had done well at school and was hoping to go to university to study languages, but they couldn't afford it. That was before Bronwen had won the lottery. Since then, neither had called on her and she guessed why. They didn't want to appear avarice. She decided to send each of her cousins a cheque for five thousand pounds and to help further with Hannah's education. Joan was too principled to ask Bronwen for money, unlike the so-called relatives, who had called on her since winning a fortune.

Stella realised that Bronwen wasn't yet asleep. 'Penny for your thoughts, Bronwen,' she whispered. 'I hope those hypocritical bastards haven't upset you.' Stella used strong language when she was anxious or angry. By apology she explained that it eased her stress.

'Bronwen, let me take you up to your room until supper time. It won't hurt you to miss tea.'

'I'd like that, Stella, but it's your day off, love. I can manage on my own.'

Bronwen transferred herself onto her wheel chair and Stella pushed her towards the lift. 'No, love, they haven't upset me, just got me thinking of this, that and the other. And don't use swear words in front of Mr Lloyd-Davies, will you? You know he doesn't like it and it makes him have to go to the toilet.'

Stella chuckled. Mr Lloyd-Davies's attitude to her swearing was a joke between her and her close companions. Bronwen often had to remind Tom, too. He could come out with a few choice words when angered; such as when he wanted to have a cigarette and had had them confiscated because of carelessness. Not because it was bad for his health. He made it clear, in no uncertain terms when feeling intimidated, that he was aware of that. Whatever bad effect tobacco smoking had on the lungs had been done. He didn't expect a cure. His argument was that he should have been told that smoking was bad for the health when he was 15. It was believed in those days "that it was good for the nerves". The damage had been done—he was addicted, and his choice was for no one to change his habit now. He enjoyed his smokes.

Stella talked as she steered Bronwen's wheelchair towards the lift. 'I want to ask you something, so I'll settle you down for a doze before I explain. That's why I've popped in now. And good thing I did, too. I'd bet my last penny that when the next Chronicle comes out people are going to try to swamp you, right, left and centre. They're going to be disappointed, because we're going to stop them. You really do need a bodyguard, but meet Kevin Grant before you make up your mind about it.

'He's taking me to that nice pub, The Bluebell, for a drink later and I've coaxed him to come in to meet you before we go. We'll only stay for five minutes after you've had supper. He took a lot of coaxing; he's a bit shy.'

'Have you told him what we want him for?' Bronwen asked.

'No, because if you decide you don't want him, he won't be disappointed. Geraint and Tom will be here, and Mary. Tell Geraint and Tom not to make it obvious and tell Mary to say nothing until asked.'

Bronwen chuckled at Stella's mistrust of Mary, but she was right. Mary was known to them all for her lack of tact and slow wit.

It took Bronwen only minutes to fall asleep after Stella tucked her in and closed the door quietly after her. She slept for over two hours.

She would have missed supper had not Geraint knocked at her door to awaken her. It would have meant one of the carers having to bring up a tray with her supper and medication.

'Matron doesn't have enough staff to allow for individual treatment, even for millionaires,' he teased. 'Come along now, Mrs Dew.'

She was pleased Geraint had alerted her; she was to meet Kevin Grant. She hadn't seen him since he had scuffed knees wearing short trousers. She tried to imagine how much he might have changed.

After supper, later that evening, Bronwen, Mary, Geraint and Tom were sitting in a group. They talked about plans for buying a suitable vehicle, going on a short cruise when the time was right and the changes that were being made at Bronwen's house in Queen Street.

Tilley was close enough to hear all what was said and spoke only when she had something useful to say. Having had a stroke, not only did its paralysis affect the side of her body but affected her memory of words.

Bronwen nor Geraint or Tom minded the residents being involved in the discussion, but interest in Bronwen's millions seemed to have waned. However, Bronwen had told Matron Helen Phillips that if any of the residents needed anything which involved money, she was to be informed.

Christmas was just weeks away and the coming of the New Year, 1999, would be celebrated in style at the home. Bronwen decided she would make it as special as possible with Stella's and Matron Phillips' help. Geraint and Tom wouldn't be much use. She hoped Mary would.

'When are we going on a cruise, Mammy? Will it be around the world?'

'No, Mary, that would take too long, and we won't be going away on a cruise until after Christmas and the New Year. We must be here for those occasions. They are special.'

Geraint agreed with Bronwen. 'Your mother's right, Mary. We've told you before, but I expect you've forgotten. A world cruise would be too long a time. Next year maybe, but we must start in a small way. A liner called The Gladiator is sailing from

Southampton early in March, when the weather in the Mediterranean will be warming up. It will stop off at different ports, I can't remember which ones, and takes only fifteen days. After three days at sea, we'll be in spring-like sunshine. That would be better for your mother, Tom and me; not too hot. You must remember, we're not as young and fit as you.'

'I agree with you there, Geraint,' Bronwen nodded. 'It means we'll spend Christmas here, at home, and it will give us time to get the right sort of vehicle—big enough to take all of us, our luggage and our wheelchairs.'

She was about to suggest a trip to a big shopping complex Stella had heard of, when she was overshadowed by someone standing next to her. She looked up to find Kevin Grant towered over her. Stella was dwarfed beside him.

When the couple walked into the big lounge, some of the residents looked up and took interest in the big man, following close behind Stella as she led him towards Bronwen.

'By God,' one of the men said. 'He's a big bugger. I wouldn't like to be on the other side of his fists.'

'Shut up, Brynly,' Stella frowned in the direction of where the voice came, 'Or you'll be on the end of mine.'

Some of the other residents laughed at the picture that her remark conjured up in their minds.

Bronwen guessed who Kevin was but wouldn't have recognised him. 'Duw, duw, Kevin, you must have grown six foot since I last saw you.'

'Stopped growing upwards since I was about eighteen, Mrs Dew. Only grown outwards since,' Kevin's voice was deep but unobtrusive.

His nose had obviously been broken, as Tilley had said, but he was still handsome in a rough sort of way. He had a kind face, bright, wide-apart blue eyes, shoulder-length fair hair which Bronwen thought was overdue for the barber. He had a pleasant smile and a body to compete with Goliath, had he still been around.

'Well, you know each other then, but Kevin, you don't know Mr Geraint Lloyd-Davies nor Tom Daly.' Stella pointed to the two men, one legless in a wheelchair and the other leaning on his Zimmer frame.

'An' I'm Mary Dew,' She gazed at him in wonder. 'But I know you. I've seen you about an' I've seen you wiv Stella.'

'That's right, Mary. I didn't introduce you because I knew you knew Kevin and I didn't think he'd forgotten you.' Stella put her arm across Mary's shoulder in a friendly manner and hugged her. 'We're best friends,' Stella added, 'but no one would think so, because I'm always nagging her about something.'

Mary smiled; Stella made her feel good. Mary was glad she styled her natural, tawny-coloured hair modestly and dress in loose fitting clothes, as Stella suggested. They didn't conceal her over-weight frame, but they didn't exaggerate it, as did the clothes she chose. She had, many times, promised herself to diet until she became as slender as her mother. But as yet, hadn't done so.

Tom nodded to Kevin. 'Going out for a drink together, are you?' he said. 'Nice. They'll have their Christmas lights up now, I expect.'

'Aye, aye,' Kevin replied. 'Christmas around the corner again and 1999 on its heels. Big night that should be. And bigger next year, the Millennium, 21st Century.'

Tom interrupted. 'That's a long way off. Let's hope we'll all be here.'

Geraint couldn't think of a suitable remark, but he nodded to Kevin. 'Nice to meet you, Mr Grant. I hope we'll see more of you.'

Bronwen joked. 'We don't really want to see more of you, Kevin, there's enough of you as it is,' they all chuckled, 'but we will see you again, I hope.'

'Stella insisted that we call in before going to the pub. She said there was a reason for her wanting me to meet you all but hasn't let on what the reason is.'

Stella interrupted before Mary innocently told him. 'Come on now, Kevin. Let's leave everybody in peace to carry on the chat. Anyway, I'm dying for a lager.'

Kevin followed her like a pet puppy. 'She's a bully,' he turned and said. 'I don't know why I put up with her.'

As they walked to the exit, one of the two carers who was stationed in that lounge called out to Stella. 'Where did you find your little boyfriend, Stella?'

She was insolent. Seventeen-year-old Megan, caring for the elderly and infirm for nursing experience before entering professional training in the coming April.

Stella pointed a threatening finger at her. 'Wait till I get you on your own.'

Megan laughed, as did the other carer, Dora, who was standing nearby.

'Don't take any notice of the cheeky little devil, Stella,' Dora said. 'But when you've finished with him, I'll have him.'

When they were outside, Stella apologised to Kevin for the rudeness of the carers. 'They can be too much of it sometimes, but they're a smashing lot, really.'

'Of course,' he grinned, 'you're one of them.'

'Well, now, if you play your cards right, you might be soon. If this rattle trap of yours can get us safely to the pub, I have something very important to ask you.'

They walked toward Kevin's old car. He was so taken up with curiosity, he drove to The Bluebell Inn's car park faster than he should have.

Back in the lounge of the nursing home, Bronwen and her companions went on planning the future: what was to be bought, where they would go and when. They talked about money as if they were thieves planning how to get it; not how to spend it. Certainly, lives would be changed, and minds broadened. Bronwen felt her life had changed already, yet the furthest she'd been, since receiving her fortune, was down to the town to put it in the bank.

Through her, Martha Tate's life had changed. And, as yet, not a week had passed. By coincidence or the effect of the new bed and mattress, she seemed to have picked up. She was taking more fluids and managing to take a small amount of soft diet. To Bronwen, she seemed to be more responsive to what she was saying to her. She couldn't have been imagining it because other carers noticed the same changes.

Geraint's life had changed. Prior to him having the interest of keeping account of Bronwen's millions, he had spent hours in front of his computer, but there had been no real reason. Now, he felt a sense of purpose. He enjoyed the challenge and he looked forward to travelling with Bronwen and their companions.

She had told him to go ahead and book them on a beautiful liner, The Gladiator, and to ensure they had the best cabins available, irrespective of the cost. That would not be a concern again.

'But the trip is going to be in the region of fifteen to twenty thousand pounds, Bronwen. Are you sure?' Geraint was apprehensive. He wasn't used to spending large sums of money; certainly not for pleasure.

'Dear God, Bronwen, Tom gasped, 'that's a bloody fortune. You'll soon get through your money at that rate.'

Geraint frowned at Tom. 'Now, let's keep civil tongues in our heads. It is, indeed, a lot of money, but a fleabite to what's in the bank. According to the figures on my computer, it will have accumulated almost that much in interest by the end of next month.'

'Sorry, Mr Lloyd-Davies, it's just that I'm not used to that sort of money talk,' Tom apologised. 'But I only said bloody. That's not a bad word.'

'None of us are used to dealing with lots of money,' Geraint replied, 'I know it's doing no good sitting in the bank doing nothing. It has to be spent and that's that.'

'We'll have to learn about it,' Bronwen added. 'Including Mary.'

Mary hadn't spoken since the meeting began. 'I can't make 'ead or tail of it, and I'm all of a dither. I could manage what I 'ad in my purse every week and knew when it was gone it was gone.

'As Mr Lloyd-Davies said, none of us are used to it, love,' Bronwen tried to comfort Mary. 'But you'll soon get the hang of it and enjoy it. You've never shown fear of spending money before, even when you got us into debt.'

'It was easier,' Mary grunted.

Bronwen pretended she didn't hear the sound of Mary's disgruntlement; she steered the subject into a different direction.

'Anyway, we've all met Kevin now. How do you feel about him being asked to come with us on our cruise as a helper and carer? I would be more satisfied because I know I will be needing to be picked up bodily at times and I think he'll find it as easy as my Lewis did when moving me from A to B. Another thing is, we hear of such awful things happening to people when they travel abroad: muggings, theft and even worse. I think Kevin would be a deterrent.'

'You'll be paying, Bronwen, but since you ask, I will say I agree with you. The girls, that is Stella and Mary, will want to go to places that we won't. Kevin will be able to watch out for them. For instance, I won't want to go to those nightclubs, discos and karaokes, or whatever they're called. Then again, you might want to go to those places. You're so much younger than myself.'

Bronwen chuckled. 'Don't be daft, Geraint, of course I won't. But that's settled, Kevin comes with us—if he will want to, of course.'

The thought of her mother at a karaoke sent Mary into a fit of giggles.

Bronwen wasn't amused. 'Mary, it's time for you to go, now. It's time for closing down for the night. I feel a need for my bed. I expect you two do, as well.' Bronwen spoke to Geraint and Tom.'

'Yes, Bronwen, you're right. I'll spend a bit of time on the computer and take another look at the people-carriers before I settle down,' Geraint yawned. 'Are you coming, Tom?'

'Not tonight, Mr Lloyd-Davies, if you don't mind. The old diabetes has been playing up today, but I wouldn't mind a smoke. Will you supervise me in the front hall, Bron? Don't want to upset Matron.'

'Of course, Tom. I'd rather you ask me before lighting up and someone coming to get me if you fall asleep, as it looks like you might.' Bronwen looked hard at Tom. She sensed he had something special to discuss.

Bronwen and Tom manoeuvred their wheelchairs to the back of the entrance hall, not to get in the way of the carers moving back and forth between the two lounges.

'What's the matter, Tom? What's troubling you?' She stroked the side of his face. Something was clearly tormenting him.

'Bronwen, you know me too well. Sometimes I think you can tell what I'm thinking. But, then, we've known each other a long time.'

'Well, I don't know what you're thinking now, except I think leaving the security of this home to come on a cruise isn't up your street.'

Tom looked surprised. 'Yes,' he said, 'how can you tell?'

'Because you've shown enthusiasm about everything that we've talked about since I've won this blooming money, except coming away with us.'

'It's not that I don't want to come,' Tom went on. 'I'm grateful for your kindness, but just look at me. Take a good, good look. I have no legs—I know you don't have a good pair, either, but you've learned to cope. The stumps of my legs are breaking down, there's abscesses coming on them because of the diabetes. I have to watch everything I eat, or the cook does. I have to take a ton of pills and I have to have insulin jabs morning and evening. Stella is a great nurse, but I can't expect her, or anyone else, to take that on. Another thing, my sight is going. I was warned about it years ago. I would spoil it for everybody and to tell you the truth, I would be afraid to leave here. I'm not fit enough to come with you, and you must see that,'

Bronwen's eyes welled and tears trickled down her cheeks. 'Oh, Tom, I'm so sorry. But it's all right, I understand. You can stay here with your mobile phone and we can keep in touch until we're all back. And I'm not giving up my room here because I know that in the end, it is here I will be. Geraint too. I'm going to reserve our rooms indefinitely.

'I wish I could do something for you, or give you something. Listen now,' she sniffed and apologised for not having a tissue. 'I heard you and Brynly talking about those marvellous mobility scooters that go on their own. Let's get one of those for you. It would be such fun and it will save your poor hands.'

He looked up with a less dejected look about him. His face, too, was wet with tears which he wiped away with the sleeve of his shirt. 'It didn't occur to me to get one,' Tom smiled, 'but I wouldn't mind having a go. Me and Brynly can share it.'

'We'll get the company who sells them to bring one here to show us. And if it's all right, you and Brynly will have one each. It'll get rid of some of the money. In fact, I might have a go of one for myself. Perhaps Geraint will have one and do away with his Zimmer. Matron is on in the morning. I'll speak to her about it. If she knows nothing about them, I'm certain sure she'll know someone who does.'

They were both cheered. 'I think you're quite right about not coming with us, Tom. I was wrong to expect it. As we've agreed, you're safer here with your cigarettes, your mobile phone and the television. You can go on trying the lottery.'

Tom grinned with relief. 'I'm glad I've talked to you, Bron. I'll sleep easier tonight. I thought you'd be offended by my not wanting to come with you.'

'You know me better than that, Tom Daly. Come on, let's get to bed.'

At the Bluebell Inn, Stella and Kevin sat at a table in a corner where they were unlikely to be interrupted. She sipped at a Pils lager, Kevin at a pint of the pub's best draught.

'Well now, what secret was it you were going to share with me?' Kevin asked. 'I'm hot under the collar with curiosity.'

Stella replied with a further question. 'What would you say if you were asked to go on a fifteen days' Mediterranean cruise on a luxury liner?'

Kevin replied by posing yet another question. 'Is the Pope Catholic?'

'What the hell has the Pope got to do with it?' she snapped. 'Of course the Pope is Catholic. What a daft question.'

'No dafter than your question,' Kevin snapped back. 'What would I say about a Mediterranean cruise? Firstly, I'd make sure I wasn't being wound up, then say yes, yes, yes, then ask what the catch was. Chance would be a fine thing.'

'Well, you've got that chance, and right; I'd expect you to ask me what the catch was before you committed yourself.' Stella smirked.

'No, I wouldn't because I'd know there was a catch. Why did you ask me that?' He sounded disgruntled.

Stella decided it would be best not to hold out any longer but come straight to the point by putting the important proposition to him.

'You know Bronwen has won millions of pounds, don't you? Kevin nodded, looking pensive as he waited for Stella to get to the point.

She went on, 'Well, she has to change her life a bit now, and the first thing she's going to do is go away while Colin does magic to her house in Queen Street. She wants to go back, but it must be made suitable for her to live in with me and Mary looking after her. She needn't live in a nursing home any more, not that there's anything wrong with that when the need is there, but with Bronwen it isn't any longer. She can live a normal life in the community as long as she is safe and comfortable. She is so rich she hasn't yet been able to get it straight in her head. Neither has any of us, but changes have to be made and we want you to be involved in those changes.'

'Me?' was Kevin's startled surprise. 'What are you telling me? I feel something is brewing in that scatty brain of yours.'

'Because you're big and strong and we'll need a... well, a bodyguard, for the want of better words. You can help me with the driving—when we've got the right sort of car. It will be one which will take wheelchairs. You'd be needed to help move Bronwen from A to B when there is no ramp for her wheelchair. And generally, watch out for would be troublemakers getting at her for her purse.'

'That's all I'd have to do for a free trip around the Mediterranean?' Kevin spoke with a raised tone of surprise. 'I could carry Mary from A to B if the need arises. But you're having me on, aren't you?'

'Stop making this difficult for me, Kevin. No, I'm not and there will be a wage. Bronwen wouldn't expect you to do it for nothing. But it might mean you'd have to give up your job at The Tower Colliery.'

'That would be a blessing; I hate the coal mine,' Kevin shrugged. 'I've been thinking about it for a long time, as I think I've told you, but I have to get something that will bring me in a living wage. I couldn't live off Cath and Dennis.'

'Well think about it,' Stella suggested. 'We'll be going in the new year, February or March, when the weather there will be beginning to warm up. You'll have time to work your notice and have Christmas at home with Cathy and Dennis.'

'And I should be away soon after her baby is born and be out of their way for a bit. I've felt a bit like a gooseberry since they got married but the house was left to Cathy and me, as you know.'

'That's it then, I can tell Bronwen and the others you will come, can I?'

Kevin looked confused. 'This is a bit quick, love, but I suppose so.'

'Right then. I'll tell her. She'll be pleased. You'll be the only one to carry her since Lewis died.'

Chapter 9
Scooters

The days of the rest of the week came and went as they normally did at The Sunshine Mount Nursing Home.

Mary came every evening after supper, as usual, but her appearance had changed, somewhat. She was dressed and shod more suitably for her age and size, as Stella had advised, and had resisted going to any of the hairdressers in town.

'You're looking so nice, Mary,' her mother repeated several times. 'Your hair is shining again. Your natural colour is much prettier than those funny colours you used to have.'

'Yes, Mary,' Tilley nodded. 'You look a bit more as you should, now.'

Mary wasn't quite sure what that meant. 'It seems daft,' she frowned, 'now I've got the money to have anything I like done to my hair I'm not allowed to.'

Bronwen smiled and patted Mary's hand. 'Living with Stella and her brother is doing you good. By the time we go on our cruise, you might have lost a bit of weight, as well.'

'Yes,' Mary replied, looking pleased as she patted her oversized abdomen. 'I think I've already lost a couple of pounds. Stella's stopped me having Mars bars an' fish-and-chips from the chippies.'

The weekend was different. Bronwen had several would-be visitors; some distant relatives she'd never known or heard of. However, they weren't allowed to see her. Matron lied and had told them that Bronwen was busy, not available, or out. The "relatives" were invited to leave their names and make appointments to see Bronwen, if they so wished.

One of the visitors told Matron Phillips she'd already written to Bronwen telling her she and her husband would visit her. Matron's response was explaining to the strange visitors that Bronwen had had hundreds of letters since winning a fortune on the National Lotter; Mrs Dew's accountant and her daughter couldn't have yet come upon your letter.'

Bronwen had asked Helen if she wouldn't mind telling a few little white lies because she couldn't cope with a score of visitors every afternoon and evening. They were after money and she felt she should give them all a handout to go away and leave her alone.

When Stella was on duty, no one got past her to pester Bronwen. She told them, in no uncertain terms, to leave the premises. Her choice of words annoyed Geraint when he was in earshot.

'Bronwen, will you tell that Stella to wash out her mouth with strong soap. That's no way for a lady to talk,' he shouted loud enough for Stella to hear.

'Sorry,' Mr Lloyd-Davies. 'I know I'm no lady but better than those scrounging bastards who try to get at Bronwen.'

He stamped his Zimmer frame in anger, knowing he was powerless to change Stella.

Bronwen calmed the situation. 'She has apologised, Geraint. She wouldn't have used those words if she knew you would hear.'

As well as agreeing to help to keep the unwelcome visitors from bothering Bronwen, Helen had agreed to contact a company which dealt with electric scooters. Bronwen explained to Helen what Tom had said about them.

Helen made the call on a Friday, asking the company for information, including prices, of their electric scooters. She achieved their added interest when she said there was a possibility of four scooters being purchased.

The following Monday was a dull, damp, late November day when a big white van stopped on the forecourt of the nursing home. The vehicle's company's name was painted across it in bold, black and orange print: T.G. Todd, Independent Mobility Ltd.

A man in a smart dark, blue suit, shirt and tie and a second man wearing a white boiler suit got out of the van. The one in the smart suit rang the doorbell. Carer Megan Jones answered the door. The man in the suit explained who he and his colleague were, where they were from and asked if they could see the person in charge.

'Matron Phillips is in charge,' Megan said in a false cultured voice. 'Come in and I'll tell her you're here. Are you expected?'

'She won't be too surprised by our visit,' Mr Todd, the man in the smart suit, said. 'We were contacted last week by Matron Phillips, asking for information about mobility aids. We, also, have a number of battery-run wheelchairs to demonstrate.'

Megan showed the men into the hall, directed them to chairs before she made her way to the office to tell the matron that they were here. Megan knew that Bronwen wanted to get some special mobility aids. It was the talk of the place.

Matron instructed Megan to show the men into the office. She did so and shut the door before running up the corridor to tell Bronwen.

Bronwen was just about to take an afternoon nap. Her eyes snapped open and, immediately, she became alert.

'Tom!' she called across the room where, he too, had settled down for forty winks. 'The people with those scooters and special wheelchairs are here. We'll want you to come and see. And call Brynly.'

She turned to Megan. 'Would you mind going upstairs and telling Mr Lloyd-Davies they're here?'

Megan didn't need to be directed. She dashed from the room in the direction of the stairway. She didn't bother waiting for the lift. She could be heard pounding up the stairs and along the corridor towards Mr Lloyd-Davies's room. Having delivered the message, she fled back. She didn't want to miss seeing the special scooters.

When back in the wide hallway, she found Tom and Brynly sitting beside each other, puffing at their own brand of tobacco smokes. Bronwen was in the office with the two men and Matron. They could be seen through the glass partition of the office, displaying their brochures and discussing matters. The movement of lips, the shaking and nodding of heads, but no sound of agreement or otherwise, was frustrating.

Eventually, they came out of the office and asked Megan to let them out through the front door. They went to the back of their van and reappeared, each riding an electric scooter, as the vehicles were referred to. They were a recent innovation to help the immobile. At least, they were new to Bronwen.

In the hallway, the salesmen demonstrated how the machines could be folded to fit into a car-boot or for easy slotting into the back of a car. They demonstrated how they functioned.

By then, a number of residents had gathered in the hall to watch the display. They were enthralled. To Bronwen they looked like mopeds which she remembered being used about Pendarren before she came to The Sunshine Mount Nursing Home.

There was a handle bar, a padded seat and a space between where the legs and feet went. There was no resemblance to the wheelchairs she and Tom used, and the function was different. They went on their own without being manoeuvred by hands and shoulders. Bronwen's shoulders sometimes ached at the end of the day, especially if she had moved about the home more than usual, or if she had been taken into the town on the minibus. She had to wander up and down the pavements, as she was able. Going up the slopes was strenuous, and there were many of those in the streets of Pendarren.

'Try one, Tom,' she called out.

'Yes, go on, Tom,' Brynly encouraged.

'No, you have a go first,' Tom responded, looking at the battery driven vehicles with suspicion.

'Why don't we take them outside and have a test drive?' Mr Todd, the salesman, suggested. 'George here will help you.' George was the man in the white boiler suit.

'Aye,' he said. 'Let's take a couple of the scooters outside. They have different attachments, but if you can drive one you can drive any.'

With the men leading, Bronwen and Matron close behind and Tom and Brynly following it was like a troop of people on a march.

Those remaining in the warmth were happy to return to the lounge and watch through the windows.

What fun Tom and Brynly had! They found the electric scooters easy to manoeuvre after a short lesson. They drove in circles and figures of eight around the forecourt. They yipeed, hooted, whistled and laughed and everybody laughed with them.

Those watching were amazed at the versatility of the electric scooters.

No one had ever seen Brynly's head above his forehead, he always wore a tweed flat-cap. It was revealed that afternoon because it fell off and trying to retrieve it he nearly fell off himself. Megan picked up the cap and chased after the scooter. She caught up with Brynly and slapped his cap on a totally hairless head. 'Mustn't catch a cold in your head, Brynly,' she shouted.

'Well done, Megan,' Bronwen shouted. 'Brynly wouldn't have enjoyed the drive without his Dai-cap.' She could hardly speak for laughing.

This is better than the dodgems at Barry Island fair,' Tom shouted. 'Come on, Bronwen, have a go.'

Matron and Megan pushed reluctant Bronwen forward. 'Go on,' Matron ordered. 'All this is your doing, so have a go on one, because you'll be getting one for yourself, I'll be bound.'

Bronwen was bullied into hoisting herself onto a wheelchair that had been brought from the back of the van. After a few words of instruction from George she was moving. She was glad she had on a pair of trousers that were tight about her ankles, so her legs couldn't be seen. However, Megan took the shawl Bronwen had on her shoulders and folded it about her knees as she sat in the scooter.

Bronwen screamed with excitement as she rode around the concrete forecourt. 'My goodness, I feel like a ten-year-old.' She thoroughly enjoyed herself and her companions did, too.

Tom and Brynly took themselves back to their own wheelchairs and let Matron and Megan ride the incredible wheelchairs that, at the touch of a lever, moved on their own. The carers who were at their posts inside the home had their faces at the windows, peering out and enjoying the unexpected amusement.

The show had to end. The late afternoon air held a chill; not good for the elderly. Matron ordered everyone in, including the two salesmen, and asked them to bring the scooters back into the hall.

She ordered a tray of tea to be brought into the office, over which the purchase of the scooters could be discussed. She praised the two men for their skilful handling of the machines and thanked them for their caution with her elderly, immobile residents.

'I think they've got a sale, haven't they, Mrs Dew?' Matron assumed.

'Yes, indeed,' agreed Bronwen, 'but cost has to be discussed. If we bought two, how much discount would you allow?' she addressed the salesman in charge.

Mr Todd was prepared for the question. 'Five percent off.'

'What if we bought four?' Bronwen added.

'The same. Five percent off,' was the reply. 'That would be a fair exchange, I promise you.'

Bronwen didn't know whether it was a fair exchange; bartering wasn't her forte. It embarrassed her. 'That's it, then, we'll have four. I know your starting price, so send us ones like you showed us today as soon as you can.'

Matron interrupted. 'The ones we've used today I can see are your demonstration models. Make sure we have brand new ones.'

'We'll do that, Matron. George will deliver them on Friday. Two red, one green, one blue. Plus, an electric wheelchair. That all right, George?'

'Yes, sir, Mr Todd. And thank you, ladies. I haven't had such a laugh in a long time. You run a very happy home.'

'Make sure the invoice is made out to me, won't you, Mr Todd?' Bronwen emphasised.

He nodded, 'Yes, I will. You're the one with the money, are you?'

Bronwen, Matron and Tom and Brynly, who had been sitting in the hall puffing at their cigarettes, watched as the white van drew away and disappeared down the hill. They chatted about the electric scooters; they were impressed and agreed that they would like one each, but would share with other residents who had the ability to use them.

Mr Geraint Lloyd-Davies appeared looking flustered and none too happy. He stopped and banged his Zimmer frame angrily on the floor in front of him.

'Why didn't someone come and get me?' he fumed.

'Megan came up for you Mr Lloyd-Davies. We wondered what had happened to you,' Tom cringed. He thought Mr Lloyd-Davies was about to hit him with his Zimmer.

'She did, but not soon enough, it seems. The men with the electric scooters have come and gone and I didn't see a thing.'

The truth was that Megan had, indeed, called on Mr Lloyd-Davies just minutes after the white van appeared. He was so anxious to get down to be involved in the demonstration that his prostate gland became acutely sensitive and he had to go to the toilet twice on the way to the lift and when he was on the ground floor. He had wet his trousers and had to go back to his room to change. He couldn't find a clean pair of trousers and searching for them took too long.

He was bouncing with anger and disappointment.

'Don't worry, Mr Lloyd-Davies,' Brynly said, 'they've ordered a scooter for you.'

'They've what!' he shouted. 'Ordered me a scooter? I can walk.'

He continued to stamp his Zimmer frame on the floor and thrust it in their direction as if it were a defensive weapon.

'Eh, butty!' Brynly shouted back. 'Just because you are Mr bloody Lloyd-Davies, you don't threaten me with that thing that props you up. If I could get out of this bloody chair, I'd rattle your guts. It's not our fault that you couldn't make it to this afternoon's performance.'

Geraint calmed and looked to his feet. 'No, that's right,' he said with humility in his tone. 'I apologise, gentlemen. It's myself I'm angry with, not you. My little physical problem held me up. I'm sorry.'

'That's all right, Mr Lloyd-Davies,' Tom said. 'That's all right.'

Bronwen and Matron Phillips left the office and walked into the hall. They had been chatting, discussing the method of payment for the electric scooters. It would be by cheque, in the region of twenty thousand pounds, they guessed.

'My goodness, Bronwen,' Helen said, shaking her head. 'Who would have thought it?'

'Not me,' Bronwen replied, 'but the money is here and I'm going to do my blooming best to spend it—with the help of others.'

They felt the tension in the hall and looked from one face to the others for clues of the reason for the sour atmosphere.

'I was disappointed at missing the demonstration of the battery-run vehicles, Matron. Anger at myself for being incapacitated was vent out on Tom and Brynly. I'm a stupid old man.'

With shoulders hunched over his Zimmer frame, he walked slowly away in the direction of the lifts. Bronwen knew he was about to shut himself away in his room with his computer and miss supper. She hurriedly manoeuvred her wheelchair and caught up with him. 'Thank you, Matron,' she said as she went.

'Geraint, it's all right. Stella and Mary weren't here for the demonstration of the scooters, either, and they'll have to know how to work them since we'll be taking them on our cruise. The men who are bringing some new ones on Friday will show us again how to operate them. I'm having one of them fancy hi-tech wheelchairs, too.'

'Yes, of course, Bronwen. I'm ashamed for talking to Tom and Brynly the way I did. It's just that my blooming prostate acted up. I had a little accident and I took a long time to find a dry pair of trousers. Circumstances, just circumstances. I won't be like that when we are away, I promise. You know, I can't wait to get away for a short while.'

'Don't worry, Geraint. Tom and Brynly will understand. And, yes, it will be good to get away for a while. We've been here a long time without a change of walls. And I'm grateful to you for arranging things. I just don't know what I'd do without you.

'Go on now into the lounge. I'll join you for supper. I'm just popping in to say hello and good night to Martha. She's picked up a bit; she'll appreciate the company. I'll tell her about this afternoon. If I can get through to her, I know she will be laughing, even though she can't show it.'

'You are one kind, lovely lady, Bronwen. Do you know that?' Geraint stroked her shoulder; it was as much touch as he allowed himself.

'Well now, thank you, kind sir. You're not so bad yourself.'

Tom telephoned Stella before supper was served. He was delighted to have a legitimate excuse to use his new mobile phone.

She was in the toilet when her landline telephone rang. She became anxious; she always responded to the dialling tone immediately. She was frustrated at not being able to get to the phone in time. Any call could be important these days.

It was partly because her outlook on life had changed since Bronwen became rich, though Stella wouldn't have admitted to that. As well as loving Bronwen as she had her mother, she was her carer. She nursed and protected her.

Stella's involvement with Bronwen's newly found wealth was spontaneous. She no longer had to worry about paying her bills, maintaining her old car, which was about to stop and not start again, or about her increasing overdraft at the bank. She used the same bank as Bronwen, so it was not a complicated administrative arrangement for Bronwen to transfer enough money into Stella's account. It cleared her overdraft and put her over four thousand pounds in credit.

Stella's heart had pounded when she discovered Bronwen's kindness. Being so inculcated with not accepting charity, she wasn't sure of how to accept it. Bronwen knew how Stella felt by the expression on her face and the humility in her eyes. If she tried to explain to Bronwen how she felt, she would fail. Anyway, there was no need. Bronwen helped her out.

'Stella, my lovely, I know how you feel about accepting money,' she had reassured her. 'There's no need. I'm lucky to have you with me to help me out with the spending of this blooming money which has been sprung into my hands. You'll never want for money again, if I can help it. So, try to get used to it, as I have to. And I rely on you to get my Mary to accept it. We both know that she's going to need a lot of support.'

Stella had hugged Bronwen and walked out of the lounge with tears in her eyes.

As she sat on the lavatory, she was thinking of her healthy bank account when Tom's telephone call went on ringing. She guessed it was him because no one else would let it ring so insatiably. She hastily pulled up her pants and jeans, ran down to the living room where the phone was and snatched it.

'Tom, is that you?'

'Yes, it's me, Stella.'

'Hang on a minute.' She hadn't washed her hands.'

She ran into the kitchen, washed her hands in the sink there. She hurriedly ran back to the phone as she wiped them with pieces of kitchen roll.

'Sorry, Tom. I was in the loo. Anything new happened, or are you just calling to test your posh mobile?'

She heard a touch of Tom's low toned laugh before he answered. It didn't take much to make Tom laugh. It didn't take much to make him angry either, but Stella sensed he was in good humour and had something special to tell her.

'Well, Stella, you missed something big here today. I've not had such a laugh since my step-father fell down the back steps and broke his leg.' Tom began laughing loudly; it stopped him talking.

'Stop your chortling, Tom, and tell me what happened. Or do I have to come in on my day off again?'

'That company Matron got in touch with about electric scooters sent two salesmen who brought some to show us. We all had a go; me, Brynly, Bronwen and even our Matron. It was like the dodgems in the fair.'

'Never!' Stella gasped and she, too, had a fit of the giggles. 'Trust me to miss that.'

'Never mind,' Tom went on, sounding excited, 'they're coming back on Friday with four. Bronwen's going to buy four.'

'Four!' Stella shouted down the mouthpiece. 'That'll cost a fortune.'

'Well, Bronwen's got one. One of them is for her. The others are for me, Brynly and Mr Lloyd-Davies, only he's none too pleased about it. Says he'll walk wherever he goes. I think he's forgotten what it's like to walk a bit of a distance. If his legs will take him, his prostate won't.'

'I'll have it if he doesn't want it,' Stella said. 'Anyway, Tom, thanks for calling. Ring off now or you'll run out of credit of what you have on your phone. Give Bronwen my love. Mary'll be in her usual time this evening. She's out buying new clothes and having a couple of sneaky Mars bars, I expect. She's not allowed them when I'm about. See you tomorrow.'

When Tom clicked off his phone, he realised all those residents around him were silent. They had been listening to his conversation. Thoughts of the afternoons' scooter show on the forecourt of The Sunshine Mount Nursing Home were on their minds and continued to amuse them.

Bronwen was at the other side of the room from Tom. Too far to hear what he was saying to Stella, but she guessed how the conversation went from his mannerisms and intermittent loud laughter. He had told her he intended to call Stella to tell her about the scooters.

The supper trolley trundled into the room with Carer Dora Evans behind it and all thoughts turned to what was on the menu.

'Same again, I expect.' Tilley, sitting near Bronwen, mumbled. She always complained about the food when she had nothing else to bother her. With one hand paralysed, she had difficulty with some food items. Bronwen always cut her meat for her and helped in any other way.

The menu was different every day of the week; except on special occasions, or when the cook decided to give a surprise meal.

If any of the residents didn't wish to participate of the expected day's meal, they were able to ask for something on toast. Scrambled egg, beans or a boil egg with bread and butter, which Bronwen often did. She was careful with her diet; the restricted mobility of the wheelchair was inclined to spread her hips.

She wondered what sort of chairs would be constructed in the elaborate people-carrier vehicle that was next on the list to consider.

She had no idea yet, but she was confident that with advice, the right one would soon be parked outside The Sunshine Mount Nursing Home.

Chapter 10
The Runaway Scooter

There were several important points to consider when selecting a people-carrying vehicle for going long distances. It had to be elegant and suitable for Bronwen, herself, and all who travelled in it. Several extras would be added. It was expected to be costly, but who cared? Bronwen didn't, as long as no mistakes were made. Selecting the right one to buy was not easy. There were many on the market to choose from.

Bronwen had to be sure to choose the right one for carrying them all in comfort and which allowed space for a wheelchair, a lot of luggage and, of course, electric scooters. Geraint and Tom helped in the selection, but they were as much in the dark as she was. The big decision was left to Colin and Kevin.

When the new mobility aids were delivered, she and her companions planned to go on a shopping spree to one of the big shopping precincts. She was determined she would remain a size twelve to get some lovely clothes for going on that Mediterranean cruise. She wouldn't have to depend on anyone again to choose her clothes. She would do so by going to the shops herself. With one of those new electric scooters with carrier baskets attached, it would be much easier.

She was lucky to have had Stella to do this in the past, and she knew Bronwen's taste in clothes was of elegant style and quality. God forbid that she had to rely on Mary. She couldn't suitably choose for herself, let alone for her mother.

Recently, Mary had Stella to choose for her, and she already began to look a different woman. A smarter one.

Bronwen was especially looking forward to seeing Mary that evening. She had gone shopping for new clothes and she would certainly be laden with her purchases when she came into the lounge. She felt more confident of the fact that she wouldn't have to hide her dislike of Mary's choice and she hoped this evening she wouldn't be disappointed. Mary was always delighted in showing her new clothes to the other residents. Some were outspoken enough to tell Mary what they thought of them and it wasn't always flattering. Bronwen was left with Mary's hurt pride to deal with.

She would tell Mary of the fun she and the others had when trying out the electric scooters that afternoon. She didn't think Mary would be able to visualise the event, so wouldn't appreciate the humour. However, Bronwen would insist that Mary would be at the home on Friday, when her new wheelchair and the four new scooters arrived. She would be shown by George how to switch on, off, drive, steer and stop. She would insist that Mary understood how they functioned. She assumed it wasn't difficult, and she would, no doubt, ride one herself. She would need to know for when they were on the cruise. Mr Todd said they were designed to carry people of up to eighteen stone or more, so Bronwen guessed Mary's weight would be no problem.

She was wrong.

George, who had accompanied Mr Todd on his previous visit, and the company's smart delivery van, arrived at two o'clock on the following Friday, as arranged. The deputy Matron was on that day; she had been told by Matron Phillips to expect delivery of the electric scooters. Geraint would be prepared to sort out the paper work and Bronwen would stand by with her chequebook. However, she wouldn't make out the cheque until Geraint had checked for exactness.

Mary arrived during the lunch time period. She waited in the hall. She would have avoided that, had she known she was too early. The residents in the lounge of The Laburnum Unit could be seen through the glass partition which divided it from the office and the hallway. It upset Mary to see the very debilitated and elderly people there. Some of the residents needed help to move in their chairs. From time to time she saw the carers helping those to stand for a few minutes. One old lady did so reluctantly and tried to hit those who were helping her.

Some of them had to be taken to the toilet every one or two hours. They were taken in wheelchairs or walked, very slowly and carefully, with a carer supporting each side. When in the toilet, a carer would remain with him or her, having closed the door. For safety reasons, there were no locks on toilet doors in nursing homes. Mary decided she would never use a toilet with someone watching her. She didn't realise that one day she would be old—God willing.

Most of the residents were too old or too ill to communicate and sat in the same chair, day in day out, except when the carers sat and talked to them, or they had visitors, which for some, was rare.

Mary was not an intellectually bright person, but like her mother, she was sensitive to others misfortunes. She had respect for the carers who did their jobs skilfully and were always cheerful and friendly. Some of them appeared and sounded uncaring—hard on the outside but with compassion and understanding of the needs and behaviour of the elderly.

One such person was Stella; though she sounded strict on the outside, she didn't look it. Quite the contrary; she was beautiful. She was Mary's role model.

Mary was glad when the lunchtime session was completed and Deputy Matron, sitting in her office writing her never-ending reports. She nodded to Mary, giving her permission to enter Willow Lounge.

Those residents who hadn't settled down for their afternoon nap greeted Mary.

'You're early today,' Tom said. 'You going to have a try on our new scooters?'
Mary shook her head. 'I don't know, Tom. I might be too 'eavy for 'em.'

'No, you're not,' he replied. 'That Mr Todd told your mam.'

'Did he?' Mary said with surprise. 'Well, I will if Mammy lets me.'

Mary's speech and mannerisms were that of a young person; not of one who had entered her thirties. She had lived a very closed life, rarely seen the outside of Pendarren, and hadn't socialised enough with people of her own age when she was younger. Bronwen knew she was partly responsible for this. Mary's incapacity had limited her life experiences. Things should change now she had the money to travel and change her life-style—but not too much, Bronwen decided. Mary wouldn't be able to cope with too much change.

She smiled happily when she saw Mary. She was dressed in a loose, pale blue rainproof jacket and a pair of dark-blue loose slacks which didn't cling and exhibit her obese thighs and buttocks. She had on a pair of flat, sensible shoes, for trying out an electric scooter.

Her hair looked as if it had been cut with a knife, but it would soon grow. Then she would get it properly cut and shaped. At least, it was now clean and glossy. Her skin was smooth and flawless, as was her mother's, and when she smiled her teeth gleamed white. She'd had a multi-millionaire mother for less than a month, yet she was already looking wealthy. Stella was a good influence.

'Hello, my lovely,' Bronwen smiled. 'You look nice.'

'Well, Mammy, it's raining a bit, so I thought this would be right.' Mary referred to her smart jacket. 'Stella told me to.'

'Good for her, but I expect you knew it would look nice. Have you seen Stella yet? She's on duty. She was on the early shift. You must have been fast asleep when she left the house.'

'No, I haven't seen her yet. She's looking after Martha Tate and those in bottom lounge, poor things. Mammy, you'll never get like any of them, will you?'

'Yes, Mary, I'm afraid I will, if God allows me to live long enough. You will, too.'

The double-doors of the lounge were still wide open after the meal trolleys had been taken through. Stella came along and shut them to allow as much of a quiet atmosphere as was possible for the residents to have their afternoon nap.

They were fire-prevention doors, which by law, should have been kept closed at all times, except for exit and entrance. No one seems to take heed.

Stella walked across to the big television screen and switched off the picture; the sound had already been turned off. She then went and sat beside Bronwen and Mary.

Tilley and some of the others had chosen to be taken to their rooms for the afternoon's siesta. It was quiet in the lounge. Stella whispered, respecting the tranquil atmosphere. 'Bronwen, the man with the scooters has arrived. He's waiting for you in Matron's office. Mr Lloyd-Davies is already there. The scooters are in big boxes in the hall. I heard him tell the man, George, the boxes will have to be unpacked and the scooters put right and tested before payment is made.'

'Very well,' Bronwen began to get agitated as she clutched her handbag and made to leave the room. 'My cheque book is in here,' she said, clutching her bag tighter.

'Shush, no rush,' Stella said quietly, 'you're the buyer. He'll wait, won't he, Mary?' She looked Mary up and down with surprise. 'My word, what's happened? You look nice.'

Mary smiled. 'Well, I did as you told me,' she whispered, before adding, 'You and me will have to ride the scooters to make sure they're all right for Mammy and Mr Lloyd-Davies; but it's raining.'

'Yes,' Stella agreed, as she took the handles of Bronwen's wheelchair and manoeuvred it towards the exit. 'It's only raining a bit, but I'll put a jacket on.'

'We'll have to ride them up and down the corridor,' Mary said. 'We can't ride on them out in the rain, can we?'

'Yes, of course, you can,' Bronwen replied as she was being wheeled down the corridor. 'We won't always be out in dry weather. I hope these scooters will allow us to go anywhere in sunshine or shower.'

George greeted Bronwen as if she were an old acquaintance, having met her a few days before. Matron had introduced Mr Lloyd-Davies to George and explained that he was Mrs Dew's accountant and financial adviser. She knew how to make Geraint feel important.

'One of the scooters is for Mr Lloyd-Davies,' Bronwen said, turning to him. 'You must have a go on one, Geraint.' But Geraint excused himself. He needed the lavatory.

'I won't be long,' he said as he turned away.

'Right, then,' George said, taking a large pair of scissors out of a pocket of his boiler-suit. 'I'll make a start on these. These boxes, being left here, will be in the way of your residents. The scooters will take up less room when they're set up.'

Stella set about helping him with her small scissors which she kept in her uniform pocket.

'Mary,' she ordered, 'go to the kitchen and ask Cook for something that will open these boxes. You can help us then.'

One of the nurses standing in the hall, watching the goings on, also took out a small pair of scissors from her pocket and began cutting the tape from the covering of the boxes.

It wasn't long before the electric mobility scooters were erected. They gleamed with newness.

'In they nice?' Mary gloated. 'I've seen people on 'em in town. Can me and Stella go outside and try 'em out, Mammy? It's stopped raining.'

Bronwen consented. 'Yes, but make sure you know what to do first. They're quite simple to use but you'd better be told first. Easy when you know how.'

George explained to Stella and Mary how to start, drive and stop the electric scooters. 'The top speed is within the safety limits,' he said. 'I find, though, they can shoot away pretty sharply until you're used to them. We would never be able to manufacture or sell them for the disabled unless they were hundred percent foolproof. Much of the cost of them is not so much for their construction and use, but for the technology that's involved. They are great little machines. Have given millions of people the freedom to leave their homes, independent of having to manoeuvre their wheelchairs or have someone push them.

'They are used mostly for going out, not for use inside, because the seating isn't comfortable enough for long periods and, of course, they can't be used at table for dining.'

Whilst he was explaining the details, Mary approached a scooter and sat on its seat. It seemed like a toy to her, but circumstances which followed changed her thoughts.

She had listened to George describing the simplicity of manoeuvring the scooters. She was too excited; she couldn't have listened close enough, although her bottom lip drooped with concentration.

'Close your mouth, Mary,' Stella reminded her, as she often had to when Mary was concentrating hard, 'your tongue is dropping out.'

Mary snapped her mouth closed. 'Come on then, Stella, you try one until Mr Lloyd-Davies comes.'

When outside on the courtyard, Stella and Mary took to their motor scooters like two champions approaching their vehicles.

George stood beside Stella and set her going before he helped Mary on her way. Stella was already half way across the forecourt before Mary had the hang of how to start her scooter. When she did, she shot from her starting point at the top speed of the motor. It was designed to travel at a maximum speed of eight miles per hour, but the darting effect took away Mary's confidence and she forgot all George had taught her.

Instead of following directly behind Stella, who was about to turn back, Mary's vehicle veered to the left, towards the steep hill, and down she went.

She screamed with fright, 'I can't stop, I can't stop!' She had lost control of the scooter.

She realised if she went all the way down the hill, the speed of the vehicle would gain momentum. It would run freely across the main road at the bottom and crash into the brick wall. She thought the lever she kept her finger firmly on was the "stop" lever rather than the "go" one.

Everybody who had been standing in the hall and just outside the front door ran to the top of the hill to witness Mary's distress.

She heard Stella shout, 'Turn to your right and go into the fence!'

At the edge of each side of the hill was a narrow bordering of garden which was flowered in spring and summer. Beyond the patch on the right side of the hill was a rough, rotting-wood fence which divided the home's ground from that of the town's allotments.

Bronwen's heart was turning somersaults as she watched her daughter's predicament. 'Oh my God,' she gasped. 'She's going to break her neck.'

Everyone was silent with eyes agog of the scene, except George. He repeatedly said, 'It's all right, the scooter is strong. It'll be all right.' He was more concerned about ending a successful business transaction than Mary breaking her neck.

Mary did as Stella had suggested and steered right across the mud of the garden-border and crashed into the fence. The fact that the fence being rotten and the flower bed muddy was Mary's salvation. That part of the fence into which Mary crashed gave way. It collapsed flat on the ground and the scooter trundled over it. It stopped as it landed in a heap of compost which had been piled against the fence. Mary fell off sideways and the scooter landed on top of her.

Stella dismounted and ran down the hill to help Mary. She was covered with soggy muck; her jacket was torn, and she was crying.

'Oh, my arm, my arm! I've broke my arm and my jacket!'

'Never mind your bloody jacket, you daft lump. Stay still a minute,' Stella snapped angrily. She needed to find out if Mary had any injury which would warrant calling an ambulance, or if she could deal with the situation herself. The scooter burped and became silent.

Stella leant at the side of Mary and looked her over. 'Where else are you hurting beside your arm?' Stella asked with some urgency in her tone.

'Nowhere, only my arm, but it's hurting terrible, Stella. I've broke it, I know. I 'eard it crack—an' felt it,' she whaled louder, 'Look at my new jacket. It's ripped, and it was thirty pounds.'

'What!' Stella screamed, 'Thirty pounds!' She would have gone on complaining about Mary's extravagance had there not been a more important matter to attend to. Mary might well have broken her arm when she fell onto the blade of a garden spade that had been left at the side of the compost heap.

'Hold your right arm, that is your hurt arm, with the other arm and stand up slowly,' Stella instructed clearly so that Mary wouldn't get the arms confused. She cried loudly like a child all of the time.

'And shut up your whaling!' Stella shouted. 'You're getting on my nerves and we've got to get back up the hill!'

'What about the scooter?' Mary sobbed.

'Do you want me to carry that as well as half of you?' Stella's anxiety was making her angry.

By that time several people who had witnessed the accident from the top of the hill had run down to help—led by George. He went straight to the scooter but stopped at the edge of the compost heap. He looked down at it, and then cast his glance down his pristine, white boiler suit before attempting to retrieve the expensive electric scooter.

He picked up the scooter and carried it to the road before returning to help Stella and Mary.

He supported Mary on her uninjured side until they had walked over the muck and collapsed fence and got to the road. There, two of the carers were waiting with a wheelchair to push Mary up the hill.

'Mary!' one of them shouted. 'You must have broken your arm. You poor thing. You'll have to go to 'ospital.'

They each took a handle of the wheelchair and pulled it up the hill to the front entrance and into the hall. Deputy Matron Banding took one look at Mary's arm before instructing Stella to go to the treatment room to get a splint and a crepe bandage. Matron then began taking Mary's jacket off, starting with her good arm then, carefully, threading it off her injured arm. The forearm was misshapen and inflamed.

'Stella,' Matron said, 'you must take Mary into Casualty. Take her into the bathroom and wash her first. She can't be seen covered with that compos muck with her. She'll need it X-rayed, set and plastered. I'm pretty certain she's broken it.'

Matron skilfully applied the splint and bandage to Mary's injured arm.

'How will you manage with one short for teas and bedtime, Matron? Perhaps Dora will come in for a few hours. She lives nearby; just across the road. I won't expect to be paid for this afternoon.'

'Never you mind about that,' Matron said. 'You just drive slowly not to cause much movement.' She looked at Mary and stroked her brow. 'It won't be long before your arm will be put right,' she advised the simpering Mary. 'Try not to move it until you get to the hospital.'

The splinting seemed to have eased the pain, but Mary was clearly in shock. Her, normally, pink cheeks were the colour of chalk, and she shivered.

Bronwen had stood by watching everyone helping her daughter whilst she could do nothing. She was frightened; pale and trembling.

'Thank you, Matron,' Bronwen said. 'She'll be all right, won't she?'

'Of course, she will.'

Stella washed Mary as best she could before going to the staff room to get her jacket. She kept on her uniform. She thought the casualty people would consider her an emergency and not keep her waiting too long.

'Bronwen, thank God it's only her arm. It could have been much worse.' It was Matron's way of comforting Bronwen.

More people had gathered in the hall to view the proceedings; Geraint was among them, standing beside Bronwen.

They watched two of the carers help Mary into Stella's car.

'It's a good thing I didn't finalise that booking on The Gladiator,' he said. 'If Mary's broken her arm, it'll be in a plaster cast for weeks. Poor thing.'

'At the moment I don't care a toss about the cruise, the fancy wheelchairs or anything, except my Mary. You know, Geraint,' she said with a trembling voice, 'there have been many times when I've wished I had legs, but never have I felt so bitter about being without them. I feel useless.'

'My dear, that's the last thing I'd say about you. Your legs may be useless, but God has given you all the good things to make up for his mistake. You're the loveliest woman I've ever known—except for my Eleanor, of course, but she's in Heaven now, so you're top of the list.'

Bronwen touched his hand that was resting on her shoulder. 'Thank you, Geraint. Now they've gone, you'll be needed in the office. We have to pay for these scooter things.'

In the office George handed the invoice to Geraint, who had put on his spectacles that had been dangling on a fine chain about his chest, before studying the document closely.

'That's right,' he said, 'that's what we agreed.'

Bronwen took out her chequebook and was about to sign a cheque. She wanted to get the business over with quickly; her thoughts were on Mary.

Matron interrupted. 'What about the one that's damaged, George?'

'It's not damaged,' he replied, 'these scooters are tough little things. It just needs a cleaning.'

There was a pregnant pause. George sensed that his good customers weren't entirely satisfied. He didn't like that because he expected the present good business to be an outlet for much more.

'I tell you what, then, I'll do you a favour. Settle the invoice now, I'll take the used scooter back with me; I see no reason why it can't be put on sale after it's been cleaned up, and I'll send you another one. Boxed up as these were, completely untouched. Will you be happy with that?'

His suggestion satisfied everyone, so the invoice was settled. Geraint ensured it was receipted correctly.

George seemed glad to leave. He had been shaken by the accident.

The residents who had been standing in the hall soon forgot about Mary and the mobility scooters. It was near teatime. They dispersed and went to their separate tables.

Bronwen had no appetite. Her thoughts were on Mary and Stella, wondering how far they had progressed towards getting Mary treated.

'I wonder what time they'll be back.' Bronwen said to Tilley, who sat opposite her at the lunch table.

'God knows,' Tilley replied. 'You know what it's like in that Accident and Emergency place. They could be hours. But never mind, Bronwen, they're in the right place.' Bronwen was slightly reassured.

Stella returned to the home ten hours later. She guessed Bronwen wouldn't have gone to bed. She had called Tom's mobile phone with her own. It was highly sophisticated, she could make a call and receive one, but she hadn't yet mastered its many functions.

She told Tom to tell Bronwen that Mary was all right. She'd been X-rayed; her right arm was fractured. It had to be reduced and plaster of Paris would be applied. She didn't know how long it was going to take.

Bronwen remained in the lounge, sitting with her eyes closed, her open book just about to slip off her lap. Stella touched her gently on her arm and she awoke with a start.

'Stella, my lovely. How are things with Mary? What would I do without you?' She stretched her neck to look behind Stella, expecting Mary to be following.

'She's all right, Bronwen, but they're keeping her in overnight in case her arm swells under the plaster. She has a cast from here to here.' Stella pointed out that the plaster was from Mary's hand to her elbow.

'I'll go and get her tomorrow; I'm off duty. But I'll be honest, Bronwen, I can't think how she's going to manage, her being right handed. We both know she's going to have trouble managing.'

'I've already thought of that,' Bronwen said. 'I've asked Matron if she can have the one empty room here for as long as it takes. I've offered to pay double for the room, if needs be, and she's agreed, thank the Lord. But I need you to make sure she doesn't get the carers waiting on her hand foot and finger. She must fend for herself as much as she can. Thank God, she's alright. I've had visions of her arm ending up like one of my legs.'

Stella laughed, but she didn't feel like laughing. She was exhausted and hungry.

'Thank you for looking after her and coming back to tell me.' Bronwen repeated, 'I don't know what I would do without you.'

'I wish you would stop saying that. You would manage quite well.' Stella embraced Bronwen and kissed her cheek.

'She'll be all right now. I'm off home to a hot bath, some fish and chips from the chippie and then to bed. You must do the same. Do you want me to take you up and settle you?'

'My goodness, no. You go and let me know when you can go to get Mary tomorrow. You have a lie-in first.'

Stella and Mary arrived back at the home during the early afternoon. They'd had lunch in the hospital dining room. Stella had telephoned Tom to tell Bronwen.

Bronwen, who had her own phone chosen by Tom, hadn't yet used it. She had chastised Tom for getting phones so complicated.

'Well, Bronwen, using a phone isn't rocket science, you know. You'll soon get the hang of it. And you want one that you can use when you're away on the cruise and stopping at ports, don't you? One of you will have to have one.'

'Yes. Quite right, Tom. You must show me how to use it tomorrow.'

'You said that yesterday,' Tom replied. 'Read the instruction booklet.'

'I have, and it might as well be in Chinese.'

Bronwen was pleased to see Mary's healthy colour had returned and she seemed proud of her shining white plaster of Paris. She had on her left arm a jacket which Stella had taken from the wardrobe at home. It was slung casually over Mary's shoulder of her right side. When it slipped off, she had difficulty getting it back with her left hand. Stella helped her before picking up Bronwen's pen and signing her name on the plaster-cast. She, also, drew a funny face with Mary's name to it.

Mary's plaster of Paris wasn't shining white for long. It became covered with names, sketches and words which Mr Lloyd-Davies blacked out.

She moved into the home, as arranged. She ate wholesome food at correct times of the day and began to lose her excess weight. It motivated her to lose more. She enjoyed the company of the carers and residents, but Bronwen didn't intend her to get too used to it. It wasn't the right atmosphere for a young person.

When Tom and Brynly went out on the scooters, she insisted Mary went with them. They didn't go far; they circled around and back and forth the forecourt. The weather wasn't yet good enough for them to go further but they became used to the scooters and enjoyed them. Mary hated them.

Chapter 11
Travelling in Style

At the end of November, a magnificent metallic silver, six-seater hatchback Mercedes was parked in all its glory outside the main doors of The Sunshine Mount Nursing Home. It was an "automatic", which was not understood to most who gazed, wide-eyed upon it. The upholstery was of the finest pale grey leather, the windows were of tinted glass, a ramp at the rear for taking on wheelchairs, and a roof-rack for extra luggage.

Bronwen was astounded at the extra, inside, luxury fittings, though she considered the roof-rack superfluous; it wouldn't be needed for the amount of luggage they would have when they went away. She was wrong.

On Colin and Kevin's advice, Geraint and Tom had ordered the vehicle two weeks ago and it was delivered to a garage in Cardiff. Stella and Kevin had taken a taxi to the garage and Kevin drove the grand car back. He'd wanted Stella to take the wheel for part of the way; she'd have to get used to it.

'What a superb piece of motor engineering, Stella,' Kevin said. 'It practically goes on its own. This Mercedes is absolutely fabulous. It even smells of wealth.'

'Mmm,' Stella had sighed. 'It is lovely, but you drive now. I'll enjoy the ride. To get used to it, I'll drive about the roads I'm familiar with.'

'Fair enough, then,' Kevin agreed with anything Stella suggested.

When Kevin drove it up the hill onto the forecourt of the home, the residents who caught sight of the magnificent car through the windows were astounded, and beckoned all others, who were able, to join them. One elderly lady with memory-loss passed comment.

'Who is it come to see us?' she asked. 'Is it Prince Charles?'

The man beside her laughed. 'No, Cissy. Him and the Queen are coming tomorrow. It's Bronwen's day today. Look at her new car,' he pointed out of the nearest window.

'Duw, duw. It's big enough, anyway,' Cissy remarked.

Some of the residents came out onto the forecourt to have a good look around the car and to touch it.

'Mind you, don't dirty it,' Tom teased, 'or you won't have a ride in it.'

Bronwen couldn't believe her eyes. 'Well, who would have thought it? You and Kevin made a marvellous choice.'

'I thought it too extravagant when I paid for it.' Geraint frowned as he sucked his teeth, thinking of the cost.

'Stop worrying about the cost, Geraint,' Bronwen responded with some irritation. 'We have plenty.'

'Yes, I know. And the cost of it is just a fleabite of what you have. Trouble is, like you, I'll never get used to not having to consider cost.'

'Yes, Geraint. You're right, as always,' Bronwen nodded and enjoyed seeing Mary sitting in the driving seat with her plaster of Paris dangling out of the window.

'Watch you don't scratch it with that plaster, Mary!' Stella shouted. 'And stop showing off!'

Mary didn't want to annoy Stella. She got out of the front seat and took a seat at the back. 'It's as comfy as a' armchair,' Mary went on. 'Come on, Kevin, take us for a little run,' she was surprised that Stella agreed.

'Yes, come on,' Stella said as she prodded Kevin. 'Lift Bronwen onto one of the seats. Mr Lloyd-Davies can get in on his own as long as he has his Zimmer.'

Geraint strode over to the car, stroked it as if it were a pet and sat in one of the seats. He was ready to try out the vehicle.

'Room for a couple more,' Kevin said. 'I'll take them up the main road for a couple of miles. Won't be long, Matron.' He looked towards Matron, hoping for her agreement. She nodded and made a gesture with her hand for him to go.

She was in the hall, near the office in case the phone rang. She positioned herself so she could see what was going on in the Laburnum Lounge. Megan, the young, cheeky carer, approached Matron.

'Matron, can I please go? It won't be long. I'll be back long before teas.'

'Go on then, you young madam. You can keep your eye on Bronwen.'

Megan made a dash for the seat beside Mary, slammed the door shut and made herself comfortable. The beautiful car purred from the courtyard and down the hill towards the main road.

'Oh, Geraint, isn't it lovely?' Bronwen swooned. 'It's worth every penny.'

'I agree, wholeheartedly.' Geraint was enjoying every minute.

'Do you want to have a try at driving now, Stella?' Kevin asked.

'Oh, no, not now. Another day. I know I have to get used to it.'

'You better had,' Bronwen said as she tapped Stella on her shoulder. 'It's only about three weeks before Christmas and we have a lot of shopping to do.'

'Why don't you go to Cribb's Causeway in Bristol, Mrs Dew?' Megan suggested. 'I've been there with my mam and dad and it's fabulous. You'll spend a fortune, though.'

'Good idea, Megan. We'll go a week on Saturday. Stella will have to request an off-duty day. Will you be working, Kevin?' 'No,' Kevin answered. 'That'll be smashing. We can all buy things for the cruise. I don't have a thing for going away.' He then took a quick glance sideways and alerted Stella. 'You and I will spend this weekend, when you are off duty, to practice you driving this. Honest, it's so easy.'

Stella reluctantly agreed. 'All right, Kevin. But you'd better turn back now. Megan will be needed on the unit.'

As he drove, pedestrians and people in other cars glanced admiringly at the shining, silver car. It purred back up the hill towards the forecourt of the nursing home, stopped silently in front of the doors and everyone got off. Kevin cradled Bronwen in his arms as if she were a kitten and put her gently onto her wheelchair in the hall.

It reminded Bronwen of her life with her dear Lewis and for a few seconds she yearned for him. Kevin seemed to handle her easier than Lewis had, but then he had been smaller than Kevin.

That evening in the lounge, there was much chat about the new car and the plans for a shopping spree.

Mary said she wanted a new bathing suit; she hadn't yet been able to get one suitable that would fit her. She recited a number of things she would buy, including the most beautiful evening dress she could find.

'I'll be getting a bikini for the swimming pool on the ship,' Stella said with glee. 'I might get two—one for best.'

Bronwen laughed. 'Do you think I can afford two?'

'Will you help me to get a bikini?' Mary asked. Stella was at a loss of how to respond. Bronwen noticed her look of reluctance and answered for her.

'Not yet, Mary, love. You haven't quite lost enough weight. The way you're going it won't be long, though. In the meantime, stick to what Stella thinks looks nice on you.'

'All right, Mammy,' Mary pouted. 'I know I'm still too fat.'

Bronwen seemed to have said the right thing. She then decided to talk Geraint into being more enthusiastic about the clothes he should take.

'You'll need a new suit, Geraint. A lounge suit and a formal evening suit and new shirts and ties.'

'I have both suits upstairs that are good enough, Bronwen. No point in spending for spending's sake,' Mr Lloyd-Davies often used that cliché.

'Mr Lloyd-Davies, if it's the evening dinner jacket and trousers you showed me, they were smart years ago. It was green, not black.' Stella had helped him to look through his clothes to decide what he should buy. She thought he needed a whole new wardrobe, but she didn't express her opinion; she avoided offending him.

'Only a bit of mould,' he said. 'It'll brush off. I'll go and try on what used to be my business suit now, so that you can all see for yourselves.'

He went to his room and was out for over half an hour. Stella realised he was having trouble getting his suit out of the wardrobe, undressing and putting it on. She went up to help him. She tapped on his door.

'Need any help, Mr Lloyd-Davies?'

'Just coming, Stella, I couldn't find it. But I've got it on now. I'm just coming down.'

When he walked into the lounge, Stella walked in front of him hoping the residents would look at her; not him. She was disappointed. He reminded her of a comedy character portrayed in an old Charlie Chaplain movie film. He heard some cutting remarks and stifled laughter.

His suit was a dark blue, wide pinstriped, double-breasted coat with padded shoulders which drooped down his arms, the too-long sleeves covering his hands. The trousers were many sizes too big; his body mass had, inevitable, shrunk with the ageing process, and the turn-up trouser-legs dragged on the floor. If it weren't for his Zimmer frame he would certainly have tripped.

'Good God,' someone said, 'here comes Al Capone.'

'I thought he was dead,' someone else said.

His close friends, Stella and Mary, passed no comment but their look said all.

'That suit is no good for you, Geraint,' said Tilley, sitting close by. 'I don't even think Oxfam will take it. It's too old fashioned.'

Bronwen fingered the material. 'My word, Geraint, the quality of this cloth is of the highest. It must have cost a lot of money when you bought it and you really must have looked quite dashing in that when you were in business.'

'Thank you, Bronwen, my dear, but I don't feel that it's suitable now. You're right; I'll have to get a new one.'

'You'll get a lovely one when we go to the big shopping place near Bristol. Kevin will be with you. He'll be getting one as well.' Stella thought it would lessen Geraint's disappointment if he knew Kevin needed a new suit as well.

Geraint sat in his chair and waited until the lounge was empty before going up to his room. He didn't wish to make a second embarrassing appearance. Bronwen felt sorry for him. She tried to think of something to say which would boost his deflated morale, but couldn't. She was glad he was the type of person who would soon bounce back from upset and bare no grudge.

She told him of her decision to buy a Christmas present for every resident and hoped he would help her to find out what people wanted. She conjured up in her mind methods of finding out what everyone would like.

She told him she was getting a good fob watch for him. He was pleased. He had one, but it was tainted, and the clockwork rusted.

Before she went to her room that night, she went across to see Martha Tate to ask her what she would like. She sensed that Martha heard her but couldn't respond.

'I'll buy you a compact disc with something I think you will like,' Bronwen told her. Martha had soft music playing all day. She loved music. She had told Bronwen some time ago that it was her love of music which prolonged her life. Bronwen hoped, again and again, that Martha was still able to hear.

She, herself, had soft music playing when in her room. She liked the ballads she and Lewis used to listen to and sing together. He had a melodious singing voice and Bronwen knew Mary had a sweet singing voice, which she must have inherited from her father. However, Martha would like something more classical than Bing Crosby or Jeanette MacDonald and Nelson Eddy.

Bronwen asked Stella to seek help from the carers. They handed out coloured strips of paper, to those who could still write, to put down what each would ask Father Christmas for, if he existed.

She had some laughable responses. Tilley Tittle-tattle asked for a toy boy. One of the men asked for a life-sized, rubber blown-up figure of Marilyn Monroe. Two requests on pieces of paper which arrived on Bronwen's lap were unmentionable, so she tore them up. A few asked for watches with big faces and big figures so they knew what time of the day it was. All the clocks in the home told a different time. Quite a few asked for expensive perfumes and make-up—easy requests. One piece of paper had written words on it in large scrawled, child-like writing, "A miracle". It saddened her; she knew who had made that strange request and knew it was made in earnest.

One sad resident, forty-eight-year-old John Drake, a victim of Huntingdon's chorea, was severely physically incapacitated, yet he was compos mentis. He knew what was said to him and knew what was going on around him but was unable to respond. He lived a life of continuous frustration. Anger and aggression were his only release.

He sat on a wide, well-padded settee for his protection and to allow him enough room for his spontaneous, irregular movements.

The carers looked after him with compassion and talked to him in a way which didn't need him to respond, because he was unable to. The men sitting near him, like John, were football fans and understood his condition. Although incapacitated themselves they, no doubt, felt lucky when compared with him.

John had been a coal miner and had played football for his hometown. He had loved the football matches and was a fervent follower of those shown on the television. He stayed awake long enough to watch "Match of the Day" and, also, watched the games during the afternoons, when they were on. In his own way he managed to cheer or boo with the men with whom he watched the games.

When Bronwen knew there was no football match on the television and John was in his usual position in the bottom lounge, she went to talk to him, as she often did.

To get some idea of what gift he would like, she decided to try to get some response rather than choose herself. From the small handbag which she always had with her, she took out the piece of paper on which John could write his choice of gift. His tremors eased as he looked into Bronwen's eyes and she into his.

'Look at these, John,' she removed the shawl wrapped about her knees and raised her trousers enough to display her ugly legs. 'If I could buy a miracle, I would for myself, now I am rich. If I won a million, million pounds, you know I couldn't buy a miracle. No amount would, you know. If some magic happens that will allow me to, I promise, you and I will be at the top of the list.'

88

She felt as if she were making excuses for how life had cheated her as it had to him. He responded in the only way he knew how and Bronwen recognised it.

'You'll get something from Father Christmas. You wait and see. He won't forget you.'

She decided to get him a pair of football boots and socks the colours of Cardiff football team. He could only look at them on his feet, but he could dream.

The same applied to two elderly women who sat next to one another in the opposite corner of the room. They each asked for a glamorous pair of shoes with diamante straps and three-inch high heels.

'But you can't walk well enough to wear them,' Dora said as she stood beside Bronwen. 'You'd fall.'

'Don't want 'em to dance or walk in, do we?' the elderly woman challenged Dora. 'Can't walk in any shoes. Just put 'em on and look at 'em. We're over the hill but we can still dream as well as you.'

Bronwen smiled her understanding and said to Dora, 'Why do people pay thousands and thousands of pounds for beautiful paintings by the famous old masters, Dora?'

'Well, Bronwen. I think they just like to look at them.' Dora paused to give the question a little thought and grinned. 'Yes, Bronwen, I see the point.'

Bronwen made a list and set about getting the gifts. Stella took her and Mary into the nearest towns out of Pendarren, whenever time allowed. Some of the items she was able to acquire, but there were things she would have to get when they went on a big shopping spree, near the city of Bristol; the one Megan, the young carer, had recommended. By then Stella was able to handle the big car expertly, but only on familiar territory. She was still apprehensive of driving on the fast motorways. However, she agreed with Kevin; it was a pleasure to drive and, being an automatic geared engine, it practically went on its own.

On a Saturday, ten days before Christmas, Kevin drove them to the popular shopping arcade, Cribb's Causeway. Mary, of course, had her plaster cast still in situation on her right arm, but it didn't spoil the excitement of the trip for her.

'I notice you can spend as much with only your left hand as you did when you had both hands functioning,' Stella teased.

She sat in the front with Kevin, Bronwen and Geraint behind and Mary in one of the back seats. Behind her was the folded mobility scooters and Geraint's Zimmer frame, leaving ample space for whatever else.

'What do you want your Zimmer for, Geraint?' Bronwen asked. 'The two of us are going to use the scooters when we get there. That's what they're for.'

'I'm going to walk on my own two legs for as far as I can,' he replied with a tone which indicated he wanted no contradiction.

Stella was in the driving seat. 'I'll drive as far as the Seven Bridge, Kevin. We'll stop at the first roadside place for whoever wants to use the toilets. I will for a start. Then you can drive the rest of the way because of the traffic.'

'Well, all right, but you'll have to start driving in traffic at some time.'

'Yes, I will,' Stella reluctantly agreed.

'You said that yesterday and the day before,' Kevin grinned. He knew she wouldn't be pushed.

Stella steered into a parking space allotted to disabled people, near the entrance of a motor roadside service station.

Geraint was first out of the car. He grabbed his Zimmer frame and made for the entrance to the service station's main building

'Thank goodness,' he mumbled, 'I feel near to bursting but, I expect, it will only be a trickle.' He made for the gents' toilet at a remarkable pace for a man passed eighty. He never ceased to amaze Bronwen. She thought he might go even faster if he didn't carry the Zimmer frame in front of him; as if it were a guard to protect him, rather than to help him to walk.

They used the toilets and had a short look around the shops. Bronwen was amazed at the facilities; she'd never been in a motorway service station. She hadn't been out of her hometown since Lewis died. She had been warned that she would find a lot of changes after ten years.

Stella and Mary each bought a bag of sweets; Mary had her wrist slapped when she reached out for the Mars bars.

Kevin drove the rest of the way to Cribb's Causeway. He, again, managed to find a spot designated for the disabled, near a lift which would take them directly down to the arcade of shops.

Stella brought the two mobility scooters out of the back of the car, set them up and checked that they were safe to use. Kevin cradle-lifted Bronwen from her seat in the car and set her down happily on her scooter.

'You can fold mine back up and leave in the car, Kevin,' Geraint said. 'I'm quite happy with my Zimmer.'

'But Mr Lloyd-Davies, you'll be on your feet for hours. There's a lot of walking to be done,' Kevin sounded concerned.

'I'll be all right,' Geraint insisted, 'for as long as I can I'm going to use my legs.'

'Geraint,' Bronwen said in an unusually sharp tone. 'You are not a young man; however young you may feel. The amount of walking we'll do will tire you and spoil the day. And we can't expect Kevin to walk all the way back here to get your scooter if you change your mind.'

'Oh, very well,' Geraint reluctantly agreed, clearly irritated having to face the truth. He mounted his scooter and drove off. He was first at the lift and pressed the button before the others caught up, relieved that he had seen sense.

It was a tight squeeze with the two scooters in the dimly lit lift. When the door opened onto their first glimpse at the entrance avenue of the arcade, it was as if God's finger had switched on sunshine.

There was a hush between the group. They were amazed at the brilliance of the light fittings. There were gasps of delight at the sight of the glass-domed ceilings, the colours and magnificence of the dozens of shining shops and stalls down the long, wide arcades.

'Good Heavens, I can hardly believe my eyes,' Bronwen was in awe. 'I feel as if I've walked into the future. How absolutely beautiful. No wonder Megan said you could spend a fortune here.'

Stella and Kevin had been in such places before, but Bronwen, Mary nor Geraint had. Bronwen realised, that to the young, this is how the world is and accepted it as the norm. It hadn't dawned upon Stella or Kevin that the experiences of Geraint and Bronwen, for the past ten years, were limited to their immediate locality.

'My goodness,' Geraint gasped. 'I'm glad you won't be paying the electricity bill for this, Bronwen, or you fortune would soon be gone.'

Being a Saturday, the arcades were busy. Hundreds of people scurried to and forth, bristling with confidence. Some were loaded with bags on their way back to the car park. Others were empty-handed, about to start their shopping, as Bronwen and her companions were.

People moved out of their path as they made their way down the arcade. Glances lingered on the unusual group; Bronwen on her scooter, with Stella strolling beside her,

Geraint on his, with rotund Mary beside him with her one arm in plaster of Paris, and the tall, stalwart man at their rear. They were a rare-looking group. Kevin was wearing a padded jacket which emphasised his size. Stella told him he looked like Man Mountain. He wasn't sure whether to take that as a compliment or not.

Their wide-eyed glances darted from right to left, peering through the large, gleaming windows, or at the entrance of some shops with no frontage but still managing to look elegant.

Goods were displayed so skilfully they became magnets to those who were easily tempted to take out their bulging purses or fat wallets. They wouldn't be bulging or fat when the owners walked in the opposite direction.

They arrived at a place where the arcade branched to the right and left as well as going straight ahead. In the centre of the way was an embellished, eye-catching stall. It had narrow multi-coloured frills around its top and a counter at each side, displaying a mass of gleaming, eye-catching items.

Mary immediately went into her shoulder bag which she could manage with her left hand. She was drawn to it as if she were on an elastic band, but Bronwen dissuaded her.

'There'll be plenty of time for buying, Mary. Don't waste time and money buying the first thing you see. You'd better concentrate on what you've come to buy.

'I suggest we split up and make this our meeting place. Anyone lost; straight back here and wait.' Bronwen was referring to Mary, but she didn't emphasise the point. 'Stella, you and Mary go your way. Kevin, you go with Mr Lloyd-Davies and help him choose a suit—two if you have time; a day one and an evening one. Get what you want for yourself, of course, and I'll go on my own into one of these open-front shops, so I can get things for the residents at home. We must meet here in no longer than two hours and go somewhere nice for lunch. No "help yourself" place today; we'll go somewhere posh.'

'Yes, Captain,' Geraint mocked with a smirk as he saluted.

Kevin saluted, too. 'Yes, Ma'am. As you say, Ma'am.'

They all laughed at the facetiousness of the two men but agreed and, eagerly, went their separate ways. Bronwen went into the first big open-fronted shop she came to. It seemed to stock everything; she expected to get many of items on her Christmas list there.

She saw Geraint and Kevin go into Marks and Spencer's, a short way up the arcade. They looked an odd couple; a giant and a gnome, making their way, side by side, up the arcade. She smiled to herself. Being on his scooter, Geraint's head reached no higher than the top of Kevin's long leg.

It was more than two hours later when Bronwen went as fast as the surrounding crowd of shoppers allowed. She made for the fancy stall where they had decided to meet. She was covered with a variety of shapes, sizes and colours of plastic bags and would have had more had she been able. The basket on the front of the handlebars of the scooter was piled high and her lap was covered up to her chin.

She thought she'd be told off for being late but not one of the others were at the designated meeting place. For a minute her gut churned; she was lost. She must be at the wrong stall. They all looked much alike.

She wondered whether she should go searching at the other pretty stalls that were scattered up and down the arcade but decided against it and waited where she was.

After about ten minutes a wave of relief passed over her when she saw Geraint's scooter emerge from the crowd. If she had the wrong place, then so had he.

'Where's Kevin?' Geraint asked, looking peeved. 'And where are the girls?'

'I've got them all in one of these bags,' Bronwen said, looking none too pleased. 'How should I know where he is when he is supposed to be with you?'

'He might be waiting for me outside the shop,' Geraint said, 'I'll go back and look for him. You were right about the scooter, Bronwen, I'm glad I brought it.' He too, was laden with purchases and the bags were big, so Bronwen guessed they held men's suits and a number of other items.

He turned back and disappeared among the crowd.

About ten minutes later she spotted Kevin's head towering above those of the crowd. He was hurrying back towards the stall where she waited. People had been looking at her strangely, wondering, thought Bronwen, whether she'd been abandoned—a poor crippled woman.

'Where's Mr Lloyd-Davies?' Kevin asked, looking daunted. 'I waited ages outside the shop for him. When he didn't come, I guessed he was back here with you. And where's the girls?'

'They've just been taken away in a black Mariah.' It wasn't like Bronwen to be sarcastic. 'How should I know where they are?' Kevin guessed she must have been waiting a long time.

'I'll have to go back to look for him,' he tutted.

Before Bronwen had the chance to tell him to stay put, he turned away into the crowd again.

About another ten minutes later, Stella appeared with both arms full of a variety of bags, as Bronwen had been herself. Trailing at her heels, Mary huffed and puffed. She was exhausted but had still managed to load herself with bags of new clothes and whatever else. Her right arm in plaster was hidden under some of them. Her jacket was, miraculously, still attached to her body.

Stella was breathless from hurrying. 'Sorry we've taken so long, Bronwen, but she got lost. I eventually found her on the verge of tears down in the basement. She'd pressed the wrong knob in the lift when she went down to the toilets and couldn't make out where she was. I told her to stay by me, but I might as well have talked to the wall. I've been so busy looking after her that I haven't got half I wanted to.'

'By the look of the number of bags you have, you haven't done too badly,' Bronwen remarked. 'I'm fed up of waiting for you all. Kevin's gone back to look for Geraint, who went back to look for him.'

Mary flopped on a bench at a nearby stall. It was positioned there for tired shoppers. 'I'm tired, hungry and thirsty,' she moaned.

'We're all bloody tired, hungry and thirsty,' Stella shouted. 'If you had listened to me and not buggered off on your own, we'd have got here sooner.'

Kevin and Geraint appeared. Bronwen hoped Geraint didn't hear Stella's angry tongue running away with her or he would have gone on at her, and she wasn't in the mood for it. She would have sworn back at him and made him more agitated. Then his prostate would have played up and he would have become desperate for the toilet.

Luckily, he was too taken up with the argument between himself and Kevin about whose fault it was they became separated and lost each other.

Kevin flopped on the bench beside Mary, almost causing it to collapse. It creaked, the seat warped, and it sounded as if one or two of the wooden slats had snapped.

The young, pretty woman at the stall gave him a threatening look.

'Other people like to sit there, you know,' she snapped. 'We have enough of vandalism without people like you causing damage.'

Kevin leapt from his seat and strode towards the woman who was protected by her counter of bric-a-brac. He looked as if, with one push, the stall would have tottered and collapsed as easily as the bench had, but with her inside. The woman looked terrified.

Stella approached Kevin, grabbed the sleeve of his jacket and pulled with all the energy she had left. It didn't budge him, but he realised he was letting his anger get the better of him. Stella had never seen Kevin angry.

'Sorry,' he said to the woman. 'I'll pay for the bench. How much is it?'

'I don't know,' the woman trembled. It's not mine.'

Stella interrupted. 'If it's not yours, why the hell are you making such a bloody fuss?'

'Sorry, Stella. Sorry, Bronwen.' Kevin had become the gentle giant that he was. He was afraid Stella would shout a mouthful of obscenities at the woman and draw more attention to them than they already had.

Bronwen realised they were all hyped up and decided to cool the situation.

'Right,' she said, 'now we're all here we can go and get lunch. I think we'd better go into the first café we come to. Once we've all had something to eat, we'll all be in better moods.' She spoke as if the stall wasn't there, or the woman, or the bench, on which Mary was still sitting. She spoke as if nothing had happened.

They went into the well-known Debenham's. 'Great,' Stella said. 'There's a lovely restaurant here and place to put our bags and things whilst we have a meal.'

Stella's idea was accepted. In single file, they trooped through the wide doors of the fine restaurant.

Geraint added his mobility scooter to the bags and took a seat at a table which could seat all of them. Kevin cradle-lifted Bronwen onto a chair at the table. Her scooter was put out of the way; beside Geraint's.

The food was excellent, and they loitered over the meal. Happiness and contentment were restored. They talked as they ate, anxious to find out what had been bought for the cruise.

They each discussed what had been bought, compared prices and tried to work out how much had been spent.

Bronwen called for the bill and sent Stella to the checkout to pay. They all took their time loading up again and, inevitably, the bags got mixed up.

'Never mind,' Bronwen commanded, 'just get the bags and we'll sort them out when we get home.'

The time had flown by. It was well into afternoon by the time they were back in the arcade to begin a second round of shopping.

'We might as well make tracks for home, Bronwen,' Stella suggested. 'We just can't carry anymore.' She and Mary had added some of the bags onto Bronwen's and Geraint's already overloaded trolley attached to the back of his scooter. Bags kept falling onto the floor.

'Yes, I think you're right,' Bronwen replied. 'There are just two more things I must get, and I'd like you to come with me, Stella. I'm looking for a shoe-shop that sells lovely women's fancy shoes. Kevin can take the others to the car.'

Everyone agreed. Kevin, Geraint and Mary went forward whilst Bronwen and Stella turned back. They didn't have to go far before finding a brightly lit shop-window with ladies' shoes so expertly placed, it was eye catching to all who passed it. But most people did, in fact, pass it, because of the high price of the shoes glistening in the cleverly lit mirrored window. Bronwen decided to go in.

'Bronwen,' Stella warned, 'this shop looks as if we have to pay five pounds each to go in, let alone buy their shoes.'

'Never mind that,' Bronwen replied. 'We're too tired to go looking anywhere else. Anyway, I think I'll get just what I'm looking for here.'

They went in and a glamorous lady immediately sprang to their aid.

'She's buying,' Stella pointed to Bronwen. 'I'll help her choose, thank you.'

'Does Madam have anything in mind?' the shop assistant smiled at Bronwen.

'Yes, thank you, I have. A pair of those, size five, please.' Bronwen pointed to a pair of three inch, high-heeled, evening shoes of fine strips of cream leather decorated with white, blue and red imitation diamonds along its straps.

'And a similar pair in a different colour,' Bronwen added.

The assistant took down the shoes from the stand and put them into Bronwen's hands before walking across the shop to take down a similar pair from a small crystal-glass display shelf. Stella thought them exquisite but not the type for Bronwen to wear, although she always liked pretty shoes at the end of her wasted legs.

'This is size five, Madam. I'll just peep into our room at the back and check if we have the size you require. We stock only two pairs of each style of our shoes. They are quite unique, you see.' The assistant disappeared through a door at the back of the shop.

'Oh, Stella, just feel this shoe. It's beautiful.' Bronwen handed the cream leather straps and sole. 'They are fit for a princess.'

'Yes,' said Stella, 'and a price only a princess can afford, I expect.'

The shop assistant returned with a black patent pair, similar to that which Bronwen had chosen and which had been put back on its crystal shelf.

'You're in luck,' she said.

'How much are they, please?' Bronwen asked. She didn't get a straight answer.

'As it happens, they are on special offer since they are the last of that type we intend to stock. They are rather beautiful, aren't they? I take it they are to be gifts for some lucky ladies.' The assistant didn't consider Bronwen, nor even Stella, to be the type to wear such beautiful shoes.

'Yes, that's right,' Bronwen said as she continued to admire the shoe in her hand.

'How much are they?' Stella repeated.

'With thirty per cent reduction they are a hundred and five pounds.'

'Each?' Stella gasped.

'Yes, of course,' the assistant was surprised Stella would expect the two pairs for that amount. The assistant's smile, which didn't reach her eyes, faded. She resigned herself to a no-go sale.

'Thank you,' Bronwen said, 'I'll take them both.'

Stella gasped. 'Bronwen, are you mad?' She knew Bronwen wanted them for two elderly residents who had requested them as a Christmas present from her.

'That's over two hundred pounds for shoes that will never be walked on.'

'No, they'll be dreamed on.' Bronwen didn't look at Stella but at the assistant. 'Pack them separately in your lovely boxes, please.'

Bronwen paid by credit card; she was getting used to it and even began to enjoy the ease of it.

'You must be bloody gaga,' Stella said. 'For God's sake don't tell anyone else what you paid for them shoes. It's a disgrace.'

Bronwen laughed. 'You're a bit like how Geraint described him and me the other day; we'll never get used to not looking at the price tab. You'll have to change, Stella. I have millions of pounds and though we're spending like we've never spent before, we've hardly scraped the surface—so Geraint tells me, and he's the one who knows.'

When they got to the car park, they couldn't find the car until Stella discovered they were on the wrong level. When they eventually found it, Mary, Kevin and Geraint were beginning to get agitated.

'They on'y went for two pairs o' shoes,' Mary said. 'They must 'ave bought the shop by now.'

'Won't get the shop into the car,' Kevin responded.

Geraint laughed but the wit was lost to Mary. 'What're you laughing at, Mr Lloyd-Davies? I don' fink it's funny.'

He was about to explain the humour of what Kevin had said when Bronwen and Stella arrived.

'And about blooming time, too,' Geraint complained. He was tired and getting irritable.

'We thought you was lost,' Mary frowned.

'You thought we were lost,' Bronwen emphasised the "were".

'Yes, we did,' Mary went on, missing the correction of her grammar.

Kevin said nothing as he gently took Bronwen from her scooter and carried her to the comfort of the car seat.

'Thank you, Kevin, love. Sorry to keep you waiting. It was my fault. I had to buy two very special pairs of shoes.'

'That's all right, Bronwen. We should get home in an hour and a bit if we're not held up. We might just miss rush hour.'

Stella folded up Bronwen's scooter before putting it in the back of the car. Mr Lloyd-Davies insisted on folding his own, but Stella had to lift it into the car before she made herself comfortable beside Kevin to apologise.

'Sorry, Kevin. Those shoes took longer than I expected. Do you mind driving all the way back?'

'Do I have a choice, then?' He switched on the ignition and made for the car-park exit.

'No,' Stella yawned. 'Shopping's hard work. Did you get what you and Mr Lloyd-Davies wanted?'

'We didn't do badly. I got a few things I need for going away; lovely pair of trainers, underwear and tee shirt stuff but the important thing is Mr Lloyd-Davies got a lounge suit, evening suit and some very smart shirts. They didn't have anything near my size. They said I'd have to have the suits specially made.'

Geraint was listening to Kevin and interrupted. 'You see, Stella, it seems you can buy off the peg if you're dwarf size but not giant size.'

They all laughed, except Mary. All relaxed and prepared for the journey home. Geraint went on. 'But the trousers of both suits will have to be shortened.'

Bronwen responded to what was being said. 'You'll have to get measured for suits then, Kevin. Do you know a good tailor? He can shorten Geraint's trousers, as well.'

'Yes, Bronwen, but that costs the earth. Not for the likes of me. I've only ever had one suit. My mother bought it for me, and when I grew out of it, I didn't bother to get another. I've got a posh jacket for when I have to go to funerals, but that's not often. Not often enough to pay the earth for a dark suit, anyway.'

'What d'you mean, "not for the likes of you"? You're as good as any man.' Stella sounded peeved. 'You just get yourself some proper suits. I'll pay out of what Bronwen's put into my bank account. That's all right, isn't it, Bronwen?'

'And if that's not enough,' Bronwen answered, 'just let Geraint know and he'll sort you out.'

They arrived back at the home much too late for tea but Mary, Geraint and Bronwen caught supper. They didn't loiter in the lounge afterwards but went to their rooms. They were exhausted, but very pleased with the day's achievement.

Matron Phillips organised two of the nursing team to unload the Mercedes and carry everything to Mary's and Bronwen's rooms. Stella and Kevin sorted out what they thought was theirs, to be left in the car to take to their own homes. Inevitably, they became mixed up.

Among Mary's things were Geraint's pants and vests and she was missing a glamorous under-slip, pants and brassier which ended up with Kevin's things.

Stella told Kevin to stop at the chippies. They had fish and chips for supper.

The Mercedes ended the day parked outside Kevin's home, to be taken back to the car park at The Sunshine Mount Nursing Home.

The following morning Kevin's neighbours couldn't believe their eyes on seeing the magnificent motor in their street, although they had heard about it. And of course, everyone for miles around knew about Bronwen, the elderly lady at the nursing home, who had won a fortune on the National Lottery. Since then, many people had doubled up on the number of tickets they bought.

Teenager, Darren, living next door to Kevin couldn't help but admire the beautiful vehicle and mentioned it when he saw Kevin getting into it to drive it away. 'Good God, Kevin. Won the lottery, have you?'

'No, but I know someone who has.'

'Ye'. Bronwen Dew. I wish she knew me.'

Chapter 12
A Merry Christmas

The days running up to Christmas were hectically busy for Bronwen. All the presents had to be packed and clearly tagged. It wouldn't do for someone to get the wrong present.

She had plenty of help. Stella spent her meal-breaks and much of her off-duty time packing parcels and organising the carers who had volunteered to help. She had a copy of Bronwen's list so knew what was to go to whom.

Bronwen, herself ensured she packed John Drake's football boots, socks and scarf. She knew he supported The Bluebirds—Cardiff City football club. He wasn't able to stand unless supported, but he could wear the boots and socks and enjoy just looking at them and having the feel of them. She had bought the men who sat with him watching the games, Cardiff City bobble caps and scarves.

She wrapped the beautiful, delicate shoes in gilded paper for the two elderly ladies who requested them. She sealed the parcels with glittering bow-clusters. She hoped they would have the effect she expected.

Bronwen's pretty shoes were a size four but her feet looked much bigger at the bottom of her spindle-like legs. Before she met Lewis she always wore black, lace-up shoes, which were considered sensible—even though she couldn't walk. He bought her first pair of glamorous shoes and insisted her feet were always prettily shod. They were never worn out because, of course, they weren't stood on, except for a few seconds at a time. Yet she had a different pair for every day of the week and "her best ones" for when they went somewhere special.

She remembered Lewis always taking her, and her mother and father, to the pantomime in the city, usually a little while after Christmas; in the New Year. It was a tremendous treat. Her spirits began to drop as she thought of Lewis. She still missed him after all the years, and always would. She hoped, if he was watching her from the land beyond, he would approve of what she was doing.

The Sunshine Mount's Christmas decorations were kept in the attic which was accessible by putting a chair on a table and one of the carers being supported as she climbed up through the hatch and handed the boxes down. They were decorations which had been used for years and had become dilapidated. As well as that, the Christmas lights for the tree and above the doors, and other such places, were broken.

On Stella's off-duty day Bronwen had asked her to go into the town, some six miles farther than Pendarren, to get as many Christmas lights as she could carry. She intended to see the place more brilliant than it has ever been. Stella delighted in the quest. When Dora came off-duty during an afternoon, they went into town together in the Mercedes and bought a generous amount of Christmas lights, baubles and Christmas trees. The tall, wide firs had to be delivered the following day.

The Sunshine Mount Nursing Home must have been the most well decorated home in the whole of the county.

Matron Phillips, Deputy Matron Banding, Bronwen and the team of carers thought of everything to make Christmas the best. They thought Bronwen would move out soon and wouldn't be there the following Christmas. However, that was twelve months away and there was no knowing what would happen before then.

There were three Christmas trees; one in each lounge and one in the main hall, with every branch laden with fairy lights and tinsel. The hall and passageways were a blaze of glistening colour and light.

When the big day arrived, breakfast was served as usual. Afterwards Dora dressed as Father Christmas handed out the presents. Bronwen and Matron read out the names on the tabs, so everyone was sure to get what was asked for.

Most of the residents of Laburnum Lounge needed help to unwrap their presents. Bronwen watched Megan tearing open John Drake's present. Megan knew what it was and wanted to enjoy his delight when he saw what it was. He didn't realise they were for him until she and another young carer helped to put on the socks and boots. The spontaneous, irregular movements of his arms and legs necessitated two people to put them on.

John showed his pleasure in laughing in the only way he knew how. He looked at Bronwen and when their eyes met, she knew she had done right.

He held out his hand to Bronwen in an effort to hold it but had difficulty. Bronwen managed to grab it for a few seconds.

The joy was shared by the men sitting near him who had received Cardiff City bobble caps and scarves.

'Smashing, Mrs Dew, smashing,' one of them said.

John wore his boot all that day and many days afterwards.

By the time she got to Gwen and Hilda, who had asked for glamorous high-heeled shoes, they were already on their feet. They moved their feet about as much as they could to watch the coloured glass designs glittering.

Matron Phillips joined them, looking festive in her Father Christmas hat.

'Aren't they beautiful?' she said. 'Be sure you take them off when you are taken to the toilet, though, won't you?' They didn't understand but they enjoyed the shoes.

The traditional Christmas turkey and pudding were served. A few elderly residents, with memories worn thin by the contingency of ageing, mightn't have understood that the lunchtime meal was any different to other days. But then, they might have. It might have jogged memories of a normal, happy past.

There were crackers to be pulled and paper hats to be worn. The carers helped with the pulling of the crackers and all wore the Santa-style hats. Christmas carols were played softly in the background throughout the festivity.

Later, many of the residents' friends and relatives, some who hadn't been seen before, arrived in response to an open invitation for tea, mince pies and whatever else was available. Alcoholic drinks were disallowed but Bronwen noticed favoured tipples appearing from somewhere and caution had to be taken to ensure the residents who were taking heavy medication didn't, out of kindness, have it given to them.

The celebration took place in Laburnum Lounge, where all special events took place. It was near the kitchen; easier for the catering.

Matron Phillips, Deputy Matron Banding and Bronwen provided the gayest Christmas possible. Those who were as independent, or nearly, as independent, as herself from Willow Lounge, entered into the festive spirit.

A few were too old, frail and mentally infirm to realise what was going on, but the carers included them in the fun, even though no emotion was shown.

There were a few wet blankets, mostly the men, who remained in the bottom lounge sipping their brew, smoking their cigarettes or the annual Christmas box of cigars. Brynly had asked Father Christmas for a box of Havana cigars. He was surprised when he got them.

Geraint sat in a corner, trying to be invisible. He sipped from a small glass tumbler; something he shouldn't have done in case it would interfere with his medication.

He was doing what he liked doing best; looking at rows of figures, working out how much was spent and what was likely to be spent. He was in the darkest corner of the room, hoping not to be seen. He didn't choose to go to his own room in case of being recognised as being a wet blanket, which he was, and to avoid being called a miserable old party pooper, which he wasn't. He was happy and enjoying himself in his own way.

Bronwen couldn't blame him. It was noisy in the top lounge and overcrowded with people. Joan and Ruth, Bronwen's cousins and their husbands were there with two grandsons.

Bronwen noticed that, like herself, the elderly liked having children about them. She guessed it reminded them of their own youth or their own children, especially those children who seemed to have forgotten about them.

Bronwen had presents for her cousins' grandchildren. She apologised to the husbands for Father Christmas forgetting them.

Friends and relatives, many who hadn't been invited, turned up to enjoy the celebration. Some, as usual, overstayed their welcome.

Gladys Higgs, a ninety-two old resident became irritable and shouted out her usual continuous lament. 'What's going on, what's going on, what's going on!' no matter how the carers tried to sooth her.

The guests didn't seem to hear her, but they did hear the usual response from ninety-year-old Eddy Bull, the man near her. 'Would somebody shut her fat mouth before I do?' He continued to describe how she was getting on his nerves in no uncertain terms. The string of foul Anglo-Saxon terms that spilled from his mouth didn't offend any staff member; they'd heard it many times. Eddy couldn't put his hand to his own mouth, let alone anyone else's. Conveniently, visitors' heads turned, and it seemed his dirty-worded threat was a cue for them to leave.

Bronwen saw Stella kneel beside Gladys and try to quieten her. Not successfully. 'Piss off and leave me alone,' she told Stella.

'All right, Gladys,' Stella said, as she took her hand and kindly stroked it. 'But try to shout quietly. You're annoying Eddy Bull again.'

Kevin had called in earlier to find out what time Stella would be able to get away.

'Not for hours, yet,' she had told him. She gave him a glass of stout and told him to go to The Colliers and wait there until she came. However, she left the home too late to go to the pub. She went straight home. It had been a long happy, but hard day. She rang him on her mobile phone. Tom had taught her how to use it, though she wasn't yet able to make use of all its facilities. She was as bad as Bronwen. Surprising everyone, was the fact that Mary seemed the best at getting the hang of it.

The elderly residents, who were the more infirm, became fatigued at the same time as they did every night. They didn't watch the clock. Stella and the carers on duty at that time helped them to bed and settled them.

By then the night staff had come on duty and before the hand-over, the two Matrons and all the staff present had a celebratory drink. Those carers who remained were pleased their working day was over. Christmas day had been a big success, but they were worn out.

The kitchen staff had cleared away the tables, disposed of the waste and salvaged what could be used another day. Not much, but enough for the staff to enjoy a good Christmas meal during the night and for lunch the following day.

Bronwen was the last resident to turn in. Willow Lounge was silent and in darkness. She wondered where Mary had got to and it was a good thing she had. She went to the big, comfortable chair where Mary usually went to hide. She'd hardly seen her since after breakfast, when the presents were given out.

She heard her snoring and found her where Geraint, earlier, had been doing his sums. He'd turned in for the night as soon as he found a carer free to help him to change into his pyjamas. He was reluctant to admit that when he was tired did he need help.

Mary would have been there all night had Bronwen not found and roused her. She had her plaster-cast arm resting along the back of an armchair and herself curled up on it. A wave of soft emotion overcame Bronwen and she felt guilty for not having given time to her daughter. She justified her neglect by reminding herself that Mary was a woman past her thirty-first birthday and should be completely independent of her mother or anyone else. But she wasn't and it constantly bothered Bronwen. She wondered if it were her fault. Where had she gone wrong, if anywhere?

Wednesday 27th December 1998, was a sad day. Martha Tate died. She passed away peacefully in her sleep. She was cremated two days later and her remains put into the graveyard of the chapel at the top of the hill of The Sunshine Mount Nursing Home.

Martha had been an only child and hadn't married, having given her life to caring for her parents and music. As far as was known, she had no living relatives, but Bronwen was surprised to see many people at the chapel funeral service.

Having been a musician, chapel organist and teacher, as well as having been involved in a number of charitable organisations, Martha Tate was well known in the area. Many came to pay their last respects.

All the carers, except those who were on duty attended the service. There was much weeping into soft paper tissues. Most of the nurses, who were off duty and were able to attend, did so.

All the residents who were able, went to say their last goodbye to Martha. Geraint attended, carrying his Zimmer frame. Tom and Brynly attended on their scooters. They were given spaces at the back of the little chapel.

Matron Phillips stood on the dais and read a passage from the Bible and paid tribute to the lovely lady, Martha Tate.

Bronwen missed the time she spent with Martha. She always spoke to her assuming she could hear and understand. Martha was the only one with whom Bronwen shared her deepest thoughts, including her worries.

The door of the room which was Martha's was closed, and the special bed and mattress stripped bare, waiting to be prepared to comfort whoever would be next to use it.

The days up to New Year's Eve and afterwards were bland.

On a Sunday early in the new year, when Stella was off duty, she and Kevin had been asked by Geraint if they could be at the home to discuss an important matter. They sat in a circle with Mary, Tom, Bronwen and, of course, himself.

The gathering was opportune to discuss the availability of passports. He, nor Mary and Bronwen had passports, which were essential to arrange the Mediterranean cruise.

'Bronwen,' he said, 'I have to ask you to do something.' He sounded as if he were about to ask her to do something which she wouldn't want to. 'You, Mary and I have to apply for passports. I understand Stella and Kevin already have them.' He looked at Stella and Kevin and they nodded.

'Well, I've completed the forms to acquire them,' Geraint went on, 'but we have to get passport photographs.' A pregnant pause followed.

Stella spoke up, 'That's easy enough. There's a passport photo kiosk in the main post office in town. I'll take us one day during the week.'

'I'll be working,' Kevin offered, 'otherwise I would take you, but Stella is all right driving the Merc around here.'

'We'll go on Wednesday afternoon,' Stella announced. 'I'll get off early so we can go straight from here.'

'That will be fine. Thank you, Stella.' Geraint looked relieved. 'I can't confirm any booking until I have our passport numbers. I'll stress they are urgent, so we should have them in about ten days.'

'What about me having my photo taken?' Mary pouted. 'I've got this dirty plaster on my arm.'

'It's only dirty because you let all and sundry draw on it. Anyway, it's a photo of your face is needed, not your arm. I'll do your hair nice for you and make up your eyes a bit.'

Mary smiled. 'Thanks, Stella.'

On the following Wednesday afternoon, Stella had a quick snack for lunch. She was still chewing the last of a pie as she went to the staff room. She changed out of uniform into something suitable for a cold, dismal day. She made her way to the car park at the side of the forecourt where the Mercedes was parked. Just before three o'clock, she was at the main exit of the home. Bronwen, Mary and Geraint were waiting in the hall.

As she drove slowly through the town towards the post office, the beautiful car caught many admiring glances. She drove into a parking space which was designated for disabled citizens, opposite the post office. She hoped there wouldn't be a queue at the photograph kiosk.

Geraint alighted the car easily and used his Zimmer for support. It was more complicated for Bronwen. She had used the ramp to drive her scooter into the back of the car outside the home. She remained on it, then manoeuvred herself down the ramp and onto the pavement when they arrived at their destination.

'That was easier than I thought,' she grinned, 'but I'm glad we have Kevin. I wouldn't enjoy travelling long distances on the scooter.'

They walked across the square to the post office and found the passport photograph booth was free.

Bronwen had to hoist herself from her scooter onto the chair in the booth. She followed the instructions clearly written on the side of the booth, followed them, and then there was a short wait for the photograph to be processed before dropping into a slot at the outside of the booth.

Success! Bronwen had a strip of passport photographs.

Geraint and Mary went through the same process. Mary had to repeat it because she pressed the wrong buttons. Certainly, no photographs appeared the first time round. Stella squeezed herself beside Mary in the booth, pressed the correct button and leapt out before it would be spoiled again.

They were relieved that they had three sets of suitable photographs. They were unflattering. Bronwen looked as if she were in shock at seeing something horrible when the machine clicked on her. Geraint looked like a worn-out convict and Mary's frowning face and double chin did nothing to boost her morale.

'They're awful photos.' Stella screamed with laughter and startled a passer-by. 'They're awful. I thought mine was bad enough,' he chuckled as he stretched his neck to see Mary's photo.

'They never make you look like a film star, love,' the intruder said. 'Not cheap, either.'

101

The nearest café was chosen for tea. It looked smart and appealing with its pseudo-Continental appearance. They had tea and cakes and afterwards, decided to do a little shopping since the town was reasonably quiet.

'I'll come into Burton's with you, Geraint, and help you to choose a couple of casual shirts.'

'I have enough, Bronwen. I'm not spending for the sake of spending,' he objected, 'but I'll buy another tie.'

'That's the point, Geraint,' Bronwen argued, 'all the shirts you have need ties. But men don't wear shirt and tie all day now. Let's go and see.'

The four of them reached the main shopping street at the end of the side street where they'd had tea before separating. Mary and Stella went one way and Bronwen and Geraint the other.

Bronwen was successful in coaxing Geraint to get a couple of casual shirts. He took a fancy to a multi-coloured tie which made her cringe. It was not his usual choice of style.

'Don't you think you're a bit too old for that sort of tie, Geraint?'

He nodded and looked disappointed. 'Yes, I suppose so.' He picked out a plain dark blue one. Bronwen wanted to say that was too drab but she decided not to comment.

On his way to the checkout, he picked up a pack of four underpants.

'This pack of underwear is size extra-large, sir. Is that what you want?' the smart shop assistant asked.

'Good Lord, no,' Geraint objected. 'Bronwen, what size do I want?'

'These,' Bronwen said, putting a pack which she had selected onto the counter. 'Small men.'

Outside the shop Geraint looked pleased as he hooked the bag onto his Zimmer. It fell to the floor.

'Here, let me take it,' Bronwen said. She squeezed it into the basket on the front of her scooter. 'Now you stand here while I go in that women's shop across the road. Now don't move.'

'All right, all right. I don't need telling.'

That area of the town was pedestrianised so there was no difficulty steering across the road.

After about twenty minutes, having bought herself an elegant evening blouse and a trouser-suit, she got back to where she expected Geraint to be waiting. He was not.

She wasn't peeved. She went into the men's shop where Geraint had bought his shirts and bought the bright coloured tie which had appealed to him. She returned to where she had left him and waited a further ten minutes. He didn't appear, and she began to lose her patience.

'Blow him,' she said to herself. 'I'll wait in the car.'

She got back to the car and he too was waiting there.

'Why didn't you wait for me outside that shop, as we agreed,' she snapped.

'Well, Bronwen, you were such a long time I thought you must have forgotten, so I decided to come back here.'

They stood around the car becoming cold and impatient.

'Oh, them blooming girls.' Geraint stamped his Zimmer hard with frustration.

'They'll be here in a minute,' Bronwen said calmly, disguising her impatience.

It was a very long minute before they caught sight of Stella running towards them, laden with bags. Mary struggled behind trying to keep up.

'Wait!' she shouted. 'Wait! I'll fall if I come any faster.'

'It's about time, too.' Geraint spoke angrily when Stella got to the car. 'We're perishing cold. It's photographs we came for, not more frocks.'

'By the look of all those bags, you've been on a spending spree yourselves,' was Stella's retort, as she clicked the central locking of the car-key.

The all alighted, Bronwen to the back, the others to the front.

'What did you buy, Mammy?' Mary asked.

'You just wait and see,' Bronwen smiled. 'It's a lovely evening blouse and matching trousers.'

'Well, I'm glad to hear it,' Stella said. 'When we were in Cribb's Causeway, you got hardly anything for yourself.'

'I've got some casual day-shirts like Kevin's.' Geraint sounded pleased with himself.

'And this.' Bronwen handed to him the tie which she had rejected.

He was delighted. 'Thank you, Bronwen. 'You really shouldn't have.'

They got back to the home in time for Bronwen, Geraint and Mary to sort out the purchases and organise themselves before supper.

Stella parked the Mercedes in its usual place and approached her ten-year-old Austin Mini.

'It's about time you got shot of that old car and got a new one,' Bronwen had suggested to Stella before she left them.

Stella realised Bronwen was dropping a hint. She wanted to get her a new car. She couldn't understand why she should buy another car when she could drive the Mercedes. She was about to say this to Bronwen when Mary interrupted.

'Stella, can I put my new clothes in your car for you to keep them at your 'ouse? When this comes off, I'll be coming back to you and Colin, 'on't I?'

Mary referred to the plaster cast on her right arm. 'Yes, all right, my lovely. That'll be a trip before long—getting that thing off.'

'Yes,' Geraint frowned. 'I hope that won't cause a complication when I complete the forms.' He pointed to Mary's arm. 'Give me your passport photographs now, Mary, in case I forget to ask you later, or in case you lose them. I'll have yours as well, Bronwen, please. I will send the applications tomorrow.'

Mary's appointment to have the plaster of Paris removed from her arm was in the middle of January. It was for ten o'clock. Stella arranged for an afternoon shift so that she could take Mary to the fracture clinic at the local hospital and be back with time to spare before she went on duty.

Bronwen hoped there would be no complications. 'At last, you'll be relieved of that ugly cast and be able to dress yourself properly without help. You'll be able to cut up your own meat at meal-times.'

Mary was nervous. 'I wonder will it 'urt, Mammy?' she asked.

Tom had joined them. He responded to Mary's question. 'Yes, it will, Mary. It would be best if you kept it on forever. At least, until it drops off. Trouble is, your arm might drop off with it.'

Mary's eyes popped as her jaw dropped. Her anxiety increased.

'Don't listen to him, my lovely,' Bronwen comforted, 'he's teasing you.'

'Do you know how they get it off, Mary?' Tom went on.

'No,' Mary shook her head. She thought it would slip down her arm like the sleeve of a coat.

'They saw it off with a round electrical saw and sometimes they go too far and cut the arm off.' As Tom spoke, he chuckled. 'Have you heard how they sometimes saw the wrong arm or leg off?'

Mary began to tremble. 'Oh, Mammy, I'd rather keep the plaster on.'

'Don't be so daft, Mary. Can't you see he's teasing? Of course, your arm won't get sawn off.' Bronwen threw her current novel, which she kept beside her, at him. It hit him in the chest, just missing his chin.

'Stop it, Tom. Can't you see she's frightened enough without you getting at her?'

Those in the lounge all heard Tom's bantering and the room was filled with the sound of laughter.

'Shut your silly mouth, Tom,' Geraint's small voice shouted, 'or I'll come and stuff something in it.'

Tom could barely speak for laughing. 'Never mind, love, they'll give you a false arm. When you've got your coat on, no one will notice the difference.'

Mary was crying when Stella appeared. 'What on Earth's the matter?'

'Tom said they could make a mistake and saw my arm off,' Mary sniffed.

Stella went to Tom and punched his arm. Not hard, but enough for him to raise his arms to his head for protection, in case the following punch would be to his face.

She moved closer to him and whispered in his ear. 'I'll knock your fucking block off if you tease her again.'

But her words didn't escape the keen hearing of Geraint.

'Ugh,' he gasped. 'There's just no need for them filthy words. Bronwen. You need to do something about that girl's tongue.'

Bronwen was too concerned about Mary. 'Come on, Stella love, or she'll be late for her appointment.'

Bronwen felt the initial, innocent teasing, was turning nasty so it was best if she hurried Stella and Mary on their way. She clicked off the brake of her wheel-chair and was first through the double doors of the lounge to manoeuvre down the corridor.

As she waved them off, she couldn't help feeling worried. Tom's words had frightened her. She was, indeed, aware of very rare incidents when limbs had been amputated in error. It was obvious which of Mary's arms needed attention and Bronwen knew a mechanical saw was used to remove plaster casts. The knowledge began to conjure up all sorts of horrible incidents.

She would be happy to see them back. She returned to the lounge to wait and as she waited Tom tried to convince her that everything would be all right.

And it was. A smiling Mary and Stella came into the lounge in time for lunch.

Bronwen liked the sight of Mary with both arms in her jacket. Stella stuck out her tongue to Tom and cocked a snook. It set him off giggling again.

Mary took off her jacket and held out her arms to Lillian. 'Look how thin it is,' she said, 'and it's a funny colour.'

Tom was able to see too. 'Looks like something that's crawled from under a stone,' he said. It was an apt description, so Stella, Bronwen and Geraint ignored him.

'The colour will soon return to normal, my dear,' Geraint reassured. 'It's because it's not seen sunlight for many weeks.'

'Which one do you think is the right size?' Stella asked Mary.

Mary's eyes jerked from arm to arm, wondering which one she should choose to keep in view. Stella tapped Mary right arm. Well, it's that one for the time being, but when we've managed to get more of that blubber off you, they'll both look like that.' She pointed to the left arm. Stella realised she exaggerated but succeeded in enticing Mary to remain on a diet to reduce her weight.

Having lived at the nursing home for several weeks, being served smaller meals than she was used to, her weight loss was noticeable. All her clothes became loose on her heavy bosom and podgy hips. She was motivated to go on trying to achieve her correct weight. She found it hard sometimes, but the discomfort of being deprived of the many Mars bars, chocolate biscuits, crisps and fish and chips was made up for by having to buy new clothes to replace those that no longer fitted her. The amount she spent on clothes made Geraint suck his teeth many times.

'It's a good thing your mother is a millionaire, my girl,' he said, 'otherwise you and she would be in jail for debt.'

'But I am, Geraint,' Bronwen interrupted. 'And you need to get more for yourself before we go on that cruise.'

'Pot calling the kettle black.' Geraint tried to make a point. 'You've got hardly anything for yourself. You must get yourself some nice things.'

'All right, Geraint,' Bronwen replied. She was feeling good having Mary back with her two arms intact. 'We'll go on another shopping spree.'

'Good,' he said. 'And good, I can hear the lunch trolley coming. I'm ravenous.'

The feeling was mutual, and all moved across to the dining tables at the other side of the big room.

Stella went to the staff room to change into her uniform. She told herself she needed to keep her mind on her job; not let it wander on thought of what the future might bring.

Chapter 13
Confirmation

Ten days later the passports arrived. Geraint was excited. When he received the important-looking envelope, he had to go to the lavatory before he opened it. He examined each one to ensure the details were all correct. He took a hard look at the unflattering photograph of himself. However, he felt a wave of importance run through him. He wished his prostate gland would stop playing up. He hoped it wouldn't let him down when he was away.

The last time he had papers about his person, which held important details, was when he was an army officer in the last war. They meant little to him then, though they were imperative to his position in awful circumstances. This time, having a passport gave him pleasure. Getting them for Bronwen and Mary gave him a sense of importance that he hadn't felt for over forty years.

Having examined the passports to ensure all the details were correct, he took a note of the details he needed to confirm a booking for the cruise with P &O Cruises.

He did that using Tom's mobile phone. He spoke to someone dealing with the reservations and gave Bronwen's credit card number to cover the deposit. He was told the balance would have to be paid before he would receive the tickets. Then, he would receive information about travel insurance as well as the facilities on board. Excursions that would be available at nominal fees when the cruiser docked at the various ports. Geraint thought to himself that P & O's idea of a nominal fee wouldn't be his.

The cruise was booked for 15th March, when The Gladiator would sail from Southampton across the Mediterranean, docking at five ports. Geraint became excited and his prostate started to play up. He had to make extra dashes to the toilet, but he was determined not to let it beat him. He would be certain to take the medication that had been prescribed and use incontinence aids if necessary.

When he came out of the toilet, he decided he might as well go down to lunch. Since breakfast, he had been at his computer, looking at the places The Gladiator would stop at. There were pictures of the type of suites they would be granted.

He could now tell Bronwen and the others that the cruise was confirmed and show them the pictures in the colourful brochure he had received.

He was pleased he had decided to get himself a computer though its cost was a big chunk out of what he was saving for a rainy day. It had given him more pleasure than he had expected, and its use since Bronwen won the lottery, was insurmountable.

He hadn't yet shown them the pictures in case the arrangements fell through, and that would have been disappointing. He decided to ask Tom to view them, even though he had decided not to accompany them on the cruise. Geraint regretted that, but understood. Geraint was grateful he was still fit enough to live a good life, though Bronwen had told him often enough he was inclined to forget his age.

He thought it a good thing that Kevin was coming with them. Not only would he be helpful, but he was another man in the group. Stella was on duty when Geraint went down to lunch, so she would be pleased to have the date of the cruise confirmed, to let Kevin know.

Geraint went into the lounge as the tables were being set for lunch. Bronwen, Mary and Tilley were in their usual places. Tom and Brynly were doing a large jigsaw puzzle at one of the dining tables that wasn't needed.

'Why is it you are so late coming down, Geraint? I was just about to send Mary up to your room to find out. You feel all right, I hope.' Bronwen looked concerned.

'Never felt better,' Geraint replied. 'I've been at my computer and working at your accounts. Doing it often makes it easier to keep up to date.'

'Since you do it umpteen times a day, I doubt you'll let it run behind. Thank you for looking after it for me, Geraint, but don't let it trouble you.'

'Don't thank me, Bronwen. I should be thanking you, because I'm in my element. If you didn't have me, you'd no doubt have a high-flyer accountant who would be younger and more up-to-date with things than I am.'

'There's no one better than you, Geraint,' Bronwen said with sincerity.

Geraint nodded and grinned. 'Anyway, I've got some interesting information for you—the cruise is now confirmed. We sail from Southampton on 15th March.'

'My goodness,' Bronwen put her hand on her heart. 'My goodness. That won't be long. You and I must really get ourselves sorted out and get what we need. Trouble is, I don't know what to get.'

'You will,' Geraint went on. 'It won't be long before I'll get all the information we need on what to take. As for paying for it, Bronwen, I've given your credit-card number to cover the deposit. The remainder will have to be paid just before we get the tickets.' Geraint sucked his teeth; thinking of the large amount to be paid hurt him.

'No need to worry about cost, Geraint. I had twenty and a half million. We haven't yet managed to make a hole in the half. What was it now; five hundred thousand? It's so much I can hardly say it.'

'I expect our spending will gain momentum as time passes,' Geraint declared. 'Starting when we go on the cruise. A good sum will be spent on the ship, I expect.'

'I hope so,' Bronwen said. 'No one, including you, must stint on things, Geraint. We have no need to. I've learned that much. Another point I must mention is that a good sum must be spent on a little car for Stella.'

Bronwen spoke quietly, not wanting anyone to know her decision before Stella did. She knew that if any of the residents overheard, he or she would have blurted it out as soon as Stella walked through the door.

Geraint looked surprised. 'Why don't you tell her to use the Mercedes, Bronwen? It's standing there in the car park outside most of the time. I've wondered why she doesn't use it more.'

'Don't be daft, Geraint. How would it look to others when a nursing assistant runs about in a colossal Mercedes and parks it on the pavement outside her house? It just isn't practical.'

'Mmm.' Geraint looked thoughtful, 'I see your point.'

'Never mind now; the lunches are coming. We've got a bit of talking to do later. Stella is on the afternoon shift today. I'll break it to her gently, after the lottery numbers have been drawn. It usually goes quiet after that—unless someone wins a fortune.'

Geraint smirked. 'Aye, that would be a turn-up for the books, wouldn't it?'

Later that day, when the National Lottery numbers were being announced on the television, the room fell to silence, as it usually did at that time.

Since Bronwen won the lottery, everyone in that bottom lounge bought tickets. It was thought, if Bronwen could win a fortune, anyone could. Even those residents who hadn't before made the gamble, did now. Those who had, bought more lines. Some spent more than they should on the lottery tickets.

Bronwen's good luck had travelled to all other nursing homes in the area and indeed, for miles around. The event of buying the mobility scooters, the magnificent Mercedes and plans to travel, had become widely talked about. Bronwen changed the face of "getting on in years" and was good publicity for Camelot.

She had her lottery tickets on a newspaper on her lap. Mary, Geraint and Tom were beside her with theirs. Tilley wasn't far away; she didn't have a lottery ticket, which surprised Bronwen. She thought Tilley mightn't have had enough money and if that were the case, she would soon put that right. She decided to ask her when the lottery programme was over.

As the numbers were called, Bronwen had her fingers crossed behind her back. She didn't want to win. She could just about manage with what she had won.

The announcer started. 'And the numbers are…' and so it went on until all numbers had been called. The silence stopped, and the room became alive.

'Only one bloody number I got.'

'More than me. I didn't get one.'

'I got two. One away from winning ten pounds. Better luck next week.'

'I got six but all on different lines.'

One resident had three numbers up and was as delighted with winning ten pounds as Bronwen had been when she won twenty and a half million.

'Tilley, why didn't you try the lottery?' Bronwen asked.

'In case I win,' was Tilley short sharp reply.

Bronwen eyed Tilley with surprise. 'Wouldn't you like winning a lot of money, Tilley?' she asked.

'No, I wouldn't.'

'Why not?'

'Because I can see the bother it's causing you.'

Geraint and Mary eyed Tilley with surprise. 'But if you win you could share it between your family,' Geraint suggested. 'You have seven children. They would all be delighted.'

'Aye,' said Tilley, 'and they'd be fighting between themselves until the whole bloody lot was gone. Excuse the language, Mr Lloyd-Davies.' She nodded to Geraint as she went on. 'By then they wouldn't be talking. Split them up, it would. Not worth it. They're all in debt now and they help each other out. I'd rather it stayed that way.'

Bronwen and Geraint nodded. 'Yes, Tilley, I see your point,' Bronwen said, before leaning over to be as close to Tilley as her restricted movement allowed.

'But if you need a couple of quid for yourself or your kids, you let me know, will you? You'd be doing me a favour.'

'Ay,' she slowly nodded. 'I will.'

Shortly afterwards, the room's atmosphere returned to normal. Some went on watching television, some snoozed until it was time for them to be helped to their rooms and become settled for the night.

Stella pranced into the room looking prim and as fresh as a daisy, as if she were starting a duty, instead of coming to the end of a hard day.

'Nearly done,' she said. 'What news, then? Anyone win another fortune tonight?'

'No,' Geraint answered, 'and Bronwen's fortune is still intact. It's not easy; spending a fortune. But we do have some news.'

'We're going on the cruise on 15th' March,' Mary shouted with excitement, before Bronwen or Geraint could get any words in. Stella looked at Geraint with raised eyebrows.

'I've confirmed the booking today, Stella. And Mary is right, it's the 15th. The 15th of March. That's in, roughly, eight weeks' time.'

'Hell,' Stella gasped as she put her hand on her chest. 'My heart's going aflutter with excitement. That's smashing,' she hugged Geraint. He pinked with pleasure. He was excited too.

Stella went on. 'Now Kevin will know when to put his notice in and get measured for an evening suit. He wouldn't do that until he was sure.'

Stella put on her bossy voice. 'Bronwen, that will give us time to get you what you need for the trip. You've been so wrapped up in getting for others that you've left yourself out. You will need a few more things, too, Mr Lloyd-Davies. I'll be taking you shopping. I'm quite happy driving the Merc now. In fact, I love it.'

'I'll come,' Mary broke in.

'Yes, you will,' Stella stressed, 'but not for yourself. You'll come to help your mother and Mr Lloyd-Davies. They're not so good at shopping as you are.'

Bronwen and Geraint chuckled at Stella's pointed remark.

'What are you giggling about?' Mary asked.

'Nothing, my lovely, nothing. We'll be glad of your help.' Then Bronwen looked hard at Stella. 'And there's a shopping item of special importance that we want you to get for yourself.'

Stella's eyebrows again arched. She wondered what that might be.

'A new car for yourself. That old banger you run about in is not safe. It rattles along as if it's about to fall to bits.'

'A new car for myself? Why? I can manage the Merc now.'

'Why are you and Mary going home in that one of yours, which is way past its "sell by date"?' Geraint asked.

Bronwen and Stella were amused at Geraint's description of her old car.

'Well, because it's smaller and easier to park outside our house, for a start,' Stella replied. 'And it's all I've been able to afford.'

'Oh,' Bronwen huffed with frustration. 'All you can afford, indeed. If I hear any of you say that again, I won't be responsible for my actions.'

'You'll chop Stella's hands off, would you, Mammy?' Even slow-witted Mary chuckled at her own remark. 'I can't imagine you even cuttin' 'er finger nails off.'

'Cutting "her" finger-nails,' Bronwen corrected Mary's grammar.

'Yes, all right,' she tutted before questioning Stella, who was still taken aback by Bronwen's offer. 'What car will you get, Stella?'

'Good God,' Stella replied. 'I haven't the foggiest.'

'Ask Kevin,' Geraint suggested. 'Or Colin, your brother. They'll know what would be a good little car for you. They were right about the Mercedes and Bronwen is right about your cars falling to bits. And the Mercedes isn't really built to be a little runabout, is it?'

'No, I suppose not,' Stella spoke with her thoughts confused. 'Me? A new car?'

She rose sharply from her seat. 'Anyway, I must go. I'm not off duty yet. The night staff are just coming on; I'll have to hand over before I change out of uniform. Be ready to come home, Mary. I'm knackered.'

Geraint frowned at her. 'Not a nice word for a lady to use, Stella.'

'Sorry Mr Lloyd-Davies.'

He tutted as she pranced out of the room.

When Mary and Stella got home, Mary was entrusted to make toasted bacon sandwiches whilst Stella bathed away the day's toil. It had been a long, hard one and she would be glad to get to bed. She would have gone straight to bed without eating had Mary not been hungry. However, Stella thought it was best she had something in her stomach. She hadn't eaten since mid-morning. She didn't mind, she wanted to lose a few pounds herself before going on the cruise.

She looked forward to it and so did Kevin. She reminded herself that she must contact him first thing in the morning to tell him about the confirmation of the cruise being March 15[th.] She'd let him have a lay in first, it being a Sunday. She couldn't herself because she was on the early shift. She would call him on her mobile during her morning break.

She ate and enjoyed her bacon sandwiches and was pleased to leave the bit of washing up to Mary. Colin was still out; at the pub, no doubt, and wouldn't be home until the small hours. He stayed on at the pub after last orders on Saturday nights. He played cards with a few regulars. He didn't mind breaking the law, but he wouldn't be pleased to come home to a greasy frying pan and plates in the sink.

Stella must have been over-tired. She couldn't sleep; so many thoughts were circling in her mind. She heard Mary snoring through the thin partition of the bedrooms and she thought it sounded course. She had advised her to try to stop it; it wasn't sophisticated.

Her aim for some weeks had been trying to smarten Mary and continued to get her to adhere to a slimming diet. In both she had succeeded and was delighted. All her clothes were beginning to feel loose. Stella also aimed at making her more articulate. Bronwen did too, and between them both there was improvement.

Stella had on her mind the renovation of 22, Queen Street. It mightn't be ready by the time they got back from the cruise, so it was a good thing Matron Phillips arranged for Bronwen and Geraint to retain their rooms.

Matron's brother, Colin, was an experienced master builder. What he didn't know about building, so people had told Stella, wasn't worth knowing.

Her part in the renovation was choosing the soft and hard furnishings: curtains and window blinds, carpeting, beds and bed linen and everything needed for a perfect home. Selecting bedroom, lounge and dining room suites was a big undertaking. She hoped she could do it, and do it well. She would hate to make a mess of things for Bronwen.

When Stella's marriage broke up, Bronwen's support was her salvation.

Steven left her after four years of marriage. She had to go back to living with her parents and Colin. The home which, when her parents died, was bequeathed to herself and Colin.

She was glad to be without Steven and wondered what she saw in him in the first place. However, at the time he left her for another woman, she was heartbroken; as was her pride.

She remembered Bronwen saying, 'Don't grovel my lovely. Keep your pride. If he intends to leave you, no amount of pleading will make the slightest bit of difference; he will go. You are young and beautiful; you will find someone who deserves you.'

Too late. Stella had grovelled and she regretted it; but it was a long time ago and the damaged pride had healed. Bronwen's shoulder was always available to cry on. Bronwen had cried on Stella's shoulder too. She always worried about Mary and her lack of coping ability. Stella helped to look after Mary in a way Bronwen couldn't, being crippled and having to reside in a nursing home.

Stella didn't regret the selling of the house in which she and Steven had lived. She could have kept it, but she didn't want to live with memories of what, she thought, was a happy marriage. He had found someone else. Someone, no doubt, who could give him children.

When she moved back to her old home, Colin was pleased to have his young sister there, where he could look after her.

Stella's sad regret was not having a child. At her age now, it didn't seem likely that she would, unless she met someone with whom she would fall in love with immediately, and he with her. As well as that, she would have to rely on Mother Nature allowing her to become pregnant.

She thought she most probably wouldn't marry again. There was Kevin, of course, who would marry her tomorrow, but that wouldn't be right. She didn't love him as he did her. Beside which, she considered herself too old for him. She was of the opinion that the man should always be the older. He was three years younger than she. To him, that was irrelevant, but she didn't feel the magic she hoped to in real love. However, she married Steven without it, thinking it would develop, but it didn't. She thought herself lucky that he was gone and glad she had Kevin. She didn't love him, but she couldn't do without him. Faithful Kevin was always there for her.

The house she and her ex-husband had lived in was sold and the proceeds divided. She was able to help Colin to buy expensive equipment for his job and the car which now, both Colin and Kevin, considered not road-worthy.

It was four years old when she bought it, so it had given her good service. Bronwen had told her to get rid of it and get a new one. That was another thought which was keeping Stella awake. She felt humble and found it hard to accept such a generous gift. However, it would be good to have a reliable car when they arrived back from the cruise. It would be needed when she moved in with Bronwen and Mary when the renovation of 22, Queen Street, was complete. That gave rise to a further problem—how would Colin feel about her moving out of their home.

He had never married, and Stella thought she was the reason for it. He wasn't the most handsome of men, but he certainly wasn't unattractive. He had a pleasant smile, a good sense of humour and a flourishing business. She thought, perhaps, when she left, he would marry and create a family of his own. She would like that, but the initial wrench, she feared, would hurt him, and it worried her.

She decided to cross that bridge when she came to it. At present there were too many other issues to be considered, but she wished Mary would stop snoring. It kept her awake until she fell asleep.

The following morning, during her break, Stella called Kevin on her mobile phone, which she was beginning to get used to. She told him they would be sailing from Southampton on 15th March. He was delighted.

'Stella, love, that's great news. I'll put my notice in tomorrow. I hope I won't ruffle any feathers. I might need to go back there, but I can't wait to get out of that black hole, even if it'll only be for a break.'

'Yes, it will be good to get out of that for a while. I'm sure they would take you back any time, but let's hope it won't come to that.'

Stella went on. 'Now there are two points I must put to you. I have to be quick about it; it's very busy here. First, get yourself measured for evening and lounge suits and order your size in shirts, or whatever you can't get in your size, and don't argue about it.'

'Stella, a made-to-measure evening suit is not far short of three hundred pounds. You know I'm just not that sort of bloke. Can't I get a dark lounge suit that'll do for all occasions?'

'Shut up, Kevin. Stop worrying about the cost. Bronwen has given me more than enough, so get them, d'you hear?'

'Yes, all right. What was the other thing you were going to tell me?'

'You'd never guess. Bronwen wants me to buy myself a car, because the Merc's too big for a runabout and my old car's falling to bits.'

'Good Lord, that's incredible. But she's right, that old rattletrap is not safe anymore, and you know Colin agrees with me. I'll most probably be able to get fifty pounds for yours, selling it for scrap and spare parts.'

'Well, think of what car I should get. I haven't a clue.'

'Ask Bronwen then,' Kevin suggested. 'No, ask Geraint about how much Bronwen wants you to spend.'

'Will he or Bronwen have a clue? I doubt it. They'll leave it to me. We'll talk to Colin this evening, after I've come off duty and had a nap.'

Stella hurriedly switched off. A resident was calling her from the toilet area.

Before Stella went off duty, she sat beside Bronwen for a while, as she always did. That day she talked to Bronwen about a car. When should she get it? Before the cruise or after? And how much should she spend on it?

'Get it now,' Bronwen insisted. 'The sooner the better. You'll, then, have a nice car to come back to. And as for how much, ask Geraint to look on his computer. You and he can pick one out tomorrow. Ask Kevin to think about it, as well.'

'Yes, all right,' Stella sounded hesitant.

The lounge was quiet with most of the residents dozing, reading, or doing jigsaw puzzles, so there were few to hear the conversation between the two women. Some of those who could hear shouted suggestions.

Tom shouted across the room, 'Get a Rover, Stella.'

'Get a Jaguar,' Brynly shouted.

'Get a Volvo, Stella,' someone else called out.

'Shut up the lot of you,' Stella snapped. 'You're making me more confused.'

Bronwen attempted to ease Stella's confusion. 'Don't let it worry you. Let Kevin and Colin pick one out for you. Geraint will arrange paying for it. Tell them to get it and put it outside your house.'

Stella went home feeling more at ease but physically and emotionally drained. She was longing to put herself between cool sheets, her head on a soft pillow and having, at least, two hours sleep. She didn't have difficulty dropping off, as she had the previous night.

A week later a new blue Volvo Estate car was parked outside Stella's home. It was bigger than she had initially decided upon, but Kevin and Colin advised her to get such a vehicle, so she could accommodate Bronwen's wheelchair. The front seat had to be big enough for Bronwen to cross onto from her wheelchair.

Stella's eyes gleamed with amazement. Never did she think she'd see a day when she would own such a vehicle. It was something exciting to come back to after the cruise.

Chapter 14
Away We Go

On Wednesday of the following week, Bronwen met with Mr Malik Shar, the managing director of The Sunshine Mount Nursing Home. It was one of four nursing homes which his company owned.

The meeting had been arranged through Matron Phillips, who knew Bronwen would be reluctant to meet him. She thought it best to agree to see him and listen to what he had to say, in view of the fact that at varying times their rooms would be retained.

Geraint and Tom guessed Mr Shah would want to talk finance, having heard that Bronwen had won a fortune on the lottery.

Bronwen met him in Matron's office at coffee time, eleven o'clock. It was hoped he wouldn't mention the retention of hers and Geraint's rooms, so she was relieved that he didn't. Matron had ensured them that their rooms would always be available to them, so that issue was off his agenda. Matron thought he might have simply forgotten what, to him, was an unimportant matter.

He sat in Matron's chair, behind the desk; she on the left with an elegantly set tray for coffee on the desk in front of her. Bronwen sat opposite Mr Shah on the other side of the desk.

They greeted each other. He stood and shook Bronwen's hand across the desk.

He opened the discussion.

'Firstly, I must thank you for your most generous donation of a very expensive, much needed therapeutic bed and mattress and the mobility scooters.'

Bronwen decided that if it were much needed, it should have been available before she bought it for Martha Tate. He didn't seem to know, or care, how many mobility scooters were bought; four or forty.

Bronwen felt disillusioned. He seemed to have misunderstood the purpose of the gifts.

'There is no need for thanks, Mr Shah. You nor your directors need have a sense of obligation because they were gifts to my friends, not a donation to the home. But of course, my friends will share them. Anyway, one of them was for me.'

'Then, I will thank you for putting The Sunshine Mount Nursing Home, "on the map", so to speak. Not only are all our rooms occupied, we have a waiting list.'

Bronwen had heard that the story of her winning a fortune had spread throughout the county. It had become recognised as a lucky home and had motivated elderly people into trying the National Lottery themselves and to dream of how they would spend it. Bronwen had put a new face onto being elderly and disabled.

'Good,' Bronwen responded. 'But what is it you wish to discuss with me.'

'Well now, my directors and I have decided we should invite you to become part of our enterprise and offer you a position on the board. You would have to buy yourself in, of course, but I understand that would be no problem to you. It would mean that your investment in our business would be most profitable to you in the long run. Your capital would benefit substantially.'

'I know nothing of business, Mr Shah, especially of the proposition you have put to me. I think I had better consult my financial adviser, Mr Lloyd-Davies.'

Mr Shah had heard of Mr Lloyd-Davies's expertise and his involvement with Bronwen's twenty point five million pounds. He preferred not to deal with him.

'But this is private business between you, myself and my directors. There is no need to involve a third party.'

'But I would prefer to,' Bronwen insisted, as she looked at Matron Phillips. 'Would you mind asking Mr Lloyd-Davies to come in?'

Matron nodded and walked to the office door. As soon as she opened it Geraint walked through. He had been sitting in the corridor directly outside. A carer had brought him a chair.

Geraint strode in wearing his new dark grey suit and looking buoyant with expectancy.

'How do you do,' he greeted Mr Shah. 'I've assumed you wish to involve Mrs Dew in business.'

'Yes,' Mr Shah said with surprise in his tone. He didn't expect sharpness of mind from a man of over eighty. He went through what he had put to Bronwen.

Geraint responded. 'That's good of you, Mr Shah, but the answer must be, no. You see, we don't choose to be implicated with the pressures of making profits. Mrs Dew has a great deal of money which, for the rest of her life, she intends to spend on pleasure. That means involving those who are nearest and dearest to her.'

'The answer is, no!' Mr Shah repeated, sounding somewhat angry. He expected Bronwen to be flattered by his offer and wouldn't hesitate but to accept.

'But you are invited to be involved in a directorship of The Sunshine Mount, which wouldn't prevent you enjoying life. Don't you think you should, at least, think about it?'

'Thank you, Mr Shah, but I need not think about it because my mind is made up, and I'm grateful for Mr Lloyd-Davies's explanation to you.' Bronwen's voice remained contained but she was wanting the meeting to close.

Its ending was brought about by angry shouting in the hall outside the office. Its distraction was timely. It was Tom in one of his rages. He and Bronwen had exchanged glances through the glass partition which divided the hall from Matron's office.

Tom had known Bronwen since she was a little girl and he was used to recognising her mood from her attitude. She had the ability to hide her feelings from most people, but not from him. She and Tom were sensitive to each other's emotional ups and downs. He recognised a definite discomfort from Bronwen's expression as he and Brynly sat in their wheelchairs puffing at the stub ends of their cigarettes.

'I want my packet of cigarettes!' Tom shouted. 'Will someone fetch my cigarettes? I paid for them; they're mine!'

'All right, all right.' Dora tried to pacify him. 'Wait a bit, will you, Tom Daly? You've just chain-smoked three. You're not only killing yourself, you're giving the rest of us lung cancer.'

'I don't give a shit what I'm giving you, I want my bloody fags! Where's Bronwen? She'll get them for me.'

'Bronwen is in an important meeting. Now be quiet, will you? She'll be out soon.' Dora cast her eyes through the glass partition and caught Bronwen's eye.

'What's wrong with that man?' Mr Shah asked. 'He shouldn't be allowed to use those words here.'

Matron, Geraint and Bronwen looked at each other. They were amazed at the man's naivety. The Sunshine Mount Nursing Home belonged to him and he knew how its administration functioned but, obviously, little of the people who were responsible for its true viability.

'They're only words,' Mr Shah, 'but we don't all use them.' It was surprising that a man whose command of English was hesitant, knew that the words Tom used were not socially accepted.

'If you'll excuse me, I will go to him. I understand him; we've known each other and have been friends for many years.'

She and Geraint shook hands with Mr Shah and left him with Matron to drink their coffee. Geraint nor Bronwen managed to sip theirs.

Geraint Zimmered up the corridor towards the bottom lounge. Bronwen loitered in the hall, braking her wheelchair beside Tom. She went into the small handbag she always carried and brought out a packet of cigarettes. She took two from the packet and gave one to Brynly and one to Tom. They had their own lighters.

'Here you are, Tom,' Bronwen said kindly, 'but this is your last one until after lunch.' She winked and smiled knowingly at him. Tom knew that this was her way of saying thanks for rescuing her from an awkward situation.

'But Tom, you know Dora's right. And you, Brynly. You both know about passive smoking and the possibility of it affecting us.'

'Bull shit,' said Tom, quietly.

'Bollocks,' Brynly added, also quietly.

The hall became clear of people; it was nearing lunchtime. Everyone returned to their usual places.

Mr Shah didn't stay long with Matron Phillips. Bronwen manoeuvred herself near the front window where she was able to see him depart in his smart car. It seemed he didn't stay to finish his coffee. That's good, she thought. Matron Phillips wouldn't have wanted him to stay for lunch.

Thursday, 15th March 1999 dawned fine and bright, but with a late winter chill in the air. Warm overcoats, hats, scarves and gloves was the dress of the day.

Kevin had been at the home long before anyone realised. He had brought the Mercedes to the front door to begin loading the luggage.

One of the carers had let him in so he was able to take the mobility scooters from under the stairway and pack them tightly and safely in the boot of the car, leaving space for Bronwen's folded wheelchair. It was a good thing it could be folded because Kevin expected a squeeze to get everything on.

Bronwen's and Geraint's luggage was in the hall. They'd had it brought down the evening before. His, Mary's and Stella's cases were already in the car.

He looked at all the luggage and scratched his head. There was so much of it. How would he get it all on and leave room for the passengers?

For the best part of an hour Kevin loaded and unloaded, pushed, pulled and manoeuvred the suitcases of various weights and sizes in an attempt to get them all slotted in.

It was a cold morning, but he became hot and sweaty with effort. Drops of perspiration trickled from his hairline down his close shaven face. It was a good thing his, almost shoulder length, fair hair was tied back with an elastic band. It was bunched at the nape of his neck, otherwise is would have got in his way and looked scruffy.

Bronwen had thought he should have taken himself to the barber's, but Stella liked his hair on the long side, especially when it was tied back. He always did what pleased Stella.

When Bronwen, Geraint, Mary and Stella appeared expecting to get into the car, ready for the departure, they were surprised to find Kevin still struggling with the luggage.

Bronwen had to admit she had been wrong about the roof-rack. She considered it spoiled the overall appearance of the car. As she watched Kevin struggling to get everything on top of and inside the car, with Stella's help, Bronwen realised the roof-rack was an essential extra. It was detachable and hadn't been used until that day. She had thought the car was so big, it surely would accommodate their luggage, themselves, the wheelchair and the mobile scooters with room to spare.

Geraint, with his Zimmer frame in front of him as usual, approached the vehicle with the intention of helping. Bronwen grabbed the back of his coat and pulled him back.

'Leave them, Geraint, you'll only get in their way.'

Geraint tutted. 'Ridiculous,' he muttered, 'anyone would think we were going for a twelve month.'

Besides a small piece of hand-luggage each of them had, Bronwen and Geraint had three cases between them, Stella had two suitcases, one large, one small, and Kevin had one suitcase and a grip. Mary had four suitcases. Her hand-luggage was a grip and a handbag, twice the size of her mother's and Stella's.

'Mary, it looks as if you've emptied your wardrobe and all your bedroom drawers. You'll not need all that,' Bronwen criticised tactfully.

'What the hell have you got in them big cases,' Stella rebuked. 'We're only going for seventeen days, not a couple of years. Why didn't you ask me to help you?'

'Well, I packed when you wa'n't in the 'ouse,' Mary looked dejected. 'I packed wha' I fought I'd need.'

Kevin snapped before Bronwen had chance to correct Mary's grammar.

'Too late now. They're on the roof rack. I'm not going to take them down for Mary to unpack and pack again. We don't have time.'

'That's right, Geraint said, 'we're boarding at four o'clock.'

The home was abuzz with excitement. Those carers who were on duty faced the window, watching the packing being stacked on and in the car. All those residents who were mobile were in the hall or standing on the forecourt. Bronwen's cousins, Edna, Ruth and Daniel, Ruth's eight-year-old grandson had come to wave them off. He was a clever boy, small for his age. He strolled around the big vehicle, peering with avid interest, until his grandmother called out to him.

'Come here, Daniel. You're getting in the way.' The boy did as he was told.

Matron had already wished them *bon voyage* and was watching through the window of her office. The task of getting all the luggage successfully packed, she thought of cliché, "fitting a pint into a half-pint pot". It was a good thing Kevin was a tolerant man, as well as being big and strong, though she recognised his dander beginning to rise. He heard people shouting advice to him on how to slot everything in.

Little Daniel appeared to be bored, seeing the cases go in and out of the car. He decided to escape. Bronwen gave him money to go to the nearest shop to get some sweets and a comic. There was a newsagent's shop at the bottom of the hill which sold sweets and cigarettes as well as newspapers, comics and all sorts of magazines.

'Go on, then, Daniel. But don't be long or you'll miss them leaving.' his grandmother warned.

'If they do, Gran, I'll see them as I'm coming up the hill,' Daniel ran off. 'It looks as if they'll be a long time yet.'

Geraint attempted to remain aloof, as adults should, but his diseased prostate gland made it difficult. He was as excited as everyone else. Matron Phillips had whispered to

Bronwen that she had attached a disposable urinal somewhere between the cases. She couldn't explain exactly where. She thought he might well need it between stops.

The only person who didn't seem thrilled about the trip was Kevin. On the contrary, he was agitated having to fit all the luggage into and onto the car. Stella helped to fit cases inside the car whilst Kevin struggled with the roof-rack.

Eventually, the almost impossible, was achieved. All the luggage was settled. He secured that which was on the roof-rack with the provided straps. There was just enough length to bind the mound of luggage.

Bronwen noticed Tom had tears in his eyes which led to her feeling tearful.

'We're only going for seventeen days, including two days motoring, Tom. Not for good,' she tried to make light of it.

'I know, I know,' he replied. 'I'm being daft; I feel I won't see you again.'

'Yes, you are being daft,' Bronwen sniffed. 'Of course, you'll see us again.'

Tom was disappointed that he wasn't making the trip with them, as Bronwen had expected; his condition was too complicated to leave the security of care at the home. He knew he had made the right choice and tried to hide disappointment with amusing remarks.

'You look as if you're taking up residents in the North Pole,' he called out.

'That's how it feels,' Kevin frowned.

'Don't get lost, Mary,' Tom went on. 'If the natives find you, they'll put you in a pot, cook you and gobble you up for supper.'

'Shut up, you,' Mary pouted. His teasing had the desired effect; she was frightened. The huddle of people there was amused by Mary's response. Their laughter was humiliating.

'You won't get lost, love,' her mother reassured. 'If you do, you have plenty of money in your purse to get a taxi back to the ship.'

Geraint carried his fine, new leather briefcase containing all the documents and a wallet packed tightly with sterling. He didn't intend letting either out of his sight.

Everyone's purse was stuffed with money. Bronwen insisted on that, in case someone got lost when they went ashore at the various ports of call. She, of course, had Mary in mind. Bronwen had shared her concern with Stella.

'Now don't you go worrying about Mary getting lost, Bronwen,' Stella stressed. 'I'll stick to her like glue.'

Bronwen was as amused by Stella's remark as she was relieved. Stella made her laugh when she needed to. She went on. 'And if she falls overboard, I'll jump in after her.'

'You won't swim far with Mary on your back,' Bronwen added with a grin

'Then I'll get Kevin to jump in and get her.'

Eventually, an hour later than planned, they were ready to set off.

Kevin cradle-lifted Bronwen from her wheelchair onto the comfortable, leather-upholstered seat, behind the passenger seat where Stella would sit. She folded the wheelchair and slotted it into a space allotted for it at the back of the car. She swore silently; the gap was obstructed by Geraint's Zimmer. It slotted in, but she daren't let him hear what she thought of it.

The back of the car was crammed; it was a jumble, but she guessed it could be sorted out when they were in their cabins.

Mary and Geraint were settled in their seats waiting for Kevin to switch on. Instead of Stella getting in at the passenger side of the car she went to the driving seat and ordered Kevin to move across to her seat.

'I'll drive until the traffic gets heavy,' Stella said. 'You've been a real sport handling all this luggage, Kevin. I'd like you to sit back and relax a bit.'

Kevin was taken aback. He was already less tense and prepared to drive to Southampton. 'It's all right, love. I'll drive. I don't mind.'

'I know you don't,' Stella replied, 'but I want to drive, so move over.'

Kevin was too big to squeeze across to the passenger seat. He had to get out of the car and walk around. He did as Stella bid. He didn't want to argue; there was no time for further hold-ups.

By the time the big, over-loaded motor rolled away, more people had gathered outside the home to bid them farewell. Residents, friends and carers crowded together outside the home. There were loud cheers, wishes for a good journey, a good holiday, reminders to send post-cards, advice not to get lost, watch the dangerous roads and don't forget to come back.

In a little more than two hours Stella had arrived on the M4 going south to Southampton. Kevin was watching the road to ensure Stella went into the right lanes. The atmosphere in the car was of excitement and buoyancy. Everyone was relaxed in the safe hands of Stella in the driving seat. Mary started a sing-along; music from the shows. She had a sweet singing voice—one of her few attractive characteristics. Bronwen, Geraint and Kevin joined in for much of the time, but they were happy simply listening to her.

Geraint waited for a pause between Mary's songs to announce he would like to stop at the next motorway station to go to the gents' toilets before partaking of the contents of a package that Cook had put on his knees. She plonked it on top of his briefcase as they started off from the home. It was an assortment of sandwiches, slices of her special sponge cake and a few bottles of sweet drinks.

Geraint was relieved to get it off his knees. He wanted to get to his briefcase to check the documents for an unnecessary number of times. He was beginning to get hungry as well as wanting to go to the lavatory.

Stella drew into the station after crossing the Severn Bridge. They all went to the toilet before returning to the car to tuck in to al fresco.

'It doesn't make sense,' Bronwen said. 'I have millions in the bank and here we are sitting in this car eating sandwiches out of cling-film. Nice though it is, we have to become a bit posher.'

'That sounds snobbish, Bronwen,' Stella said. 'Don't you mean we have to become a bit more sophisticated?'

'Same horse, different jockey.' Kevin helped Bronwen with what she was trying to explain.

'Right you are,' Geraint said, as he munched at a small pork pie. 'I know what you mean, Bronwen. But if you don't mind me saying so, I've always tried to be as well-bred as I was brought up to be.'

'Well, if that's the case, Geraint, you can help the rest of us,' Bronwen responded. 'You won't find me being any different to what I am,' Kevin looked around at the faces behind him.

'Nor me,' Stella supported Kevin, 'but I know what you mean, Bronwen.'

'Nor me,' Mary added.

'Yes, you will,' Stella said with determination. 'You need a bit of polish in your corners and I'll see you get it.'

'Good,' Bronwen agreed, without further comment. Mary expected her mother to add a few words in her defence, but she was disappointed this time.

They left the service station to continue the journey with Kevin in the driving seat. Stella took the map, but she was no map-reader and they got lost. She told Kevin to go straight on when he should have taken a left turn.

However, they were soon travelling along a road which was parallel with the magnificent liner, Gladiator. It indicated that Kevin had to turn right. Thereafter, there were ample signs directing them to the dockside.

'My word, isn't it beautiful?' Bronwen gasped. 'How Lewis would have liked to see that.'

'Magnificent,' agreed Geraint. 'Absolutely magnificent.'

'It's much bigger than I expected,' Stella said. 'We'll be days finding our way about.'

The anxiety about being late and the liner going off without them was unfounded. They arrived outside the departure lounge with time to spare. As Stella and Kevin alighted, a porter came up to the car to help them with the luggage. The porter's eyes widened with amazement as he scanned the mound of luggage.

'I'll go and get one of my mates to give me a hand with this lot,' he said as he looked up at Kevin. He was a small man and seemed as amazed at Kevin's size as he was about the amount of luggage.

'We'll need another luggage trolley, too,' he said. 'Would you try to grab one?' He had his hands already on the handle of one trolley.

Stella had some difficulty getting Bronwen's wheelchair from the back of the car because Geraint's Zimmer had its legs firmly embedded in the luggage. She managed to dislodge it and stood it on the pavement where Kevin had begun to stack the luggage. She had her eyes on the back of the boot to organise Bronwen's wheelchair and the scooters.

Bronwen had surveyed the activities from her seat in the car until Kevin knew it was safe to help her. Without obvious effort he lifted her and gently lowered her onto her scooter. She ensured the bottom of her slacks was well down to her feet. There were lots of people about. She didn't mind anyone seeing her smart shoes, but not an inch of her abnormal legs.

Kevin continued to help the two porters to unload the last of the luggage from the roof rack. The two men eyed the car with invisible pound signs floating in the air around them.

Before the luggage was taken away to be put on board, Kevin gave twenty pounds to each of the porters. Bronwen had slipped the notes into his hand to remind him to give them a good tip. He thought that was too much, but he couldn't argue.

A man came to drive the car to the car park. Kevin handed him the keys and explained the driving mechanism. It was not the usual kind.

'Thank you, sir. I'll be here when you and your party return. Have a good cruise.'

People looked with amazement at the amount of luggage. Kevin was embarrassed. 'It's not all mine. 'There are ten of us,' he lied. One of the onlookers nodded understanding.

Geraint chuckled at Kevin's exaggeration as he took his Zimmer and tottered off towards the checking-in counter to be there first, since he had all the documents.

He had ensured every piece of luggage was well tagged with names, addresses and other bits of information, in case of loss. He'd put one on his Zimmer as well as on the mobility scooters. He hadn't forgotten to put one on Bronwen's wheelchair. He had ordered the others to secure labels on their hand-luggage.

There were hundreds of people queuing in the departure hall. Everyone had to report at one of six desks with two women behind each one. The queues meandered along rope-formed divisions. It reminded Bronwen of when Lewis used to take her to the cattle-market to see newborn lambs being bought and sold.

She was pleased when her group were beckoned to the end desk where the disabled were booked in. But she felt guilty, too. She saw people with children waiting in the queues as well as others; as elderly as she and Geraint. It didn't seem fair, and she expressed her feelings to one of the officers beside her.

'It's all right, Ma'am,' he reassured. 'They'd prefer to wait than be disabled. Anyway, you've paid well for it. You're first class, aren't you?' He had spotted the cabin numbers on the luggage tab of her scooter. He knew they were one of the best suites.

Geraint put down his Zimmer frame as he reached the desk. He dealt with the documentation and when all was completed, they each were given two small plastic cards which were to be carried on their person at all times. Each card served two purposes: identification and to allow credit, the other card allowed access to their cabins.

Bronwen was doubtful about Mary taking responsibility for these cards; she was apt to lose them. She would keep an eye on her. She realised Stella would be aware of the likelihood of her putting them somewhere and forget where.

From that desk they were led away, through double-doors to another desk which dealt with security matters. Bronwen was embarrassed when one of the female guards fumbled up and down, inside and outside her legs. She apologised for having to do so.

'It's all right, my dear,' Bronwen said. 'It's good to know that we're being cared for so well.'

When through security, they all had their photographs taken.

'What do 'e wan our photos for, Mr Lloyd-Davies?' Mary asked.

'I think they take photos of everyone, my dear. It's a record of who is on board if the liner gets into trouble and sinks, or something.'

'Sinks?' she said with horror. 'I can't swim.'

Kevin was amused. 'I'll bet any money you'll swim if the liner sinks, Mary. Especially if a shark is chasing you.'

Kevin's teasing frightened Mary. She moved to beside her mother, who was concentrating hard on manoeuvring her scooter between the long winding designated way.

She was concerned about Geraint. He was actually using the Zimmer to help him along. He insisted his scooter remained with their luggage, which would be taken to their suites. The circumstances at the time prevented Bronwen from arguing with him. It would be a long walk to the suites and he was already finding it hard. She decided she would insist upon him using his mobility scooter thereafter.

'Wha' 'f the boat do sink, Mammy?' Mary asked. Bronwen heard her but was concentrating too much on Geraint to be bothered with a reassuring answer.

'What if the boat sinks?' Stella corrected. 'You must speak nicely, Mary. And don't be daft. Of course the boat won't sink. It's not The Titanic. Don't listen to Kevin; he's teasing you.'

When they got to the gangplank, they all had to show their identity cards for the first time. Mary couldn't find hers. Stella helped her to go through her pockets and bags. It was found in the top pocket of the jacket she was wearing.

'Come on, you dopey bugger. You're holding everybody up,' she snapped at Mary.

Geraint was too worn out to criticise Stella's coarseness.

Bronwen found the gangplank steep for her scooter. Kevin pushed it by its backrest until they stepped onto the carpet of the liner.

The deck area was beautiful. The officers welcoming them were smart and professional. It was a strange party they greeted; a handicapped couple, a frowning fat lady, a beautiful woman with bright intelligent eyes and a long-haired, stalwart man who towered over them.

They were shown to the lifts by a young Asian man in pristine, white uniform who guided them to the top level of the liner. From there they were shown down a soft-pile, carpeted corridor to their cabins.

Their luggage had already arrived; scattered in the cabins, and two of the bigger ones in the corridor.

The guide recognised the excess amount of luggage and before leaving them, addressed Bronwen. 'When help is needed with your unpacking, Ma'am, please let your steward know.'

'Cor!' Stella and Mary chorused. They were astounded at the splendour.

'Bronwen, my girl, this is living,' Geraint gasped.

'My God,' Kevin said, 'this must have cost a fortune.'

'I have a fortune,' Bronwen said, 'and we're all going to enjoy it. This is mine, Stella's and Mary's cabin. You two men go and look at yours.'

The deco of the cabins was magnificent, and the crystal light fittings discretely designed. Each cabin contained furniture of the highest quality with ample wardrobe and drawer space. A lounge contained fine upholsters chairs and settees. The furniture was of the finest mahogany, including a wide screen television cabinet. There was a television in each bedroom and in the bathrooms. A large bowl of fruit was on one table and two bottles of champagne in an ice bucket on another.

The carpets, curtains and other soft furnishings were the most beautiful they had ever seen. The luxurious fitting of the toilet area, shower and bathrooms were similar to those seen on glamorous films. There was a fridge-freezer, a well-stocked bar and big vases of fresh flowers placed at a number of strategically positions throughout the rooms.

French doors opened out onto spacious balconies, also furnished for leisure and comfort.

'I don't want to go out anywhere,' Stella said as she looked around in awe. 'I'd be quite happy to stay here with a couple of magazines and one of those bottles of champagne.

'You'll have to go out to show off that smashing bikini you bought,' Kevin reminded her. 'And what about your lovely new evening frocks. And what about my evening suit. I'm not going out in that on my own.'

'You go' a bikini for yourself, did you?' Mary pouted. 'Why di'n't you le' me ge' one?'

'Shut up unless you speak properly,' Stella snapped to change the subject. Bronwen helped her.

She sighed. 'I'm so thrilled to see you all delighted,' she said with a broad smile, lighting up her kindly face. 'If this is being rich, we'll soon get used to it.'

'When you know the cost of it all at the end,' Geraint said, as he also looked about him, 'you'll know you have to be rich to afford this.'

'Don't be such a wet blanket, Geraint. Enjoy yourself as the rest of us intend to,' Bronwen insisted.

'Don't you worry, Bronwen, my beauty—I will,' he smiled one of his rare smiles.

'I can't remember being called a beauty, Geraint. Makes me sound like a racehorse. And that makes me think of a good way to spend money—we can buy a racehorse and go to the races. Only the wealthy do that.'

Geraint grinned. 'Do you think I could ride our horse in the Grand National, Bronwen?' She laughed.

She was back in her wheelchair to help with the unpacking. With only Mary's cases opened and unpacked the room became a jumble. There was such a large amount; Mary looked at it with bewilderment. She didn't know where to begin.

'Stella, shall you and I help her to put away her things before we open our cases?' Bronwen asked.

'We'll have to, Bronwen, otherwise we'll be in a hell of a mess.' Stella pursed her lips as she looked at Mary. 'Most of this can go back in that big case and put somewhere out of the way, because you won't need it.' She pointed to the biggest of Mary's suitcases. 'Those two big jackets can be put away for a start. It's not likely to snow. And you have almost a dozen pair of shoes. You just pick out six pairs of what you want, and the rest can be put out of the way.'

'All right, Stella,' Mary pouted agreement. ''Ow was I to know?' She was glad of the help.

When all of Mary's things were neatly put away, there was ample space left for Bronwen's and Stella's things. The room was designed with plenty of space for personal clothing; it was planned for the rich.

'Shall we unpack yours now, Bronwen?' Stella suggested, 'because some of Mr Lloyd Davies's things are in one of your cases.'

Bronwen was able to pick out garments which went into drawers she could reach. Stella and Mary put garments on hangers in the wardrobes and on the shelves.

'Yes, all right,' Bronwen agreed. 'It's his best suits; one on top of each case, not for them to get creased.'

Stella put her hand on her hip with irritation. 'Oh, and it doesn't matter about your things getting creased, does it?'

'Mine don't crease,' Bronwen replied, just when a loud voice came over the Tannoy system.

'*This is your captain speaking. I have an important announcement to make.*

At 18.00 hours, eight blasts of the whistle will indicate that all passengers should proceed to their muster stations for emergency drill, taking their life jackets with them. Life jackets are on the top shelf in the corner of your cabin. You will be instructed on the use of your life-jackets in the unlikely event of an emergency.'

The voice went on to explain why the exercise had to take place, where and how to get to the muster stations and safety measures to be taken when walking to the muster stations. He ended by wishing everyone an enjoyable cruise.

Robot-like, three pairs of busy hands, sorting out the unpacking stopped abruptly.

Three faces stared at the Tannoy system in the ceiling above the main cabin door.

'Do we have to go?' Stella asked. 'We haven't finished our unpacking yet.'

'Of course, we have to go,' Bronwen said. 'Think of The Titanic.'

Stella and Mary remembered the film of the sinking of The Titanic. They made a dash to get the life jackets as Bronwen manoeuvred her wheelchair to look at the notices on the back of the door.

Before she got there Geraint burst into the room.

'Come on, quickly, you three, we have to go to another landing to the exercise.' He held his life jacket on his chest with one hand, his Zimmer with the other. Kevin behind, pushed Geraint further into the room and went to Bronwen.

'Bronwen, it will be easier if you use your scooter. It gets around bends better.' He cradled her to her scooter which was parked out in the passageway.

They were directed to one of the theatre halls where the safety lecture took place.

Mary couldn't manage her life jacket. One of the crew, a handsome man in uniform, helped her. She blushed; too shy to thank him.

There were at least a hundred passengers at the drill. Everyone was chatty and in holiday spirit. Bronwen was pleased to see she wasn't the only one on a mobility scooter and there were several people in wheelchairs.

The safety drill fascinated them. They arrived back in their cabins, happily prepared to complete the unpacking; but not Mary.

'I'm starving,' she said. 'Can' we go and 'ave some tea before we finish.'

'Have some tea,' Stella corrected. 'Not a bad idea. Aren't you feeling a bit peckish, Bronwen?'

'Mmm,' Bronwen replied. 'The Conservatory is the dining area. It's on the floor above us, I think.'

They had no trouble finding The Conservatory. The lift was full of passengers going to the same place. Bronwen was given priority and room was made for her and her scooter.

The grandiose of The Conservatory and the selection of the finest teatime food, was beyond expectations. It was arranged in buffet style and Stella had to restrain Mary from overloading her plate.

'Well, I'm 'ungry,' Mary pouted, and we don't have to pay, do we?'

'Mary,' Bronwen whispered sharply, 'behave yourself. Do as Stella says. We don't want to let ourselves down.' Mary was too busy munching to take notice of her mother's advice.

She and Stella enjoyed their tea, too, but ate with dignity, being surrounded by many other passengers. The individual tables were all taken and Bronwen noticed that some of them weren't as elegant as she'd expected. She assumed they would all be rich on such a cruise, and everyone to be elegant and smart.

She didn't know then, that first class passengers dined at a more refined area. She guessed Geraint knew but hadn't, yet, got around to that issue.

On return to their cabin they continued with the unpacking. They called in on Geraint and Kevin on the way from the dining area and found them both dozing on their beds. Their room was as neat and tidy as when they'd arrived, except for a few bits and pieces on the dressing tables. Their cases had been emptied, the clothes put away, and the cases hidden away in the cupboards which were meant for them.

'Don't be too smug about finishing your packing before us, Geraint,' Bronwen said. 'Remember some of your suits are in the case in our room.'

'I'll come for them afterwards,' Geraint said with half closed eyes.

'I can see you don't need them now,' Stella said. 'You look like one of the Muppets in that dressing gown, Mr Lloyd-Davies.' He was wearing one of the soft, white terry-towel bathrobes that was hanging in the gleaming bathroom. Only the top of his head and part of his face could be seen.

'That robe is about ten sizes too big for you, Geraint,' Bronwen exaggerated.

Kevin had his on, too. It was about ten sizes too small for him. It didn't reach around his large, muscular frame and barely reached his knees.

He yawned. 'I'm going to ask for a bigger size,' he said.

Mary was amused by their appearance. 'Why don't you swap? You look like two Yogi Bears,' she laughed. It was unusual to hear Mary laugh. It was contagious. The other women laughed, too.

A programme of all the events going on aboard was in each room and declaring the mode of dress; casual, semi-formal or formal. That evening the dress was to be casual.

When the unpacking was complete, Bronwen had a shower with Stella's help, before she had a bath. Afterwards there was time for a short rest before dressing for the evening.

Mary went out to explore the ship whilst her mother and Stella rested. Stella was too tired to go with her.

'Oh, God, Bronwen, I hope she doesn't get lost,' Stella said with a sound of hopelessness.

Mary got lost. She hadn't returned by seven o'clock and they'd planned to go to one of the smart, cocktail bars for an aperitif before going into the dining room at half-past eight.

'It's no good me going out to look for her, Bronwen. I'll get lost myself,' Stella said. 'I'll go and tell Kevin to go.'

Just as she spoke, a knock at the door startled them. Bronwen opened it to find Mary standing in the corridor with a uniformed young man. She was crying.

'I forgot to take my key,' she sniffed, 'and I forgot the number of our cabin. I've been round and round this blooming ship hundreds of times looking for you.'

'Here we are, Ma'am,' the young man said. 'Safe and sound.'

Bronwen thanked the young man. The fact that her adult daughter got lost embarrassed her. Mary wasn't a young girl but an over-weight, thirty-one-year-old woman. The young man would have had to be blind not to realise that. Bronwen shut the door before chastising Mary.

'Didn't you see our scooters outside when you went around and around a hundred times, you silly girl. But never mind, you're here now. Dry your eyes and get washed and dressed to go out. We don't want to be late to the dining room on our first night.'

'Silly girl!' Stella shouted, 'Bronwen, she's a woman, and it's about time she acted like one,' she glared at Mary. 'I told you not to go, and as for walking around a hundred times, that I would like to see. Go in the bathroom and start washing. I'll pick out some clothes for you.' Stella was angry.

'Now, now, Stella,' Bronwen said calmly. 'We're here to enjoy ourselves. You help her wash and do her hair and I'll get her clothes.'

Soon the five unusual passengers trooped from the majestic, staterooms ran down the long corridor to the lifts. Bronwen led them in her mobility scooter, followed by Stella, then in front of Mary was Geraint, carrying his Zimmer frame. At the back was Kevin. He had looked at a map of the ship and selected a bar at the front which appeared interesting. They left the lift and walked a short distance down a carpeted incline into The Tree Tops bar. It was large, beautifully furnished and carpeted. Its glass roof of twinkling lights gave the impression of sitting in the sky. Bronwen and company caught people's attention as they made their entrance. They were bid a good evening by many. People were friendly, and the waiters made them feel like royalty.

Kevin had a can of beer, but the others selected elaborate cocktails from an elegant menu of drinks. Soft music in the background, from a grand piano, enhanced the atmosphere.

Dinnertime was announced over the Tannoy, which indicated they should make their way to the dining room. They followed other people who had chosen second sitting. Some of them were at as much of a loss as Bronwen and her party, but there were those who had cruised many times before.

The enormous dining room amazed them. Dozens of handsome young waiters pranced about, skilfully missing tables, chairs and passengers.

Stella whispered, 'Don't look surprised. Make out we've been here lots of times.' Mary couldn't manage that. Her eyes widened, her bottom lip dropped, as she looked about her.

Stella nudged her. 'Mary, shut your mouth,' she obeyed immediately.

Bronwen was on her mobility scooter which didn't fit at the table. Kevin cradle-lifted her onto a chair and the scooter was taken out of the way, by one of the waiters. He made no attempt to disguise the fun he had in parking it.

Those passengers at the nearby tables admired the skill with which the big handsome man handled the lovely woman.

Bronwen chose for Mary from the six-course menu. It concerned her that Mary couldn't read well enough to choose. Besides that, she didn't want her to eat her way through the menu.

Geraint chose the wine since he was the only one of them who had knowledge of the grape; but little. He put on his professional face, hoping he looked as if he knew what he was choosing. Stella couldn't suppress a giggle and Geraint looked down his nose at her. The meal was of the best quality and the presentation matched its surroundings. Although the portions were ample, they weren't overmuch, but Bronwen nor Geraint managed to fully partake. Their digestion was unused to it, having lived in a nursing home for ten years or more, where the meals were arranged to suit an elderly palate.

After dining, they followed a group of people who seemed to know their way to the theatre. The P & O's entertainments group put on a colourful, first night variety show. The colour and spectacle were magnificent and ended the first day aboard with joy and happiness.

When they got back to their cabins, they found the upheaval they had left behind in preparation for the evening had been cleared. The curtains had been closed, the lights dimmed, the towels in the bathroom changed. Their bed-covers had been turned back and a chocolate put on each of their pillows to remind them that someone had been there to make them comfortable.

They'd had the most enjoyable day since Bronwen had become a millionaire.

125

Chapter 15
The Stowaway

The cruise became more enjoyable as they became more familiar with their surroundings. The following two days were filled with new experiences and all the "family" wallowed in the luxury. Every day, morning, noon and night, there was some form of entertainment.

After breakfast on the second and third days, Mary and Stella attended line-dancing. Kevin jogged around the deck and Bronwen and Geraint attended the lectures and discussions. There was a well-stocked library which they all used, except Mary.

During the afternoons of the first two days the excitement and entertainment continued. Kevin and Stella attended the gleaming, up-to-date gymnasium and encouraged Mary to go with them. They taught her how to use the treadmill. Although she found it hard going, she enjoyed wearing her athletic clothes and being part of an athletic group. She met other unmarried people of her age group. Some younger, some older. They were friendly and didn't seem to notice she was fat. A few of them were fat; one man was obese. It didn't seem to bother him.

Stella whispered to Mary, ensuring they were out of the hearing of anyone else. 'You'll be as fat as that if you're not careful.' Mary was aghast and shook her head vigorously.

Kevin looked dashing in his new sporting gear. Stella didn't like the admiring glances he had from many female eyes. The glamorous gymnasium staff approached him to pamper and flatter as he worked out. He had understanding of all the equipment because he attended the gym twice a week at home. He enjoyed the fluttering about him, which he didn't have at his local gym.

However, during the evening times at the bars, it was Stella who had the admiring glances from men with or without wives. It didn't miss Kevin's notice.

Mary, Kevin and Stella took to the Jacuzzi during the afternoons before teatime, whilst Geraint and Bronwen rested in their rooms with their library books. The weather was yet too cold to sit on the verandas or out on the decks. That would come later as they went further south.

Bronwen intended to use the Jacuzzi. She would wear a suitable pair of long, white trousers to keep her legs hidden. Kevin had assured her that he could easily carry her in and out of it.

Their first days aboard were the most enjoyable any of them could remember. They would have liked it to go on for a long time; not just another thirteen days. It is said that all good things must end, and it almost did on the third day at sea.

When Bronwen and Stella opened their eyes on the third morning of the cruise, they were surprised to see land outside the window. Mary didn't awaken until Stella went across to her bed and shook her.

'Mary, look. We've docked at Vigo. We're all going ashore to see what it's like. And it's a lovely day. We'll have to wear something cool.'

'We're going after breakfast, though,' Mary yawned. 'I'm starving.'

'You always are,' Stella replied, before stirring Bronwen into action. She helped her out of bed onto her wheelchair. Bronwen had strong arms, having always to rely on them for moving. She was always aware of having to avoiding strain on Stella.

'Do you want to bath or shower, Bronwen?' Stella asked. 'And what shall I get for you to wear? You know you thought so much about others before this trip that you haven't brought enough clothes for yourself, have you?'

'No, I haven't,' Bronwen agreed. 'I thought I had, but seeing how smart everybody is, I realise I'll have to get more. There are some beautiful frocks at those shops on this ship. They'll be seeing some of my lottery winnings. How lucky we are to be rich.

'I'll have a shower, please, Stella. I'll get what I want to wear while you start getting yourself ready.' She looked out of the wide window and beyond the veranda before e adding, 'How lovely to see bright, warm sunshine.'

The telephone rang. 'It'll be Geraint, I expect,' Bronwen rolled her eyes to the ceiling. 'He'll be telling us to look out the window for a surprise. He'll think we'd not noticed.'

'It won't be Kevin, anyway,' Stella said, as Bronwen picked up the phone. 'He won't be back from his jog yet. He runs for half an hour, at least, before breakfast.'

But it was Kevin. 'Bronwen, are you all up and decent in there. I need to come in immediately. You'd better prepare yourself for a shock.'

'No, Kevin, we're not. Give us five minutes,' she slammed down the receiver. 'Quick, the pair of you, get something on. Kevin is in a bit of a stir about something and is coming in now.'

Mary jumped out of bed as quickly as her tardiness allowed and scrabbled into a flowing shift that covered her from neck to feet. Her soft, terry-towel bathrobe was on a hook inside the bathroom. Bronwen already had on a multi-coloured kimono, covering her lap and legs.

In little more time than a blink of the eyes Kevin knocked the women's door and stormed in.

His tee shirt was stained with sweat and his shoulder length hair, loose and tousled after a quick rub with a towel. Behind him, holding his hand was a small boy.

'Daniel! Daniel!' Bronwen screamed. Bronwen never screamed. 'Daniel, where are your mam and dad?' A look of fear was about her; she dreaded the answer.

'In the house, Aunty Bronwen, 'and I want my mam,' he sniffed; he'd clearly been crying.

His light grey sweatshirt was dirty and torn as were his jeans. His face looked as if he hadn't been washed for days and had white streaks where tears had tumbled down his cheeks. He had on only one trainer; its lace undone. The sock on his other foot was soiled and had a big hole at the heel.

'Where…? What…?' Bronwen was at a loss for words as she looked at Kevin for answers. He had been right to warn her about being shocked.

Stella was almost as dumbstruck. 'Ruth's grandson?' she reminded herself. 'How did he get here? He could never have got through security.'

'No, he didn't have to,' Kevin began, 'he found another way to get here.'

'Well, there's nice to have you, Daniel. We can look after you,' Mary sounded pleased.

'Shut up, Mary. Don't say another word,' Bronwen snapped, surprising Mary, who wondered what she had said to offend. 'Where was he, Kevin? How did you find him?'

'I didn't find him, he found me. He was chasing after me calling my name as I was jogging around on the promenade deck. I wondered how he knew my name. I couldn't remember him until he told me you were his aunty and Ruth is his Gran. He managed to hide in the back of the car when Stella wasn't looking, jump out at the checkout when she had her back towards him sorting out your scooter. He sneaked up the gangplank where the men were loading on the kitchen stuff. Once he was on board no one questioned him. Why should they; they didn't know he sneaked aboard. As far as everybody knew he was with family.'

Daniel was eight but small for his age. Bronwen realised he could easily have snuggled up between the luggage in the back of the car and not be noticed.

Under the back seat of the car a wide enough gap accommodated Daniel's small frame. The two folded mobile scooters were propped against the back of the chair. Daniel must have crouched behind the scooters with his legs under the seat. Getting the car loaded with luggage was such a topsy-turvy task, no one bothered to check.

Daniel went on from where Kevin had left off. 'When the men who were carrying in the cabbages and things, when they went to their big van for tea and sandwiches, I ran up the gang-plank and hid on one of them big boats hanging on the side in case the ship sinks. But I was cold, and I wanted my mam,' Daniel burst into tears.

Mary went and hugged him. 'Don' worry, Dan, we'll look after you until you're back with your mam.'

At that point Geraint burst into the room. His ablutions had held him up; he didn't knock. His anxiety mounted as he tried to comply with the needs of his prostate. He hurried frantically to be in the next room to hear why and how the boy was there.

'Isn't this your cousin Ruth's grandson, Bronwen? What on earth is he doing here? You'd think his parents would have told you they'd be on the same cruise as we are. I had a few words from him which didn't make sense before Kevin brought him in here.'

'They're not with him,' Bronwen said with worry creasing her brow. 'You sit down a minute, Geraint, and let's listen to what's happened before we decide what to do.'

He did as Bronwen suggested. He was clearly worried. He had guessed from the little he'd heard when Kevin brought the little boy to their room that something very serious had occurred.

'Why did you follow us, Daniel, love?' Stella asked. 'You should've let your Gran know.'

'I heard Mr Lloyd-Davies say you'd see the apes in Gibraltar. I wanted to and the only way I could was to sneak away with you. If I asked to come with you, I know I wouldn't be allowed. And my dad had smacked me for being clumsy and my mam said I was always naughty. Nobody wanted me, so I thought I would come with you. They wouldn't care.'

'Of course, they would care. Come over to me a minute,' Bronwen hugged him and beckoned him to sit on the floor beside her. 'Your mam and dad love you. But Stella is right, Daniel, you shouldn't be with us. For a start, you have to go to school and a little boy like you shouldn't leave home without letting someone know. Anyway, how did you manage without anything to eat and drink once you managed to sneak on the boat?'

Stella interrupted. 'We can see you got dirty because you couldn't wash, but how did you manage to go so long before coming to your

Aunty Bronwen and us?'

'I waited until there was nobody about and I sneaked from the boat and walked around. Nobody noticed. Then I watched people going up to them eating places and having food for nothing, so I did. I asked for burgers and hot-dogs and stuff like that. Them nice waiters who clear the dishes away helped me to get drinks, 'cause I couldn't reach the machine. They all thought I was with grown-ups until yesterday.'

'What happened yesterday?' Mary asked, intrigued with Daniel's survival story.

'Well, one of them looked at me and saw my dirty face and clothes and asked where my mam was. I said she was outside having a smoke. He looked out and couldn't see anyone, so he told me to sit on one of the tables and he'd be back in a minute. He asked my name and I said I'd forgot so he gave me a dish of ice cream to eat when he was gone. Then I thought I'd be caught and have to pay for me being on the ship, so I ran and hid and waited for Kevin. I saw him running in the mornings.'

'Well, you're a very naughty boy,' Geraint pointed a threatening finger at Daniel. He was in a nervous state. He looked about the room at the faces with eyes staring at him, waiting for a solution to the predicament. 'Do you all know the penalty for harbouring a stowaway?' he asked gruffly. 'No, neither do I, but it won't be light. We could all end up in court, fined and possibly imprisoned.'

Daniel burst into tears again; he was terrified. He appeared so small, no one doubted his ability to have crouched between the luggage, however tightly Kevin had stacked the car.

'Shhh,' Kevin interrupted. He'd been sitting with his head in his hands, thinking while the banter was going on. 'Shhh, or we'll be heard.'

'Well, Kevin,' Stella said, 'do you think we're going to keep this quiet,' she pointed to Daniel. 'I can't see P & O keeping him aboard. His parents will have to know.'

'That's strange e,' Bronwen said, 'I've talked to Tom on the telephone yesterday and the day before and he didn't mention anything about Daniel being missing from home and yet I know his family will be beside themselves with worry. They'll be looking for him.'

'The whole of South Wales police will most probably be looking for him,' Geraint said in a tone as if it were everyone's fault but his.

'My God.' Bronwen paled at the possibility of a police dragnet to find Daniel. 'Geraint, you're exaggerating.'

With Daniel and Mary whaling, Stella was folding and unfolding her arms with agitation and repeatedly rubbing her brow. Geraint was now up from his chair; he and his Zimmer began pacing the floor. Kevin sat on the edge of Stella's bed combing his long hair with his fingers.

Bronwen lost the cool, calm temperament that was always her. 'Stop it, all of you!' All eyes turned to her with surprise. 'We're all overreacting. Daniel is here, he's alive and well. He could have fallen into the sea when he was getting in and out of those boats. He could have broken a leg or something when jumping on and off that boat, but he hasn't. Now, what we have to do is to get him back to his parents as soon as possible.'

'And how are we to do that?' Geraint snapped, 'Take his little hand and walk him back? I'll remind you that out that side is the sea and out that side is a foreign land,' he indicated each side with his Zimmer. 'We'll have to contact the captain and own up right away, otherwise I'm afraid an accusing finger might be pointed at us.'

'For goodness sake, Geraint, try to calm down. You're right; we must contact the captain or some official and explain what's happened. First, though, I'm going to contact Tom at the home to see what's been going on. He didn't say anything about this when I rang him yesterday. Thank goodness, I've got a phone.'

'Good idea,' Geraint agreed, as he made a dash for the toilet.

Bronwen looked at Stella. 'Geraint hasn't had his morning medication, Stella. Would you sort that out and mine as well?'

Stella was glad of something positive to do. She went to a cabinet in the corner of the room, unlocked it and took out a white, metal box which she also unlocked and began taking out Bronwen's and Geraint's medication. An important task which she did every morning and evening.

'Sorry, Bronwen, I'd forgotten about them.'

Bronwen didn't hear; her ear was against the telephone. She told the operator that her call was of great urgency before she asked for Tom's number. It took a long time to get through but, at least, it gave everyone a little time to unwind.

Kevin took Daniel's hand and led him out onto the veranda to view the dockside and the bit of Vigo that was in view. He thought it best not for him to hear the conversation Bronwen was about to make.

Eventually words were exchanged. 'Tom. Tom. Is that you?'

Tom answered. 'Yes, Bronwen, it's me. You rang me yesterday; I didn't expect to hear from you for a few days.' 'I had to. Something unbelievable had occurred. Young Daniel, my cousin's grandson has turned up here, in front of our eyes, on The Gladiator. We know how he got here but we can't understand why no one has missed him.' Bronwen was shouting down the mouth-peace to ensure Tom was hearing every word.

'My God, Bronwen! He's safe with you when all the county is out looking for him. I didn't tell you yesterday because I knew you would worry. You gave him money to go down the shop to get sweets and a comic the day you all left, and he hasn't been seen since.'

A crackling and a long bluuurrrrr was what Bronwen heard. Those in the room heard her say. 'Please don't let us be cut off. Tom, are you there?' Another frustrating period of crackling followed.

'Yes, I can still hear you. His mother and father are going off their heads with worry. It's thought he must have been picked up by someone when he was on the way back from the shop the day you left. There's a hell of a to-do here. The coppers are questioning everybody who knows you, his parents, his granny and some of us in the home. There's a lot of suspicion and hard feeling. You'll have to let them know that you've got him. Haven't you seen the papers? And it was on the Welsh news.'

Bronwen realised she hadn't looked at a newspaper since being on board. She had been enjoying herself, taking part in all that took her interest. She hadn't looked at the television and neither could the others have done, otherwise they would have picked something up.

'We must get Matron to get in touch with his parents to say he's safe and well, and we'll see he's sent home as soon as we can.' Bronwen had no idea how she was to get Daniel home. Those around her saw Bronwen's expression change from surprise, to stress, to anger.

'It's not our fault he sneaked into our luggage and got on the ship on his own and turned up here to us because he wanted his mam.'

'Then Bronwen, that little bastard is causing you, Mr Lloyd-Davies and…'

'Tom! Tom! I'm still here… Damn! We've been cut off,' Bronwen sagged with frustration.

The voice of the operator broke in. 'I'm sorry, Mrs Dew, but you've been cut off. Circumstances beyond our control. The only alternative is our emergency telecommunication. You'll have to try again later if you wish to continue.'

'Then I'd like to speak to the captain, and I assure it is a matter of urgency that I wish to do so. Would you put me through to him, please?'

'He's not available at the moment. I'll get back to you.'

'Then, Miss or Mrs, or whatever you are, you better had.'

Geraint, Mary and Stella were looking at Bronwen with wide eyes of expectancy. Stella didn't bother to tell Mary to close her mouth. She had her own open.

Bronwen held her hand to her mouth and closed her eyes. For a minute or more her mind was in too much of a turmoil to announce that the situation was more serious than at first thought.

'He's a missing person,' she began, 'missing since we left, Thursday. The whole county's looking for him. The police are scouring the immediate area and questioning anyone who might give some indication of where Daniel is, including the staff and some residents at the home. His parents are in a terrible state and if I know Ruth, she is too. And I expect she feels she is to blame because he was in her care. I remember her saying his mother kept him from school that day because he said he had a headache, so Ruth had him for his mother to go to work. I'd say he didn't have a headache at all; he'd planned to come with us.'

Geraint hobbled over to Bronwen. He was distressed at seeing her so worried, as he was, of the possible consequences of Daniel being on the ship with them. He put his arm across her shoulders.

'It'll be all right, Bronwen. It's as if you're taking this problem all on yourself. You mustn't. If anyone's to blame, there's Daniel and the rest of us. And you're right, it's a good thing we have him. God knows what could have happened to the little boy. He's only a scrap of a thing.'

Bronwen tapped the hand that was on her shoulder. 'Thank you, Geraint. I know we're all in this together. They, whoever "they" are, can't possibly blame us.'

The glass doors to the veranda were ajar. Though Kevin couldn't hear what was being said in the cabin, he glanced in and saw the dismay depicted on everyone's face. He realised the situation had worsened. He and Daniel went back into the cabin to find out.

'He's reported missing, Kevin,' Stella blurted. 'The whole police-force is looking for him as well as the locals. His parents are beside themselves with worry,' she was on the verge of tears. 'Look what it's doing to Bronwen.'

'It'll be all right, Bronwen,' Kevin sounded more confident than he felt.

'Everybody will be so relieved that he's safe with us, that it will just flitter out.'

'Yes, that's right,' Daniel whaled. 'I want my mam.'

'You want a wash, too,' Bronwen forced a smile, 'and some new clothes. Mary, when you've been in the ship's shops, have you noticed clothes for children?'

'Yes,' Mary nodded, 'plenty of tee-shirts and shorts but no trousers.'

The atmosphere needed brightening. 'None of us have had breakfast,' Stella remarked, 'I'm going to ring for room-service to bring it up for us. Speaking for myself, I don't feel like going anywhere until we've sorted Daniel out.'

'Good thinking,' Geraint said, 'just a pot of tea and toast for me. The same for you, Bronwen?' She nodded but she certainly didn't feel like eating.

'Ask for some sausages, Stella,' Mary said with a smiling face, as if everything was normal.'

Stella frowned at Mary and shook her head. 'Yes, but don't you expect a plateful.'

'I'll ring again to speak to the captain,' Bronwen said.

'Yes,' Geraint agreed. 'Tell him there's a stowaway on board and we've got him here. He'll be down in a flash.'

The person Bronwen spoke to sounded officious and Bronwen had to warn her that if she didn't comply with her request, she would report her for incompetence and hold her responsible for a law-breaking offence. 'We have a stowaway in our company, you insensitive girl.'

Geraint was right. The captain and an entourage of two officers arrived at the cabin before the breakfast trolley.

Stella let them in and asked them to join the others in the lounge area of the suite. The three officers removed their elaborate peaked caps; an abundance of shining buttons and braid remained decorating their uniform. The captain was a tall, well-built man with a pewter-coloured beard and moustache.

He introduced himself and his colleagues. He spoke with a Scott brogue. They were clean-shaven and appeared small beside the tall captain.

'I'm Captain Alistair Stewart, this is First Officer John Cross and First Officer Jonathan Briggs. I understand you have a stowaway in your company, Mrs Dew,' he sounded sceptical. He looked from face to face. 'Where is he, or she?'

Daniel was sitting on Kevin's knee. He stood and positioned Daniel against his leg with his hands on the little boy's shoulders. The two First Officers looked up at Kevin with astonishment.

'This is he,' Geraint said, directing them to look at Daniel. 'He made himself known to us this morning, when he ran after Mr Grant when he was exercising on deck.'

The captain's scepticism changed to disbelief. 'That's most odd. What's your name, laddie?'

Daniel clung to Kevin. 'Daniel Palmer, Mister,' he replied. 'I come on the ship when no one was looking and hid in one of them big boats you keep in case you sink.'

The captain looked aghast. 'That's impossible, sir. No one would stand an earthly to get through security on my ship.'

The two first officers looked at each other. 'Impossible,' one of them said. 'The boy must have had help.'

'You think we hid him in one of our suitcases?' Kevin asked, a thunderous look appearing in his eyes.

'Not at all,' the other officer said. 'Because even then he would have been discovered coming through.'

'Then how do you think he got to us?' Bronwen asked with her eyes darting from one officer to another. 'I can assure you, the first thing we knew about Daniel was when he called after Mr Kevin Grant early this morning. Just look at the state of the lad. Do you think we would have kept him looking like that if he was with us?'

'Not at all, Mrs Dew, not at all. Not to worry, we'll get things sorted,' the captain then turned to one of his officers. 'Jonathan, go and check whether Daniel Palmer is on our passenger list. Come back immediately.'

'Yes Sir,' Jonathan left the crowded room. Although the suite was large, the lounge area felt crowded, in spite of there being one less person.

'You don't believe me, Captain Stewart?' Bronwen looked hard at him. 'That disappoints me; and indeed, hurts me. I, nor my companions, are liars.'

'But I must consider all possibilities,' the captain replied. 'I would ask you to consider my reputation as a captain of this vessel, should its security fail in any way. If it does, what could happen does not bare thinking about.'

'The captain is right, Bronwen,' Geraint intervened.

'Yes, of course,' Bronwen said. 'My mind is in turmoil as I think of how his parents and grandparents are suffering. Please let our local constabulary know as soon as possible that Daniel is safe and well.'

The captain's attention went back to Daniel. 'Daniel, laddie, will you explain to me how you came aboard The Gladiator on your own with no one to help or look after you?'

Daniel repeated the story of how he had hidden in the back of the Mercedes. He had jumped out when Stella's back was turned, and I ran up the gangplank of the ship when the men who were loading were in their lorry having something to eat. Then, he climbed across into one of the rescue boats before most of the passengers were on board and lay

132

low until evening time. He described how he managed to get something to eat and drink. But he became cold and frightened so decided to get to his Aunty Bronwen and the others.

'She's not my real aunty but my mam said she's like an aunty and she's a nice woman,' Daniel ended on the brink of tears again. 'I'm sorry I worried my mam. Can you get me back to my mam?' he asked the captain. 'You're the big boss, in you?'

'Of course, you'll get back to you mammy, laddie, but you must understand you have been bad, and you've broken the law. Do you know what that means?'

The captain's Scottish brogue became more pronounced. Bronwen thought he sounded a kind, understanding man. She also knew that he had a duty to find out how Daniel came aboard. How had a little boy managed to overcome the strict barriers?

'No, I don't,' Daniel answered. 'I won't go to jail, will I?'

The captain laughed. 'No, of course you won't; you're too young, but if you were a man, you might. Being a stowaway is not good.'

John Cross, the First Officer interrupted. 'Excuse me, sir. May I ask Daniel a question?'

'Go ahead but be tactful, Mr Cross.'

'Daniel, did anyone meet you when you got on board?' John asked.

Daniel paused, he looked confused. 'Not straight away. Not until those nice foreign men talked to me and gave me burgers and sausages.'

'Who helped you get from the life boat onto the deck? It's not easy to get across, I know.'

Daniel thought before he answered. 'Nobody. Nobody knew I was there.'

'But Mr Grant passed the boat where you were hiding. You said you called out to him.'

'Yes, I did. Kevin brought me to Aunty Bronwen,' Daniel became frightened. He was afraid he was giving the wrong answers.

'It sounds likely that Mr Grant knew you were hiding; and that was for two days until you were cold, and you told him you wanted your mother.'

John Cross was a short, lean man with a head which appeared too small for his highly embellished hat. Kevin crossed the room in two large strides. He grabbed First Officer John Cross by his neat uniform lapels, his tightly knotted naval tie and crisp white shirt collar. He lifted his feet off the ground and shook him as if her were a rag doll. John's feet did a wiggle as he struggled to keep them on the floor. His hat fell off.

As Kevin shook him he shouted. 'What are you suggesting, you little shit,' he pulled back a ham-sized fist to throw it hard into his face. 'Perhaps you'll ask straight questions of me when I've knocked your teeth out.'

Stella darted across the room and forced herself between the two men and held back Kevin's fist. 'Don't, Kevin. Please don't. You'll floor him. The runt is not worth the trouble you'd have.'

She saved John Cross having a pulverising blow but didn't stop his dentures being dislodged. His full set of top teeth projected and, luckily, dropped onto the soft carpet, so didn't break. Kevin dropped Mr Cross. He landed like a sack of sand on all fours. He crawled to reclaim his dentures, which had landed partly under Geraint's chair. He slipped them, surreptitiously, into his mouth.

The atmosphere in the room was tense as Stella attempted to cool Kevin's temper; a rare occurrence. It took a lot to rile gentle Kevin. Bronwen and Daniel were frightened by the turbulence in the room and clung to each other

At that moment Jonathan returned with the information about the passenger list. He knocked the door and walked in uninvited.

'No, sir. Daniel Palmer is not on the passenger list. But there is some disturbing information regarding the little boy. The Gwent police in South Wales are looking for him; scouring the area. He is a missing person causing much concern there. He's been missing since the 15th, the day we left Southampton. His missing has been announced in the local press and on local radio bulletins, but as yet the incident hasn't reached the national press.'

'Thank God for that. We must contact the lad's town constabulary to let them know he's safe and well, and to get news to his parents. Hopefully, we can get him home and settled before this affair can become more widely broadcast. We, or I, will have some difficult questions asked about this little lad being able to get aboard under the noses of our security checks. John, you find out the time of the next flight out of Vigo. I believe it's this evening; I hope I'm right.'

'And now you have established what we set out for you to do,' Bronwen said, with a touch of acidity in her tone, 'I'll be grateful if you leave us to make plans of our own. If Daniel is to be taken home this evening, he'll need to be washed, dressed and given some comfort and reassurance. He's had a most traumatic experience. He must be the first consideration. Then, Captain, I assure you we will do our utmost to prevent your unblemished reputation not to be tainted with something which was beyond your control.'

The captain rose from his seat, nodded and put on his high-status symbol hat. Was it Bronwen's imagination that he looked smaller and older?

'Thank you, Mrs Dew. I apologise for the unpleasantness, but there were questions that had to be asked and I must prepare you, there will be many more asked. With your permission, I'd like Daniel to take one of my officers to the place where he came aboard to verify it is the place, so that his words can be put on record. Then I will ask you to add your signature to verify it is a true statement. Would it be possible for you to accompany Daniel and my officer on this mission? I will return to my office and begin writing the report.'

Bronwen replied. 'I will, indeed, Captain. I would like to see for myself. If Daniel is to return to the U.K. this evening, it will have to be in the next three hours or so. In which case, Captain, I need a little time to see that Daniel is properly dressed and clean.' Bronwen then stressed, 'he hasn't washed or brushed his teeth for days.'

Geraint had passed small remarks from time to time and asked questions himself. He had another comment to make.

'Captain Stewart, as Mrs Dew's accountant, financial adviser and more importantly, her companion of many years, I would ask you to put your questions to me whenever possible. She is a compassionate, kind, wise and wealthy woman, but as you see she is physically handicapped and has been for over fifty years. That is enough to bear in this life. Also, questions to the others of my companions must be put to me so that they may enjoy the pleasure of your magnificent liner.'

The captain nodded. Thank you, sir. Then would you go with my officer, Daniel and Mrs Dew, say in about two hours? I will select one of our female officers; one who will see Daniel back to his parents. It will be a good thing for them to meet before the departure.'

'Yes, sir, I will. And now I will see you and your officer out,' Geraint shook the captain's hand and saw him and his First Officer, John Cross, out of the room. He didn't shake his hand.

When they left the room, Mary and the others began tucking into the trays that were brought for breakfast. The toast was cold, but the croissants, butter, cheese and cold meats were taken with relish by all but Bronwen. She had no appetite. Her mind was too full of what was to happen to Daniel.

'Stella,' she said, 'as soon as you, Mary and Kevin have had something to eat and drink, would you mind going ashore at this place, whatever it is, and get clothes for Daniel. I can't see them having all he needs at the shops here, but there will be shops on shore that will. You'll have to be quick though, otherwise he'll be in those rags when he shows the officer how he managed to hoodwink the lot of them and got ashore on his own.'

They all agreed with her and grinned as they chewed the late breakfast.

'I'm glad you didn't mention me going to Vigo with them, Bronwen,' Geraint said. 'I'm not interested in seeing the place, and from what I've heard from others who've been here before, Vigo isn't one of the best places. I'll save my energy for the other ports we'll be docking. At the minute I feel quite exhausted. This sort of excitement is too much for an old codger like me.'

'You use your age to suit any circumstance, Mr Lloyd-Davies,' Stella reminded him. 'You're too old for any event which you don't fancy and as fit as you ever were for those that appeal to you.'

'I don't blame him,' Kevin said. 'I'd be the same in his shoes.'

Daniel sat on the floor beside Bronwen asking her questions she couldn't answer. He wanted to know what was going to happen next because he'd been naughty.

'I don't know, my lovely, but I don't think you're going to get away scot free. I don't think any of us are. I'd give anything to know exactly what's going on at home. I'll ring Tom again this afternoon.'

Mary, Stella and Kevin were soon off the ship and on their way to the shopping centre of Vigo. The captain had given strict instructions not for Daniel to leave Bronwen's suite.

Mary, Kevin and Stella were back on board sooner than expected and they had managed to get suitable clothes for Daniel. The little boy brightened when he was given the new clothes Stella had chosen for him: fancy underwear, a bright yellow sweatshirt, jeans and a smart new jacket.

Mary bought herself a white tee shirt with the word Vigo written across its front in big red capital letters. Stella allowed it because it was large man's size, so it didn't cling to her oversize frame to exaggerate her flabby bulges.

Geraint and Bronwen used their mobility scooter to travel along a deck of the liner with Daniel and First Officer Christine Stone. Daniel liked her, and Bronwen felt satisfied that she would be the one to take Daniel home. They walked up and down the dockside, past all the gangplanks of the ship to find out which one Daniel boarded by. Christine took Daniel up each one and entered the ship for him to look around the entrance. They all looked the same to him and he couldn't say, for sure, which one it was.

Geraint began to get annoyed with Daniel. 'Daniel, surely you can remember where you got on the ship? Think boy, think. It's very important that we know.'

'I'm trying my best, honest, Mr Lloyd-Davies. They just look all the same. And I was so afraid of getting caught I didn't take a good look at things.' The little boy was agitated and the more he tried to find the entrance they were looking for the more confused he became. Christine decided the quest had to be abandoned; time was getting on and there was a deadline. She and Daniel would be flying back to the U.K. in a matter of hours.

It was now accepted there must be loopholes in the security system of boarding passengers but only someone as small and wilful as Daniel could possibly get through them. The fact that he had boarded, in spite of the rigorous eyes of the security team, meant an investigation would take place so that it couldn't happen again. It put the captain in an embarrassing and precarious position.

He was glad that Bronwen Dew, like himself, wanted the whole business settled and over with as quietly and quickly as possible. It was the intention of both to avoid interference by the police and the press as far as was possible. It was too late to avoid that back at home. Bronwen decided to find out what was happening when she telephoned Tom later on—when Daniel was on his way home with Christine Stone.

Bronwen ask for the name of Captain Stewart's immediate superior. She intended, with the help of Geraint, to write to him to explain her side of the event and to obviate any blame from Captain Stewart. She wished to point out her high regard for his professionalism.

Bronwen and her group went to the landing where Daniel was being taken by the hand of Christine, to the waiting taxi at the dockside. They were all down in the mouth.

'Stella and I will take you for a long ride in the Merc when we get home, Daniel. Your mam and dad as well, if they want to,' Kevin said.

Daniel pouted. 'Thank you, Kevin. I'm sorry I got you into trouble.'

'You didn't get anyone into trouble,' Bronwen lied as she put an envelope into the top pocket of his jacket. 'Be careful you don't lose that. It's a lot of money; some for you and the rest for your mam.'

Mary was crying. 'Pity you gorra go, Dan, but you'll like it on the aeroplane, won' you? Your mam will like your smashing new jacket.'

'We'll get another one for you when we're at home. It won't be long,' Geraint said as he ruffled Daniel's hair.

They waved him off and returned to their rooms. They were the only ones in the lift at the time. All the passengers were back on board and in their cabins having a short nap after their visit to Vigo. The ship was about to sail.

'Now that's all over,' Bronwen sighed with relief. 'Daniel is on his way home so we will continue with our lovely holiday. I'm now going to ring Tom to let Daniel's mother know he's on his way home, have a short snooze, then ask Stella to help me dress in my finery for a lovely dinner.'

The atmosphere became lively; Stella smiled. 'Right, Bronwen. I'll do that before tarting up myself up.'

'The dress is smart-casual tonight,' Mary said with a thrill in her tone. 'And there's a magician on in the theatre. I like seeing a magician.'

'A magician, is there?' Geraint repeated. 'I was going to have an early night, but shall we go to see him, Bronwen?'

Bronwen giggled. 'Yes, Geraint, but don't spoil it for me by telling me how his tricks are done.'

When Stella was taking a bath and Mary a shower, Bronwen telephoned Tom. She had difficulty controlling her impatience whilst the operator was clearing the lines to get through to him. Her anxiety to know what was going on at home regarding Daniel made it seem an age.

It was suppertime at the home; Bronwen hadn't reckoned on that. Tom wheeled himself from the table to speak to her with privacy. Not easy in the home, but the corridor was empty of residents during the mealtimes.

'Bronwen, I've been waiting for hours for you to call. Where's Daniel? Matron's phone hasn't stopped ringing.'

'He's fine, Tom. I haven't been able to ring you sooner; things have been pretty tense here, too. Daniel should be back with his family in a matter of hours. He's on the way to the airport now. The ship's captain arranged it and he's spoken to the police back there. I expect Geraint and I will have the third degree when we get back home.'

'Daniel's parents are fine. They don't blame you and he's going to get a tanned arse when he gets home. It's the police who will have the questions to ask. They're wanting to know for sure if Daniel actually did sneak off with you or if one of you arranged it. They must be daft. The Chronicle's article was headed by, "Eight-year-old boy lured away by his aunt's millions." Have you ever heard such rubbish? We're all laughing our heads off.'

Bronwen laughed at Tom's information but her gut churned; she was hurt. She didn't want Tom to know she was upset so she made no comment.

'Never mind, Tom. We'll cross that bridge when we come to it. Daniel's all right and I think he's learned a lesson. Tell Matron I'm sorry for all the bother. She has enough on her plate without us adding to it. But who in the world would have thought Daniel would do such a thing? Never did I think I'd have to be on the lookout for stowaways. If that is what being rich means, I don't want it.'

She heard Tom chuckle. 'Serves you right for being a big spender. But Bronwen, it's just a hiccough. Enjoy the rest of your cruise and give the others my best. I miss them, even Mr Lloyd-Davies. I miss you most of all. Ring off now or this phone call will cost you your fortune. And you can stop worrying about the Daniel Palmer business. Enjoy yourself, my lovely, life is too short not to.'

'Good night, Tom. Give my love to them all,' Bronwen had tear-filled eyes. She sensed some sadness in Tom's tone. Or was it her mood?

She didn't want Mary and Stella to see she was tearful. She told herself to pull herself together; they'd be away only for another twelve days not twelve years. It had been a bad day; a stressful day. Tomorrow would be back to normal.

Bronwen was right. The following morning, after breakfast, she and Geraint went about the liner discovering all sorts of interests. There were discussions and lectures available to attend before lunch; and after lunch, if they so wished.

Bronwen saw Geraint into his suite as they had to pass it before she got to hers. An official-looking envelope had been pushed under her door since they had left. She picked it up with her "grabber", a special instrument, which more often than not she carried with her for picking up things from the floor. She had discovered, the more she couldn't lean over to pick things up, the more they dropped.

Its envelope was addressed to her, from Captain Stewart. He thanked her for the immediate information of

Daniel turning up and for her understanding of his, rather stringent, attitude about the little boy stowing away. Daniel would arrive safely back to his home in Wales, which was the most important issue. He admitted that the event would cause difficulties for him but that was his problem, not hers. However, he warned her to expect an approach which might be offensive. There would be many questions the police would ask of her and her companions. It was a comfort to Bronwen to read the captain's words which indicated he didn't expect her daughter, Mary, to be bothered by formal questioning. This pleased Bronwen because Mary had a knack of saying the right things in such a way that made them seem wrong.

He closed the letter by saying that he felt honoured by meeting such a fine lady as herself, that she should endeavour to enjoy the remainder of the cruise and to ensure that the rest of her group did. He offered to make himself available should she wish to discuss the matter further, but if not, she wouldn't hear from himself or any of his team again unless it would be regarding something pleasant.

Except for a few unexpected experiences, she and the rest of them would enjoy the remainder of the tour more than expected. They discussed taking further cruises. Kevin, Mary and Stella continued to take in the sunshine and all the pleasures the liner offered.

During the evenings there was always plenty to amuse the younger people: dances, discos, gambling casinos and karaoke shows. Theatre and cinema for the older, and more genteel passengers.

The night following the stop at Vigo was a "formal" night. Everyone dressed up in their very best. Bronwen wore blouse and matching trousers which she had bought at the Gladiator's shops that morning and a neat pair of diamond earrings.

'Whoever would have thought I would have real diamonds,' Bronwen sighed as she put them into her neat earlobes. 'I hope Lewis is watching me. He always said I deserved diamonds.'

Geraint spoiled the thrill. 'I don't think they are real diamonds, dear. That really would make too big a hole in your fortune.'

The cream and silk, exquisitely designed outfit, she thought was far too expensive on the day she bought it. She had to be bullied into buying it. Stella was determined she would have it and Stella was skilfully persuasive.

'Don't be daft, Bronwen. If it cost ten times as much, you can afford it. You have money to spend. No pockets in shrouds, remember. You've told me and Mary often enough.' Stella won; Bronwen bought that and a number of other garments.

She had to agree she had used that saying often enough about there being no pockets in shrouds, but she intended to leave enough of her fortune for Mary. She'd mentioned this to Geraint, and he used words to her reassure her.

'Bronwen, you had twenty and a half millions of pounds. What you've spent so far has just skimmed the surface. Please, leave the possibility of overspending to me. I'll let you know soon enough, but I can't ever see it happening.'

'Thank you, Geraint. Whatever would I do without you?' Bronwen repeated words which she had put to him many times.

For dinner that night, Geraint was in his dress suit, frilled evening shirt, red bow tie and matching handkerchief.

'Mr Lloyd-Davies,' Mary gloated. 'You look smashing.'

'Thank you, Mary. You look very nice, too,' Geraint returned the compliment with the usual lack of expression but, obviously, appreciated.

Stella had chosen loose, flimsy material gowns for Mary, which not only tried to disguise her size but made her look almost pretty. Her hair had grown to its natural colour, shoulder length with a fringe above her eyebrows. It was the most suitable for her eyes and mouth, which were her best features.

Stella looked stunning in her plane, tailored black, subtly touched with lace and sequins which showed up her perfect figure. The neckline was low, but not too low. It allowed a teasing cleavage. She caught many a male admiring glances, including Kevin's.

'Don't you think that neckline is a bit low?' he frowned as he stared upon it. 'Can't you pull it up a bit?'

'If you look around you, you'll see I'm showing far less than a few others and from the lecherous look on your face you're enjoying them.' Stella knew that Kevin was jealous of the admiring glances she was having. She was pleased, because when he walked into the bar he caught many admiring glances.

Having been out of the mines for a short while and being out in the cool sunshine of the Mediterranean for a few days, his face took on a tan. His brown hair had lightened and the style of it, being bunched from his shoulders to the back of his collar, looked more elegant than Stella had anticipated, when she advised him to do it that way. In his expertly tailored, silk, evening suit, she thought he looked handsome. His hands had become softer. He no longer had to scrape his nails to get out the coal-dust until they were sore.

Stella stroked the back of them as they sat in The Treetops cocktail lounge waiting for their drinks. 'Well, you mightn't like the way I look but I think you look absolutely fabulous.'

Bronwen and Geraint, at the other side of the table looked at them and enjoyed what they saw. 'You both look like something on the fancy American shows we watch on the telly,' Bronwen said.

They had a most enjoyable evening. It was as if Daniel Palmer didn't exist. He wasn't mentioned, but each one of them couldn't help but think of him before they slept. Bronwen especially wondered where he was at that moment as she lay between fresh cotton sheets. She thought of what had happened during the day and what would be the repercussions when they got home. He must be almost there now. She thought by morning he would be in his parents' kitchen, warm and safe. Disappointed perhaps, at not having seen the apes of Gibraltar, but happy to be at home. He'd never forget his illicit experience on board the luxurious Gladiator. It wouldn't have happened if Aunty Bronwen hadn't won the lottery.

Chapter 16
The Apes of Gibraltar

When the liner docked at Gibraltar, Bronwen and Geraint didn't get to see the famous apes, as they had planned. Though there was a transport system from the main street to get to the spot, Bronwen and Geraint decided to stay in the town.

'Kevin is taking his video camera with him. We'll see the apes in comfort when we get home.' Bronwen justified her lack of enthusiasm by saying she would hold them up by being slow. There wasn't all that much time; they had to be back on the liner at the latest by six o'clock.

She wanted to do more shopping for presents for her friends at the home. It included six packs of two-hundred duty free cigarettes for Tom, some special perfume for Helen Phillips and others, before sitting at a café to wait for the other three. That suited Geraint; he had no special shopping to do but he did buy some expensive after-shave lotion for himself. He said it would last him a year since he needed to shave only twice a week now. Once a week when he was at the home.

Kevin and Stella knew the café to meet Bronwen and Geraint when they would return from The Rock, where the renowned untethered apes were allowed to romp among the tourists. Mary knew, too, but Stella wouldn't lose sight of her because she wouldn't remember which café it was.

The last thing Stella wanted was for Mary to get lost in the streets of Gibraltar. She did, however, lose sight of her when she rolled down a small embankment at the tourist area, to escape an ape which seemed to have taken an unusual liking to her.

Lillian and Geraint had a long wait. They had completed their shopping, had coffee and cakes, did more shopping, went back to the café and had lunch. It was a late lunch; they expected to see the others to have lunch with them. The wait was too long. They began to wonder what possibly could have happened. They were due back on board before six o'clock.

When the hands of Bronwen's wristwatch were moving past five o'clock, she and Geraint began to get worried. He persisted in telling Bronwen that they would be along at any minute; there was no need to worry.

Yet he had to use the restaurant's toilet a number of times. His prostate gland had sensed something was amiss.

'Come on, Bronwen' he said, 'we'd better make our way back to the liner. They'll know where we are, and they can move faster than we can on these things. He referred to the mobility scooters which were designed to go no more than eight miles an hour. Neither he nor Bronwen had had experience of them going at that rate. The only one who had gone faster on one, as far as they knew, was Mary. That was down the steep hill outside the home, which resulted in her breaking her arm.

'If you say so, then,' Bronwen replied, feeling none too sure about Geraint's decision. 'Trouble is, I'll need Kevin's help to get onto the shuttle bus.'

'There's bound to be someone there who will help,' Geraint said. 'I'll find someone. I wish I'd used my Zimmer today.'

'Do you think you would have managed to walk up and down this street the way we have on that old Zimmer frame. Of course, you wouldn't.' Bronwen was getting jittery. Geraint sensed it, so didn't argue.

'I suppose not,' he agreed reluctantly, as he began stuffing the shopping into the basket on the front of his scooter and down the side of him. 'Good thing I've not got much beef on my bones.'

Bronwen did the same but there were still a number of items she had to put between her legs. 'And a good thing I don't have any beef at all on my legs,' she said. Geraint was amused, as she meant him to be. They both laughed but didn't feel like laughing.

Just as they were about to set off down the street towards the bus terminal, they saw the three of them running up the street towards the café. Kevin was in the lead with his hand in Mary's pulling her as fast as her legs would carry her. Faster, in fact. She was shouting at him to slow down. Stella behind was pushing her.

Kevin's tee shirt was soaked with sweat and droplets fell from his forehead. Stella's cotton top was wet with perspiration. But Mary looked as if she had been mauled by a wild beast, which indeed, she had. Except that the beast was considered to be tame.

Her loose cotton blouse was torn, as was her multi-coloured flared skirt. She had a bruised lump on her forehead and a number of scratches on her face. She looked as if she hadn't had a bath for a week and she was in floods of tears.

'Mammy,' she wailed, 'I was nearly killed. A big ape attacked me. I rolled down the mountain and lost my handbag.'

'No time for explanations,' Kevin held up his hand to her. 'We have to hurry. We have to get to the liner quick or they'll be sailing without us.'

'Don't exaggerate, Kevin,' Stella gasped. 'It can fucking well go without us. I've just got to have a rest.'

'You can stop your foul words, Stella!' Geraint shouted. 'It disgusts me! People can hear. And you haven't got time for a rest. We have to move.'

Bronwen was shocked by the sight of Mary. 'Let them sit down for five minutes, Geraint. That should make no difference.'

'You sit then, for as long as you like. I'm off,' Geraint grabbed the starter of his scooter and went as fast as he could down the middle of the street. It was late, so there weren't many shoppers. Those that were, moved out of his way.

'Come on, Bronwen, let's go. We'll just move in the right direction and take our time until those three have caught their breath.'

When the shuttle bus was in sight, they put a spurt into their steps. Geraint was sitting on his scooter at the pavement beside the bus. He had pleaded with the driver to wait a while until Kevin and the three women arrived.

When the three arrived at the bus, Kevin carelessly snatched up Bronwen, took her onto it and transferred her to the nearest empty seat. Bronwen hadn't before known him to be rough with his handling of her. Stella folded her scooter with the presents still on its seat. Two dropped off. Mary glanced at them and wondered if they'd have to be left behind.

'Pick them up, you dozy lump,' Stella snapped. Mary did as she was told.

Geraint got onto the bus leaving his scooter for Kevin to fold and put into the luggage space. He ensured that all the presents stayed crunched in the scooter. He decided that if anything got broken, it was just too bad. After the experience with Mary and the apes, he was in no state of mind to humour anyone.

Nothing got broken. The duty-free spirits were in the baskets. The items being crushed on the scooters were beautiful lace blouses, collars and tableware.

'Why you have to buy things here because they're cheaper than at home beats me,' Geraint commented.

'As you've pointed out, Geraint,' Bronwen reminded him, 'we'll never get used to not looking at the price tags.'

They arrived at the dockside and aboard the liner with minutes to spare. The officers at the check-in welcomed them; they were relieved to see them.

The first thing Stella did when she got into her cabin was to fill a small basin from the drink's cupboard with ice from the freezer to make a compress for Mary's forehead. She took a wadded pad from her first-aid kit and put it onto the ice to cool, whilst Mary soaked her aching body in the bath. She said she ached all over, as Stella helped her into her bathrobe. The clothes she'd had on when among the apes were thrown into the waste bin. She lay on the settee in the lounge area of the suite holding the cold compress to the lump on her forehead, looking sorry for herself.

Kevin and Geraint showered and were relishing the comfort of their snug, now fitting, terry-towel bathrobes as they sat on the lush, lounge chairs with their feet up on the smartly upholstered footstools.

When they were all gathered in Bronwen's suite, having sorted out the purchases, they relaxed. Not until a tall, double-tiered trolley of a late tea had been delivered from room service did Bronwen and Geraint hear about Mary's narrow escape from the grasp of a big, persistent ape. Kevin, Stella nor Mary had eaten since breakfast so little talking took place until the first pangs of hunger were satisfied. Mary's took longer than the others and Stella couldn't be bothered to remind her of her restricted food intake.

Bronwen sat near Mary stroking a bruised arm and commiserating with her. Her, normally, pink cheeks had paled with shock.

'Now,' Bronwen asked, 'what happened?' Bronwen and Geraint listened to what happened to Mary among the apes on the Rock of Gibraltar.

Apparently, Mary and Stella were standing close together on The Rock for Kevin to get them into the background of the snaps he was taking. He aimed at getting as many apes in the frame as possible. It wasn't difficult because there seemed to be scores of them; all with the same faces and buttocks but different sizes, from sweet-looking tiny ones to big one; as big as Kevin.

Mary had screeched with laughter when she saw the apes approaching the tourists, jumping on their shoulders and taking things from their baskets. A handbag was taken from one lady. One of the men in charge of the apes had to rescue the bag and scold the ape with a loud slash from a fierce whip, until it ran away, looking angrily at its keeper.

Some elderly people were frightened and made their escape. Stella was glad Bronwen and Geraint had decided not to come.

Kevin had to cling tightly to his expensive camera after the first part of a reel was taken. One cheeky ape tried to take it from him. He put the camera into its case and slung it across his shoulder for safety.

The laughter dropped from Mary's face when one of the bigger apes seemed to take a liking to her. It ran towards her and began pawing and scratching at her feet and legs. Her multi-coloured cotton skirt reached the middle of her calves. The ape wasn't doing much harm at her feet, but she didn't like it.

Stella and Kevin were creased with laughter. 'Watch out, Mary, he seems to like you.' Kevin called out between fits of laughter—until one jumped onto his back. He pushed it off and hit out with his fist which the ape dodged. Kevin mumbled some strong language No one made out what he said except Stella.

'I'll tell Mr Lloyd-Davies what you said,' Stella laughed.

142

She kept her back against a low wall with her bag behind her. Her hands were free to fight off any ape which attacked her. She had on dark colours and it seemed the apes preferred the bright shades of Mary's skirt and blouse. The ape jumped onto her back and began pulling at her hair and clothes and, it seemed, trying to put his claw into her ear. She screamed but the ape held on. She tried walking away, but he still clung to her, having taken her handbag, which she had hit him with. He threw it into a clump of bushes on the embankment nearby. As he alighted from her back, he took a length of the cloth of her blouse with him, grabbed her skirt and dragged her to where he had thrown her handbag.

The laughter now had fallen from Stella's face. She was terrified of what was happening. It seemed to her that the ape was making sexual advances to Mary. She was glad of there being few people watching.

Most of the tourists were gathered around the keeper listening to his story about the apes of The Rock.

'Kevin!' she shouted, 'for God's sake get that fucking ape off her.'

Kevin tried to get the ape off Mary, angering him as he tried to pull Mary further away from Kevin. Mary was pulled towards the embankment and rolled down the incline, ending astride the bark of a tree which luckily stopped her tumbling further. On the way down her head hit a small rock embedded in the earth. Her, now, ragged skirt was around her head allowing a good view of her heavy thighs and frilly, blue knickers.

A few people who witnessed what was happening sniggered behind their hands at the sight of Mary's legs in the air and the sight of her thighs and fancy knickers.

Kevin trundled down the incline to help Mary, but the ape wouldn't let him near her. It wasn't as tall as Kevin but looked too fierce for Kevin to try to fight him off.

The keeper heard Mary's screams and Stella's shouts for help. He came running, the tourists following. They saw Mary, screaming for dear life and watched the keeper beat off the ape with his whip and helped Mary up onto her feet. She was a weeping, ragged wreck as she scrambled up the short incline, forgetting her bag.

By that time a second keeper arrived. He said something in a foreign language with an angry tone.

'Yes,' the other keeper said, 'that one will have to go.' He spoke English with a broad accent, looking at Kevin whom he assumed was in charge of the two women. 'Sorry, man. It 'appen often. One of our man, he gone. A lot of ape here for two, yes.'

'Yes,' Kevin agreed as he concentrated on Mary. 'She's in a state, Stella. What will Bronwen think of us? We should be looking after her.'

'You bring de lady wit' me,' the keeper said. 'She sit in cool room, have drink, rest a while. Maybe go to 'ospital,' His tone told Stella and Kevin that he hoped it wouldn't come to that. It didn't appeal to Mary either.

'I'm not goin' to no 'ospital,' she shouted with tears flowing down her sore cheeks. 'Stella, le's go down to find Mammy and Mr Lloyd-Davies. Le's go back to the ship.'

'All right, my lovely,' Stella placated. 'But do as the gentleman suggest. Let's go somewhere in the cool, have a drink and a short rest for you to recover. Then we'll go down.'

After a drink of tepid water and a tidying up from Stella, Mary stopped crying and lay down on the rough couch. She was in a state of shock; it took more time than they could spare. They were due back on board before six o'clock.

Kevin went looking for Mary's handbag. He was away for, what seemed a long time, and returned without it. He looked rough, too.

'I can't find it,' he held out his hands with hopelessness. 'It's nowhere to be seen. Either someone's picked it up and kept it, or the apes have chewed it to bits. It's gone and that's that.'

'Never mind,' Stella said, 'it's just a bag. We'd better get back, Kevin. Time's getting on. But I hope she didn't have her credit card and a lot of money in it.'

'No, I didn't 'ave my credit card in it,' Mary said. It sounded as if she were recovering a little. 'Mr Lloyd-Davies said it wouldn't be safe for me to 'ave it in case I lost it. There was money in it, though, but I can' remember 'ow much.'

'Never mind the money, my lovely, as long as you're all right? Are you ready for us to go now? We're very late. Your mother will be worried and Mr Lloyd-Davies's prostate will be playing up.'

By the time they were down in the main street of Gibraltar, Mary had recovered enough to run, but not fast enough. Bronwen had to push and Kevin pulled. When they arrived at the spot where they were to meet, Bronwen and Geraint looked horrified.

'My God, what's happened, now?' Bronwen gasped. 'She looks as if she's been mauled by a herd of apes.'

'Not quite,' Kevin replied, 'but you're on the right track. You know the story from there.'

Some hours later, Mary hadn't regained her rosy cheeks, but had her appetite. The repeated swabbing of iced packs Stella applied to the lump on her forehead was effective and the swelling had subsided. The bruising Stella noticed which was scattered about Mary's body would take longer. Cuts and bruises on her face and arms were much in evidence but a thick application of pan-stick make-up on her face would disguise them enough for Mary to dine at the restaurant that evening. Stella decided not to warn her that the following morning she would be aching in every muscle.

She'd have to be excused the treadmill at the gymnasium for a few days. She mentioned this to Bronwen.

'She'll get over that,' Bronwen said. 'I only hope the experience doesn't affect her emotionally. From what you and Kevin have told me, she was frightened half to death. It might take a long time for her to recover. However, she's seen the apes of The Rock and no doubt, come tomorrow we'll all laugh about it.'

'There's something else, Bronwen. She had money in her purse; no credit card, thank God, but she can't remember how much there was.'

'Not much more than two hundred pounds,' Bronwen volunteered.

'Oh, no,' Stella gasped. 'I didn't think it would be that much because she'd bought some expensive perfumes.'

'Stella, for goodness sake,' Bronwen jokingly slapped her wrist. 'It could have been two thousand, I couldn't give a toss. I am tempted to use a stronger word, but Geraint wouldn't like it.'

Their loud laughter reached Mary as she slept in the next compartment of the suite.

'Wha' you laughin' about?' she said as she ambled into the lounge.

'Nothing much, my lovely. It's now time we got dressed for dinner. Stella, go and knock on the door to make sure Kevin and Geraint are awake.'

Stella used the telephone in her room to ring the room next door to awaken the two men. She knew they would be fast asleep. Geraint awoke with a grunt, startled to wakefulness.

'Who the heck is this?' he grumbled at he picked up the receiver. Then, 'Stella, couldn't you just walk a few yards and knock at the door to tell us it's time to dress for dinner?'

Stella replied. 'The answer to that is, no. I'm in my bra and pants.'

It wasn't too long before the two men were knocking on Bronwen's door, freshly washed, shaved and raring to go. They decided, as usual, to go en masse to The Tree Tops for their cocktails before being summoned to the dining room.

Usually, they all went to the theatre after dinner. However, Bronwen and Geraint retired for the night whilst Kevin, Stella and Mary went on to the clubs and bars. The night entertainment was the best they had ever known.

Bronwen always used her scooter. Geraint was adamant about sticking to his Zimmer, unless they had to walk long distances. When back in his suite, he was sprightly enough to prepare himself for bed. The luxurious living made him more independent than he was at the home. Bronwen managed, as she always did, and was glad she was able to, however crippled her legs were.

The night of the unpleasant event on The Rock, Mary declined going around the entertainment halls with Kevin and Stella. She limped back to her suite. Bronwen noticed her wince with pain and knew she would be worse in the morning.

Normally, Bronwen would get help from Mary, as long as every step was explained to her. She would, at least, take Bronwen's clothes and hang them in the wardrobe. That night she didn't even pick up her own clothes from the back of the chair, or from the floor. She groaned as she fell into bed. Bronwen was left to her own devices.

Mary always needed a few prods to get out of bed. Bronwen guessed the following morning, especially, she wouldn't want to arise. She would have to be bullied to move about, painful though it be.

Bronwen hoisted herself from the mobility scooter onto her wheelchair. It was easier for getting about the room and for transferring on and off the toilet, back onto the wheelchair. Bronwen was adept at this procedure; she'd been doing it for most of her life.

She kicked off her shoes, undressed and went into the bathroom to wash her hands and face. She took out her dentures to soak them clean under the running water of the tap before putting them into their container to soak overnight.

She put on her nightclothes and was able to hoist herself onto the bed. Every evening the steward would have tidied up their suite and pulled back the sheets, so it was easier than usual. The gesture of him laying a single Continental chocolate on each of their pillows every night was appreciated. Bronwen didn't eat hers; she was still digesting her dinner, but Mary usually ate it and her own. However, she didn't the night she was suffering the after-effects of the ape's assault.

Stella enjoyed doing things for Bronwen. She was a good nurse but that wasn't why she did it. She loved Bronwen and the feeling was reciprocated.

Bronwen appreciated Stella's loving care but often declined unless absolutely necessary. She was young and beautiful and Bronwen preferred her to be out having fun. Stella took her responsibility of being carer to Bronwen and Geraint too seriously sometimes. Each evening she ensured their medication was on their bedside tables before they went out and emphasised that they were to be taken before they went to sleep. She would check, when she came in, that they had been taken, no matter how late. It was often in the small hours.

That would have been too late for Bronwen's peace of mind had she not know she was with Kevin. He wouldn't let her out of his sight. Bronwen laughed at one of Stella's recent remarks. 'He's like a bloody jailer. I can't go to have a pee without him watching me go in and out the lav.'

Kevin dearly loved Stella and Bronwen sensed that her feelings for him went deeper than merely friendship. The cruising holiday seemed to be bringing them closer together.

If only Mary could find someone, Bronwen thought. Perhaps when she had lost more weight and continued to wear her hair, make-up and clothes as Stella bullied her into doing, someone might come along who might want to spend his life with her. It seemed highly unlikely, but then, Bronwen thought, she had never expected anyone to fall in love with her. Yet Lewis had come along, and he did. She was in love with him before he declared his feelings for her and asked along her to marry him. They had had a wonderful life together. They had Mary, the gift from God, but the complications of her birth resulted in her not being bright and of normal intellect. They had concerns about her future.

When she left school, she could barely read, and writing was even more beyond her natural abilities. Nature had been cruel, but having won the lottery and becoming rich, by their standards, seemed to be part of the solution.

Bronwen looked across the room to where Mary was curled up fast asleep. She tried to be a good girl but, somehow, so much went wrong. The fact that the big ape went for Mary, when she was with Stella and Kevin on The Rock, was typical. If anything was to happen, it happened to Mary.

Bronwen sighed deeply before she fell asleep. She heard Stella come in and check that the medication had been taken, but she was too far in slumber to respond to her.

Chapter 17
A Foreign Police Station

The following day was at sea. After breakfast Stella and Mary usually went to the line-dancing class whilst the others enjoyed themselves watching until coffee time.

Stella caught on to the steps quickly and went swinging along without falling over her own feet too often. Mary had difficulty. She shuffled to the right instead of the left and visa-versa. She cha-cha-chaed to the front instead of to the back and visa-versa. Bronwen, Geraint and Kevin, watching in the audience were creased with laughter. However, before the holiday was over Mary had improved and was pleased with herself.

After the amusement of viewing the line-dancing, Geraint and Bronwen attended a discussion group whilst Mary, Kevin and Stella enjoyed the other forms of entertainments on board. Their enthusiasm and obvious joy told Bronwen they were having the time of their lives.

Mary didn't attend the line-dancers on the day after her tussle with the ape. She ached too much. She remained in bed until lunchtime. Stella thought she must have been aching badly to forgo the sumptuous breakfast that was laid on every morning.

Stella and Bronwen made her get up for lunch to take some exercise. They explained to her that she would seize up like an old car if she didn't encourage her joints to function normally. They had to disguise their shock when they saw how bruised Mary's body was. Stella hugged her to say how sorry she was. Mary winced and moved away. She could tolerate no one touching any part of her; not even her mother.

Geraint suggested she should see the ship's doctor, but she adamantly refused.

''E'll expec' me to take my cloves off,' she pouted, 'an' I don' wan' 'im to.' Mary's poor control of language became worse when she was upset. Stella and Bronwen continually corrected her and she was improving, but it wasn't apparent that day.

She recovered enough to go to dinner and enjoyed the condolences she received from other passengers. Bronwen and her group had become friendly with many. The holiday atmosphere was everywhere and the friendliness of everyone made the cruise all the more enjoyable.

Somehow, people found out about Mary's experience with the apes on The Rock. She was talked about. There must have been a number of people from The Gladiator on The Rock at the time. They hadn't been noticed by Mary, or Stella and Kevin. They were too busy rescuing her.

'God Almighty,' Stella muttered, 'the bloody gossip here is nearly as bad as at The Sunshine Mount.'

'Stella, keep a civil tongue in your head or we'll be talked about and it won't be nice talk, either.' Geraint stopped munching his fillet steak to chastise Stella.

'Sorry, Mr Lloyd-Davies.'

'No one heard her, Geraint,' Bronwen said as she winked at Stella. They both had to stifle their humour by turning their attention to the waiters who were serving them.

'Madam,' one startled waiter said to Mary. 'Your head. You fall down?'

'Yes,' Mary replied. She adored the handsome, brown waiters. They made her, as they did everyone, feel special. She didn't want them to know she had been ravaged by an ape. They had heard what had happened but were too polite to let Mary know. Anyway, the funny side of the story had worn thin and to them, it wasn't funny anymore.

The following morning, they looked out of their windows to find they were docked.

It was special for those who were fit and able to make a long journey in-land, to the city of Rome. There they could enter the Vatican and view the famous, world treasured chapel.

Bronwen and Geraint decided not to take the arranged tour because they had planned to make a special trip to Rome at a later date. They would spend more than one day there. It deserved more than a day. Mary didn't understand the value to the world of The Vatican, and she was still in too much pain to make a long journey to view something she knew nothing about. Stella and Kevin had heard Bronwen and Geraint discuss a possible visit to Rome in the future and they would go with them.

They simply viewed the shops and roadside cafes. They bought tee shirts which would advertise the fact that they had been there, but they spent most of the time in the cool shade at the cafes. Many passengers they knew did the same.

Mary spent a boring time reclining on deck with her mother and Mr Lloyd-Davies, going through, yet again, her girlie magazines and journals. Mary was apt to forget that she was beyond the age of magazines for the young. She was in her thirties and her behaviour and overweight frame made her seem younger. Resultantly, everyone treated her as being younger. But how much younger? That was a question for the individual. It was never answered, as far as anyone knew.

When the ship was in dock, the liner's shops, library and other places of entertainment on board were closed. So, except for the time she went with her mother and Geraint to the dining areas to take lunch, she mooched about. She got on Geraint's nerves. However, it allowed her time to overcome the pain of her injuries. When tired of her magazines, she took a Jacuzzi before going to Deck 5 to wait for Stella and Kevin to return on board.

The liner was quieter and more peaceful when most passengers took the opportunity of going ashore at the foreign ports. Bronwen and Geraint enjoyed it. It gave them time to discuss finance and the future—yet again—without interference. However, by the time everyone was due on board they had missed the lively company. So, either way, it didn't matter. They were having a lovely time. More than once, Geraint mentioned his Eleanor; how she would have enjoyed being there with him and Bronwen.

'And my Lewis would, too,' Bronwen added. 'He would have loved to travel.'

'Yes,' went on Geraint, 'from what you've told me, Lewis was the adventurous type, but didn't have the chance to spread his wings. Wasn't given it. You have, though. Where shall we go next, Bronwen? Rome?'

'I think we'll do a little settling down at home next,' she answered. 'Life there is going to feel strange, for a while.'

'Yes. Quite right. Anyway, let's get this trip over with first. So far, it's been grand, hasn't it? Accept for the little trouble with Daniel. And isn't it a wonderful way to spend your money?'

Excursion trips were arranged from the next port of call. Passengers would be taken on sightseeing tours, but a long time would be spent on a coach, and that didn't appeal to Bronwen and Geraint. His prostate wouldn't endure a long time away from a lavatory, so they all remained on the coast, enjoying the pleasant sunshine of the sea front. They sat at a boulevard for coffee before exploring the quaint narrow streets.

They met a number of fellow passengers of The Gladiator who stopped and chatted. Bronwen's party became well known on the ship and were known as the "Nice Odd Group". People tried to work out the relationship between them, but no one could. No one dared ask.

There were those who were veteran cruisers and enjoyed giving others the benefit of their experience:

'Keep your wallets out of sight, hang on tight to your handbags, check your change. When you buy something, don't pay the first price they ask. Haggle a bit and they'll drop the price.'

Bronwen admitted enjoying the camaraderie and believed the others of her group did, too, though wouldn't admit it.

'Why don't they mind their own fucking business,' Stella frowned, forgetting not to swear in front of Mr Lloyd-Davies.

'They must think we were born yesterday,' Kevin added.

'They're only being friendly and trying to be helpful,' Bronwen said

Mary couldn't resist the small tourist-trap shops. She didn't haggle and, no doubt, paid double the going price of items. She bought yet another tee shirt and a trinket to go on her dressing table at home. She was reminded by Stella that, as far as she knew, she didn't yet have a dressing table. Colin threw the one that was in her bedroom onto the rubbish skip and Stella hadn't had time to complete the ordering of the furniture for 22, Queen Street. When Bronwen and Geraint told her to get a new car, her time was taken up by that. Anyway, she wanted Mary with her when she chose the furniture; and Bronwen, as far as was possible.

They loitered over a fresh fish lunch at a smart restaurant in the town. At least, the menu offered fresh fish, caught that morning, but Bronwen could tell the texture of fresh fish before and after it was put into the pan. She, certainly, knew when it wasn't fresh. However, it was enjoyed with a bottle of white wine which was shared between four. Mary drank three cans of Coca-Cola. Stella wouldn't allow her a fourth.

'Mary, you're cutting down. Remember? You've at least another two stones to lose.'

Mary groaned at the thought of the long struggle but decided not to complain. 'Yes,' Stella, alright.'

For much of the cruise the itinerary included a day at sea before each port of call. That suited them well.

Between meals, Bronwen and Geraint liked to sit in the shade on deck, take the air, read their books and talk about the previous day ashore. Geraint kept Bronwen up to date with her financial affairs. More than once he told her that what she had spent to date didn't have a great deal of impact on the amount remaining.

'You'll be saying that when the coffers are empty, Geraint,' Bronwen chuckled. 'Don't worry, I won't mind as long as there's a bit left for Mary.'

As long as Geraint did the counting, she took little interest and would change the subject. The conversation usually ended with the same words from Geraint.

'It's a good thing you can trust me, Bronwen, but you must take an interest. I won't always be around, mind.'

'Don't be daft, Geraint. You're as fit as a flea except for your old prostate and that can be seen to, if it gets a real bother to you. I think you'll last longer than my money.'

They were glad Kevin took dozens of photographs; they would enjoy seeing them when they got home and showing them to their friends at The Home.

Whilst at sea, Bronwen and Geraint went to lectures or discussion groups when the subjects were of interest to them. At other times they wandered around seeing what Stella, Kevin and Mary were doing. It would be deck-quoits, swimming and sun-tanning, working out at the gymnasium or participating in the games and competitions that took place.

Bronwen hadn't before seen Mary enjoying herself so much. She was always poor at socialising, but there she was mixing with other friends and family groups.

She seemed to have lost some of her shyness and had gained confidence. If being rich would continue to help Mary live a normal and happy life, then being rich was good. Stella and Bronwen agreed that Mary could be left to herself. She became part of a group of people younger than herself. Because of her manner of speaking, her sense of humour and her general behaviour, they didn't realise she wasn't of their age group. She had the good luck of her chubby face making her look younger.

One of the ports of call was Calvi on the coast of Corsica. Bronwen and her group went ashore there. Not all ports accommodated as well as they would have liked for the disabled. This one was different, as the way of getting ashore was by shuttle-boat and they didn't want to miss the fun

That day the sea was choppy; there had been a storm during the night.

They went to Deck 5, where all passengers going ashore were accounted for.

When Bronwen saw how the shuttle boat rocked and moved away from the edge of the dock, she was about to change her mind. Even with Kevin to lift and carry her, and although with plenty of sailors to help, she remained apprehensive about getting onto the shuttle.

'Oh, Bronwen, what a pity,' Geraint said. 'Yes, I can see the danger, but never mind, I'll stay on board with you.'

'Shut up the pair of you,' Kevin interfered. 'We're all going ashore on that shuttle. Just leave it to me.'

He told Bronwen to take her scooter to the edge of the liner before he scooped her up in his arms and handed her across to a sailor almost as big as himself.

He was waiting with open arms on the shuttle. The pitching of the shuttle made the sailor stagger, but he laughed as he put Bronwen onto the nearest seat.

'She feels like feathers,' the sailor said with a strong accent.

A man, one of the passengers, moved quickly out of that seat so Bronwen could be gently put down on it. Kevin jumped on the shuttle with ease carrying Bronwen's scooter in his arms. A loud cheer came from the passengers on the shuttle boat.

It was almost as difficult for Geraint to step from the liner onto the shuttle but, at least, he had two functioning legs to rely on. He tottered and swayed and would have fallen, had not the big sailor grabbed him in time. Geraint's face was a picture of fear but when he landed safely, he laughed loudly. Bronwen couldn't remember Geraint laughing so heartily, and all those about him laughed.

Then it was Mary's turn. The big sailor's jolly smile dropped. It went through his mind that if he tried to catch her in his arms, they would both end up in the sea. He thought, this one must weigh more than a sack of coal.

'You go first, Stella,' Mary pushed Stella too far forward for her to change her mind. She leapt across from the liner onto the shuttle with ease. She stood at the edge of the shuttle facing Mary.

'Now come on,' Stella shouted. 'You won't fall. The platform is there to stop you.'

Mary was almost in tears with fear. Fear of Stella, fear of falling.

She was in luck. A swirl of the sea pushed the shuttle right up to the platform of the liner, so she stepped over with ease. She flopped with relief into the nearest available seat.

'Well done,' Bronwen praised. 'Well done. I knew you could do it.'

150

Stella sighed. 'Who'd think we were doing this for bloody pleasure. It reminds me of the pictures I've seen of The Battle of Dunkirk.'

The trip across to the main land was well worth the risk of getting on the shuttle. Bronwen, especially, loved the spray swishing high at the windows and the sea-swell breaking over the front of the boat. She was surprised by its size. When she looked about her to give waves to the people she knew, she was surprised to see that there must have been eighty people, at least.

Getting ashore didn't pose the difficulty it did getting onto the shuttle. Kevin was one of the first ashore because Bronwen was in a front seat with her mobility scooter beside her blocking the gangway. He unfolded the scooter and carried it ashore before carrying her and settling her on its seat.

'Thank you, Kevin,' Bronwen said. 'I hope I won't break your arms one day.'

'Like the man over there said,' Kevin reassured, 'you feel like a bag of feathers. A small one, at that,' Bronwen nodded her gratitude.

The five of them gathered together and decided, first, to find a café for coffee. As at the other places they'd docked at, the boulevard was quaint. Lots of pretty cafes, souvenir shops and stalls of locally made wares, enticed the tourists to dig deep into their pockets.

They came across one of many inviting-looking cafés with a table for five in the shade of a palm trees, overlooking the marina. There were hundreds of colourful yachts of all sizes moored there. Bronwen remarked on how smart and well cared for they appeared.

'That's something confined to the wealthy of the world,' Geraint remarked. 'Some of the owners of them have more than you have in the bank, Bronwen.'

'What a pity,' Bronwen replied, 'I was thinking of getting one to take home for the pond in the park.'

Geraint, Kevin and Stella laughed at Bronwen's cynicism, but not Mary.

'Wha' you laughin' at?' she asked.

'You mean, what are you laughing at,' Stella emphasised. 'Stop clipping the ends of your words.'

'I try not to,' Mary pouted, 'but I forget. What were you laughing at, then?'

'At your mother saying she'll take one of those boats home,' Kevin explained, as he pointed across the road to the beautiful yachts.

'How could she take one of them home?' Mary looked puzzled. 'We go' too many cases as it is.'

Her naivety brought on more laughter and she walked off in a huff.

'I'm going up here to buy a tee-shirt, Mammy,' she said, making her way up the pavement.

'You already have more than a dozen tee-shirts, Mary,' Bronwen remarked.

'Yes, but I'm makin' a collection of everywhere we go.'

'That's a good idea, 'Stella nodded, 'but watch you don't forget where we are and get lost, Mary. Especially if you go up one of the side streets. All these cafes look alike.'

''Course I won't forget and get lost,' Mary frowned.

Bronwen wished she wouldn't go but she didn't want to undermine Mary's growing confidence.

Mary got lost.

An hour later the four of them fidgeted in their seats, looking up and down the boulevard, hoping to see her walking towards them. They'd had several drinks to justify taking up a table; the headwaiter began to give them unwelcoming looks.

'We'll stay here and have an early lunch,' Geraint suggested. 'We daren't move because if she comes back and find us gone, she'll be frightened.'

'That's a good idea,' Bronwen nodded. She called the waiter across and asked for the lunch menu. His manner changed and gave Bronwen a big toothy smile.

'Your sister?' he asked. 'She come back?'

'She's not my sister, she's my daughter and we hope she comes back soon, or we'll assume she's lost.'

He understood only the words explaining Mary was not Bronwen's sister.

'My, my, Madam. You look too young. Yes, I get menu.'

'Smarmy bastard,' Stella muttered. Kevin gave her an elbow dig as he looked at Geraint, hoping he hadn't heard. He'd heard but could say nothing except give Stella a look of disgust.

'We're all getting a bit jittery,' Bronwen said. 'I know I am. After we've ordered, will you two, Kevin and Stella, go and have a look around to see if she's lost her way?'

'We'll both have fish and chips. You order for us,' Stella said as she and Kevin got up from their seats. Kevin went one way, Stella the other.

They had gone more than half an hour and arrived back together having met up at the bottom of the square near the front promenade. Their fish and chips had gone cold and the flies had feasted from them.

'Not a sign of her,' Stella clenched her fist and banged the table. 'I'll throttle her when she gets here.' She was clearly worried, and her manner made Bronwen more worried.

'We saw people from The Gladiator,' Kevin said. 'One group said they saw her passing about an hour ago but nothing since.'

'We'll have to go to the police station,' Geraint suggested, looking at Stella. 'But I'll do the talking. I'm apprehensive about what might come out of your indelicate mouth, young lady. You let yourself down, and us.'

'You'll do best to stay here with me, Mr Lloyd-Davies. Stella knows when she must conduct herself properly, don't you worry about that,' Bronwen said. Her anxiety was clearly increasing.

'Yes, I know that,' Geraint replied.

The waiter was giving them dirty looks again, making Geraint and Bronwen uncomfortable. Geraint wanted to use the toilet; the anxiety had affected his prostate gland problem, yet he was reluctant to ask the waiter for permission to use their facilities. But where else should he go?

'Don't worry about that squirt,' Kevin said. 'We've just spent a lot of money here—more than we should have, no doubt,' he whistled and beckoned the waiter across.

'We're going to be here for a while,' Kevin said slowly glaring at the man. 'We're waiting for someone. Is that all right by you?'

'Noooo,' the waiter replied. 'Busy lunch time. You finish, you go.'

Kevin arose from his chair, stood his full six feet five inches and stuck out his chest. He put his spade-size hand on the little man's shoulder with a force which pushed the man down, making him dwarfish beside Kevin. He grabbed the clothing of the waiter's shoulder and slowly pulled him up to his size again.

'You've got a nice little business going here,' Kevin said. 'Pity if it got smashed about a bit. Now, my friend and I,' he pointed to Stella, 'are going to the police station for help to find one of our party who's got lost. In the meantime, our two disabled friends here, are going to wait at your dirty table until we get back. Have you got that?'

The waiter's smooth, brown face became drained of colour and he shook as he shrugged back the clothes about his shoulder.

'But yes, of course,' he trembled. 'No problem, you stay, you welcome.'

'Right,' Kevin nodded, 'now you, or one of your minions, will take this elderly gentleman to your toilet. And make sure you're nice to him and the lady, Mrs Dew, until we get back. Got it? She'll be wanting to use your toilet, too. I hope they're clean enough for her.'

The headwaiter, who was obviously the owner of the café, bustled off toward the inside of the café and soon a youth came out to escort Geraint to the toilets. If Bronwen hadn't been so worried about Mary, she would have laughed.

Before Stella went off with Kevin to find the police station, she helped Bronwen to the toilet and used it herself. Bronwen then sat beside Geraint at the table, made herself comfortable and prepared herself to wait.

All sorts of things went through her mind of what could have happened to her daughter. Geraint put her thoughts into words. 'I hope she'd not been kidnapped, Bronwen. Word might have got around that you have money.'

'Don't be daft, Geraint. Who'd want to kidnap my Mary? She got lost and is now, most probably, waiting at the police station for one of us to get her,' Bronwen was clearly very anxious. Geraint regretted his words.

'Yes. She'll be all right. Kevin and Stella will find her—when they've found the police station. It might be miles away.'

Geraint was wrong. The police station wasn't far off. It was up a side street off the boulevard. There was a traffic warden strolling up and down the parked cars, licking his fingers of the pages of his parking-ticket book. He pointed Stella and Kevin in the right direction. He explained the way, too, but neither of them understood a word he said. However, they found the police station.

They pushed their way through shabby wooden swing-doors into a cold air-conditioned room and there was Mary sitting on a bench, trembling with fear. Two uniformed policemen hovered about her, speaking loudly in their own tongue with a spattering of English.

When she saw Stella and Kevin, she leapt at Stella with relief and hugged her, squeezing the breath out of her. Stella angrily pushed her off.

'Where the fucking hell did you get to?' she shouted.

Kevin hoped the English vocabulary of the policemen didn't include Stella's swear words.

'Some boys chased me,' Mary whaled. 'They tried to take my handbag, but I hit them with it, and they ran away. But I didn't notice where I ran to and then the policeman came, and the boys ran away. The policeman brought me here and I asked to be taken back to where the shuttle boat will pick us up, but they didn't understand. I couldn't remember the name of our ship.'

'You couldn't remember the name of our ship, you daft dollop?' Stella shouted. 'The Gladiator! The Gladiator! We've all been worried out of our minds.'

Kevin shrugged his shoulders and held out his hands in apologies for Stella's bad behaviour. He towered over both policemen who decided they wouldn't upset him; he looked very powerful.

'Ah, from Gladiator?' the policeman said. 'Why she not tell The Gladiator.'

Kevin had the understanding that the policemen would have taken Mary to the jetty had they known she had come off the liner. They took it that she was a tourist. They feared they'd have to keep her there for an indefinite period. Her whaling was irritating them.

'Eh, you woman,' the policeman addressed Mary. 'You go now.'

'Thank you, Officer,' Kevin said as he reached into his side pocket and took out his wallet. The two policemen looked at the wad of notes with beady eyes.

Kevin first handed out the value of ten pounds sterling. They smiled and would have been satisfied. He took out another ten pounds. They were delighted and took Kevin, Mary and Stella back in their duty car. They drove slowly up the boulevard, giving Stella and Kevin time to recognise the café where Bronwen and Geraint waited.

Mary leapt out of the car with unusual dexterity, ran to Bronwen and hugged her before going to Geraint and hugging him.

'I fought I'd never see you 'gain,' she sniffed.

Bronwen and Kevin shook hands with the policeman and they both mimed their appreciation.

Mary babbled to her mother about her frightening experience; about the awful gangster boys who tried to rob her, but she got away. Stella flopped onto a seat at the table and looked as if she was unable to move.

'I'm bloody knackered,' she muttered. 'Sorry Mr Lloyd-Davies. Good job you're here or this air would be blue, I can tell you.'

'Well I can tell you something,' Geraint snapped. 'You can get up from that chair and be prepared to be off. The last shuttle leaves in less than twenty minutes.'

'My God,' Bronwen panicked. 'It never ends. Open my scooter quick, Stella, and you Kevin get me onto the thing. Geraint, I said you should have come on your scooter, didn't I?'

'I'll carry your Zimmer for you, Mr Lloyd-Davies,' Mary volunteered. 'You'll be able to walk faster without that to carry.'

'Don't be silly, girl. I can walk faster with it. Why do you think I have it,' he snapped?'

'I don' know,' Mary wondered what she had said to upset him.

The last shuttle hadn't left but was about to. The officer in charge looked none too pleased as Bronwen and her party arrived at the jetty. He saw them hurrying when they were many yards away, but he swung his arm at them in a gesture to hurry them further.

'It's a good thing for you I have a good memory,' he said, 'otherwise you would have been left behind. What were you thinking of, leaving it as late as this?'

He directed his anger at Stella and Kevin.

'Don't look at us,' Stella replied. 'Look at her,' She pointed to Mary who looked at her feet with embarrassment. 'She went and got lost. We found her in the police station,' her voice was rising as was her temper.

Bronwen pushed herself nearer. 'We're so sorry, Officer,' she said in the gentle tone that was always Bronwen. 'We've had a harrowing time and were so afraid you wouldn't miss us and go.'

As always, her manner cooled the situation. 'No, Mrs Dew, we wouldn't have gone without you. It's just that The Gladiator has to leave on time, or we could be fined by the authorities. Come on now, let's get you aboard.'

There were two other couples on the shuttle boat. They looked worried. They wouldn't have minded the shuttle going without Bronwen and her group.

On stepping aboard, it was just minutes before the Tannoy announced departure.

'By golly,' Geraint remarked. 'We didn't leave it a minute too soon, either.'

There was relief on getting back to the comfort of the suites. There was time left to have a short rest before getting ready for the evening's meal and entertainment.

The dinner was as luscious and as beautifully presented as always but appreciated more; they were all hungry. Mary, Stella and Kevin hadn't eaten since breakfast. The waiters noticed the meal was taken with particular relish and had heard that they were late getting back because Mary had been lost. Second helpings to whoever wanted them were offered. Kevin accepted. Mary wasn't allowed to.

They all went to the theatre afterwards and laughed with the audience at a comedienne who told jokes that hadn't been told before. They listened to her beautiful singing of songs that were popular during the war. Songs of an era appreciated by the elderly.

As usual Stella, Kevin and Mary went to the "hot-spots" afterwards and Geraint and Bronwen went back to their suites. They sat for a while on their joint balcony, sipping a liqueur from the well-stocked bar.

'Well, Geraint,' Bronwen sighed. 'If this is what it means to have money, then I like it. Life is just beginning for you and me, you know.'

'Aye, Bronwen. You're right and it's been another stressful but interesting day.' He paused as he thought of how to describe the "interesting day", except for the hitch of Mary getting lost.

'Another restful day aboard tomorrow, Bronwen.' Geraint went on. 'Then Barcelona. Barcelona is a big place, so I'm told. If Mary gets lost there, it could be a week before we find her.'

Bronwen chuckled. 'She's learned her lesson. You're more likely to get lost than her.'

'What, me get lost!' Geraint was astounded. 'Geraint Lloyd-Davies get lost? That'll be the day.'

It was the day. Geraint got lost.

Chapter 18
Locked in the Lavatory

At Barcelona they all stayed together. Mary, especially, didn't budge from the side of her mother's scooter until she followed Stella into a baby-wear shop. They both loved looking at the tiny clothes and Stella bought a few items for Kevin's baby niece. He stood behind the two women, listened to the chat. He wouldn't admit to it, the little garments intrigued him, too.

'Stella, you've already bought a load for Cathie's baby. Remember, we didn't have any room to spare on the Merc when we came.' He saw her eager eyes on every baby dress she took from the hangers.

'Get on with you, Kevin. Look at them. How much room will these take?'

'The three you've got for three-month old and the six you've got for six-month old, not much. But you've got loads more. Wherever we go you buy something.'

'You'd better take us out of this shop, Kevin, or I'll buy a ton of things. They're so lovely.' Stella's face was aglow with delight. Kevin noticed it, as he had when she looked at other baby clothes. It saddened him. Stella would make a perfect mother.

Bronwen had been looking forward to going to Barcelona. It was the last port of call before returning to Southampton. She had seen pictures of it in the travel brochures. She had read its history and had been told by a number of people on board, who had been there before, that it was well worth a visit.

They all went up to the conservatory for a full breakfast. They had learned there was no telling what might happen before their next meal. Afterwards they went to their suites to prepare themselves for going ashore at Barcelona.

Cool, light clothing was worn to suit the sunny, pleasant weather. The climate was perfect; just like a warm spring day at home. Mary took a small case on wheels to carry hers and everyone else's shopping.

Geraint warned everyone to be aware of pickpockets and to keep a good hold of handbags. 'And for goodness sake,' he added, 'don't anyone get lost.'

He referred especially to Mary but didn't say so; he wouldn't hurt her feelings.

'I know you mean me, Mr Lloyd-Davies. Don' worry, I 'on't ge' lost again.'

'I won't get lost. Won't,' Bronwen emphasised. 'Stop clipping the ends of your words.'

'I di'n't know I did,' Mary replied, looking confused.

From the liner they were taken to the main thoroughfare by bus. It stopped outside a large supermarket, opposite an outstanding monument. The driver had to shout instructions above the noise of friendly banter.

'To return, you wait over there,' he pointed to the other side of the road where some Gladiator passengers were already sitting on a low wall waiting to return to the ship.

'They didn't stay long,' Kevin said, looking at the driver. 'We heard that Barcelona is well worth a visit.'

'Is nice city,' the driver replied. 'They come by early bus; eight o'clock. Very cool, then. Bus every two hour', last one five o'clock. You not miss 'im, eh.'

'They've only stayed a couple of hours,' Bronwen assumed. 'They most probably just came to say they'd been here. It's not eleven o'clock yet.'

'Just in time for coffee and doughnuts, before we go sightseeing. We'll get a taxi to that museum we were told about, shall we?' Geraint had had enough of looking at shops. 'I just must just get a few boxes of good cigars to take back. Someone told me there's a superb selection here.'

They crossed an impressive cobbled square before entering the main street. It was wide and a scene of life and colour. The wide pavements were taken up with tables and chairs spilling over from the cafes. In the middle of the road were rows of market stalls tended by gaily-clad people shouting their wares.

Bronwen was amazed by the many flower stalls. Mary couldn't resist loitering by the sparkling, dangling, bracelets, necklaces and earrings stalls. There were stalls selling wide, locally made skirts and gypsy styled blouses. The lengths of silks and lace caught Stella's eyes and there were a number of stalls selling baby clothes. She loitered there; Kevin had to drag her away, but not before she bought an expensive lace shawl.

'You can be pleased our leader has enough money to allow you to be a big spender, Stella. How are you going to thank her?'

'By being a bigger spender,' was the reply.' Stella justified the buying to Kevin. 'Cathy, your sister, will love it.'

'If it gets to her. How the hell we'll get everything in or on the car, God only knows. I certainly don't.'

Geraint loitered at a stall where original watercolour paintings were on view. They were authentic. The vendor spit on his finger and rubbed it across the picture of a dancing girl's skirt and the colour smudged.

'We'll buy some of those,' Bronwen said, 'but not the one he spat on. I would like some nice prints for the walls of 22, Queen Street.'

'Oh, yes,' Stella responded. 'You know, I hadn't thought that far of the setting up of the house. You choose three, then, and I'll choose three.'

Bronwen nodded. 'Yes, all right, but let's not be hasty. Choosing from all these is not going to be done in five minutes,' she then looked at Geraint. 'Shall we have a look around here, then have lunch before getting a taxi to the museum?' she asked. 'We'll still have plenty of time. We'll skip coffee and cakes and have an early lunch, shall we?'

Geraint agreed. He was as taken by the atmosphere of Barcelona as they all were. He thought the people most welcoming and many of the stall-keepers spoke enough English to hold a short conversation.

Kevin took dozens of photographs, always attempting to get everyone in the frame, as well as the surroundings; not always succeeding. He caught Stella buying a colourful tinkling mobile. Stella had to enlighten Kevin; he didn't recognise it as the sort that dangled over a baby's cradle.

She wore a white, full-skirted frock, down to the calves of her shapely legs and a wide brimmed straw hat. Kevin thought she looked prettier than the models on the fronts of the hundreds of magazines in the shops they had passed.

Bronwen wore the same sort of hat which matched her white, cotton, sleeveless blouse but with a light shawl about her shoulders that she moved to her lap, when the need arose, to ensure her legs were hidden.

Having missed the coffee and cakes at mid-day, Bronwen claimed "to be a bit peckish". Since the feeling was mutual it was decided to look for a restaurant as they moved further up the wide, cobbled boulevard. They found a bright, clean-looking pizzeria about half way up the square. The main road in the distance appeared to branch into two.

Bronwen was adventurous when it came to choosing menu items. She and Geraint had tasted a variety of foods on this holiday they hadn't heard of before. They had been surprised at the enjoyment. However, if either of the group didn't fancy what they saw being served at other tables, or what was particularly foreign to them, they stuck to "good old British fare". There weren't many places that didn't cater for the mundane taste of the British tourist.

They went inside the pizzeria rather than sit outside. It was cooler and away from the fumes of the street, which at times weren't all that sweet. Geraint suggested it was the result of old sewerage drains which needed replacing.

His prostate had led him to a number of different lavatories in the different places they had explored. He was about to have an experience of yet another one.

After enjoying the chosen pizzas, it was agreed any of them had ever tasted, followed a large variety of ice creams. Afterwards came the coffee, over which they lingered. Geraint didn't take coffee; he decided to go to the lavatory whilst the others lingered. It would avoid them waiting for him.

'It'll save time,' Geraint said, 'I'll be back by the time you've finished.'

'Hang on, Mr Lloyd-Davies.' Kevin wasn't interested in having coffee, either. He took a last sip of his beer. 'I need to go, too. We passed a gents on the way here. It was down there on the left,' he pointed. 'At the end of a side street. Not too far but you'd better use your scooter.'

Geraint was getting increasingly more dependent on his mobility scooter. Carrying his Zimmer-frame through crowded streets was cumbersome and he found people moved out of his way when on the scooter.

'Right-o,' he said.

'No good for you, Bronwen,' Kevin added. 'It's down some steep stone steps.'

'I can go when we get to the museum,' Bronwen replied 'We'll manage fine, Kevin. I expect Geraint will need to go again.'

Kevin stood close behind as Geraint waded through the crowd of locals and tourists, dodging in and out of each other on the crowded pavements. The toilets were further away than he expected.

They arrived at the top of a flight of steep stone steps which led down to the toilet area. Geraint had to park his scooter at the top of the steps. He looked with an expression of confusion and distaste when he recognised the sign on the wall. It indicated the conveniences were for the use of both sexes.

'This is used by women as well,' Kevin had seen the sign, too. 'Make sure you lock the lav door, Mr Lloyd-Davies. I don't expect there'll be men's urinals here.'

He was right. There were three toilets but no male urinals. There were sinks for hand-washing and a grubby towel on a roll for wiping them. They heard each other's bolt click when they locked themselves in.

Kevin was out of his toilet first. He spoke through a narrow slit at the top of the lavatory door where Geraint was. 'I'm not going to wash my hands here, Mr Lloyd-Davies. Stella and Bronwen have some antiseptic hand-wipes in their bags; I'll use one of them.'

'Right-o, Kevin. I'll do that, too. You go on, though, I'll be a few minutes yet.'

Geraint was always longer than others in the toilet. His prostate problem didn't allow a healthy flow of urine and he needed to ensure his bladder was empty before he left the toilet, or he'd be looking for one again after a short time.

He heard Kevin's steps fade away as he got to the top of the steps. Geraint hoped no women came in whilst he was using the toilet. He would have been embarrassed, should they happen to see him.

When he felt he'd relieved himself of enough urine to satisfy his prostate, he pressed the flush and turned to let himself out. He would be glad to be back up in the street; the toilet wasn't clean, and the smell was unpleasant.

He grabbed the metal knob and turned it to pull back the lock. It wouldn't budge. He thought he must be turning it the wrong way, so he turned it the opposite way. It didn't function. He turned it this way and that, pulled and pushed it, all to no avail.

'It's stuck good and proper,' he said to himself.

He tried to move the bolt many times; until his fingers became sore. He decided to give the knob one last try and if it didn't work, he'd wait for Kevin to come back for him. The knob came off in his hand.

'Well that's that and all about it,' he said to the four walls of the tiny room.'

As he was deciding not to mutter to himself again in case someone came in, heard him and thought him mad, he heard the trip-trap of female high-heeled shoes coming down the steps.

Two women gabbled to each other in their own language, but he got the gist of what they were talking about when he heard a loud sniff and a female voice.

'Pooh,' she said as she pushed the door behind which Geraint remained silent, except to shuffle his feet for the women to know someone was using that toilet.

He thought it strange that she tried his door when the others were ajar. They used the toilet each side of him and loudly relieved themselves. They continued conversing over him through a narrow slit at the top of each dividing partition. He noticed they didn't lock their doors; he didn't hear the click of the locks.

They didn't press the flushes, either, and walked out of the toilets without washing their hands. He guessed they must carry hand-wipes, as he knew Bronwen and Stella did. He was glad they were gone. He heard their footsteps fade as they got to the top of the steps.

He could faintly hear the sound of people passing to and forth at the top of the steps. For what seemed an age, no other person came down them. Actually, only about fifteen minutes had passed before he heard the heavy clump of a man's feet descend the steps. He was muttering gruff sounds with no meaning as he pushed the lavatory door, behind which Geraint was beginning to perspire and have the need to pass urine, yet again. He sat on the pedestal pan which didn't have a lid, as he was used to. He felt a need to sit; his legs had become unsteady.

The man, instead of entering one of the lavatories with the doors ajar, thumped on the one Geraint occupied and continued to voice annoyance in guttural tones.

Over the malodour of the toilets, a strong waft of alcohol reached Geraint through the slit at the top of the door. He wondered if it would be safe to call out for help from this man. He was obviously in his cups and more than just "tipsy".

Geraint began shuffling his feet on the floor to let the man know that the toilet was occupied. He shouted, 'I can't get out. The lock is broken. I need help!'

Geraint could sense the man pause and look about him. He'd heard the call for help, but in his drunken state he couldn't make out where it came from.

He mumbled something in a guttural language before entering one of the toilets next to Geraint. At that moment the man felt it more important to answer the call of nature than reply to Geraint's call for help—though he didn't recognise it as a call for help. He thought he was imagining another man's voice.

When the sounds and smells of the man emptying himself were over, Geraint called out again.

'Can someone let me out of here? Oeuvre la porte.' He and Eleanor had gone on a short holiday to Normandy, many years ago. He had brushed up on a few phrases of his

159

school days' French lessons. He remembered a few and used them, though having little hope that they were of any use now. They weren't of much help at the time.

The man heard and realised where the sound came from. He stood on the seat of the lavatory pan he'd used and peeked through the slit in the wall. He saw Geraint sitting on the lavatory seat.

The man gasped. 'Oh, lo sielento, Senior. Pardon, excuse,' he thought Geraint was shouting for peace and privacy whilst he used the lavatory.

Geraint shouter loudly, 'I can't get out! The lock is stuck!'

The man shouted his apologies for disturbing Geraint. 'Lo siento, Senior,' he fled, leaving Geraint in a state of despair.

'Where is Kevin?' he shouted and threw a punch at the door.

It wasn't too long before he heard loud voices at the top of the steps. Some lads seem to be loitering there, wondering whether they would use the toilets or not. They were boisterous and laughed loudly at their own youthful behaviour. At the top of his voice Geraint shouted for their help. He didn't care if they were a gang of hooligans; that's what they sounded like. All he wanted was for one of them to force open the door and release him from his imprisonment in the lavatory.

The hustle-bustle of gabbling people, and the sound of the traffic passing by, drowned out Geraint's cry for help.

The youths made a lot of noise and passed comment in their own language that he couldn't understand, or care about, before they scuffled away. It dawned on him that they might steal his mobility scooter. That they did.

With bravado, Geraint's scooter was driven down the street by one youth at a time, the others squabbling for their turn.

Geraint's frustration became profound. Claustrophobia and the stench of the toilet area were beginning to shatter his self-control. He lowered himself onto the lavatory seat again and waited for Kevin.

Bronwen and the others must be wondering what had happened to him. He'd been away for more than half an hour; it felt eternal. And they had, no doubt, expected him back on the heels of Kevin.

'Where on earth could he be until now?' Bronwen wondered. 'You say he told you to go on because he'd be a little while longer in the lavatory, Kevin?'

She knew Geraint was a private man. He was conscious of his prostate problem and tried to confine the inconvenience to himself. He had been told by the doctors that sometime in the future he might need an operation to relieve his discomfort. It seemed to her that the time had come. Geraint was eighty-one. How much future did the doctors think he had? She would speak to him about it. He wouldn't mind speaking to her. She and Geraint had no secrets from each other.

'Kevin, love, time's getting on. Would you mind going back to see what has happened to him.'

'Yes, Bronwen. I was just about to. Those toilets weren't all that you could expect; not a place to linger, anyway. I thought he might have gone back to get some more of them cigars.'

'Shall I come with you?' Stella said. 'He might have been taken bad.'

Kevin agreed, 'That's a thought. Yes, you better had.'

They left Bronwen and Mary sitting outside the restaurant at its roadside accommodation. The couple who ran the restaurant realised they were waiting for the old man and had no qualms about the table being used. The lunchtime busy period was over, and Geraint, who held the purse strings, had spent a hefty sum on their meal.

When Kevin and Stella arrived at the roadside toilets, Geraint's mobility scooter was not at the top of the steps where he'd left it. The thought that it had been stolen didn't cross their minds.

'He must have got a bit disorientated and went down to the left instead of coming up to us on the right,' Kevin surmised. 'We'll have to go down looking for him, Stella. You take this side of the road and I'll take the other. We'll meet where each side of the road opens up into the square, but for God's sake don't you get lost, will you?'

'Don't be daft, Kevin. Of course, I won't get lost. He couldn't have gone far, and he shouldn't be hard to spot on that scooter, should he? I haven't seen any others here, anyway.'

It took Stella and Kevin over half an hour to search the street before meeting in the square. Each expected the other to be with Mr Lloyd-Davies.

'Haven't you found him?' Stella sounded as if she were blaming Kevin.

'No. And it doesn't look as if you have, either.'

'I've been in and out of these shops like a bloody yo-yo,' Stella complained, 'and not a sign of him. He'll have more than a few dirty words said to him when he's found.'

'If he's found,' Kevin emphasised. 'When I asked people if they'd seen an old man on a scooter, they've looked at me as if I am mad. He could be dead in a gutter somewhere.'

'Oh, Kevin, don't say that. I'm frightened enough without you making things sound worse.'

Kevin sighed as he put his arm across her shoulders. 'No, all right, love. We'll just walk up your side of the street now, because that's where I left him, and hope he's back with Bronwen. If he's not, it's no good, we'll have to go to the police station; he might have collapsed somewhere.'

'Oh, God, I hope not,' Stella said. 'When I looked forward to coming on this cruise, I didn't expect to become familiar with the inside of a foreign police station. I hope he's all right. He's no youngster, although he thinks he gives the impression of being one.'

They arrived at the entrance to the narrow ally-way down which the public toilets were, where Mr Lloyd-Davies was last seen.

'Kevin, I'm bursting for a pee, what are these toilets like?'

'It depends on how desperate you are. You'd better go. I'll wait here at the top and keep my eyes peeled on the middle of the road. He might be at one of the stalls, though I doubt it; he wouldn't lead us on this goose chase deliberately.'

Stella's heels tip-tapped down the stone steps into the toilet area. She found the middle door shut and the two doors either side wide open. She guessed the closed door was in use and went into the end one, missing the one in which Mr Lloyd-Davies was trapped. He recognised them as being female steps but wouldn't have cared if she had three legs as long as she would use one to kick the lavatory door in.

Stella closed the door of the lavatory she chose to use but didn't click the lock. It was rusted, and she didn't trust it to unlock. She didn't like the look of the toilet seat, either. She decided not to sit on it but to squat whilst she relieved herself, irrespective of the position being hard on the legs.

When the tinkling sound of her urine into the pan stopped, she heard a whimpering coming from an adjacent toilet. She quickly pulled up her pants and her skirt down and paused to listen; it sounded ominous. She thought, perhaps, it would be a good idea, after all, to lock herself in and call out for Kevin. Her common sense overcame that thought; she had to get out. The whimpering continued.

Geraint didn't realise he was whimpering. In desperation he began talking to himself thinking the last toilet user had gone.

161

'God help me, God help me.'

Stella recognised his voice immediately. She screamed out, 'Mr Lloyd-Davies! Is that you?' A pregnant pause followed her shout.

'Yes, yes. It's me, Stella. Oh, thank you God, thank you.'

She pushed the locked door with her fingers. It didn't budge; she lunged into it with her shoulder. 'It's all right, Mr Lloyd-Davies. Try to keep calm, we'll get you out.'

She darted to the foot of the steps and called out at the top of her voice. 'Kevin, Kevin, come down here quick!'

She feared Mr Lloyd-Davies had had a stroke or a heart attack. She dreaded to think of the state he'd be in having been cooped up in that stinking toilet for nearly an hour. She stood on the seat of the pan in the next lavatory and peeped through the slit between the two thin divisions before speaking through it.

'Hold on, Mr Lloyd-Davies. You'll soon be out.'

'Stella,' he responded with faint words, barely audible. 'The lock broke.'

Kevin descended the steps in three strides. Something had happened to Stella?

'He's in there!' Stella pointed a finger on an outstretched arm. 'Mr Lloyd-Davies is in there, in a bad way.'

As Stella had, seconds before, Kevin pushed the door with his hand. It didn't budge. Kevin knelt on the floor on all fours and peered under the narrow slit at the bottom of the door and spoke through it.

'Don't panic, Geraint. I'll soon get this door open. Get as far back to the wall as you can. I'll have to break it in.' Kevin rose to his full height and told Stella to stand back.

He spat on his hands and rubbed them together as he poised to kick the door in. He did so at the level of the lock and a mighty crash resulted in the splintering of wood as the door broke away from its jamb. Kevin completed the opening with a pounding lunge with his tough shoulder.

For a few seconds Stella and Kevin stood in awe as they watched the old man cringing with his hands flat against the wall with a look of terror on his grey, parchment-like face, broken only by red-ringed orbs of eyes.

Stella went to him and helped him squeeze through the narrow space between the wall and the toilet pan before throwing her arms about him in a comforting embrace. He continued to whimper.

'Hush now, Mr Lloyd-Davies. You've had a terrible time. You're overcome by it, but you'll be all right. Let's get you back to Bronwen for her to know you're safe, and then we'll all get back to the ship.'

'Thank you, Kevin. I hope you didn't hurt yourself. The lock was rusty, and the knob came off.' Geraint's words were faint but audible; he was beginning to recover emotionally, but he could barely walk.

'Could happen to anyone,' Kevin replied. 'Try to pull yourself together. I'll carry you on my back to where Bronwen and Mary are waiting.'

'I'm too heavy for that, Kevin,' Geraint shook his head. 'I'll totter back somehow.'

'And that would take a week,' Stella said. 'I can assure you that Kevin has carried twice your weight on his back. And I can help support you from behind.'

'Can you manage with help to get on the third step here?' Kevin pointed.

Stella supported Geraint to the third step and turned his frail old body around until he faced Kevin's broad back.

'Come on, up you get. It's a long time since you had a piggy-back, but I don't expect you've forgotten.' Stella half guided, half lifted him, like a sack of potatoes, onto Kevin's back.

'Put your arms around my neck, Geraint, and try to relax,' Kevin said. 'You're not too heavy. In fact, there's hardly anything of you.' Kevin hoped to ease Geraint's guilt about being a burden. 'We'll soon get there. It's not far.'

When they got to the top of the steps, Geraint became more alert when he saw that his scooter was gone.

'Oh, dear,' he whaled. 'Those big boys have stolen my scooter.'

'That's what put us off the scent of finding you. When I saw your scooter had gone, I thought you'd gone off to get some more cigars and took a wrong turning.'

As they made their way up the street towards the café where Bronwen and Mary were waiting, a number of people stopped to gaze in wonderment at the threesome. Some smiled broadly, some laughed, some looked with surprise, wondering what they presented.

At the bottom of the street a number of people were dressed up in strange costumes. It was a show to entertain the tourists. A few had painted their bodies to represent fictitious characters. Some did somersaults, some sang and recited; all part of the attraction of the lovely city. It seemed as if people thought Stella, Kevin and Geraint were trying to draw the attention of the crowd. Kevin was embarrassed and hastened his steps.

By the time they reached the roadside table where Mary and Bronwen were waiting, Geraint had fallen asleep. Stella nudged his buttocks to alert him.

Mary leapt from her chair to help Stella lower Mr Lloyd Davies from Kevin's back onto the ground and guide him to a chair at the table. Mary embraced him tightly—too tightly as she burst into tears.

Stella nudged her off. 'Don't choke him now we've found him, Mary love.'

The creases of Bronwen's worried expression deepened when she saw the poor condition of Geraint. 'Dear God,' she gasped. 'He looks as if he's at death's door.'

'He would have gone through it if we hadn't found him when we did,' Stella told her. 'He was locked in that lavatory he and Kevin went to hours ago and we didn't look there because his scooter wasn't at the top of the steps, where he'd left it. Some thieving little bastards pinched it,' she looked at Geraint. 'Don't get at me for using language, Mr Lloyd-Davies, or it'll be directed at you.'

Geraint was past caring; he certainly was in no fit state to chastise her. 'Yes, I'm sorry, Bronwen. My scooter's gone but I can claim off the insurance,' he muttered. His speech was slurred and slow. 'Please see that this incident isn't talked about. I feel so ashamed. Make sure Mary doesn't forget herself and talk about it. She's apt to forget, isn't she?'

Bronwen looked hard at Mary. 'Did you hear that, Mary? Don't you dare talk to anyone about what happened to Mr Lloyd-Davies. If anyone asks, you say he took a poorly turn, which is not untrue. And Geraint, my lovely, come here to me and let me give you a hug and forget about the old scooter,' Bronwen beckoned him to where she sat. He had to bend a little to reach her arms and fell into them. They enfolded him, and she patted his back as she would have a child. 'You've had a terrible time, but you'll be all right once we get you back to the ship and get you in to bed.'

He slumped back onto a chair and listened to Stella. 'That's right,' she said. 'I'll give you one of your sedatives and you have a long sleep. No dining out for you tonight. You'll have something brought to your suite,' she turned to Kevin.

'Kevin, call a taxi to take him, me and Mary, to that bus stop where we got off, and another one for you and Bronwen. You'll have to see to Bronwen, and her scooter and I'd better stay with him,' she referred to Geraint who was near collapse. He was unaware that he had wet himself and no one mentioned it until Stella caught Kevin's eye. She pointed to his back. His shirt was stained with Geraint's urine from when he had carried him up the boulevard.

Bronwen noticed the communication and realised it was done discretely to avoid embarrassing Geraint any further. The taxi driver mightn't be discrete if he found Geraint had fouled the seat of his car, nor would the people on the shuttle bus, when they saw and smelled Geraint's wet trousers.

Bronwen had an idea to avoid the possibility of Geraint being embarrassed when he knew other people could see that he had wet himself. She knew he'd be horrified. She rummaged in her large, lightweight handbag and took out a white plastic mackintosh. It was tightly folded to take up a small space in a lady's bag. Stella carried a blue one and Mary a pink, in case it rained. Bronwen was pleased she had the white one, because it would look the least conspicuous on Geraint. It would protect the seat of the taxi, the bus and be out of the sights of others. She beckoned Stella to put it on him.

'Here, Mr Lloyd-Davies, put this over your clothes. You look a bit untidy after your ordeal and that's not like you. It'll keep your body heat in, too; you've had a shocking experience.' Bronwen thought Stella handled the situation perfectly.

Geraint's appearance in a plastic mac amused Mary. She grinned broadly and was about to giggle. Stella gave her a threatening look. 'You dare,' the look said.

Bronwen ordered Mary to gather all the bags together. 'Yes, Mammy,' Mary dithered as she busied herself doing what she was told. One bag fell and was unseen under the table.

Kevin responded to Stella's instruction to call a taxi. He stepped to the edge of the kerb, put two fingers to his mouth and whistled as he waved to an oncoming taxi.

A taxi appeared almost immediately. 'We want to go to the bus-stop beyond the square, where people from the big ships get on and off. Do you know where I mean?' Kevin hoped the taxi-driver would understand deliberately, slow-speaking English. He was in luck.

'Si, Senior,' the sweaty, scruffy taxi-man answered. 'I tek you.' The dilapidated state of the inside of his taxi reflected his appearance.

He waited whilst Stella and Mary helped Geraint into the back of the car. He looked him up and down quizzically and decided it was an old man's strange behaviour to wear a mackintosh when the sun was shining. Mary sat in the front, Geraint and Stella in the back. Stella held her arm across Geraint's shoulders and he leant against her. His red-rimmed eyes closed, and their eyelids blended with the parchment-grey of his face.

There was a long queue waiting for the shuttle-bus. Those standing in it recognised the crisis and ushered Stella, Mary and Geraint to the front. There they were able to get the most convenient seats. They supported him between them.

When they arrived at the pier, Stella let everyone get off before she and Mary helped Geraint off the bus. The security staff at the check-in recognised Geraint's plight and realised help was needed. One of the female officers took Mary's place in supporting Geraint; she was beginning to collapse under the burden. Stella stood up well to it, even though she had taken more of Geraint's ten stone weight.

'Nigel, get a wheelchair, quickly,' the female officer called out to one of the group of officers who was involved in the security check-in. Another officer produced a canvas, collapsible wheelchair on which Geraint flopped.

Another of the staff was designated the task of pushing the wheelchair to the suite. Stella assured him that she could manage; she was used to it. However, she was relieved.

When back in the comfort of the suite, Stella helped Geraint to undress and encouraged him to sit on a chair under the shower to wash off the grime of the Barcelona toilets. She held the container in which he soaked his dentures overnight under his chin.

He ejected them into a solution of Steredent before she put a glass of juice to his mouth. He guzzled it down. She prepared a second glass and put it on his bedside table.

'Try to drink that as well, Mr Lloyd-Davies. You must drink as much as you can until you've recovered from your awful time. Look, I've put that disposable urinal near to your hand. Matron Phillips pushed it into the back of the Merc before we left home, in case your prostate bothered you. She was right, wasn't she? It has come in useful.'

He had wanted simply to collapse onto his bed, but when the ablutions were over, and he was in bed, he was glad of Stella's ministering.

'Thank you, Stella. You have the right name; you are a bright star.'

'I'll remind you of that when you're telling me off for using naughty words.'

He recognised Stella's cynicism and smiled before sinking into sleep. He hadn't needed a sedative and he slept until the following morning; the penultimate of the cruise.

When Kevin arrived with Bronwen, her scooter and a few bags of shopping, Stella warned him to be quiet when he went to his suite not to awaken Geraint. They all decided not to call for tea in their rooms; it was too late. In a short time, they would be taking dinner in the main dining room, so they each decided to rest before preparing for the feast.

The outcome was that Bronwen and Mary decided to rest a while longer and miss dinner. They decided to call room service to prepare a snack supper. Bronwen wanted to stay near Geraint and check up on him from time to time in case he awakened.

Only Kevin and Stella went forth to enjoy the evening meal in the magnificent dining room. They, firstly, went to their favourite bar at the stern of the ship, where an enormous glass-domed roof allowed a panorama of the Mediterranean Sea, shimmering in the moonlight; calm and flat as a millpond. The stars twinkling above, looked near enough to be plucked from the black velvet sky.

The moment they settled at a window seat a smart, sleek, uniformed steward, smilingly appeared with a silver tray asking their orders for aperitifs. Stella ordered her favourite, pina colada. Kevin, as usual, ordered a beer.

'And some nibbles, Madam?' the handsome, young, Indian steward asked, looking at Stella.

'Yes, please, Ajay,' Stella replied, addressing him by his name; which pleased him. He brought a small dish of unrecognisable bits to chew on whilst sipping before-dinner cocktails.

The staff of the ship became familiar with the "odd group". Bronwen and her party were well liked for their friendliness and gratitude.

'Where are your...?' He pointed to the empty seats. 'I hope nothing wrong.'

'We went ashore,' Stella replied, 'and Mr Lloyd-Davies took a poorly turn. Mary and Mrs Dew are staying with him and eating in their suite tonight. We are all quite tired.'

'Ah, yes, Barcelona very busy. Make you wear out.' He walked away with elegance. Kevin and Stella were amused at Ajay's description of being worn out, but smiled at each other when Ajay's back was towards them.

'You look so pretty, Stella,' Kevin said when they were alone. 'Even after such a hectic day you look as fresh as a daisy.'

She was dressed casually in a blue silk blouse and black, loose-fitting crepe-de-chine trousers.

She smiled; her even white teeth gleamed against the healthy tan of her flawless skin and her wide, brown eyes sparkled bright, as they always did. She had paid little attention to her hair after washing that evening, so her unruly curls bounced about her face and shoulders in the natural way, which Kevin preferred.

'Thanks, Kevin. I don't feel like it, but once I've had my pina colada I'll be fine. I expect a beer will do the same for you. You look rather dashing yourself and your day was just as hectic. I don't know what we would do without you.'

'You'd do quite well without me, unfortunately, and I want to talk to you about that.' He looked serious.

'That sounds ominous,' she said. 'You've enjoyed the cruise, haven't you? You don't want to leave us, do you?'0

'The cruise is terrific,' he replied. 'I've never enjoyed myself so much and, no, I don't want to opt out until I feel I'm not needed. It's about you I want to talk.'

'Oh. And what might that be?' Stella's eyes widened in expectation.

Kevin went on. 'I've watched you closely when you were shopping. At every place we've stopped you've bought hardly anything for yourself; all for someone else. Especially baby clothes. I've watched the look of delight on you as you handled the tiny clothes; the thrill you obviously get buying a pile of baby clothes for my sister's baby, your friend's baby and God knows who else's baby. Stella, love, you should have babies of your own. I know your age; it's thirty-five, you have time to have ten babies, if you hurry.'

'Hell fire, Kevin, I wouldn't want ten.' She paused and looked blissfully up at the stars. 'Yes, I would like babies of my own. But there, I can't and that's that. I wanted one with Steven, but it wasn't to be. Good thing, as it turned out.'

'Has it ever occurred to you that it might have been Steven's ability to produce was at fault? From what I know of you, you were born to be a mother and you'd make a great one. I think I'd make a great father, too. Is there need to tell you I love you? You're stubborn, you're bossy, you swear like a trooper, but you're the nicest, kindest, most unselfish, caring woman I know.'

'You make...' Stella tried to interrupt.

'Just you shush for a minute or two and let me have my say,' Kevin insisted. 'I love you, always have, always will, whatever happens. I want to marry you and have a family with you. And here I am shooting of my mouth without a drop of booze inside me.' He looked up at Ajay, who had arrived with the drinks and began setting them on the table. Kevin paused before thanking him and turning to face Stella again. He allowed her to speak. 'Now then, what was it you were about to say?'

'I was about to say, you make me sound as perfect as Bronwen and I'm not. It may be that we've been close friends for so many years, a bit of her good nature has rubbed off on me, but only a little bit.'

'That's rubbish. Bronwen loves you because you are what you are. And you know, I have a lot to thank Bronwen for. It's not only for getting me out of the mines and giving me this marvellous bit of life, but because she's given me the opportunity to be near you. Think of it, Stella. For all the years we have known each other we've not been together for more than a couple of hours at a time. Being with you every day hasn't made me fed up with you but has made me more determined to have you till death do us part; if you see what I mean.'

'Yes, I see what you mean, Kevin. You are asking me to marry you again. Well, I feel it wouldn't be fair to you to say "yes". You're four years younger than I am and from the way I've watched others ogling you, it wouldn't take you long to find a young, lovely girl who would marry you and be more deserving of you. I can't say I love you, but I can say my life would be empty without you. I've come to rely on you and you're a saint to put up with me because I'm all those bad things you just listed.'

'Now what would a young girl want with a great hulk like me? You're the only one who's tall enough to reach above my shoulders and that's when you're wearing your three-inch heels. And as for being lovely, in my eyes there's no one lovelier than you.'

Stella's lips pursed in a smile. 'I know I call you a great ox sometimes, but the truth is, I admire your size and strength and I know you are gentle and kind. Tolerant too. I don't want to lose you, but I've always… I've always prepared myself for the fact that one day you would find someone worthy of you.'

'Never,' he shook his head. 'I don't expect you to make up your mind to anything until this cruise is over, but when we are back to normal, I will ask you again.'

'We'll never be back to normal, Kevin I, at least will stay and look after Bronwen and Geraint. Our life-style has already changed and I foresee it changing more. It's true what they say about money changing lives, isn't it?'

'I wouldn't expect you to stop caring for Bronwen, and Mary needs you, too. That wouldn't stop us tying the knot. In fact, I think Bronwen, and indeed, Geraint, would give us their blessing.'

'Well, all right,' Stella agreed, 'let things stay as they are until we get back home. For now, let's make the best of the end of this lovely holiday. Your beer is getting warm and in a few minutes we'll hear the call for dinner.'

Stella took a long sip of her pina colada and sighed with pleasure.

They enjoyed the rest of the evening. After dinner they strolled on deck in the moonlight. They kissed goodnight outside their suites. Stella liked it and thought hard about Kevin's proposal before she fell asleep. She decided to discuss matters with Bronwen when they were back home.

The dress was informal on the last night aboard because most of the packing had to be done during that day. The suitcases and grips were put outside the doors of their suites to be taken away around midnight.

The show in the theatre was again in the style of the old-time music hall.

Bronwen was sorry Geraint was unable to attend. He'd been looking forward to that particular show.

By lunch time the following day he had shown signs of recovery. He wasn't as bright as a button, as Bronwen told him, but certainly heading back to normal. She suggested that he try to forget his awful experience and certainly forget about the lost scooter.

'You are being patronising, Bronwen. Of course, I'd like to forget that frightful and embarrassing event. But I don't think I will.'

'Sorry, Geraint. You know I wouldn't say anything to offend you. 'But you still have your Zimmer.' Bronwen continued to be patronising. Geraint felt too weak to chastise. It was easier to let her go on. 'If the truth be told, you'd say you're happier with that. Anyway, there's not much walking to do between now and getting back to The Sunshine Mount Nursing Home.'

'Yes,' Mary pouted. 'Wish we had more days here. It's so nice. I love cruising, Mammy. Will we come again?'

'More than likely,' her mother replied, 'but we must get ourselves settled in our new Queen Street house first.'

Stella reminded them. 'We'll have the police on our backs to sort out that business with Daniel before we do anything else.'

'I'll deal with that,' Bronwen emphasised. 'I want not one of you to worry about it. Nothing is new, otherwise I would have heard from Tom. Funny thing, though, I haven't heard from him for three days. He started off answering my calls to him every day, but his phone has been switched off lately. He's worn it out, I expect. That does happen sometimes, so I've been told.'

Stella sensed that Bronwen was finding excuses to justify not being in touch with home through Tom, but she said nothing. If something had gone wrong, they would soon know.

'And that won't be long now. I wonder if all millionaires experience the same sort of life as we have, since I became one of them.'

Chapter 19
Going Home

On the last day aboard pandemonium reigned in the two suites—packing time. Kevin reminded them that getting all the luggage onto and into the big Mercedes would be a tighter squeeze than when they left home. Now there was more luggage.

'It's going to be like trying to put a pint into a half-pint pot.' Kevin moaned the usual cliché. 'God knows how we're going to do it.'

'You'll manage, love. We have every confidence in you,' Stella encouraged. 'Anyway, you can't complain too much because you've got an extra case yourself,' she was being facetious, but she was right. He'd bought gifts for close family and a couple of friends and more shirts and slacks for himself.

He scoffed. 'It's less than half the size of the one you've got. And you, Mary, could do with Pickford's removal van.' His remark amused everyone but not Mary.

The atmosphere was one of togetherness and companionship. Bronwen felt happiness surge within her and she was excited about going home. She felt as if she'd been away a long time, not just seventeen days.

Winning the lottery and making her rich had changed her life in ways far greater than she expected. Although her nearest and dearest wouldn't admit it, it seemed to be changing them. She intended, as far as she could, to ensure that it would always be for the best. It didn't occur to her that her well-meaning intentions could go asunder.

Stella helped Mary to sort out the garments she wished to keep and those that she agreed could be left behind. There was plenty of it because her things included two suitcases of clothes Stella had insisted went into the storeroom on the first day aboard.

'What a waste? Mary, my girl, you've been spending for the sake of spending. Your days of being in want are over but you will need to be more selective.'

'Yes, Mammy,' Mary replied with a sniff. She was about to cry on seeing some of her lovely clothes being left behind.

'Don't let it worry you too much, love.' Stella felt cruel, having bullied Mary to abandon a pile of clothes at the beginning of the holiday. 'They will go to the lovely people who have looked after us.'

'Yes, that's right, my lovely,' Bronwen reassured. 'I'm glad you're leaving them. I'm going to leave some things, too.'

She managed to do most of her own packing. The room was big enough to manoeuvre her wheelchair from wardrobes and drawers to the suitcases, which Stella had placed on the bed. She knew exactly what she had and what went where. Mary had forgotten much of what she had and didn't know where to start.

Bronwen shouted out instructions to her but it was Stella who did her packing. It seemed to be the expected thing for Stella to guide and supervise Mary. Her manner of speaking had improved as a result of her mother's and Stella's constant badgering. Her hair, make-up and dress always looked right with Stella's advice and Bronwen's scrutiny. Since the beginning of the cruise, even her self-confidence had improved when in company.

However, she was approaching her thirty-second birthday with the ability of an immature teenager. She was loving and sensitive and accepted insulting criticism from others without repartee. Those close to her knew that her many shortcomings and weaknesses were no fault of her own. They took responsibility for helping and protecting her.

Kevin helped Mr Lloyd-Davies as much as he was allowed. The old man liked to be independent and do all for himself but his suitcases, too, were heavier than they were when starting from home. He had attached the official labels to his and Kevin's cases. Kevin carried them out into the corridor to be picked up at around midnight and taken to the dockside at Southampton.

Bronwen, Mary and Stella, too, had Kevin to carry their suitcases out of their suite to be picked up from the corridor. Mr Lloyd-Davies had attached all their labels and checked them several times. He insisted on being in charge of all the administration.

The next time they saw their luggage was when porters appeared pushing their cases on trolleys through the massive departure area where thousands of cases awaited to be claimed by their owners.

Geraint counted the pieces of luggage and checked the labels again. Being first-class passengers, Bronwen and her company were among the first to be taken ashore. As always, having priority treatment made Bronwen feel guilty. It didn't seem right to be put before parents with children and others who were expected to wait for, maybe hours, before getting off the liner. To appease her conscience, she generously tipped the porters who attended and helped to stack their luggage on and into the Mercedes.

The grand silver car was waiting outside the departure hall. A man had driven it from the P & O dock car park. He, also, helped with the luggage.

After much putting on and taking off, of trying the cases one way and another they were finally ready to begin their journey home.

It wasn't a comfortable journey. Bronwen, with a cushioned lap, held a small, light case. As did Geraint, plus his weighty briefcase. Mary had a big case on her knees. She could barely move her head from side to side. She knew she daren't complain because so much of the luggage was hers. There was a case under her feet, too. Stella in the passenger seat had a case under her feet and on her lap.

'You'll have to drive all the way, Kevin,' Stella said. 'I can never get out from under this to do a bit of the driving and you're too big to have it on your lap and under your feet.'

'Don't worry, love, I'm quite happy to stay in this seat. From what I can see, I'm the most comfortable.'

He laughed. 'I wish I had the camera handy to take a picture of us all. Anyway, we'll have to call at a couple of motorway café places for Mr Lloyd-Davies to use the toilet—and the rest of us, if it comes to that. We can't go all the way home without a couple of stops.'

Stella groaned. 'How right you are. I feel I want to go now.'

'And me,' Mary called out from behind the case. Her hearing was acute enough to hear all that was being said in the front seats. As was Bronwen's.

'Well, you'll have to hang on,' she told Mary. 'With all that on you, you might have to wait until we get home and the unloading is done.'

By the time the car drew up outside The Sunshine Mount Nursing home, all except Kevin were inert with stiffness. However, the warm, welcome home from the staff and able-bodied residents soon made the discomfort of the journey forgotten. Even those very elderly residents, who had forgotten the recent events of Bronwen's good fortune and what followed, had been wheeled to the windows by their carers to watch the homecoming. The carers themselves wanted to see the smart car arrive and to wave to Bronwen and her companions.

A rough banner above the main door waved in the sharp breeze. It said, "Welcome Home" written with red paint. Bronwen was touched.

The carers greeted Stella as warmly as if she'd been on an altruistic mission.

'What was it like, Stella?' Megan asked, with excitement in her tone. 'Did you buy anything?'

'As much as I could carry,' Stella said. 'A load of fags for the smokers.'

'Great,' one of the smokers said. 'What were the fellas like, Stella? Did you meet anyone smashing?'

'There were plenty that would have interested you, Megan, but none good enough for me.'

There was plenty of repartee until Kevin called Stella to give him a hand. He didn't care for the carers to be asking Stella questions about other men.

The weather was early spring-like; sunny but with a bite of chill in the air. It was fine enough for a couple of residents in wheelchairs to be outside. There was a couple able to stand on their own two feet and a couple supporting themselves with their Zimmer frames. Tilley stood with her tripod walking-aid and a carer to help support her. Brynly was there in his wheelchair—but no Tom Daly beside him.

Matron Phillips was in the background, standing on the threshold. She waved to Bronwen, but she wasn't smiling. Matron Phillips always smiled. Why not now? Bronwen noticed that Brynly and Tilley were waving but not smiling. A shudder went through Bronwen. Where was Tom?

As Mr Lloyd-Davies shook hands with his old friends as if he'd been away on an expedition, rather than a luxury holiday, Bronwen hugged her friends. Kevin, Stella and Mary got on with taking the cases from the car. It was a puzzle sorting out which were Bronwen's and Geraint's to go into the home. What was left was Stella's and Mary's to go to Stella's house and Kevin's to his own home. Inevitably he got it wrong and the situation became flustered. It didn't matter; things could be sorted out the following day. He drove off with the two girls.

The welcome group broke up with the residents and staff returning to their places inside. It was near teatime and the usual quietude returned. Geraint had disappeared to the toilet and Matron Phillips beckoned Bronwen into her office. Bronwen, in her wheelchair, had deliberately loitered behind.

Matron Helen Phillips closed her office door before taking the seat behind her desk. She had a sad look in her wide, brown eyes. Bronwen expected bad news. The thought of police involvement regarding young Daniel's escapade crossed her mind, but it was worse.

'Tom Daly is in Martha Tate's bed, Bronwen,' Helen said. The expensive bed Bronwen had bought for Martha Tate's comfort in her last days had become known as the bed of the terminally ill.

The significance of her remark took seconds to accommodate in Bronwen's mind and grasp her heart. 'What are you telling me? You're telling me he's going to soon die, Helen?'

'Only God knows exactly when,' Helen replied, 'but he is very poorly. I think he's been hanging on until you got here.'

'I knew something was wrong,' Bronwen said. 'He wasn't responding to my phone calls.'

171

'He was too weak. He had a stroke a week ago. Two days later he had a massive heart attack. One of his leg-stumps is highly infected and not responding to treatment. He adamantly refused to be admitted to the hospital and we had to respect that. He lapses in and out of consciousness. As I said, I think he's waiting for you.'

Bronwen wept into her hands. 'We've been friends for sixty years. I'll miss him.' Bronwen clicked off the brake of her wheelchair and made to leave the office. 'May I see him now?'

'Of course. I'll come with you if you like, but I think he'll want to see you on your own. One of our carers is with him. I try to keep someone there all the time, but it's difficult. The door is always kept open.'

Bronwen paused outside Tom's room. She dried her eyes and took a deep breath to stem back her tears.

'Hello, Mrs Dew,' the young carer said. 'He's been waiting to see you. I've just given him a few sips of juice. I'll go out now and help with the teas.'

The putrefaction of Tom's infected legs gave the room the smell of death. The window was open a slit. Not enough to dispel the odour and not enough to allow Tom to be cold.

He was position lying on his side, facing her. She held back a gasp at the awful look of him. His eyes were hollows in a sunken, cachexic face. A carer had trimmed his, sparse grey, but once wild red hair, and taken most of his white woolly beard away to allow ease of maintaining hygiene.

His eyes were closed. Bronwen took his hand and they snapped open.

'I thought I was dreaming,' Tom said in a hush. 'But you're here. I can see and smell you. You always smell of roses.'

'What have you been up to when I was away, Tom? I can't leave you for long, can I?'

'It seems you've been away for ever.' His voice was weak; he could barely speak.

'Don't talk, Tom, it's tiring you. I'll just sit here and tell you about the cruise.'

'I must talk, Bronwen. I want to tell you something before I pass on.'

'You can't pass on yet, Tom. I've brought a dozen duty-free cartons of two-hundred cigarettes; posh ones that you like. That's over a thousand Dunhill.'

The touch of a smile crossed his lips. 'I wouldn't tell Matron, if I were you.'

'She wouldn't mind. She wants to see you get better to smoke them.'

'I won't get better,' he repeated, 'I want to tell you something. Come a little closer.'

Bronwen bent over until her head was almost resting on the pillow. His voice was no more than a whisper.

'I want you to know that I love you. I wanted to marry you, but you were too good for me. I was no more than a tramp. Still am. I would have spoiled your life. Lewis came along and made you happy, so I went away. It was my choice because my heart was breaking. I've always loved you, will die loving you,' his voice faded away. He closed his eyes and tightened his grip on Bronwen's hand.

She let her head touch his and wept unashamedly. 'Oh, Tom. Please don't die. Not yet.'

Tom died that night.

Chapter 20
Back to Earth

Bronwen's husband, Lewis, had often said that the richest man in the world is the poorest without health and happy relationships. His words entered her dreams.

Tom Daly's death had a detrimental effect on her emotions. She sobbed every day and night before Tom's cremation and afterwards. Her manner and attention to others returned to normal after being beckoned to another talk with Matron Helen Phillips, behind the closed door of her office.

'I wish I didn't have to tell you this, Bronwen, but I have to,' Helen seemed apprehensive. 'A police detective will be here tomorrow at two o'clock to talk to you. The order was given to me before you returned from the cruise, but I insisted that the death of Tom be respected, so they held off. He wants to question you and especially Kevin Grant about Daniel Palmer being missing from home, possibly kidnapped. An innocent but expensive event is beginning to turn nasty and I wanted to warn you.'

Bronwen's sorrow became anxiety. She remembered the insinuation the officer on board The Gladiator made to Kevin, and Kevin's well-founded violent reaction.

'Kidnapped! Kidnapped! Is that the word used?' Bronwen seethed.

Helen nodded.

Anger raged through Bronwen. She made up her mind; determined that no policeman would question Kevin. He would be found innocent, of course, but the fact that it had been thought that he was a possible paedophile would emotionally damage him. There would be a stigma which would never be entirely eradicated.

Bronwen clicked off the brake of her wheelchair and without politely taking leave of Matron she fled from the room. She went to Geraint's room, barged in without knocking to find him where she expected. At his computer.

'Geraint, I want you to send an urgent e-mail to the captain of The Gladiator immediately,' she ordered. 'Make sure the urgency of it is emphasised and the fact that I want a reply without delay. Tell him to explain that a security error had been made on his liner; why and how Daniel Palmer stowed away, how he was found and brought back to his parents. He won't like to have to mention the breach in the liner's security was being broken but tell him his declaration will be strictly confidential. Tell him it's imperative that I have this information today, otherwise I can see the business will become nasty for him and myself.'

She shook a forefinger at Geraint as she spoke. He had swivelled his chair around to face her with his mouth agape with surprise. He hadn't before seen Bronwen so agitated.

'All right, all right, Bronwen. Calm down. This is not the Bronwen I know. What's happened?'

'I am calm Geraint, but very, very angry. I've just been told that a detective from the county police will be here tomorrow at two o'clock to question me and, above all people, Kevin, about the kidnap of Daniel.'

Geraint's reaction was as Bronwen's was. 'Kidnap! Kidnap! Did you say? How ridiculous, how offensive! They'll not get away with that. They're looking for a scapegoat because they were unable to find Daniel themselves. I'll get the e-mail off right away. If the reply doesn't get here by two o'clock tomorrow, or better, earlier for us to study it, then you'll have to tell the detective he'll have to come back the next day. And I think you ought to tell him to get Daniel out of school to speak up for himself.'

'Good, I'll do that,' Bronwen seethed. 'And when you've sent it, you need to take your face out of that screen for a while, otherwise you'll have square eyes. Come downstairs and take a coffee break with me.'

Some hours later two e-mails arrived from Captain Stewart. One was a personal one for Bronwen, wishing her well and hoping to see her and her "family" on his liner again. The other, an official one explaining how Daniel got himself to Southampton, how he got onto the ship and how he used Kevin to get to Bronwen.

'Perfect,' Bronwen sighed with relief. 'Now I'm ready for anyone who dares to dirty what was an unusual but innocent event.'

At two o'clock the following day two officious looking policemen alighted from a police car. The ubiquitous blue and yellow striped vehicle drove into the car park some yards away from the entrance of the home. Bronwen and Geraint watched the heavily chrome-buttoned, blue uniformed men stroll across the forecourt and her gut turned a somersault. Geraint noticed Bronwen flinch. He put his hand on her forearm.

'No need to be nervous, Bronwen. You are in the right and cleverer and wiser than they are. And for what it's worth, I'll be beside you.'

She smiled at him. Her expression said all that was needed to be said.

'Since there's two of them,' he said, 'there's no reason why I can't be present. You have as much right to a second person being present as he has.' He was referring to the person who was obviously the senior officer since the second man trailed a few steps behind him. 'Matron will stay, too,' Geraint went on, 'but she must remain in a neutral stance. I don't envy her.'

The Matron invited the two officers into her office and directed them to where she had decided they would sit. They witnessed her telling a carer to let Mrs Dew know they had arrived. Bronwen kept them waiting for ten minutes before she appeared at the door. She was followed by Geraint, who had deliberately left his Zimmer frame behind. The policemen stood when he and Bronwen entered. When they were all seated, Matron got up from her chair. 'I'll leave you for a short time,' she said. 'I'll arrange some tea to be brought in.'

She'd found it difficult to keep small talk going with the arm of the law for ten minutes. It was a relief for her to get out of the office as well as to give them privacy to discuss what had become an unpleasant matter.

The senior office was a tall, grey-haired man, in his fifties, Bronwen guessed. He and his colleague, who appeared at least ten years younger, had taken off their uniform caps and rested them on their knees. The embellished uniform jacket of the senior officer appeared too tight; seeming to be having a battle with a belly-bulge of over-indulgence. However, he had a kind face and an unthreatening manner; not as Bronwen expected. She waited for him to open the discussion.

'I'm Inspector Beynon and this is Constable Browning. I was sorry to hear about the passing of your close friend, Tom Daly. I remember him from many years ago; my father and Tom were acquaintances. I'm also sorry that the unexplained missing from home of young Daniel Palmer cannot be left to rest. There are a number of gaps in our understanding of what happened, and I have been instructed to question Mr Kevin Grant directly after getting some facts from you.'

Bronwen had taken a deep breath to control and conceal her anxiety before entering the room.

174

She nodded to Constable Browning after the introduction. 'You, of course know that I am Mrs Bronwen Dew. I don't know whether you know my associate, Mr Geraint Lloyd-Davies. If you don't mind, he'll take note of this meeting. He was with us on the cruise ship Gladiator and was witness to the events concerning little Daniel Palmer. You might know there were three others with us on the cruise: my daughter and our carers Stella Vaughan and Kevin Grant. I must say at this point that I will not allow you to interview Mr Grant or any of the others. If you are concerned about this refusal, then I advise that you send your Constable immediately to bring young Daniel here. He is at school, but I'm sure he will be excuse for the sake of clearing up this whole silly business by telling you exactly what happened.'

'But, Mr Grant...' Inspector Beynon attempted to speak, Bronwen held up her hand to stop his words.

'Just one moment before you begin.' She took out a printed e-mail from her handbag which she'd received from Captain Stewart and handed it to the inspector.

'As you study this, and we discuss it, Constable Browning should shortly be back with Daniel,' she looked directly at the constable. 'Please be gentle with the little boy, Constable, we don't want him frightened. And tell him his Aunty Bronwen will reward him when he comes here to relate what truthfully and correctly happened to him,' she turned again to the Inspector. 'I have neither seen or spoken to Daniel since he left us to fly home from Vego with a very nice officer, Veronica. Nor have I spoken to his parents or grandmother. I tell you that for you to be certain that I haven't influenced, in any way what he will tell you. Now what were you about to say, Inspector?'

'I was about to say, Mrs Dew, that the little boy and your companions, were instrumental in him leaving here and getting to Portsmouth and onto a liner. It caused a great deal of trouble and stress to a number of undeserving people, and the county police a great deal of unnecessary expense and embarrassment. I'm in the difficult position of justifying that and getting to the bottom of the incident.'

'Then Daniel and I will help you to do that,' she looked at Constable Browning in anticipation of him leaving the room.

'You know where Daniel lives, don't you Constable?' the inspector asked.

'Yes, sir,' the constable replied as he stood.

'Then get the permission of his mother to get Daniel out of school and explain why?'

Near an hour went by before the constable arrived with Daniel. During the waiting time they sipped tea and nibbled biscuits, which Matron had brought into the office before taking up her position behind the desk.

There had been silence in the room, except for the noises of activity from the adjoining residents' lounges, whilst the inspector read the e-mail from Captain Stewart. He read it slowly and seemed to consider certain points as he read about them before handing it back to Bronwen.

'It's all right, Inspector,' Geraint said. 'I have it on my computer. That, you should keep for your records.' The inspector folded it and slipped it into the inside of his jacket.

For the remainder of the time they waited for the constable and Daniel to return, they had chatted about the weather and national events.

Daniel looked spruce in his school uniform, and younger than his eight years.

'Hello, my lovely,' Bronwen beckoned him to stand beside her. She hugged him and held his hand. 'Did you like that ride in the important police car? It's smart, isn't it?'

'Not as smart as your Mercedes, Aunty Bronwen,' he said, clearly feeling more confident beside her.

'Well, you must have a ride in it another day. Today, I want you to tell us all that happened to you when you had a long ride to Portsmouth. Then Stella will take you home in her new car. That's smart, too. If you can remember real good, I'll see that you are rewarded for being a clever boy.'

'I remember, Aunty Bronwen. I was a naught boy and I won't do that again. Anyway, I was frightened until I was brought to you. And I wouldn't have if Kevin hadn't seen me. I ran after him early in the morning and he wondered who I was. He only saw me once when we came to the Christmas party here. He only remembered when I told him you was my aunty and I wanted to go to you, so you could send me home to my mam.'

'How did you get to Portsmouth dock, Daniel?' the inspector asked.

Daniel looked down at his feet; he felt ashamed. 'I was a naught boy, sir. I snook into the back of Aunty Bronwen's car when nobody was looking. I was squashed but I wanted to see the apes in Gibraltar. I didn't know it would take so long before the ship got there, and I got cold and hungry. I was hiding in one of them big rowing boats and I snook out early in the morning when no one was about. Those nice serving men give me beef burgers and sausage rolls. But I wanted my mam, so I went to Aunty Bronwen and she told the captain and he told a nice woman officer to take me to the airport and bring me home. I had to show him how I snook onto his ship, but I couldn't find the place where I ran in. It all looked the same,' he was on the verge of tears. 'I'm sorry, I won't do it again.'

Bronwen took his hand into both of hers. 'It's all right, my lovely, you have done very well. You were a naughty boy but you're not now; you're a good boy and I think you learned your lesson. You know you did something very dangerous and your mam, dad and Nanna were very, very worried about you. Don't cry now. Look, I've got something for you.'

She took from her purse four-pound coins, held them on the palm of her hand and held them before Daniel's eyes. They gleamed. 'Two for telling me your story and the others for you to answer the inspector's questions.' She looked at Inspector Beynon. 'What would you like to ask Daniel, Inspector?'

'Why did those kind people give you food when you weren't a real passenger, Daniel?'

'I think it was because they thought I was a real passenger 'cause there were a lot of boys and girl having stuff off them and they didn't have to pay anything.'

'Why didn't you go straight to where your Aunty Bronwen was?'

'I wanted to, but I didn't know where to go. It would have been awful if Kevin thought I was a real passenger and told me to go away. He nearly did 'cause he didn't know who I was until I told him.'

The inspector spoke. 'Thank you, Daniel. You've explained what happened to you very well. You were very frightened and although you did wrong it strikes me you're a brave little boy, too.'

The inspector looked at Bronwen. 'I know all I need to know, Mrs Dew. It's quite clear what happened. Now I will report to my superior and, hopefully, the matter will be ended.'

'It will, indeed, Inspector Beynon. If it's not and your superior wishes to prolong the matter and cause more harassment to myself and my nearest and dearest, I will sue the county police.' Bronwen chuckled and insinuated a joke.

The inspector chuckled, too. 'I don't think it will come to that.'

'Then I bid you and your constable a good afternoon. I must see that Stella takes Daniel safely home. If I do have to sue, you might remind your superior of something.' She paused before her closing words. 'I can well afford the consequences.'

She clicked off the brake of her wheelchair and made for the door. Geraint opened it for her as Matron Phillips appeared. 'Thank you, Matron,' he said as he followed Bronwen up the corridor.

'You're welcome,' Matron Phillips grinned as she replied. 'I'll show these gentlemen out.'

'My word, Bronwen,' Geraint mumbled to her out of anyone's hearing, 'you handled that well. I didn't think you had it in you.'

'I didn't think I did, either, Geraint. It's true that money breeds confidence but I tell you honestly, my tummy was churning like God knows what.'

Stella took the happy Daniel to his home. She was glad of any excuse to drive her beautiful new car. She had been on early duty, so she had been off since three o'clock; she was waiting for the meeting to be over. She knew it was about Daniel's big adventure, but not that there had been the possibility of the police questioning Kevin on suspicion of premeditated kidnapping. She would have burst into the office and created havoc. What had been said within those four walls of the matron's office remained a secret.

Stella hadn't yet put in her notice to leave The Sunshine Mount Nursing Home. That would be when 22, Queen Street was ready for Bronwen to move in. Its completion had been delayed by Colin having to wait for planning permission to extend further at the side of the house. It was a good thing Bronwen and Geraint had their rooms at The Sunshine Mount Nursing Home. Bronwen wanted to get used to being back. Even when on the cruise she sometime had a feeling of nostalgia. However, at the home she wouldn't be far away. She could always pay visits.

Hence, when they all arrived home after the cruise, she wasn't disappointed that there remained work still to be done to make 22, Queen Street habitable. She sensed Geraint was of the same opinion.

Colin, Stella's brother, was an expert builder, but he had no idea of interior designing and hard and soft furnishings. It would take some time to complete the task of choosing and fitting the hard and soft furnishings.

Stella had chosen the type of bathroom and kitchen fittings before she departed on the cruise and Colin had excelled himself. It was perfect. Stella made a full examination before taking Bronwen down to Queen Street to see for herself. Its grandness was beyond Bronwen's expectations.

'My word,' she said with amazement. 'Even a little lift to the upstairs rooms. I assume that is mainly for my benefit.'

'Maybe,' Geraint said. 'But it will have many other uses.'

'Yes, it will,' Stella responded. 'And there's the chair-lift. Mary and I can use that when we're tipsy after The Colliers,' Bronwen and Geraint were amused.

Bronwen had insisted that Geraint was available for the conducted tour of his future home. It would be some weeks away.

The front of the house looked little different to how it always looked, in spite of its new front windows and door. However, instead of the door opening into the narrow passage as it used to, it opened into a bright hallway. It had been a small room, ludicrously referred to as "the parlour" where Bronwen's mother entertained her visitors.

The gleaming glass windows and doors were of a design and size to allow maximum sunlight in. Where appropriate, the rooms had no doors, but archways, to make movement from room to room easily accessible for wheelchairs.

The old scullery and adjoining tumble-down glass lean-to had been replace by a fine, stone and brick building. It had become an exquisitely designed kitchen and dining room.

Rooms had been built above the extra buildings on the ground. The windows of these overlooked the views beyond. A large room at the end of the extension offered a wide view of the valley.

Although the view from the front windows of the house was no different from all the other houses in the street, it looked much different at the back, because every inch of the back garden had been built on.

Those neighbours of 21, Queen Street, didn't complain about Bronwen's extended building taking away a large part of their view. They were pleased to know she was returning to her real home. They had always been good to Bronwen and Mary when, first Lewis died and a few months later, her parents.

For a number of years, they had helped with shopping and cleaning. They had done what they could to help Bronwen. She appreciated the way they tried to support Mary, when she lived at number 22 on her own. Mary didn't recognise it as a kindness.

Bronwen was now in a position to repay them for all the years of kindness. She requested to change the back of their home, adding a new kitchen and an extra building for whatever use they chose.

They couldn't believe their luck. It would be more comfortable and add value to the property for their children when it was passed on to them. Those kind neighbours refused at first; Bronwen was being too generous and there was no need for it. The gentle manner in which she suggested the proposal made them think they were doing her a favour.

She explained to them that it would be giving Colin and Kevin work when her own home was completed. Colin employed Kevin since the return from the Mediterranean cruise. He had little to do being Bronwen's human hoist and "minder", so he became Colin's "boy" to learn how to become a builder. It was a strange situation, Kevin being Colin's apprentice. Colin wasn't a small man, but Kevin made him feel small.

Bronwen discussed the matter with Geraint. 'Tell Colin to give Kevin two hundred pounds a week,' she told him, 'and arrange to give that amount to Colin to give to him. Kevin won't accept it if he knows it comes from me.'

Geraint responded with a frown, deeply wrinkling his already wrinkled countenance. 'You're being naïve, Bronwen. Don't you think Kevin will guess? Why not let Colin give to him what he would to any labourer working for him, and to add more for being good at the job, considering he's new at it.'

Neither Bronwen nor Geraint knew that Kevin's first few weeks with Colin were not incident free. Kevin was clumsy and found it difficult learning to use tools that were unfamiliar to him. There were quarrels between Colin and Kevin, Colin and Stella and Stella and Kevin.

Stella assured Colin that Kevin was a good learner and insisted that he should be tolerant of Kevin's errors: spilling a large tin of paint by letting it fall off the stepladder. Then breaking the stepladder with his clumsy tread. Kevin's cementing together the wrong bricks, knocking down walls when they shouldn't have been knocked down. Understandably, Colin became riled into frustration that he couldn't always hide from Kevin. There were some unpleasant words often exchanged.

However, Kevin, not only learned, but enjoyed the work. Bronwen saw the rationale of Geraint's suggestion and agreed that the method of payment to be Colin's.

'Well, all right,' she nodded, 'how much should that be?'

'I don't know. Wages have changed since I was working. You'll have to ask Colin.'

Inevitably, with Bronwen's gentle approach and manner, circumstances improved when Colin and Kevin worked out their differences. They became good friends.

When the building of 22, Queen Street, was complete, the result was beyond Bronwen's expectations. She was impressed by the doors being wide, so she wouldn't have to struggle to get her wheelchair through. She liked the windows being big to allow a maximum of daylight in. Some of the kitchen worktops were at a level she could reach from her wheelchair and the floors were all flat and even.

Her bedroom was on the ground floor at the back of the house, overlooking the valley with its river, old railways and green common stretching to the tall mountains beyond.

Colin had sought professional advice in the planning of the house; there were aspects that he wouldn't have thought of. Nothing, it seemed, had been overlooked.

Colin's part was over when he visited the neighbours to begin planning the extensions of their home. It would be nowhere near as large as the extension on Bronwen's house but the Coopers of number 21, Queen Street willingly agreed with what was offered.

Colin went along with the work at number 21. Geraint and he had worked out an arrangement for paying. When the work was complete, the final settlement was made. It was a staggering amount to Bronwen; she wasn't used to being responsible for such large sums. There was much sucking of teeth from Geraint, but he assured Bronwen that the amount was within their budget. A large amount of her fortune had been spent but, Geraint assured, there was plenty left.

The spending wasn't over. Bronwen and Stella looked forward to choosing the furniture, carpets, curtains bed linen, crockery, cutlery, pots and pans and every new kitchen electric equipment that was available. They, no doubt, would forget items and would be buying ad infinitum when they moved in. It was easy when the amount on the price tags didn't have to be considered.

Stella and Bronwen involved Mary as much as possible and encouraged her to make choices. She wasn't good at it. Bronwen and Stella did much discrete prompting and advising. She was allowed to choose the soft furnishings for her own room. They aimed at her feeling confident about her choices. Stella told Kevin that Mary's room would have looked like something out of Count Dracula's castle had she been left to her own devices.

'Black bed-sheets,' Stella cringed. 'Black silk sheets, she wanted. Thank God I was there before she paid for them. I know, she thought they wouldn't need changing as often as a normal coloured bed sheet.'

Kevin laughed. 'That doesn't sound too unreasonable to me.'

It took a further two months before all the furniture for the different rooms had been selected, ordered and delivered. Carpets had to be chosen and fitted, curtains made, delivered and fitted. It took longer than expected.

The enterprise provided entertainment for the neighbours. The various business cars, trucks and vans appearing outside 22, Queen Street brought people to their doorsteps to witness what came out of them. Those more curious than others came to the door of number 22 to offer help.

When Bronwen was there to help Stella with the organising, she invited those neighbours who came out of curiosity, to come in and see what was going on. Much to Stella's frustration, the proceedings were inevitably held up. She either joined in the fun or disappeared to do something upstairs.

When Bronwen brought Geraint to view his room, Stella's progress was held up even more. One of the rooms upstairs was for him. When he saw it, he was amazed at the grandness. He was humbled by the wealth which had been put into it. The apprehension he had about leaving the nursing home dissipated. He looked forward to moving in. Bronwen made every day a party day with promise of luxury.

Being there was good for Mary. She met a few neighbours who had recently made their homes at Queen Street; women of her own age and younger. Most of them were married with children. She hoped one day to be like them. She was only thirty-one. There was still time to meet the man of her dreams and have children of her own. She continued to lose weight and had gained confidence because of it. Most importantly, she was rich. At least, her mother was, and her mother denied her nothing.

The day eventually arrived for Bronwen and Geraint to move from The Sunshine Mount Nursing Home into the magnificently renovated 22, Queen Street. Bronwen had been looking forward to it, but when it arrived, she was sad. Geraint was, too, and was beginning to have second thoughts about leaving the security of the nursing home. He'd lived there for over twelve years.

'Geraint,' Bronwen remarked one day. 'It's no good; you nor I will ever get used to being rich.'

'Yes, you're right. And you know this prostate problem of mine will be more of a nuisance at our home in Queen Street. I really need to have the availability of twenty-four-hour care, until I have that operation to put me right. I'm not getting any younger; neither is my prostate.'

'No, Geraint, I know you're not, but you've been on the waiting list for the operation for over a year. You surely should have heard something by now. Perhaps others are jumping the list in front of you.' Bronwen's heart ached for Geraint. There were times when he had dreadful pain for which there was no immediate ease, except for pills which upset him.

'I don't know why I haven't heard. Perhaps they think I'm too old and let younger people go before me. But it will be too late if I don't hear soon. Mind you, I can understand those more deserving going before me.'

'Well I can't,' Bronwen's tone hardened. 'You've as much right as anyone else. Why not go private, Geraint? I understand you can be done almost straight away if you've got the money to pay. And we have, haven't we?'

'Yes, Bronwen, that's right, but that would be against my principles. I'm no saint, but I wouldn't feel right going first because we can pay,' Geraint looked sad.

'I know what you mean, Geraint, but this time my principles have flown out of the window. I'm going to speak to Matron. She'll make an appointment for you to see our doctor and tell him you want to have the operation privately. I'll speak to her today. Stella will take you to the doctor's and tell him to make the necessary arrangements. We've enough in the bank for them to put your prostate right and anything else while they're at it.'

'Well, all right,' Geraint sounded apprehensive. 'Let's go and say our farewells to our friends, then. We must come and see them often, mustn't we?'

'Yes, and I'll see that they are brought down to see us, too. It'll be somewhere for them to have a change of four walls. I hope they don't all come at the same time, though. I'll ask Kevin to bring them down in the big car.'

Geraint's characteristic chortle told Bronwen that the possibility of that amused him, and that he felt more confident. He hastened to his room to organise the movement of his computer and other equipment.

Kevin hired a removal firm to organise Geraint's and Bronwen's move from The Sunshine Mount Nursing Home. It saved him and Stella making several trips in the Mercedes and her Volvo. As well as that, they feared that their precious vehicles would be damaged; some of the things to be moved were big.

The contents of the two rooms were moved; both having lived there for over ten years. Geraint had so much equipment that only the bed and fitted wardrobe were left. He had taken over Tom's scooter but held on to his irreplaceable Zimmer frame.

Bronwen had a smart hi-tech wheelchair, but she'd kept the old one because Lewis had acquired it for her. It became of sentimental value and taken to the new home.

Bronwen had a glass cabinet, a smart, comfortable television chair and a wardrobe taken to Queen Street. She didn't care that it would look incongruous amongst the beautiful things at her new home; a home, she thought, which would be for the rest of her life—God willing.

She and Geraint felt a lack of confidence when leaving, but Matron Phillips assured them she would make rooms available to them when and if needed. She didn't think so, because Stella, on Bronwen's instructions, had hired another carer and two cleaners. They were women living in Queen Street who were well known to "the family". They were reliable and in dire need of the money they would earn.

The new employees had been unable to take a job. Having to care for their young children was more important. When working for Bronwen, their hours were arranged to accommodate their domestic commitments. They were allowed to take along their children when necessary. Needless to say, they were overpaid, and Geraint didn't agree with that.

'You are creating a precedence, Bronwen, and other employers can make trouble for you,' he warned.

'Let them, then,' Bronwen replied. 'We'll deal with that when and if it happens.'

The moving-in was celebrated with the popping of champagne corks and a heavy table of good food. Everyone who'd had a hand in the development was at the party, as well as close neighbours, Dulcie Curtis, Daniel Palmer and his grandmother, Ruth and Joan, Bronwen's cousins. Matron Phillips put in a short visit and the nurses from the home came down in turns. The party went on until the late evening.

Bronwen went to bed that night thinking she'd be unable to sleep in the strange bed; however grand and comfortable. As she waited for dreams to take her, she wondered what would happen next in this changed life of hers. Whatever it might be, it wouldn't involve the big step she had taken by moving to The Sunshine Mount Nursing Home from 22, Queen Street. And now she was back. It felt like an age ago when her purse was often empty.

Her winning of the National Lottery had not only changed her life but the lives of others. She hoped it would prove to be for the better.

Chapter 21
A Changed Life

After a few months of moving into 22, Queen Street, Geraint paid a visit to his General Practitioner. He listened to Geraint's complaints of pain, discomfort, inconvenience and embarrassment. It was known that he had been on the hospital waiting list for the operation, prostatectomy, for nearly a year.

The doctor had read Geraint's case-notes. 'Yes, Mr Lloyd-Davies. It seems you would benefit from surgery. I will contact the hospital to find out when you can undergo the procedure. The sooner the better, I would say, and I expect you would, too, but there's little I can do about the waiting list being lengthy.'

Geraint thought his manner patronising but put that down to his apparent youth and inexperience of the necessary sensitive communicative skills. However, that was of no significance. Getting an operation to improve his quality of life was the priority.

'What if I request a private consultation, Dr Mason, and am able to pay privately for the operation? How long would I have to wait then?'

'Less than two weeks, I would say. Initially, you would have a pre-operative assessment to ensure you are fit for surgery. You would put yourself in a different frame, but it would be costly.'

'How costly, Dr Mason? Can you give me a rough estimation?'

'It would depend on how radical the surgery would be. And of course, there would be a cost for the number of investigations prior to surgery and the extent of the post-operative care. It would cost anything between two and six thousand pounds, but I couldn't be sure.'

'Well then, cost is no problem, but my conscience is. It seems unfair that a man of my advanced age could be seen so quickly when another man, just as desperate as myself, would have to wait. And I am desperate. The physical problem is spoiling what life I have left.'

'If you are able to pay for your treatment, Mr Lloyd-Davies, there is no need for guilt because you are shortening the list. Someone else will take your place on it.'

Young Dr Mason hadn't been in the practice long enough to know Geraint's involvement with Bronwen. He might have heard that she had won a great deal of money, but he wouldn't know that she would be paying for Geraint's treatment.

'Then, yes please,' Geraint nodded. 'I would like you to get the matter started right away. Naturally, I am anxious about undergoing surgery; I am no longer a young man and I realise there could be complications but, at least, I can say I think I am fit, considering my advanced age. However, waiting would increase the anxiety, so the sooner it's over with, the better.'

The doctor stood and shook hands with Geraint across his desk. It was a sign that Geraint's interview was over. 'Right, sir,' the doctor said, 'you will hear something in a couple of days. If you have no preference of surgeon, I know one quite well. I'll contact him at the end of my clinic.' In little over a week Geraint was sitting in a bed in a single room of the private wing of the local hospital. He underwent a battery of tests: physical examinations, blood pathology and a variety of X-rays prior to surgery; a prostatectomy. 'A prota-what?' Bronwen asked. She visited him on the first evening of his' admission and every afternoon and evening. She took him flowers, fruit, squash and chocolates. As did Stella.

Bronwen looked startled when she saw him on the first evening. She peered above his bed at a plastic container which was attached to his arm by a long tube. 'What's that for?' she asked, sounding resentful of the fact that it was there.

'I'm sure it's there for a reason,' Geraint replied. 'Just shut up and mind your own business.'

Before the visit, Bronwen had sworn to herself and to the others, that she would reveal no anxiety to Geraint, and she expected them to do likewise. Bronwen didn't do very well herself. All the bottles, tubes and attachment on the wall behind his bed alarmed her and she had difficulty disguising her apprehension.

He explained to her, Stella and Mary, as much as he knew about what was to happen to him.

Mary gasped. 'Oh, it sounds awful, Mr Lloyd-Davies! Can you change your mind?'

Stella snapped. 'Of course, he can change his mind but he's not going to. His old prostate has been a nuisance for as long as I can remember. He'll be great when it's over, you wait and see.'

'Stella is right, my lovely,' Bronwen patted Mary's hand. 'Mr Lloyd-Davies will be as right as rain afterwards,' she looked at Stella. 'She's just nervous for him, love. She hasn't your experience, has she? You know lots of men who've had a pro… What is it again, Geraint? And, Stella, you've nursed them, haven't you?'

'Never mind that, now. You're talking about me as if I'm not here. Talk about something else.' Geraint sounded irritable and changed the subject. 'The man in the next ward has had a hip replacement. He sat out of bed the day after he had it done. He seems to be fine and he doesn't look all that much younger than I am.'

Just then, a white tunic with blue epaulettes above a pair of navy-blue slacks waltzed into the 4-bedded ward. 'Excuse me Mrs Lloyd-Davies,' she spoke as she looked at Bronwen and smiled at Mary and Stella. 'Must take basic signs. Won't take long.'

'It's Mrs Bronwen Dew,' Stella corrected, 'but she is Mr Lloyd-Davies's next of kin. His son is in Australia. Mrs Dew and Mr Lloyd-Davies have been companions for many years.'

'I'm sorry,' the nurse said, not appearing as if she were. 'I've just come on duty and haven't had time to read all the reports yet.'

'I'm his companion, too, and this is Mary, Mrs Dew's daughter.'

'Right,' the nurse said. 'I'm Nurse Ann Harvey, I'm Geraint's nurse.'

'We address him as Mr Lloyd-Davies,' was Stella's retort with an edge to her tone.

Nurse Harvey seemed to disregard Stella's remark. She concentrated on the stand which measured his blood pressure and pulse rate before taking a chart from a file at the bottom of the bed. She did some writing in it before slotting it back.

'Right, then, Mr Lloyd-Davies; that's fine. Won't bother you again for a while, unless you want me. Here's the bell.' The bell was on the bedside locker. She placed it nearer Geraint's hand.

'What're base signs?' Mary asked the nurse.

The nurse laughed. 'You mean basic signs. They tell us how Mr Lloyd-Davies's heart is behaving; and it's doing well,' she smiled without looking at anyone and left the room.

'For goodness sake, Stella, don't rub any of them up the wrong way. I'm the one having the operation, remember.' Geraint spoke as he plucked a grape off the bunch they had brought in for him—among other things. Pears, bananas, squash, bottled water, a box of Dairy Milk Chocolates and a small pot of African daisies.

'Well, I'm glad she took the hint,' Stella said. 'Nurses shouldn't call patients by their first names unless they are invited to.'

Stella remembered the teaching of her nurse training some years before. She had completed her first year when she married Steven. She discontinued the course to please him, but with the intention of returning. She never did.

'Am I going to be in here long enough to get through this lot?' Geraint grinned. He referred to his overloaded bedside cabinet. 'Thank you, ladies. You mustn't spoil me just because I'm in hospital.'

Two days later Geraint had a prostatectomy—a surgical technique to remove the prostate gland.

When Bronwen saw him the evening of the operation, she thought he was dying. The operation had taken longer than expected and, she was told, he'd lost a lot of blood. He'd had a blood transfusion, but his condition continued to cause concern.

'Of course, his age is against him,' the ward sister told Bronwen. She felt like reminding the sister that his age wouldn't have been so much against him if he's had the operation over two years ago, when the urinating trouble started, but she decided not to. Geraint had asked her to say nothing which might "ruffle feathers".

Stella embraced Bronwen. She, too, was worried, but she tried not to let Bronwen know it. 'They always look terrible strait after surgery, Bronwen. And although he's good for his age we can't expect him to look good at a time like this, can we? He looks worse because he's without his dentures.'

'Stella is right, Mrs Dew,' the sister said as she put something into the tube on the back of his hand. 'This is his antibiotic I'm giving; to prevent a possible infection. His blood pressure is coming up nicely and he has a strong, steady pulse, considering his age.'

The healthy pink of Mary's cheeks had left her. She was as white as the sheet Geraint lay on and tears filled her eyes. 'He looks as if he's dead, Mammy. I don't want him to die.'

'You're not the only one,' Geraint's voice was weak. ''Course I'm not going to die. Not tonight, anyway, but if I feel like this tomorrow, I wouldn't be too sure.'

'Geraint, my lovely, it's good to hear your voice, though it's not likely to shatter the windowpanes. Don't talk; save your strength.'

'That's right, Mr Lloyd-Davies,' Stella added. 'And if you're in pain, you ring the bell, mind. The staff nurse told me that you can have pain relief any time it's needed.'

She could hold back her soft emotion no longer, though she didn't intend to; it would have worried Bronwen more. She stooped and wept into Bronwen's hair as she stood behind her wheelchair. Bronwen patted her head.

'He's going to be all right,' Bronwen said. 'You take Mary home, now. Stop and have a drink at The Angel Hotel on the way. Just have a juice or something, 'cause you're driving. The company will be good for you. Ring and ask Kevin if he'll come and get me in an hour. I'll just sit beside Geraint and hold his hand for a bit. Will Kevin mind, Stella?'

'Bronwen, of course, he won't. You know he won't. He'll be glad to do something to help.'

Mary was pleased to leave; she looked as if she were about to vomit.

The room became silent except for mumbled voices and slight movement of the activity outside. The noises seemed far away.

'Geraint, love, I know. You are glad they've gone. You love them but all you want now is peace and quiet. Well, I'll just sit here for a bit. You needn't say a word and if I say something, it won't need an answer.'

'Yes, Bronwen,' he muttered. 'I'm going to be all right. I feel it in my bones.'

'I believe you, but I wouldn't rely on your old bones, too much. They're as bad as mine except my legs are worse. Shut up now and rest.'

'Bronwen, one last thing for tonight.' She could hardly hear him. 'This is going to cost a terrible lot of money and I don't think I'm worth it; especially if I go to my maker. Should have waited my turn on the list.'

'And one last thing from me Geraint Lloyd-Davies. You are not going to your maker yet; he's not ready for you and anyway, I need you. And if you haven't heard a single word I've said, you'd better hear this.' She bent over as near to his ear as her wheelchair would allow. 'I don't care if it costs me every last penny. In fact, getting you your operation is the best thing about winning all that money. I don't care if I'm left without a farthing. Sometimes I wonder if I'm the right person to have it.'

'Shut up. Don't talk such nonsense. Winning millions of pounds couldn't have happened to a better, more worthy, lovelier woman.' His words were muttered and barely audible. They faded away as he fell asleep, but she'd heard every word.

She sat holding his skeletal, cool, sinewy hand, hearing Nurse Harvey's feet from time to time, discretely slip-slapping in and out to peep at him and the tell-tale technology surrounding him. It wasn't long before she heard a light tap on the open door. The nurses hadn't tapped the door as they came in. Who else but gentle-giant Kevin would do that before waiting to be allowed entry?

Bronwen looked up at him and smiled her thanks. Her lovely, grey eyes were wet with unshed tears. 'Shhh,' she put a forefinger to her lips. 'He's asleep. Best not to wake him.'

Kevin nodded his agreement as he stood beside the bed and glanced at Geraint. He was taken aback. He was about to express his shock but Bronwen put her fingers to her lips again.

She leaned across to the back of a chair where she had draped her coat. Kevin helped her on with it. She held out her hand and stroked Geraint's grey face. 'See you tomorrow,' she whispered, but he couldn't have heard.

Bronwen stopped at the nurses' station on the way out. The nurse, who was obviously in charge, had her gaze on Bronwen. The nurses behind the desk were busy writing, in what must have been, patient's progress reports. They raised their eyes to Kevin. They admired his size and physique. He had retained some of the tan he'd acquired on the cruise and his corn-coloured hair was pulled back to the nape of his neck. They stopped writing to acknowledge his courteous nod and smile from clear blue eyes.

'Is Mr Lloyd-Davies progressing all right, Sister?' Bronwen asked. 'He looks none too good to me.'

'Don't worry, Mrs Dew, the doctors are quite satisfied. He's had major surgery and his poor colour can be expected. Me and my team are keeping a close eye on him and we're feeling quite confident at present.'

Bronwen wasn't sure what the "at present" meant. Did it mean that things could change?

'Thank you, Sister, I see he's in good hands, and your information is comforting. If, by any twist of fate, he deteriorates, however slight, would you please let me know immediately, day or night, no matter what time?'

'Yes, Mrs Dew. I feel confident that he will progress now the worse is over, but if the unexpected happens and we get in touch with you, how will you get here?' She was surveying Bronwen's wheelchair.

'I'll bring her,' Kevin's deep voice interrupted. 'As Mrs Dew has asked, no matter what time, day or night.'

'Kevin is one of my carers,' Bronwen said. The look of surprise on the nurses' faces could hardly have been overlooked by the astute Bronwen.

She smiled at them and again thanked them. Her tone was soft and gentle; she spoke with calmness, exuding strength and wisdom. Kevin walked beside her wheelchair as she manoeuvred it towards the lifts. The nurses left their chairs at the desk to watch the back of them, until they disappeared through the double-doors at the entrance.

When in the lift, which would take them to the ground floor, Kevin spoke the words which he almost did at Geraint's bedside.

'Bronwen, he looks terrible. He looks dying, yet all those nurses seem to think he's suffering nothing more than a cold in the nose.'

'Stella said that all people look like that for a day or two after they've had an operation,' Bronwen assured Kevin. 'I feel satisfied enough, Kevin. He'll be all right. Geraint's a fighter and he couldn't go on much longer suffering as he was. He tried to hide it, but I could tell. I've known him long enough; there is nothing we don't know about each other.'

'Yes, I know that, Bronwen. But if there is a change for the worse, I meant it when I said I will bring you night or day, whatever the time. Even if I'm at work; I know Colin will agree with me.'

Geraint recovered. After ten days he became impatient for his discharge to 22, Queen Street. He'd had a urinary catheter in situation since the day of the operation, which he hated. When it was removed, he found he couldn't control his urinary output. With help from his nurse to practice what she called, "urinary drill", he managed to overcome that. He was amazed at how well he felt. He had forgotten what it was like to pass urine without having seething pain.

He was full of admiration for the surgeons, the nurses and scientific progress—until he had the bill. It came a week after he was home.

He remembered signing a lot of papers when he was too ill to ask what he was signing for, but he trusted everyone, as Bronwen did.

'Just sign them, Geraint,' she'd said. 'No one is going to cheat us, if that's what you're afraid of. Anyway, we can pay the bill twice over if needs be.'

When Geraint, thirty years before, was in control of his accountancy business, he was used to handling large sums of money, but his values had dated. A large sum now was difficult to accept.

However, the cost of Geraint's pre-operative treatment, the operation and after-care were paid. He closed his eyes and sucked his teeth as Bronwen signed the cheque.

'That is beyond extortion,' he said. 'If I'd known, I might have had second thoughts about having it done.'

'Of course, you wouldn't have. You're forgetting how bad you felt.'

Following his discharge, a community nurse called on Geraint as part of the after care. The nurse enjoyed going to his home. It was unusual and beautiful. Bronwen made her welcome, as did Stella, who benefited from another opinion on the state of Geraint's wound and his progress. Geraint thought the community nurse's call was superfluous to his needs. He preferred to be totally in Stella's hands. As well as supervising the taking of his medicines, he was used to her seeing him in all stages of undress. Before his operation, it was Stella who ensured he always had clean, dry clothes; she understood why he frequently wet himself. She was knowledgeable enough to recognise if complications occurred. The year she had undertaken for professional training hadn't been wasted.

The amount of money paid to the hospital trust wasn't missed from Bronwen's fortune. On the remainder of the twenty million pounds, interest was gained each month. The banks were pressing her and Geraint to invest in shares, but they adhered to their decision to spend what they needed and consider alternatives of the deposits of the money after a year.

Geraint's physical condition improved. He felt well and life at 22, Queen Street was exquisite beyond his expectations, as it was for his four companions. Christmas followed shortly after his operation. He was able to enjoy the festive days without having to sit near a toilet. He found life was getting better as he grew older; defying nature. He hadn't expected to be alive to celebrate entry into the millennium.

The beautiful house was alive with laughter and good will for days before December 31st and following 1st January 2000.

That time would never be forgotten.

Bronwen had been a millionaire for over a year. A lot of her fortune had already been enjoyed and most of it was still in the bank. Her accounts were in perfect order. Geraint wouldn't have been able to enjoy his life if they weren't. Part of the joy of living was having the responsibility of being her accountant.

However, something on his mind skimmed the cream off his peace of mind. It was the thought of having to do what the banks were pressing him to do for Bronwen. He was apprehensive; the task was too big for him.

It took a lot of thought before he considered to tell Bronwen of his concern.

'I knew something was bothering you,' Bronwen admitted. 'I should have got you to tell me weeks ago, but I thought it might be a private matter you didn't wish to share with me.'

'Bronwen, for goodness sake. What on earth made you think I would want to keep a private matter from you? Did you think I had a mistress or had committed a crime? What could happen in my life that you wouldn't know about? Don't be daft.'

'A mistress, indeed!' Bronwen's laugh was unusually loud and was heard in the kitchen, where Stella, Mary and a new carer, Bethan, were busy preparing lunch. The doors were always kept open in Bronwen's new residence.

Stella, who was cleaning potatoes, dropped a large one into the bowl she was using. The murky water splashed onto her clean white tunic before she dashed through into the lounge where Bronwen and Geraint were browsing through the Sunday newspapers.

'Did I hear right?' she asked with raised eyebrows. 'What was that about a mistress?'

Bronwen continued to laugh as she spoke to Stella. 'Nothing, love, nothing. Geraint and I were just laughing over old times.'

Stella looked doubtful as she went back to the potatoes. 'Dirty talk was it?'

Bronwen and Geraint enjoyed the repartee, but seriousness returned. 'It's months from the deadline,' Geraint said.

'Deadline, Geraint? What do you mean? You're worrying me now.'

'Well,' Geraint went on, 'you're well aware of the manager of our bank and his superiors pressing us to use your money sensibly. They say it could be gaining much more if it were invested wisely. I'm not doing right for you. The truth is, I don't know the market anymore and I cannot do you justice; you need an adviser other than me.'

'That I don't want,' Bronwen sound insistent; almost as if she were chastising Geraint. 'If we said that, it wouldn't be just one man coming along here and telling us what to do but half a dozen, I expect. I don't want the bother and that's that.

'It just doesn't make sense. One minute that old Mr Clapworthy is telling us how the money is increasing due to interest and another minute he's telling us we're losing money because it isn't invested wisely. We'll stay as we are and just spend as we do and change if we see the needs. Now, you can stop worrying and tell Clapworthy to do nothing until you tell him to. And don't tell him to do anything. Perhaps, they'll just go away and leave us be.'

'Yes, Bronwen. I'm relieved. I think you're right,' Geraint breathed a sigh of relief.

Bronwen and Geraint had spoken quietly. They didn't want anyone else in the household to be thinking of money matters except the pleasant ones—spending and enjoying.

The three women, led by Stella, walked into the lounge. They looked happy; in high spirits. Stella carried a tray with a coffee pot, sugar basin and milk jug and a plate of a variety of biscuits.

'Here's for your coffee break,' Stella said as she put down the tray onto the coffee table in front of Bronwen and Geraint. 'All is done and dusted, and the lunch is on. It should be ready for the gravy in about two hours. I'm taking the girls down to The Colliers for an aperitif. And don't remind me to have a fruit juice, Bronwen, because we're walking. Colin and Kevin will be there, so I hope they'll get us something stronger. And it'll give you two chances to be on your own to talk about the dirty old days without us overhearing.'

'I beg your pardon,' Geraint gave Stella a look of disdain. 'You know different, don't you, my girl.'

Stella laughed and so did Bronwen. 'Of course I do, Mr Lloyd-Davies.'

Being a Sunday, it was a day off for the two cleaners. It was up to Stella to supervise the tidying up of all the rooms. Stella knew how Bronwen liked it and she ensured it was kept that way.

'All right, my lovelies,' Bronwen smiled. She liked to see them going out together. They bloomed with health and happiness. Smart, too. She'd never seen Mary look so bright. She wasn't sharp minded, and never would be, but she seemed to have blossomed during the past months—or was it because she had the money to do the best for herself with Stella's guidance?

Twenty-eight old Bethan was of the same ilk as Mary. She was the youngest of five daughters, born late to a mother of forty-two years of age. Bronwen knew her grandmother and decided to do something for Bethan.

She put Mary in charge of Bethan's induction to the Bronwen Dew household. She assumed it would do something for Mary's general outlook and it seemed to be effective. Discretely, Stella overlooked them all.

Bethan was sometimes so slow witted; even Mary looked puzzled at her responses. Perhaps she sympathised, Bronwen thought. Her dear Mary could relate to Bethan. She tried to explain to Bronwen why Bethan was "not a scholar".

'She was a long time being born, Mammy, like I was. An' when she was born, the cord was tight around her neck, so she couldn't breev for a long time.'

'She couldn't...breath...for a long time,' Bronwen corrected.

'Yes, Mammy, vat's right.'

Bethan enjoyed going to the pub on Sunday mornings with Stella and Mary. It made her feel good. The pub wasn't exciting enough for Mary.

'Why can't we go into town to the wine-bar?' Mary plagued Stella. She preferred the loud music and young crowd of the more glamorous wine-bar than the beer-smelling local pub.

'One, because it's Sunday morning and The Cellar's not open. Two, because I don't want to drive because I feel like a real drink. Is that enough excuses for you?'

'Yes, all right, Stella,' Mary frowned. 'Sorry.'

It was a misty autumnal day and the sharp nip of winter's promise had them running most of the way to the pub. They barged through the splintered, paint-flaking double-doors to the bar.

Colin and Kevin were playing darts. Kevin, who was about to aim at the board, jokingly turned in the direction of the three women as if he were about to throw at them.

'I think I'll aim at you Mary Dew; you're the biggest and easiest to hit.'

Mary didn't laugh as Bethan did.

'I'm losing weight,' Mary pouted, 'I won't be the biggest for long.'

Stella flew across the room and flung her arms about her brother, crushing him to her. 'Hello, my lovely brother,' she said. 'Have you found a woman to take my place at home yet?'

Colin kissed Stella's cheek. 'No, but I'm still looking. I don't think there's another Stella, though.'

'How about a big hug for me?' Kevin held out his arms.

'I can't reach up to you, you great ox. I'll do it when you're sitting down.'

They moved out of the bar into the lounge and Colin asked each one of the group what was "her poison" before listing them to the barman. Kevin was already half way through a pint of draught. He put it onto a table around which they all took seats.

'Well, what about that hug?' Kevin asked Stella as he ruffled her shining, curls. He bent down and kissed her cheek. 'Are you all right, my lovely?' He referred to Stella but looked at Mary and Bethan. 'Is she still slave-driving you?'

'Yes, she is,' Mary pouted. 'She is a bloody slave driver.'

Stella snapped. 'I'm telling Mr Lloyd-Davies you swore.'

'He'll know who taught her to have a dirty tongue,' Colin remarked as he arrived with a tray of drinks. Stella had half a pint of what Colin and Kevin were drinking and the other two women drank shandy.

They talked, laughed and sipped their drinks for longer than planned. A main topic of conversation was Mary's thirty-third birthday on the following Sunday. They decided to go to the wine-bar in town on Saturday to celebrate; the night before. Bronwen had arranged a tea party for the Sunday with a birthday cake bearing the correct number of candles.

'It'll have to be a big cake,' Kevin teased, 'you're nearing the top of the hill, Mary.'

'No, I'm not,' Mary pouted, 'and if you don't watch out, you won't be invited.'

They also talked about the extension of the house next to 22, Queen Street and what jobs Colin had lined up for when that was completed,

Stella noticed that the palms of Kevin's hands had become calloused again and his fingernails were short and chipped. When on the cruise, they were soft and his nails tipped-white. Stella picked up one of his hands and commented on it as she examined his palms.

'Better this way,' he replied. 'A proper man's hands.' She happened to catch sight of the face of his wristwatch and leapt up from her chair.

'Quick!' she ordered Bethan and Mary, 'that leg of lamb will be done to death. We've got ten minutes to get home, get it out of the oven, calve it, drain the vegetables and get it on the table.'

'We'll never do that,' Bethan gasped, 'Bronwen will be offended. Good job I laid the table before we came out.'

'What?' Kevin said with surprise, 'Bronwen be offended? That'll be the day.'

'Kevin was right; Bronwen wasn't offended. She was surprised they arrived back so quickly. She had taken the joint out of the oven, Geraint calved it whilst she made the gravy. Geraint had drained all the vegetables and kept everything on a low heat until they were ready for the table.

All Stella had to do was make the custard for the apple pie which had been warming in the oven. The kitchen had every modern convenience available. Bronwen called it a "dream kitchen". She hadn't known what was available at that time; the choices were left to Stella and Colin. Kevin helped Stella to choose the colour schemes and Colin to install them. Kevin was learning fast under Colin's supervision.

'This sort of work is a dawdle compared with being in the black hole of a coalmine,' Kevin told Colin. 'I'm grateful to you for taking me on.'

'Glad to have you,' Colin had replied. 'I needed someone who I could trust and who I know isn't afraid of hard work.'

After lunch on that Sunday afternoon Bethan went home to her own family. Geraint went for a couple of hours sleep, Mary went into the lounge to watch television, so Bronwen and Stella were left on their own.

Stella helped Bronwen to undress to take a couple of hours sleep. She had given one of her twice daily leg and buttock massages and leg bending exercises. Only Stella was familiar with Bronwen's unclothed body.

She rotated her feet at the ankles and bent her legs gently at the knees as she had been shown by the physiotherapists. It, at least, prevented stiffness.

Bronwen asked Stella a personal question. 'Has Kevin popped the all-important question since he did when we on the cruise?'

When Stella had been alone with Bronwen soon after they arrived back at The Sunshine Mount Nursing Home, Stella told Bronwen what Kevin had said about her obvious love of babies and that he thought she still had time to have many of her own if she married him soon. She told Bronwen that Kevin told her he loved her and would be prepared to marry her even though he knew she didn't feel the same about him. He would be happy to spend the rest of his life with her and give her children.

Stella couldn't explain to Bronwen her feelings for him except that she couldn't imagine life without him. They'd been going out together, off and on, for years. She had also admitted to Bronwen that her being four years older than he, made it unfair to him. He could find someone younger and prettier.

Bronwen had told Stella that she thought the age difference was irrelevant and he wouldn't find anyone prettier than her. She agreed that she was right to suggest that Stella think carefully about his proposal, before making up her mind. Bronwen thought, also, that Kevin was tolerant of Stella's attitude towards him, but she knew he loved her for some time, otherwise he wouldn't have put up with it, or she would have experienced a sharp rebuke.

One of Bronwen's many fine attributes was that she was a good judge of character. It amazed Stella how she could almost tell what a person was thinking, when she set her mind to it. After Stella had opened her heart to Bronwen she asked her the all-important question. 'Bronwen, do you think I should marry Kevin?'

'Stella, my lovely, I was hoping you wouldn't ask me that question.' Bronwen took Stella's hand and caressed it as she spoke. 'My eyes as well as my thoughts tell me that he loves you to distraction. You can tell me you don't want to lose him, but you can't say you love him, so you must decide for yourself whether you should marry him. I can't say whether you should, or not, but what I can and will say, is that I don't think you should marry him just for the sake of having children.'

'No, I know, Bronwen, you're right. But whatever I decide I would hope we can live here with you and Mr Lloyd-Davies. I can't leave you and it's not because I want to go on caring for you; anyone can do that. It's because I love you and depend on you; you are my rock.'

'To cover your first point—yes, you and Kevin will live here; there's plenty of room, and as for your second point—no one can care for me as you can. I don't want anyone else to care for me and I've known that since the first day I met you. If you have ten children, you must still look after me. And live here at 22.'

Bronwen's last remark eased the tension. They both chuckled.

'Not much chance of that,' Stella sighed. 'I'm not that fond of babies, but I would like a few.'

'You'd make a lovely mother,' Bronwen said, giving back Stella's hand. 'Can I ask you something personal?'

'Good God, no. I wouldn't want you to know anything about me,' Stella joked. 'You know you can ask me anything. Anything,' she emphasised.

'Well, I'll ask you, then. Has Kevin proposed since that night when you were together on the cruise?'

'No, he hasn't,' Stella replied with doubt in her eyes. 'I'm thinking perhaps it was the romantic circumstances of the lovely ship, the moon and stars. We'd had a lovely time. He might have changed his mind.'

'It wasn't just the result of a romantic evening together,' Bronwen remarked, 'I think he still loves you, but he said he'd give you time to think about it until we got home. I think he's waiting for you to make the first move. But I would advise you not to. Wait for him to ask you again. You'll be doubly sure that he wants you then.'

'What if he doesn't?' Stella frowned.

'Then I'd say, whether you love him or not, you've lost your chance. Now, I implore you, my lovely, wait for him to make the next move.'

Stella looked sad. 'You know I'll do exactly as you advise, and I've never known you to be wrong on any matters of the heart—or any other matter, if it comes to that. I'll go and nag Mary to tidy her room, before putting my feet up with my book. It's a good thing you don't go upstairs very often, because if you saw the state of her room, you'd have a fit.'

Bronwen chuckled. 'She's lucky she has you behind her. Don't get married if you intend to stop being her mentor. Tell her about that illocution class that's being held every week at the college, Stella. I'd like her to go but she's refused up to now. I think it's because she's afraid. Talk her into it if you can.'

'I'll try, but I hope she doesn't end up speaking as if she has a plum in her mouth. I'll get her to agree when we all go to that new wine bar in town on Saturday. She loves it and always gets a bit tipsy on a couple of gin and oranges.'

Bronwen was amused at Stella's remark. 'Watch she doesn't have too many won't you?'

'When we do all go out next Saturday night, do you want me to ask Dulcie to come in and sit with you and Geraint?' Stella asked. She was always concerned about them being on their own when she, Mary and Bethan were out late.

Dulcie Curtis and Bronwen had been friends and near neighbours since their childhood.

'Whatever for?' Bronwen tutted. 'Geraint and I are perfectly able to fend for ourselves, you know. Dulcie will pop in for a bit of company if she sees your car gone from outside, but anyway, stop worrying, Saturday is a week away.'

Chapter 22
Kidnapped

The days up to Saturday passed peacefully and happily though not uneventfully. There was always much coming and going in and out of 22, Queen Street. Bronwen had many friends who visited. They enjoyed having tea and biscuits at the lovely house and bending Bronwen's ear. They all had their different problems, but similar in that they were usually domestic ones.

Neighbours who had been neighbours from years ago wouldn't pass her door without calling in to ask if they could get her anything when their husbands drove them to the out-of-town supermarkets. It was as a matter of principle that they offered; they knew she had ample transport available to her. She had a smart Mercedes engineered to accommodate her in her wheelchair and Geraint with his Zimmer frame. Also, Stella was always at hand with her more modest, shiny new car.

Two elderly neighbours had husbands who had allotments on a piece of ground at the end of the street. They took pride in taking fresh vegetables to Bronwen. She tried to make them accept payment, but it was a matter of pride to refuse. The fact that they knew she was very rich added to their need to give—not sell. Yet, when any of the other neighbours had vegetables from them, a small charge was involved.

Mary's friends often called in with their children. When their morning's chores had been done and older children seen off to school, they had time on their hands. Mary always kept sweets and small bars of chocolate for when they called.

She took pride in taking them to her own room and showing them her beautiful clothes. At such times she was glad Stella kept her room pristine. The two cleaners who worked for Bronwen's household during the weekdays had had strict instructions from Stella and, indeed, Bronwen, that Mary was to do her own cleaning. That included the changing of her bed-sheets every week and all her own laundering. She was cack-handed at first but she, eventually, learned what had to be done.

Mary had lost over two stones in weight over the past year but was yet not as she should be. Not as sylph-like as Stella, but she never would be.

A few of Mary's friends were as overweight as she. One or two even more so. Most of them were slim. However, many of Mary's clothes could be made to fit her friends who couldn't afford lovely clothes. When a special occasion occurred for any of them: a wedding, a Christening or any celebratory night-out, they scanned Mary's wardrobe. She was willing for them to borrow any of her clothes. She was flattered and quite often she allowed her friends to keep whatever suited them. It allowed a good excuse for buying new.

When all her clothes were too big for the borrower, Stella helped out with the lovely items in her wardrobe. What was a little too big, could be taken in at the waist with a pretty belt. What was a bit too tight could be hidden with a loose, suitable blouse.

Mary was busy with callers that week after she, Bethan and Stella had gone to the pub to have a drink with Colin and Kevin.

She let her friends know about the coming Saturday night arrangement to celebrate at the wine bar. Those who were able to be there had to arrange something to wear. Mary's, Stella's and Bronwen's wardrobes were ransacked.

There was always someone making a friendly visit to the house. It got on Geraint's nerves. He was polite to everyone but invariably excused himself and went to his room to work on his computer and account books. He considered keeping track of Bronwen's financial business his responsibility. He took it seriously. It excited him, and it was the most important task of his existence.

He encouraged Bronwen to look at the accounts. He wanted to keep her as informed as he thought she should be. It bored her and she soon tired of listening to him.

'I'm lucky to have you, Geraint. You are an expert, so I know there will be no errors. If there are, it won't matter, and you must take as much as you want. If you don't, I'll have to see for myself that money is put into your bank account. I don't want to do it; I'm afraid of going wrong. And another point is, you must always have plenty in your pocket.'

'What do I want more money for, Bronwen. I have more than enough in my account and in my pocket. I have this lovely home with you, all the care I need with Stella and that young Bethan—though she has a lot to learn, and I have you for company. Plenty of other company when I want it, and when I don't, unfortunately.

I feel grand after that operation. My word, they're clever these days. But I am coming up to my eighty-third birthday. I won't last forever. I'll feel more confident with someone else knowing where you stand with all your wealth.'

'Don't talk like that, Geraint, you'll last for years yet. You told me your father was well over ninety when he passed on. Well you'll beat him, I'll be bound. But if that's how you feel, I think you ought to have a talk with Stella and Kevin.'

'Kevin is a virtual stranger; he might feel intrusive. But I'll do as you suggest. It's a pity Mary couldn't become your accountant. But we have to face it, she just doesn't have the ability. It would be impossible to her.'

'I know what you're saying, Geraint, and you're right. My poor Mary. She's doing well here, though. She's become a changed woman in the last year, thanks to Stella—and you, of course. To burden her with something which is beyond her ability would be cruel.

'But going back to Kevin, Geraint, I think he will soon be one of us. I hear the distant peel of wedding bells ringing in my ears. I think he and Stella are about to tie the knot. But you mustn't let on that I've told you. It's in the balance at the moment. I'm just waiting for the scales to tip, and she is, too. I'm not sure she would like to know that I have shared her secret with anyone—not even you.'

'Really,' Geraint said with surprise. 'I'm not so blind as to see that their relationship is beyond the bounds of friendship; I'm pleased for her. Of course, I won't let on that you've told me anything. I'll wait for her to come to me.'

'That's just the situation between them at present. He popped the question when we were on that lovely cruise but gave her time to get back here to think it over. She's waiting for him to ask again. She thinks he might have changed his mind, but I'd bet a million pounds he hasn't.'

'I hope you wouldn't gamble away a million pounds,' Geraint grinned. 'You'd have only a few left.'

His remark made them laugh.

On Saturday evening, the eve of Mary's thirty-third birthday, many people gathered to begin the celebration at 22, Queen Street. Kevin, Colin and Stella were the chauffeurs of the party-goers to the wine bar in town. The law was broken; cars were overloaded with passengers. No one seemed to give a thought as to how they were to get home; not even those who had left their husbands doing a turn of staying in with the children.

Everyone was dressed up in their finest. Some of Mary's, Stella's and Bronwen's outings were having an airing. Mary had a smart new outfit; a loose, frilly blouse and calf-length skirt which flattered her by hiding the fat-bulges which still remained from her days of obesity. Her thick, shining, tawny-coloured hair, one of her few good features, floated loose about her shoulders. Hair inherited from Bronwen, which was always well groomed in the bouffant style to frame her lovely face. It was now steel grey with hints of its original glory.

The men were dressed casually, as they would be if they were going to The Colliers' Arms.

'Aren't you and Mrs Dew coming to The Cellar wine bar, Mr Lloyd-Davies?' Colin teased. 'You'd both cut a dash there.'

Bronwen smiled and shook her head. 'You'll all have a jolly time.'

Geraint frowned. 'You're being patronising, young man. You know very well that Mrs Dew and I wouldn't enjoy that noisy place.'

Colin bent down to Geraint where he sat on the settee beside Bronwen. 'Tell you the truth, sir,' he whispered, 'it's not my cup of tea either, but I'm expected to fit in. I'm sure you know what I mean.'

Geraint chuckled. 'There are some compensations of being ancient.'

He and Bronwen were glad to see them gone and the door closed tightly behind the last one through it. Soon she would boil the milk that Stella had prepared in a saucepan on the exotic, modern cooking range. She had set a tray on the kitchen table nearby with mugs for the chocolate drinks and plates; one of neat sandwiches and another with slices of rich fruitcake. All Bronwen had to do was boil the milk and pour it into the mugs. Geraint would carry the tray onto the low table in front of the fire.

They looked forward to watching a "golden oldie" film on television. It would go on until quite late, but they would both be fast asleep in their beds before the party-goers arrived home.

Bronwen knew they wouldn't know what time that would be because they would enter the house quietly, not to disturb the old couple.

Bronwen's predictions were wrong that night. Something evil, beyond description, happened and would never be forgotten.

She and Geraint were awakened by a noisy entry to the house at around two o'clock. Stella, Kevin, Colin and a policeman went into the main lounge and stood waiting with anxiety.

Stella went straight into Bronwen's room. She awoke without being prodded. She saw Stella in a state of distress that she hadn't seen before—not in all the years of knowing her. Stella was a strong-minded character who didn't panic. Bronwen now saw her in a fearful state of panic, and she was sobbing.

'What on earth…?' Bronwen didn't finish the sentence.

'Bronwen, Mary has been taken and we can't find her. I'm sorry to wake you now, but this couldn't wait until the morning.'

Bronwen's mind was sleep sogged. Stella's words didn't register in her mind. 'What do you mean Mary's been taken? Where to? Why are you crying?'

'She went to the toilet. She was so long that I went to look for her and she was gone. One of her shoes was on the floor outside the toilet door and her handbag beside it. Her purse with all her money was gone. A man was in the car park. He said he saw a woman being dragged to a car; he thought she was drunk and was being taken home by two men, one each side of her. He was just coming into the bar. He said she was kicking and screaming but he thought nothing of it,' Stella sobbed. 'I'm terribly worried.'

Bronwen became alert; her stomach churned and she felt sick. 'Well, whoever it was will surely bring her back. She wouldn't stay away any time without us knowing.

'Look, I won't sleep now. Help me into my wheelchair. We'll have a cup of tea and talk about it. She'll be home soon, I expect. They'll bring her home, surely to God.'

When Bronwen reached the main lounge, she was surprised to see so many people there. Kevin and Colin she expected but four of Mary's friends were there, too. Not one of them looked as if she'd had a good night out. One of them, Sally, held Mary's pretty flat-heeled shoe. It was green, almost the same shade as the outfit she had on when she went out, except it had multi-coloured beads decorating it. The front of the shoe was as it was, but the back and heels had been scuffed, as if it had been dragged across rough ground.

'That's Mary's shoe,' Bronwen said, 'Is that the one that was outside the lavatory?'

'No, Bronwen,' Sally said, 'I picked this one up from the car park.'

Sally, one of the friends, began to tremble uncontrollably. 'She's been taken somewhere, and she must be terrified out of her mind. I know I'd be.'

'Sally, pull yourself together and you others.' Bronwen looked at the other girls. 'Go home to your husbands. Say nothing of this, mind. People will make too much of it. Mary will soon be home.'

Stella saw the young women out, thinking there was no hope that they wouldn't talk about tonight's incident. 'Now don't forget what Bronwen said, you lot. No gossiping, or you'll have me to answer to.'

'No, Stella.' they chorused. 'Let us know if you want to go on searching. The sooner Mary is home the more satisfied we'll be.'

When Stella returned to the lounge, she was crying again. 'Bronwen, I'm so worried.' Bronwen was too confused and anxious to respond.

'Stop your waling, Stella,' Colin snapped. 'That'll do no good.'

Kevin gave him an ugly look and put his arms about Stella's shoulders. 'Come on, love, this is not like you. We'll find her. That man in the car park was a special constable; he'll put a few feelers out.'

'A policeman putting a few feelers out!' Bronwen almost shouted. 'What do you think has happened to Mary? Do you know something that I don't?'

The doorbell rang. The shrill sound startled. The door between the lounge and the hallway was open, allowing a shuffling sound to be heard; someone pushing something through the letterbox.

No one moved.

'Who on earth could that be at this time?' Bronwen looked round at everyone but realised no one knew. 'It'll be our Mary. Her keys must be in her handbag that you found outside the ladies' toilet, Stella.'

Stella darted out of the room towards the front door. She saw an envelope on the doormat, but she ignored it to unlock the door and snap it open. There was no one there. She stood on the doorstep and looked up and down the street. She saw no one. She looked across the road to the rough patch of greenery, expecting to see someone lurking in the thick foliage. There was no one. It was as if whoever knocked on the door had disappeared like magic. It was odd.

She returned to the lounge having picked up the envelope and had begun opening it, though it was addressed to Bronwen Dew. Her intuition told her the words would be like poison and she didn't want Bronwen to be the first one to read them.

Geraint, from his room upstairs, heard the doorbell ring and became aware that something was going on down stairs. He had descended the stairs on the chair lift and had entered the lounge when Stella was scanning the street.

His feet and ankles were snuggled in a blue and grey chequered pair of carpet slippers and he was enveloped in a long teddy-bear brown dressing gown. It was tightened about his waist by a thick dressing-gown cord which seemed to stop the gown from dropping.

'Well, what is it? What did it say?' Geraint asked, wondering why Stella's hands trembled.

Kevin went to her and put his arm about her. 'What is it, love?'

Stella couldn't answer; she didn't want Bronwen to hear.

'Stella! For God's sake what is that? What does it say?' Colin snapped.

After reading it, Stella handed a single page of lined paper to Geraint. She had taken it from a small grubby envelope. She sat beside Bronwen.

'Bronwen, something awful has happened to our Mary. She's been taken by some men; kidnapped. They want money to have her back.' Stella sobbed, rubbing her eyes sore with a saturated piece of tissue.

Geraint's face blanched. 'Whoever they are, they're illiterate young thugs,' he said. 'This was written by no adult.'

Bronwen snatched the slip of paper from him and read it. The feeling of dread increased as her eyes moved slowly through the words. The serene, kind, forgiving Bronwen went into frenzied despair. Her hand, holding the letter, flopped onto her lap.

'My Dear God. Please don't let them hurt her. I'll give anything they want, everything I have. Please let her come back.'

Kevin could no longer tolerate the suspense of wanting to know what was written on the sheet of paper. He took it from Bronwen's hands and read it out.

'We ave you girl Mary. You can ave er bak after you giv us a undred thosand ponds. Thas a hundred grand. We want nots of 5 10 20 50 and 100 ponds. Get the muny and put it in a big c box on you dorstep on tewsday nite cos the banks not open til munday. Keep you frunt dor shut an sumwun wil pik it up and bring it yere. If you see woo piks it up and ask im things, you wont ave you Mary back in wun piece. We all got shap nives. Wen we got the muny the boy wil bring you a not telin you wer she is. If you folo him, you won see your Mary agen unles is in peeces.

An you won have er bak alve if you tell the polis. Remember NO POLIS.

You beta get the muny kwik lik we ask. The longa we ave er the more we will play wiv er if you see wha we meen. An rememba a undred grand.'

The spelling was bad; Kevin was hesitant in trying to decipher it. He was shaken and at a loss for words. For a time no one spoke. The only sound in the room was of Stella crying and Bronwen's laments.

Kevin was the first to speak. 'Bronwen, we'll find her. I promise you, if we don't, someone else will. We'll get her back. I promise we'll get her back.'

'It's that rotten money,' Bronwen sounded bitter. 'That rotten, rotten money. I shouldn't have taken it. Geraint, get what they want now. Don't wait until the bank is open. Find the bank manager's home number and get it.'

'Right, Bronwen, I'll do that. I'll start trying to get it now.' Geraint made to leave the room to go to his computer and telephone directories.

'Wait, now,' Colin interrupted. The room went silent, waiting for him to have his say. 'These thugs said no policemen. Well, don't forget, it was a special policeman who helped us look for her. I can't see him keeping this from the regular police. And another thing, Geraint. When you get in touch with the bank manager out of hours to arrange for a hundred grand in cash to be ready, in cash, as soon as he can, before Tuesday night, don't you think he's going to ask why?'

'Yes, you're right, Colin,' Geraint nodded. 'And knowing Clapworthy as we do, I can't see him handing over the money without being very suspicious.'

'Dear God!' Bronwen wailed, 'What are we to do. We're all sitting here doing nothing. Mary, Mary, where are you? What are they doing to you?'

Stella sniffed and stopped weeping to give her opinion. 'I think these are kids, not men,' she said. 'And what's more I think someone in this street is involved because when I answered that door-bell, whoever rang it disappeared too quickly to go up or down the street. He went into one of the houses in this street and not far away either.'

'That's right,' Kevin spoke as he went near Bronwen. He knelt in front of her wheelchair. 'Think, Bronwen. What boys in this street aged between, say, eighteen and twenty plus, could be the sort of boy to do this to Mary?'

Bronwen blew her nose on her snip of lawn-cotton handkerchief. 'Wait a minute, Kevin. I can't think straight. I'll try to pull myself together. Give me a few minutes.'

'Yes, let's all pull ourselves together,' Geraint said, still in a state of shock, himself. 'While we're doing it, I'll go and put the kettle on. We'll have some tea.'

'You stay there, Mr Lloyd-Davies, I'll do that,' Stella said as she walked towards the kitchen. Kevin followed her.

Alone in the kitchen, he took Stella into his arms. 'I hate seeing you so upset,' he said. She was comforted by the warmth of him and returned the feeling he had in his heart for her.

'Don't worry about me, love,' Stella said. 'Think how Mary's feeling. They'll rape her, Kevin. If they're anything like the rotten little bastards in this street and those around here, she won't come away a virgin, I'm sure of that; even if they know they'll get the money.'

'Things are black enough without thinking the worse,' Kevin replied. 'But the police will have to be brought in, if they're not already, and every man or boy you or Bronwen would be suspicious of will be taken in for questioning. Once that's started they'd be afraid to do anything to her.'

Stella set a tray on the low table in front of the pseudo-flame gas fire and poured each of them a cup of tea. Kevin switched the fire on. Its real flame effect put a little cheer into the room. The chill of winter had added to the gloom.

Stella put down Bronwen's cup on the small table attached to her wheelchair. It was close to her hand, which shook too much to lift the cup to her lips.

'Bronwen, let me take you to bed. The police are bound to be here in the morning and you will rest in bed even if you don't sleep. I'll sleep on the other bed in your room tonight, is it?'

Bronwen nodded. 'She may be home by then. We can but hope.'

Stella turned to Colin. 'Colin, you'd better go home and get some rest but I'd rather you stayed here, Kevin, if you don't mind. You can sleep in the room next to Mr Lloyd-Davies, to make sure you're here in the morning. The police will have to be contacted.'

'Yes, right-o,' he said. 'Come on then Mr Lloyd-Davies, you take the stair-lift up first.'

No one slept; their minds were full of the same questions. 'What had happened to Mary? Where was she? How could the money be obtained in time and handed over to the kidnappers? What would happen to her?

Chapter 23
Gang Raped

Mary was convinced she would be murdered. At the wine bar she had made the mistake of being lured out of the short passage which led to and from the ladies' toilets.

'Mary, come out and see this smashing car.' A youngish man she had seen standing at the bar held out his hand to her. She took it spontaneously and he pulled her with force along the passageway.

She wasn't thinking logically. It went through her mind that he and a couple of young men standing with him had been looking at her from time to time during the whole of the evening. She thought they were admiring her, and she felt flattered. She knew she looked nice, but not nice enough for men such as those to admire her.

When outside the building, she tried to pull her hand away. Someone from behind clamped a foul-smelling cloth over her mouth so tightly her eyes bulged. She tried to scream; it was impossible. Another man grabbed her hands behind her back and tied them together until she felt the rope cutting into her wrists. A third man grabbed her hair and began pulling her further away from the building.

'Quick, boys,' she heard another man say in a hush. 'Quick, before somebody comes out. There's no one about out here except a man who's over the other side of the car park. He'll think she's drunk and we're taking her home, or something.'

They half dragged, half carried her some yards to a car parked in the shade of a high wall which edged the wine-bar's territory.

She heard yet another man's voice; she guessed there must be a big gang of them.

'Quick, for Chrisake,' he said, 'that man over there seems to be taking a better look over here.'

'Rambo, will you stop fuckin' panicking?' someone seethed. 'Do you want her to recognise your voice? Just push her into the back of the car.'

'Easy for you to say; she weighs a fuckin' ton. 'An' it's my face she saw, none of the rest of you.'

'Look, you are the only one of us who's not from round here. When you've had your cut of the dosh, you can fuck off to Australia, like you said you would.'

Mary thought he sounded like the ringleader. He was the biggest and was wearing an ugly rubber mask as they all did. The one who lured her into the car park had put one on. She didn't recognise his face at the wine-bar. He was a stranger to her and didn't have a Welsh accent as the rest of them did. She did wrong by letting him entice her out of the wine bar passage, but he was small and seemed nice.

She felt as if she were in Hell. Her lovely shoes had scuffed off her feet as she was dragged backwards to the men's car, and her new outfit was torn to shreds. She was bundled into the back seat, without thought of how she would land. Her head thumped against the opposite door. She was dazed until one of the men pulled her up.

The car's engine was switched on and the car backed out of its hiding place and drove out of the wine-bars parking lot. It couldn't have been heard by anyone; the loud music booming from the wine-bar's disco drowned out the sound of any noise moving in or out of the car park.

Mary was tugged into an upright position with a hand bunching what was left of the front of her dress. Another hand held a dagger. The steel blade glinted in the small amount of night light that beamed into the car. A strong hand held the point of the weapon to her throat; she felt its piercing, sharp point digging into her soft skin.

'When I take this gag off your mouth and you scream or make a nuisance of yourself, I'll slit your throat. Do you get that?'

Mary nodded with hysteria and horror filling her eyes and mind. The face of the man who spoke had a Halloween rubber mask on his face. It was that of Count Dracula painted with evil fangs dripping blood. He sat beside her and another man sat on her other side. He also had on a rubber mask. It was the face of a green devil with horns. They all wore horrible-looking masks to hide their identity. Mary recognised two voices behind them, but she decided not to admit to it.

The car was an estate type. An old one; it clattered as it went along and bounced on worn-out springs. In the front, one of the men sat beside the driver, prompting him not to exceed the thirty-mile speed limit. Behind, Mary and two of the men sat. Another one squashed in the luggage space. The gang of five sounded like fifty.

The gag covering her mouth was removed. 'I won't scream, I won't scream!!' she said immediately. Too loud for Dracula's satisfaction.

'Be quiet you stupid bitch,' he said as he dug the point of the dagger deeper into her neck. With the car in motion she wouldn't have been heard. It clattered along at a steady pace; not likely to be stopped by any of the many police that paraded the town on a Saturday night.

'All right. I'll be quiet. What have I done wrong and where are you taking me?' Her words were gasping; she was too frightened to cry. 'Don' kill me! Please don' kill me! Wha' you doin' this for?'

'Your mother, the rich woman and that wrinkly Lloyd-Davies will know that, and soon. We've asked for a hundred grand for your safe return. When we get the money, they'll come and take you home.'

'My mam don't keep all that much in the 'ouse and the bank is shut?'

'We know that; we're not daft. We give 'er till Tuesday to get the money. If we don' get it, it's curtains for you.' The gang leader, the one with the knife, did the talking. His voice was familiar, but she was too frightened to make judgement.

'She'll give it to you but take me 'ome first. I'll get it for you on Tuesday.' Mary was quieter but trembled uncontrollably. 'I feel sick. You'd better stop, or I'll sick all over you.'

The man squeezed further away from her. 'Shit! Don't you spew over me or you'll get this slashed across your ugly mug.' His remark made her feel more nauseous.

The driver turned his head to glance at her. 'Sick on the fuckin' floor then, you stupid cow. I can't stop until we get there.'

'And you shut your fuckin' mouth, unless you want her to recognise your voice. And keep your eyes on the road,' the gang leader shouted.

'Where we goin'?' Mary screamed, 'Where we goin'?'

'You heard what I said about you screamin', di'n you? I won't warn you again; you'll have this.' He held the blade so close to her face she smelled the steel of its slim blade.

She sank back in the seat and silently sobbed. Her tears flowed freely and washed away the smudged mascara.

'We're going to a caravan,' the leader said. 'But it's going to be no holiday. Until we get that money from your dear mammy you're going to rough it.'

The man sitting in the back end of the car reached over and grabbed her breasts in his hands. It hurt her, and she screamed again.

'But you won't be lonely, love. We'll play with you a bit.' He leered over at her. 'She got lovely big tits, too.'

The man with the dagger got angry. 'Get back, you ram. There'll be none of that.'

The man in the back didn't sound pleased. He grabbed the one, who seemed to be the gang-leader, by the hair that protruded from his ugly, mask and yanked his head back.

'You listen to me. You may have taken the place of the boss here, but not over me. I'll fuck when I want to. We're equal shares in this, but with the dosh. I won't take any more than my share, but what extra I get out of this is up to me. Get it?'

'I get it, Jordy boy, but you damage the goods in any way, and you'll get more of a share than you bargained for.'

Mary realised why the man who lured her out of the wine-bar didn't sound as if he came from around here. He was a "Jordy", whatever that was. His rough grabbing of her breasts in that threatening way added to her fear.

The sour atmosphere in the car became silent except for breathing sounds, sniffs and occasional scraping of throats. To Mary, it was a journey through Hell and just as she wished she would die, the man beside the driver spoke.

'Digby boy, you take the next left. It's a narrow lane that will take us to the field.'

'Don't use my name, you stupid bastard. I don't want her to know my name in case she recognises my voice.'

'Sorry, Butty. Here we are, though. The surface is a bit rough. I hope the bloody car don't fall to bits.'

The driver sounded chuffed. 'Never mind. 'This is nearly its last lap. We'll all be able to buy new cars when this little lot is over.'

The description of being "a bit rough" was an understatement. The lane was made for farm tractors and herds of cows. The car stopped by a five-barred gate and the navigator got out to open it. He waved the car in before closing the gate behind it. He didn't get into the car again but walked toward the corner of the field they'd entered, to where a circle of five tumble-down caravans were parked.

The driver steered the car to between one of the caravans and a thick hawthorn hedge where it couldn't be seen from the lane or by anyone approaching the caravans.

'Here it is,' the navigator said. 'No one ever comes here, and these vans have been abandoned for years. They're not fit to live in and there's no water nearby.'

They all got out of the car leaving Mary trussed up inside. They had kept her hands tied securely and had added a gag to her open mouth. She was unable to utter a sound except for groans of discomfort.

The night was still and silent. A fog hovered over the damp grass and blanketed the sky. When the car headlights were switched off, the world was pitch black, until broken by the beams of the kidnappers' torches. Mary could hear part of the conversation.

'Jesus, Butty. You said this was rough, but you didn't say it was a load of shit. The cows have been dossing down in these vans by the looks of them. They're hardly fit for animals let alone us.'

'They were put here for farm workers. When they went away, the caravans were just left until a load of Hippies found it and formed a commune. Then it became too bad for them, so they passed on. Then these caravans were left to rot. And good thing for us they were. But with a bit of luck, we won't be here for long, either. Follow me, I'll show you the best one.' He walked toward the third one along the line.

There were three wooden steps to get into the caravan, but they weren't used; they would have collapsed. Each of the men leapt up from the ground into the rotting wooden caravan.

The floor was littered with filth—used rusty food and drinks tins, mouldy and stinking remains of meals: fish and chips, Indian and Chinese. There were rags of various clothes, sacking, soiled plastic refuse bags and a number of used condoms. Against one wall was a rolled up, old ticking, bed mattress. One of the men pulled it away from the wall, unrolled it and spread it out on the filthy floor. It was bug-infested and whatever it was stuffed with had broken through holes on its surface.

There was a broken kitchen chair and a plastic garden bench against the wall opposite the mattress which would offer no comfort to Mary's abductors.

The wood of the walls and floor of the caravan was rotten. In one place on the floor was a gaping, splintered hole where a foot had broken through. The kidnappers stepped with care in case they, too, went through the floor. Each end of the caravan was a wide gap where once the windows had been, recognisable by the flaking frames.

'Well this is her chamber and ours until Tuesday,' the gang leader said.

'What do'ye mean by 'ours'. We're not staying. We tie her up and leave her on that until Tuesday.' He pointed to the foul mattress. 'She'll get lousy with fleas but that won't kill her. Show 'er 'ow the other 'alf live.'

'One of us will have to stay with her all the time. We'll go in turns. We've all got mobile phones; we keep in touch. Better still, two of us at a time stay with her. There's five of us. I'll have to go last 'cause I'm the one with the car.'

'Well, when it's my turn,' one of them leered. 'I'll keep myself warm by rubbing against her. A bit of fuckin' will pass the time away. There don't seem nothin' else to do.'

'What you do to pass the time away is up to you, but you'd better be careful she's not damaged. We're asking for a hundred grand for her safe return, remember. Now, let's get her in here and on that mangy mattress. Watch where you tread. We don't want the floor collapsing.

'Boyo, you were in the back. There's a pack of sandwiches and a bottle of water there. Get them and put them somewhere where she can reach them. Whichever one of us is with her will have to untie her hands but watch to tie her legs first. We don't want her darting through the door, but we got to feed her and give her drink, or she'll die on us. An' we don' wan' that, do we?'

'Oh, sorry, Butty, I didn't know they were for her. I've ate half o' them but there's a bit left and the bottle of water. I'll get them. You lot can get her out of the back of the car and bring her into this lovely bed-sit.'

Mary was straining her ears to hear what was going on. She'd hear them talking about a caravan and hiding her there. In the still night the mumble of voices reached her, but she couldn't make out what was being said. She imagined they were arranging her murder and disposal of her body, but that would be after her mother paid them the money they asked for.

She realised it was late now, and she would have been missed. Stella, Kevin and Colin would know she had been taken and would be looking for her. They would never find her here; she would never be seen again. She felt despair and convulsively shivered.

Her mother would have been told by now that she'd been taken, and she would be worried out of her mind. Mary had seen this sort of thing happening on television. She guessed it was happening to her because her mother was rich, and she would have to pay to get her back. She hoped it would be soon. She would die if these men don't kill her first.

The gag in her mouth and the cord around her wrist were cutting into her flesh. She would have closed her eyes and tried to sleep and shut out the terrible thing that was happening, but she was in too much discomfort.

They dragged her along the back seat of the car until she was able to put her feet on the ground. Her eyes bulged with fear as two of the men pulled her into the caravan and the other two lifted her, having told her not to use the rotten steps. When inside, her terror-filled eyes rolled from side to side and her nose twitched as the foul smell filled her nostrils. She tried to yell but the mouth-gag was effective.

'Lie down on there,' one of the men wearing the rubber mask of an ape ordered.

She shook her head with hysteria as he pulled her towards it and pushed her. She thought it best to do as he bid. She had never experienced such filth or bad treatment in all of her thirty-three years.

'Right, since you are the one who's eaten you will be the one to stay tonight. Which of you is going to volunteer to stay with King Kong here,' Dracula ordered?

'I will,' the one called Rambo volunteered. 'I'd rather get my turn over with. But you make fuckin' sure to be here early in the morning with some grub since you're the one with the car.'

Mary realised she was to be on that mattress all night. She was already shivering with cold and wouldn't be able to tolerate being tied up and in that position until morning.

Three of the men left, leaving Mary at the mercy of the one without a mask, Rambo, who had mauled her breasts in the car and the one wearing a mask of an ugly ape. One sat on the broken chair the other on the bench.

Rambo knelt down and leered at Mary. He had acned skin, a big nose and rotten teeth. He moved close to her. His foul breath wafted to her as he spoke in a dialect that was unfamiliar to her.

'I'm not sitting on that fuckin' chair all night, Mary Darlin', I'm going to kip down here by you. And for sharing your bed with me I'm going to do something for you. I'm going to take that gag out of your mouth.' From the back of his jeans he slipped out a fierce looking blade. 'Remember, though, if you make a sound, this can cut your throat as easily as it can cut this gag.'

The ape tugged at his shoulder. 'Eh, Rambo, do you know what you're doing? If she screams, she could be heard by someone who just might be about. You never know.'

'Are you going to shout, Darlin'?' Rambo touched her cheek with the point of the knife.

'No, no,' she said. 'I won' scream. I won'.'

'There, you see,' Rambo looked up at the ape. 'She won't scream. Now I'm goin' to give her a bit of the old "you know what". If you want to watch, be my guest. If it embarrasses you, go out for a pee and make it a long one.'

'Embarrass me, like hell,' the ape replied. 'If that's in the game, I'll take a turn after you.'

Mary was pushed flat on the filthy mattress; Rambo got on top of her and wrenched her legs wide apart before undoing his belt and the fly-zip of his jeans before tugging them down about his ankles. He rose what was left of Mary's dress above her thighs and rubbed himself up and down on her defenceless, near-naked body.

He groaned, 'It's coming up lovely.' He grabbed her breasts. 'An' you got lovely big tits. Just as I like 'em.' He plunged himself inside her and she screamed. She couldn't stop herself as she fought to push him off her. Mary was a virgin and knew next to nothing about sexual intercourse.

'Shurrup!' he shouted. 'Boyo, put that gag on her again.' Her screaming and struggling didn't deter him pummelling himself into her.

The ape grabbed the twisted rag and made to put into her mouth. It was difficult with Mary squirming and Rambo lunging himself up and down on her body.

She became still, knowing there was nothing she could do to stop the despicable act. The quicker it was over the better. She closed her eyes and suffered in silence. He grunted when he reached climax.

He groaned with pleasure. 'That was great. Better if you kept still, you cow. Next time you'd better behave yourself.'

She wept, sobbed and squirmed as much as her restriction allowed. She stopped thinking, stopped feeling.

'Hang on, Rambo boy. I'll have a turn now,' the man in the ape-like mask said.

'Go on then. I want a bit of a rest, anyway. Don't be long, though.'

Having watched the act of rape, the nameless man had become aroused. He took off his trousers, lowered himself onto her and forced her legs apart with his knees. Mary saw what she considered an enormous penis, before it was lunged inside her. He bounced on her until he was fulfilled, afterwards resting himself on her, relishing the pleasure he'd taken from her.

The men raped Mary in turn until she lapsed into an unconsciousness which she had prayed for.

'Eh, Butty, I think we've fucked her to death. She's not moving, and her eyes look funny an' she's gone awful stiff.'

'Don't be daft. 'Course we 'aven't.' He looked over at her, through the eyes of the ape-mask. 'She's still breavin'. She's stiff from the cold. She been shiverin' all the time.' He was clearly worried.

'If she is, we can watch out for Digby, our mate, who thinks he's boss, 'cause he's the one with the car. Chesty bastard.'

Mary wasn't too unconscious to hear the name, Digby, mentioned. Digby Mason lived in the street adjacent to Queen Street. She thought she knew the voice but, of course, wasn't sure. He was at The Cellar wine-bar and she caught him often staring at her. She remembered he was standing next to Mickey Curtis who lived with his grandmother six houses away from where she lived. His granny often bent Bronwen's ears to share her worry about him. He was twenty-two, never had a job in his life and always in trouble with the police. He had once been imprisoned for causing grievous bodily harm.

Mary groaned. She was beginning to stir. 'I'm cold,' she mumbled. 'I'm cold.' She spoke as if she were pleading for help. In her semi-conscious mind, she had a vision of the men at the bar of the Wine Cellar. The voice of the man wearing the ape-like mask spoke and she recognised it to be that of Mickey Curtis. She hoped she wouldn't, inadvertently, address Mickey by his name. She knew, instinctively, she had to be careful what she said.

'She's still alive, anyway.' Mickey Curtis sounded relieved. 'Thank God for that. We might 'ave been sliced up ourselves by the big head. Here, give us your jacket. We'd better try to warm her up a bit.'

Rambo reluctantly removed his jacket and put it on her bruised, naked body. Her dress was unrecognisable, in tatters about her chest.

'Come on, your jacket as well. She needs it over her feet and legs. And get that bottle. We'd better offer her a drink.'

Mickey, also reluctantly, took off his jacket and put it on Mary's bare legs. 'Rambo, she can't drink with that gag in her chops, can she now?'

''Course she can't, you daft bugger. Get it off.'

The ape, Mickey Curtis, undid the knot of the gag on Mary's face. She hardly responded; she'd got used to it although it had cut into the side of her mouth. However, the second he put the bottle to her lips she greedily guzzled the tepid water. He cut the rope that tied her hands together behind her back, freeing her to grab the bottle to help herself to the fluid. When she knew the bottle was empty, she lay back on the stinking mattress and fell into a deep asleep; blessed oblivion.

'I think we can let her be for a bit,' Mickey said. 'By the look of her she's not leaving here tonight, however much it's like a slum of hell.'

Rambo agreed. 'Christ, I'm cold and hungry, too, and I could murder a pint. I hope that bastard with the car won't be late coming here tomorrow. And I hope he'll bring some grub.'

'I hope, too,' Mickey agreed. 'My granny will be wondering where I am. I shouldn't stay here all night.'

The time for the two villains dragged through the night and the following day, until one o'clock. They didn't bother to restrict Mary's movement by tying her up again. Apart from putting the bench in front of the door in case she found the energy to make a dash for it they were past caring. She was aching, bruised and injured so severely between her legs, she wouldn't have had the ability to walk, let alone make a dash. Anyway, she had no idea of where to go. She was in the hands of her captives. She prayed her mother would pay up soon to end her suffering.

When the gang leader, still wearing his Dracula mask, and his two accomplices arrived next day, Mickey and Rambo attacked him. Rambo, the bigger man, grabbed Dracula by the throat with one hand and was about to punch him with the other.

'You bastard. We're all supposed to be equal in this. Did you finally remember we were in this stinking, rat hole?'

Dracula was too sharp for him and adeptly kneed him sharply in his groin. Rambo yelped and backed off.

'We all 'ad things to do,' snarled the man wearing a devil-mask covering his face. 'We 'ad to act natural-like. An' when we passed Mrs Dew's house, we saw a white box on the doorstep. I thought I saw something like an envelope on the top of it.'

'So, Ape-face,' Dracula's muffled voice came from behind his mask, 'you'll have to pick it up and get into your house pretty sharpish, like you did when you put the note in. It may be giving us some instructions. Contact me straight away; you have my mobile number? I spoke to someone in the house this morning and he said the rich woman was in the process of getting the money. I spoke to that big guy. He looks tough, but I don't think he'll give any trouble.'

'Great, then,' Mickey replied with excitement in his tone, 'the money might be in the box.'

Dracula's glance went to Mary's moribund figure under the two jackets. He moved the one covering her face and chest. 'Jesus!' he yelled, 'what happened to her? She's half dead.'

He removed the jacket from her bottom half revealing the full extent of the manhandling she had suffered. She had fouled the already putrid mattress and lay in her own excreta. Her face was marble-like except where it was bruised. Her blue lips sagged, and her bluish tongue dropped out of them. The lids of her closed eyes were also blue. Her breathing was shallow, hardly noticeable except for the slight movement of her chest.

'She's dying of cold,' Dracula shouted at the two men who had guarded her during the long night. 'What's happened to her clothes? What the hell have you done to her?'

'Nothing except to fuck her a few times to keep her and ourselves warm. We had to stop when she pissed 'erself,' Mickey mumbled, sounding full of guilt. 'How did you expect to see her, stuck out here all night?'

'What did you expect us to do?' Rambo asked, 'light a fuckin' fire?'

'Go to the car and get a rug that's in the back,' Dracula said to the man who wore a werewolf mask, who had arrived with Dracula. 'And bring that bag of sandwiches and the drinks.'

'Thank God for that,' Mickey emphasised, 'I'm fuckin' starving.'

'They're not for you,' Dracula snapped. 'They're for her.' He pointed to Mary. 'We'd better do something to revive her. If she stops breathing and dies of cold and shock, there'll be no hundred thousand grand; we'll be on the run from the coppers for murder.'

His remark put fear into the four men. Mickey bent over Mary and spoke to her through his ape facemask. 'Mary, wake up and have something to eat. We'll be taking you home soon.'

He had no response from her. It seemed her brain had blessedly switched off from the horror of what was happening to her.

'Mary!' he called louder, 'you can wake up now and have something to eat.'

'She's in a bad way,' Dracula looked worried. 'Couldn't you see how bad she was? We'd better do something quick.'

Just then the man returned from the car with a rough, tartan wool rug. He went to put it over her.

'That's no good,' Rambo growled. 'Put it on the floor. We'll have to roll her off that stinking wet mattress then put your jackets back over her.'

They did as the boss instructed. They rolled her off the mattress onto the rug beside it. She fell onto her side.

Mickey and Rambo had been so cold they had taken their jackets from Mary for themselves. They hurriedly took them off and handed them to Dracula.

'At least you've warmed them a bit,' he said. He began massaging Mary's feet, calves and thighs before putting a warm jacket over her. He instructed the two men who had arrived with him to take off their jackets and they were put over her. He then rubbed her back and chest as far as he could and put his warm jacket over her.

'Give me the water,' he ordered. The bottle was eagerly handed to him by one of the accomplices who was silently praying that Mary would open her eyes. Dracula put the bottle to her mouth and gently tilted it. It was flavoured water and Mary's mind responded to the sweetness. She licked her lips and seemed to need more. Rambo dripped more into her mouth and she swallowed. He heard sighs of relief around him. He looked up at one of the men with whom he ordered to guard her for the next twenty-four hours.

'Don't let her get like this again,' he demanded. 'Keep talking to her and as soon as she's able to swallow properly give her bits of sandwich. The sooner we can hand her back the better.

'I'd better take these two back, now. Ape-face will have to pick up that shoe-box off the Dew's doorstep and dart into his own house before someone sees him.' He looked at Mickey. 'Do you know what I mean?'

'Yes, Boss,' he nodded willingly. 'And I'll ring you on my mobile to tell you what's in it. I know your number.'

'Right. Now we go and you two will stay with her until I come back tomorrow.' He pointed to the two men, one wearing a werewolf facemask, the other a devil. 'Keep the masks on because when she's back, she's going to be asked to give descriptions of us.'

Dracula, Rambo and Mickey jumped out of the caravan into a cold drizzle, wearing no jackets. The two men inside complained about being cold before they were left.

'Eh, Dracula Boss,' the devil-mask ordered, pointing a threatening finger. 'An' don' forget, we'll expect you in the morning and not after you've had your bacon an' eggs and a read of the paper. We got no coats and not much to eat.'

A muffled voice came from the werewolf. 'An' it looks like we won't be able to entertain ourselves with her, as they did.'

'You can put rape right out of your minds,' Dracula warned, 'unless you want to see her dead. She's barely conscious now. I hope to God she survives.'

Chapter 24
Rescued

At ten o'clock, the morning after Mary had been kidnapped, the telephone rang. Normally, Bronwen answered; most of the telephone calls were for her.

She looked at Kevin and shook her head. She was too devastated to answer. He realised she was asking him to do so. He picked up the receiver.

'Hello,' he answered, 'this is the home of Mrs Bronwen Dew.' A pause followed as Kevin listened to what the caller had to say.

He spoke again. 'Mrs Dew has already contacted her bank to arrange the sum of money you've ask for is at her disposal, but it's not easy to get such a large sum in so short on time. You might have to wait another day. Let me speak to Mary.' Another pause before Kevin went on.

'I warn you, if as much as a hair of her head is put at risk, you will be hunted down, and I swear we'll get you. And no, as yet we haven't contacted the police but, you rotten bastard, you'd better know there was a policeman in the car park who saw you take Mary. We won't be able to keep it from the police much longer.'

The gang-leader clicked off his mobile phone. Kevin immediately dialled the recall number, but the caller's number couldn't be traced.

Kevin paled and beads of sweat glistened on his brow. 'He said Mary's fine but wouldn't be unless the money is on this doorstep on Tuesday. He said to make sure there's no one watching out when the box of money is picked up. When the money is safely in their hands—there must be a gang of them—we'll be told where Mary is, so we can go and get her.' He looked at Geraint who sat beside Bronwen.

'Mr Lloyd-Davies, do you think it would be a good move to put that big shoe-box of Stella's on the doorstep with a note explaining that all attempts are being made to give them what they ask? The box will attract their attention. They're bound to pass this door sometime today and they'll get the note.'

Stella was in the kitchen. She heard Kevin's bass voice as she stood at the sink preparing vegetables. She stepped quietly into the lounge and heard the end of what he said on the phone. She went to Bronwen and embraced her. They both wept.

'Geraint, for God's sake, ring up that bank manager again to make sure he understands the urgency of this.' Bronwen was in despair. She rocked her body to and forth as if she found comfort in the movement.

Geraint was considering what Kevin had suggested. 'Yes, Bronwen, I will. I've stressed the importance as much as possible, but I'll ring him from time to time to stress the urgency. And, yes, Kevin, I think we'd better do as you suggested. The more contact we have with these evil people the better.

'But you know, these men aren't experienced criminals. The note was written by someone barely able to write and that phone call was too long. An experienced crook would have cut off after a much shorter time. He gave you time to possibly recognise, or at least, remember his voice.

'Another point is that experienced kidnappers would have asked for much more than a hundred thousand. They obviously know that Bronwen won millions but are too timid to ask for a larger six figure sum.'

Bronwen looked up with a little hope in her eyes. 'Do you think so, Geraint? Then they'd be too afraid to harm her, I hope and pray. If I hadn't won that wretched money of hell, this wouldn't be happening.'

'I'll go upstairs and type the note,' Geraint said as he reached out for his Zimmer. 'Get that box ready, Stella. They are bound to see it on the front doorstep; they'll be keeping a sharp lookout, I should think.'

'Right-o, Mr Lloyd-Davies. Then I'll get on with the meal. We all should try to eat. Other than that, all we can do is wait.'

Stella found that the box with the note attached to its lid was gone from the doorstep just after three o'clock when they were reclining after lunch. She looked up and down the street for some sign of where it had gone and who had taken it. Being a Sunday, the street was quieter than usual; the weather was cold, grey and spitting rain.

She guessed someone with a car must have picked up the box, yet she didn't hear a car engine and she had been listening hard. It suddenly dawned on her that it might have been picked up by someone living in the street, but she quickly cast the thought out of her mind as being most unlikely.

An hour later the thought returned to her and she acted on it. It was as a result of Mabel Curtis, who lived six doors away, calling in on Bronwen. She did so once, sometimes twice, every week to have a short chat. She and Bronwen knew each other from the old days when Bronwen lived with Lewis and her parents.

Mabel had lived with her parents and husband, too. She had one daughter who became pregnant in her late teens. Her daughter abandoned her baby leaving Mabel, who was by then a widow, to bring up the child: a boy, Michael, known to everyone, except herself, as, Mickey.

The shrill ringing of the doorbell startled everyone in the room and broke the silence. Very little was said as they pretended to be watching the television as the others did.

Kevin leapt out of his chair to answer the door before Stella did.

'It's only me, Kevin, come to see how Bronwen is,' Mabel Curtis said with false cheer. 'And to have a change from my four walls. Won't stay long.' Mabel sensed the strained atmosphere immediately she entered the lounge.

'Bronwen, my lovely, there's down in the mouth you seem. Not like you at all. But there, it might be my thinking because I've been worried half to death myself.'

Bronwen was relieved to gather that Mabel obviously didn't know what had happened to Mary. She couldn't tell her.

'What have you been worried about, Mabel?' Bronwen asked.

'Well, my Michael didn't come home all night and I thought he might be in the clink again. I couldn't sleep a wink for worrying. Then this afternoon he came home, bold as brass, filthy dirty and no jacket. He came in, said, "Hello Gran", and went straight upstairs to his room. I went to the stairs to give him "what for" and saw he was carrying a white box. I didn't say anything about that because I thought he'd been shopping.

'"Where've you been all night? I asked him and where's your jacket? You're soaked; you'll catch your death."

'"Sorry Gran," he stopped and said. "I had a bit too much to drink so I went home to my butty's and slept there the night. I forgot my jacket; I'll get it back tomorrow."'

'He had a wash and came for his dinner. I'd kept it warm in the oven. He said he was starving. But I feel sure he's been up to no good, Bronwen. I could tell by the state of him and that look on his face, telling me to mind my own business. He'll be the death of me that boy will.'

No one noticed Stella sit upright in her chair, eyes and mouth agog. Kevin felt her stare at him. She beckoned him into the hallway and closed the door, which was usually left open.

'Mickey Curtis, out all night,' she said in a loud hush. 'With a white box, no jacket. He was at The Cellar last night, huddled together with four other creeps at the bar. They hardly took their eyes off Mary. Quick, telephone Colin and tell him to come over here straight away. We need him to help us corner Mickey Curtis. Tell him to come straight into the Curtis's at number 16.'

Kevin called Colin from the front step of the house to avoid Mabel hearing. He did exactly what Stella asked because he realised what she was thinking. No wonder there was no sign of anyone putting the note through the letterbox, or after the box had been taken off the doorstep.

'I'm going to number 16, now,' Stella said. 'I'll go straight into the house, no knocking, and catch him unawares. I'm sure he's in on it and he'll know where Mary is. You go to his back door because when he hears what I have to say, he'll make a dash for it. He's done it before when the police were after him.'

Stella waited about five minutes to give Kevin time to run up the street, around the corner and down the lane at the back of the houses to number 16.

Stella turned the knob of Mabel's front door and burst into the living room.

She didn't waste time asking Mickey if he knew where Mary was. She wanted him to know that she knew he was guilty.

'You rotten bastard, Mickey Curtis,' she shouted. 'You'll tell me where Mary is, or I'll see that you're put behind bars for the rest of your life,'

Mickey sprang up from the kitchen chair at the table with such a start that it fell backwards into the hearth. He had a mouthful of roast potato from the meal that his grandmother had kept for him. He spat it across the table where he had sat and dropped his knife and fork with a clatter. He dashed into the scullery, opened the back door with a force that caused it to rebound on the wall behind it, onto the back yard, down the short path to the door and into the gully. He opened it and crashed into Kevin's wide, tall frame which was blocking the way.

Kevin grabbed him by the scruff of the neck and dragged him back up the garden path towards the house. Mickey wasn't a tall man but thickset. Kevin handled him as if her were the weight of a rabbit. His feet barely touched the ground as he squirmed to be free of Kevin's grasp.

'Wha' you doin'?' he screeched. 'Wha've I done? I haven't touched Mary.'

When in the kitchen, Mickey was thrown onto the chair which had toppled over. Stella had picked it up and put it in the middle of the room. Kevin loomed over him and held him by his throat.

'Now the tighter this hand gets on your throat will depend on what you tell us,' Kevin snarled. Mickey was already gulping.

Stella held him by his hair with one hand, Mabel Curtis's sharp kitchen knife with the other. 'Where's Mary?' she hissed as she dug the knife into the flesh of his cheek. 'Tell us or I'll start by cutting your nose off.'

Mickey was frightened out of his wits. 'I don' know! How should I know?'

'The same as you know about this box and the note on it.' Stella had taken the liberty of running up Mabel's stairs into the back bedroom which she knew was Mickey's. The box and Geraint's note were on the bed. Beside it was Mickey's mobile phone.

'I don' know where that came from,' he stammered. 'My gran musta put it there.'

'Your Gran's a kidnapper now, is she? Well this is not your Gran's phone, nor the last message on it. Stella recalled the phone message; it was from Digby Mason asking Mickey if he'd picked up the box and to call him back straight away.

'Digby Mason,' Stella tried to stay calm. 'That snake. You were both at The Cellar last night with some other slimy looking toads. Now, where's Mary?'

Kevin tightened his grip on Mickey's throat, and he gagged. 'You're going to tell us where she is then come with us to get her or we'll cut you up into little pieces and throw you to Dai Dando's pigs. No one will ever see you again.'

'I don' know nothing'. An' if I tell you Digby Mason will kill me.'

Stella moved the knife to his ear and run the blunt end of it over its top. Mickey screamed. 'It's Digby Mason who told us to get Mary. He made us and said we would have a share of the money.'

'We'll let the police look for that bastard.' Kevin shook Mickey and his head wobbled like a rag doll. 'Now, where's Mary?'

Stella dug the point of the knife into the side of Mickey's nose. He yelled before surrendering the information.

'She's on a' old caravan site on Carpenter's farm on the road to Newtown,' he stuttered. 'It's down a lane on the left about eight miles out. Now don't cut me. Le' me go.'

'Is that lane called Mulberry Lane where some hippies used to have a commune?' Stella asked, still with the blade on his nose.

'Dunno no Mulberry Lane but, yes, it used to be a hippy place. 'An I have'n done nuffin' to Mary.'

Colin arrived. He knocked on the front door and walked in. He was dazed at what he saw. A scene from a crime film? A young man, the victim, on a wooden chair with Kevin half choking him with the neck of the man's T-shirt, Stella holding a knife to the victim's face with a murderous look in her eyes.

'What the…?' began Colin.

'He's just told us where they are holding Mary for a hundred grand. There's a gang of them, Colin, so you'd better get in touch with that special policeman who was with us last night. You said you know him. Me and Kevin are taking this evil bastard to show us where she is, you'd better tell that man to get the police in on it. We're going on the Newtown Road to Carpenter's farm, down Mulberry Lane, to the old hippy commune.'

Colin looked dazed. Things were moving too fast for him and he was confused.

'What if there's a gang of them down there?' he asked. 'How do you think just you and Kevin will be able to get to her. If they've asked for a load of money, they'll be pretty desperate characters, I would say. And it's getting dark.'

Kevin had pulled Mickey to his feet. 'How many are with Mary?' he asked.

'Two,' Mickey trembled. 'They've got torches for the dark. They're in the caravan with the bit of light showing. But remember, I was with Mary last night and she was all right when I last saw her this afternoon.' He sounded doubtful which hastened Stella out of the house towards her car which was parked outside number 22. She was glad of the darkening, misty night; she didn't want Bronwen or Geraint to see them.

'I'll drive, Kevin, I think I know where it is. You'll have to keep him in the back of the car. Here, tie his hands behind his back.' She took from her neck a fine silk scarf which, when twisted, made a strong tie about Mickey's wrists.

'Good idea,' Kevin said, 'though I can't see this coward making a leap from a fast car. But be careful, there's a lot of sharp bends on that road.'

On the way, Mickey continually swore his innocence. His tongue loosened; the more he talked the guiltier he made himself and his accomplices.

Digby Mason was the ringleader; there were two guarding Mary now and he and his mate who looked after her last night. Five of them in all, but he didn't want anything to do with it; he was made to. He din' hurt Mary but his mate messed her about a bit.

What Stella heard put sordid and fearsome thoughts through her mind, but most of her concentration was on the road. She drove fast, skidding around some of the sharp bends making Kevin cringe and shout at her to slow down.

She slowed down when she knew she was nearing Mulberry Lane. She missed it. Mickey called out to her and she backed the car about a hundred yards. Kevin's heart was in his mouth. He silently thanked God that the road was quiet, and no other car approached during the short time it took her to find the entrance to the lane.

It was rough and muddy. She stopped when she came to the five-barred gate. It had been left open but the entrance to the field was deeply mud-rutted and she daren't risk getting bogged down.

'We'll have to wait until the police get here, Stella. I can't let this piece of shit go to tackle the others on our own,' Kevin insisted. 'I could take on the two in the van, if this one is telling the truth and there are only two there, but it would mean leaving this one with you and I don't intend to do that.'

The area used to imprison Mary was, only just, discernible by the feeble light of the men's torches within.

'Let's take him across there with us,' Stella suggested. 'If Mary has been there since last night, she will be freezing and frightened out of her mind. They might have hurt her from what this rat has been saying.' She referred to the cringing Mickey who trembled with fright.

'They'll kill me for this,' he winced.

'Save me doing it then,' Kevin said as he dragged him out of the car, through the open gate and made for the caravan. Kevin and Mickey were wearing stout boots, but Stella had on a smart pair of fine-leather court shoes. She felt the mud squelch to her ankles. She was flimsily dressed and felt the November frost bite into her.

The two men guarding Mary heard the faint sound of the Volvo's engine across the field. At first they thought it was Digby Mason returning, having received the money early. When they both stepped out of the caravan and saw Mickey with a man tugging at the back of him and a woman in a light frock showing the way with a torch, they realised things had gone wrong. They took to their heels and fled around the back of the caravans in the direction of the main road, half a mile across the fields from where the ululating sound of a police vehicle could be heard.

'Some bastard has shopped us,' one of the men shouted. 'The cops will be after us.'

Stella reached the caravan in front of Kevin and the grovelling Mickey. She took the three steps up to the floor of it, the danger of the rotten steps hidden by the darkness. One collapsed and her foot got trapped. She ignored the injury to her leg and withdrew it before making a second attempt to get to Mary.

'Dear God!' Stella screamed. 'She's dead. Oh, Mary! Kevin, dial 999 and get an ambulance quick.'

Kevin threw Mickey to the ground and used his mobile phone. Mickey didn't try to run off as his accomplices had; the police car had arrived. It was parked in the lane behind Stella's car. Two uniformed policemen ran across the field towards the caravan.

'They've scarpered,' Kevin said. 'This one told us where Mary was. She's in a very bad way; we've called the emergency for an ambulance to be quick.' Kevin had cast his eyes on Mary and gasped at the sight of her.

The police knew of the kidnapping of Mary. Colin had informed them when he called from 16, Queen Street.

'We can't all go into the caravan or the floor will collapse,' Kevin warned. 'And we'd better move the cars further up the lane to make place for the ambulance.'

Kevin and one of the policemen ran back to the lane to move the cars. The other policeman clapped handcuffs on Mickey who continually emphasised his innocence.

Stella held Mary in her arms, rocking her to and fro and rubbing her hands up and down her back. Mary's breathing was so shallow it was hardly discernible, but she was alive. 'Keep breathing, my lovely, keep breathing. You're all right now. We'll soon get you warm.'

Within twenty minutes an ambulance and two paramedics arrived. They took one look at Mary and one of them telephoned the emergency department of the nearest hospital, about ten miles away. 'A bad case of hypothermia and assault,' he said before moving Stella away from Mary.

'You'd better go outside,' he told her. 'I can't see this floor standing the weight of us and Mary on the stretcher.' The second paramedic had brought in a stretcher and positioned it to roll Mary onto it. He wrapped a thick blanket around her. Mary was carried on the stretcher across the field and into the brightly lit ambulance. In a short time the area became alight with the many bright lights. Stella was able to see the pool of mud at the gate entry but, uncaringly, waded through it.

She travelled in the ambulance. Kevin and Colin followed. She knelt beside Mary's frozen body. She wept and pleaded. 'Please don't die, Mary. I'll never bully you again. I love you, please don't die.'

For two days Mary's existence tottered between life and death. It was established that she had been raped many times. She was dehydrated and badly bruised. The hypothermia became complicated with pneumonia. On the third day, when Bronwen and Geraint visited, she was sitting beside her bed eating her lunch in a comfortable chair.

Bronwen and Stella had barely left Mary's bedside. They were exhausted. Stella insisted Bronwen be taken home by Kevin at the end of the second day, having been told that Mary was out of the critical stage. Bronwen obeyed Stella. She was taken care of at home by Bethan and Kevin. Geraint was shaken by the incident, but he put on a good front to support Bronwen. He was afraid the same thing might happen again. That had crossed her mind, and she cursed that lottery day when she had all the numbers. She feared Mary would never be herself again or, certainly, not for a long time.

Bronwen's prediction was correct. Mary recovered physically but, emotionally, she was irreparably damaged. Digby Mason, the ringleader and planner of Mary's kidnapping was arrested shortly after she was rescued.

When he responded to the sharp knocking on the front door of his home, where he lived with his wife and two children, he was aghast. He knew nothing of what had happened since he left Mary, guarded by two of his accomplices at the caravan earlier that day.

The two policemen entered the passageway, pushing Digby back before closing the door. They went through the expected form before putting handcuffs on him. He was forced out and across the pavement into the back of the blue and yellow police car. He loudly protested, insisted he was innocent and had nothing to do with the Dew girl.

'And what makes you think we are arresting you because of the Dew girl, Mr Mason?' one of the policemen asked. Digby realised that his careless words proved his guilt.

It was late and dark, relieved only by the distant beam of a streetlight. Being a Sunday, it was quieter than other nights, though the sight of the police car in the street brought a few people to their doorsteps.

Digby's children were in bed. His wife was distraught and awakened them. She brought them down the stairs to the front door. 'What has he done?' she screamed at the police. 'He's been in with us all day!' She turned to Digby. 'What have you been up to again?' she screamed.

The children stood on the doorstep, crying and trembling with fear as they saw their father being taken away.

'He is believed to have has been involved in a serious crime Mrs Mason. You'll hear more in due course but in the meantime it would be best if you went indoors and took the children.'

She didn't go indoors. She stood on the edge of the pavement until the police car was out of sight.

She wept bitterly; she knew what Digby had been up to. He was excited at the thought of having a large sum of money and couldn't resist telling her about the kidnapping. Her shopping list had already been made out and a cruise of the Caribbean planned for.

The man who had been guarding Mary with Mickey Curtis on the first night of her terrible ordeal was arrested. The two men who had taken to their heels when Kevin and Stella had approached the caravan were caught the following day. The man called Rambo returned to his home in Birmingham and was caught some days later. He was well known to the police in his hometown.

Bronwen and those of her household were given this information but she had been too worried about Mary to care about the kidnappers' capture. She was more concerned about the fact that they would be brought to justice and Mary would be expected to attend the trial. They were all worried about Mary having to attend a court of law. She wouldn't cope with going through the rigors of questioning and having the details of that terrible event brought to the surface.

Stella, Kevin and Colin agreed to attend the trial and be witnesses. Geraint made it clear to the prosecuting police that Mary wasn't in a fit state of mind to attend the court. For her to have to take the stand in a courtroom and describe the details of her being gang-raped would be critically damaging to her recovery.

Chapter 25

A Birthday and a Wedding

Stella was nervous at the thought of having to stand in a courtroom and explain her part in the rescue. She said she'd do it ten times over to prevent Mary having to do it. However, it was essential that Mary attend the court to identify the criminals.

Kevin consoled her. 'You'll be fine. They want the truth and that's what you'll give them. Bronwen's money has changed us but we're still the same people.'

'Yes, you're right,' Stella agreed, 'but to people like us, Bronwen's money is more than enough to have changed our lives.'

Kevin, sitting close to her on the settee before the fire, put his arm about her.

'We're still the same people, love. I still love you; that won't change. Have you thought any more about what I asked you when we were on the cruise? Will you marry me?'

Stella beamed as she threw her arms around him. 'I thought you were never going to ask again. That cruise seems to have happened years ago. Yes, yes, I will marry you.'

'I've held out because I thought you didn't want to. I'd rather our relationship remain how it is than not have you at all. When will you marry me? Let's do it before you change your mind.'

The glow fell from Stella's face. 'Not yet. Not until all this rotten court case is over and settled. I'd marry you tomorrow, but we can't think of ourselves just yet. We've become a sort of family around Bronwen. She and Mary are my priorities at the moment, and I hope you're behind me. We can't leave it all to Bronwen and Mr Lloyd-Davies, can we?'

'Alright, love. I see your point. We'll wait, but I hope this trial won't drag on as so many do. We won't say anything to them for the time being. I'll go on working with Colin and getting some cash together. That'll be easy; I know I'm earning more than I'm worth.'

'That's wrong. You and he make a good team,' Stella declared. 'He's told me so. Anyway, you'd better think of going home now and me to bed. I want to get myself organised in the morning before those police investigators come.'

Stella referred to the repeated questions she expected to be asked.

The good relationship between Mickey Curtis' grandmother and Bronwen was spoiled. The street gossip was rife and old friends and neighbours of Bronwen's kept her well informed of what was being said, whether she wanted to know or not. Geraint was always at her side, reassuring her and advising as best he could, to protect her from being hurt.

Some of the neighbours suggested that the family in the "palatial" number 22 might have been, somehow, to blame for what had happened to Mary. Having all that money, they had become "above" themselves.

No one who called on Bronwen reminded her that Mary was intellectually disadvantaged, so was taken advantage of by the kidnappers. She guessed it would have gone through people's minds. When Mary was a little girl, she often went home to her and Lewis having been teased and bullied by spiteful children who made fun of her slowness and tardiness.

The local press wallowed in the story of rape and kidnap. For a number of days after that horrible Saturday and Sunday, journalists loitered around 22, Queen Street, hoping to speak to one of its inhabitants.

They took pictures of the house and of people going in and out; sometimes approaching them and plying them with questions. One day, a man with a camera made the mistake of taking a picture of Stella before approaching her to ask questions. She walked up to him and punched him. He held his bruised face, staggered backwards and fell onto the hard pavement stones.

They gathered directly outside the door, until Kevin approached a man in front of the group. He grabbed him by a bunch of clothing at his neck and shook him. He dropped his camera onto the wet paving stones and it broke into several pieces.

Kevin towered above him so the man, peacefully, moved away. Kevin looked fierce, though he was averse to be aggressive, unless necessary.

Eventually, the press journalists drifted away, as did interest in the Dews' affairs. People turned their minds to Christmas.

Bronwen and Stella hoped the festive season would help Mary to recover from her terrible ordeal. Her face was constantly expressionless; she rarely spoke, took no interest at meal times and had screaming nightmares. Her manner was robot-like. Stella had to remind her to shower or bath and change her underwear. She continued to groom Mary's hair, choose smart clothes for her and help her to make-up.

Stella would awaken Mary from nightmares and comfort her. 'Shush, love. You're all right now. You'll soon forget.'

'I won't, I won't. They did dirty, dirty things to me. I'll never forget.' Mary spoke more after a nightmare than at any other time.

Geraint suggested they do what they did last year—go to Cribbs' Causeway on a shopping spree.

'She enjoyed it a lot,' he said. 'She spent enough, and I told her she'd soon make you a pauper at the rate she was going.'

Bronwen chuckled. 'Yes, she did. So did we all.'

On a Saturday early in December 2000, the Mercedes took them to Cribb's Causeway. Stella and Kevin ensured all the walking aids, shopping bags, container of biscuits and flasks of tea, coffee and fruit drinks were in the boot in case they were held up by traffic. As on the previous year, a December sun brightened the day, but the bite of winter called for warm clothing.

Mary displayed some enthusiasm, but it was forced. She knew Stella and her mother were worried about her manner, but she couldn't help it. She was deeply depressed, and she had lost the will to drag herself out of it. Stella had to remind her to pick up her handbag containing five hundred pounds and her credit cards. She had put it on the hall table whilst she donned her coat.

Bronwen reminded her to take a woollen scarf and drape it about her coat.

The arcades of shops at Cribbs' Causeway were as beautiful as Bronwen remembered. Though it was early in December, the Christmas decorations were already there, and she thought no Christmas decorations in the world could be better.

Mary didn't notice them.

She didn't get lost as it was always feared she would, nor did she buy too many clothes. She didn't buy anything. She followed Stella into the shops and slowly browsed through the lovely clothes with no apparent interest.

Stella tried dresses on and encouraged Mary to give an opinion.

'Yes, Stella. That's nice. Buy that one.'

'Remember we're coming up to Christmas, Mary. You'll need some new clothes. We've got a few parties to go to and you've lost so much weight the frocks you've got are dropping off you. We'll all have to look our very best for The Sunshine Mount do. Your mother will expect it.'

Usually, the compliment of Mary losing weight delighted her. She now didn't seem to care.

'You pick one out for me, Stella. You know I'm hopeless at it.'

'No, you're not. You used to be, but you're not now. You have good taste since you've had plenty to spend on things.'

Stella chose two dresses for Mary.

'Do you like these, Mary? They're your size.'

Mary nodded.

'Go in the fitting room and try them on, then.'

'No. They'll be all right. They're nice.'

They all met at the same stall as on the previous year. The lady behind the counter remembered them; she had thought them a strange group. The bench which she remembered collapsing under the weight of Kevin and Mary had been taken away and replaced with a new one. Stella sat on it beside Bronwen's wheelchair, but Kevin chose to stand, regardless of being laden with bright-coloured plastic bags. He and Geraint had made a number of purchases; things for themselves and Christmas presents for others.

Bronwen was loaded with bags and boxes. A little for herself but, as usual, most for others. She bought for some of the neighbours and the residents at The Home. She had visited there a number of times since she and Geraint left and had kept in close touch with Helen Phillips, the matron.

They lunched at Debenham's restaurant, as they had the previous year, but the cheerful spirit was absent. Mary ate little. She went to the toilet, came back and put on her coat.

'When are we going home?' she asked, not seeming to notice that the others hadn't finished their meals. Bronwen looked miserable. Mary's behaviour spoiled the day for her. Stella became angry.

'Mary,' she snapped. 'Take that coat off and sit down. We are not ready yet.'

She did as she was told but made everyone feel uncomfortable.

When they arrived home, Kevin dropped them off before he and Stella unloaded the boot of all the purchases. He carried Bronwen from the car onto her wheelchair. He then parked the car on the verge opposite the house.

'I'll go straight on home, Bron, and leave you and the family to yourselves for a while. Can I take your car, Stella? I'll dump my stuff at home and bring it back later.'

Bronwen looked hurt. Recently, she always had a worried frown on her face. Stella decided that if she didn't do something, Bronwen would become as depressed as Mary. But she didn't know what to do. Mary had been seen by a professional counsellor and psychologist and both had advised patience and tolerance; time would heal.

Later that evening when Stella and Kevin were alone, she expressed her frustration to him. 'Patience and tolerance be damned. If she doesn't pull herself together soon, a good kick in the arse should help. It would help me, anyway.'

'Don't do or say anything you'll regret,' Kevin advised. 'Give it a little while longer. Until after Christmas anyway. Just let things ride. We are tending to forget the terrible experience she had. If we don't do what's right, it could take years for her to be as she was. It's been known for the victims of gang rape to commit suicide.'

His words frightened Stella into submission for a few weeks longer.

216

They embarked on a few more shopping sprees; Bronwen had more presents to get. They were packed and labelled by herself, Stella and Geraint, whilst Mary didn't take her eyes from a television programme which didn't interest her. It seemed the more they followed the advice of the experts the more depressed and withdrawn Mary became.

Christmas came and went, seeing the old year out and the new year in, came and went. Before the end of February, the trial of the five criminals was over and they were all sentenced accordingly. All things should have returned to normal. But they didn't. Mary's emotional condition continued to fill the home with gloom.

Saying nothing to Bronwen, Geraint or Kevin, Stella decided to change the approach. She went up to The Sunshine Mount Nursing Home and spoke to Matron Phillips, who knew the situation. Stella told her she decided to change her stance as far as Mary was concerned.

'And it's about time, too,' Helen said. 'I've seen a change in Bronwen over the past weeks that I haven't liked. It's just not her. She blames the winning of the money, but she has it, and that's that. There's no reason for her to give it away. She's already given more than enough to charities. She should be having a wonderful life.'

'Thank you, Matron,' Stella agreed. 'You wouldn't have changed my mind about trying to make Mary see what's happening, but you've made me feel more determined.'

'Good. But Stella, go carefully at first. Point out to her what is happening; what she can't see, then put forward proposals for activities. Don't try to drag her back to reality; nudge her gently in the right direction.'

Stella thought about the matron's advice and began the transformation of Mary the next day.

Stella was out of bed by eight o'clock as usual. Bronwen was already awake.

'You couldn't sleep again?' Stella asked. 'You should have called me to get you a cup of tea or something. There's no reason why you can't take those sedatives the doctor gave you to help you sleep. They don't make you a drug addict, you know.'

'I know, my lovely. I'm just laying here thinking.' Bronwen smiled up at Stella.

'Yes, and I know what you were thinking. She'll come out of it, you see.'

'She suffered so terrible. I wonder how much I was to blame.'

'None of it was your fault,' Stella snapped. 'If anyone was to blame, it was me for letting her go out on her own.'

'She's thirty-three, Stella. Of course, she should go out on her own.'

'Try to get it out of your mind and say and do things that will make her get it out of her mind. That's what I'm going to do, anyway.' Stella was hinting to Bronwen that things would change. 'Let me help you to the commode, then you get back to bed for a bit. I'll go and make you a cup of tea before I see to your commode, then I'll go up and make sure Mr Lloyd-Davies takes his medication. I expect he's had as much sleep as you have. Mary is affecting us all.'

After Stella organised Geraint's medication and had given him a cup of tea, she knocked on Mary's door and walked in. She knew she wouldn't have had a reply, even if she'd waited for one.

'Mary, it's going on half past eight. Wake up and get yourself dressed. I need you to help me in the kitchen today. It's Monday and I have to get some shopping done. Your mother's coming to help, so you can, too.'

Mary sat up with surprise on her sleep-sogged face. 'I can't come. I'm not well.'

'Aren't you? Where do you feel bad, then?' Stella sounded sympathetic though she didn't feel it.

'I don' know, I jus' feel bad,' Mary yawned.

'You mean, you don't know,' Stella corrected.

'You haven't told me to speak proper for a long time, Stella. Are you going to start again?'

'Yes, and you're going to stop feeling sorry for yourself. You're making us all miserable, especially your mother. Can't you see how worried she is?'

'But they did such awful dirty, dirty things and hurt me terrible. I nearly died, din' I?'

'Didn't I,' Stella corrected again. 'Yes, you did, but do you think you're the only one that's ever happened to? It happens to hundreds of women every day.'

'Do it?'

'Does it, I've told you that a hundred times. Yes, it does, and not just by two men but a big gang sometimes, and then the woman has to go home to a rotten husband who hits her about, and she has to work hard. You have a lovely home and family, plenty of money to spend and you're making all of us as miserable as sin. You spoilt Christmas for all of us with your long face and self-pity.'

'Did I?' Mary replied sleepily, 'I din' notice.'

Stella didn't bother to correct her speech. 'No, because you were wrapped up in your own feelings. Now it's your mother's seventieth birthday next month and you and I are going to plan a surprise party for her. Do you understand?'

Mary became more alert. 'Stella, if you hadn't reminded me, I would 'ave forgot my mother's seventieth birthday. Tha' would have been awful.'

'You would have forgotten your mother's seventieth birthday and that would have been awful.' Stella emphasised the words Mary had clipped.

'You do it. I don't feel well enough.'

'Oh, no, my lovely. You're going to do your bit. So, you'd better think of what I've said and pull yourself together.'

Mary fell back onto the bed and made to pull the pretty blue and pink duvet over herself.

'Oh, no you don't,' Stella said as she tore back the duvet. 'You get up, wash, clean your teeth and dress. I'll expect you down in the kitchen in half an hour.'

Stella stood with her hands placed threateningly on her hips, sounding angry and determined. 'Now, get up!' she shouted.

Mary shot out of bed and ran into the adjoining bathroom suite. 'I'm not well,' she whined. Stella followed her.

'There's nothing wrong with you that a good kick up the arse wouldn't cure and that's what you'll get if you continue to worry your mother half to death and make us all miserable. I warn you Mary Dew, if you make Bronwen ill, I'll never forgive you.'

Mary looked shocked and frightened. The first signs of emotion shown in months. Stella felt she was getting through to the numb mind. She stood in the doorway of the bathroom. She had a grin on her face.

'And I've got a secret, but you mustn't breath a word to anyone until I tell you,' she said. She was surprised to notice she'd aroused interest in Mary. She stopped wiping her hands and face.

'What? What secret? I promise I won't tell anyone.'

'After your mother's birthday party, because I don't want to take interest away from that, Kevin and I are getting engaged.'

Mary dropped the towel onto the floor. 'That means you're goin' to get married?'

'Yes,' Stella responded, with joy gleaming in her bright brown eyes. 'And who do you think will be maid of honour?'

'I don' know.' Mary's bottom lip sagged, her mouth opened.

'Shut your mouth, Mary. It's going to be you, of course. You've lost all that awful weight, you'll look lovely in a blue velvet bridesmaid's dress.'

A spark of excitement appeared on Mary's face, pushing away the last signs of sleep. 'Oh, that will be lovely.' She smiled; the first time in weeks.

'And we're going to have a baby straight away and two more later. I'll need you to help me look after them.'

For a few seconds Mary's smile broadened; then it fell from her face and was taken over by an expression of doom.

'I'm not well enough,' she whined. 'I'll drop them.'

'Don't be daft. Of course, you won't. They won't be as big as Kevin to start with. Now stop that mooching.' Stella raised her voice. 'And don't forget it's a secret for the time being. Don't you dare forget and tell anyone; not even your mother.'

Mary actually chuckled at Stella's remark about the baby's size. 'I won't, I won't, Stella. I swear I won't tell anyone until you say I can.'

'That's my girl. Now get dressed. Come down and have breakfast with the rest of us. And eat your breakfast. Don't just fiddle about with it. I must dash now; I've been up here ages and there's a lot to do before we go to Waitrose.'

Mary dragged herself down to breakfast and for a while lost the expression of blankness and actually spoke a few words. She asked her mother what time she would be going out shopping because Stella said she must go.

Stella stopped chomping into her thick piece of buttered toast, looked around the table at everyone as she thought of an explanation.

'That's right,' she said. 'I would like you to come because I can leave Bethan to watch out for the washing machine to finish and to put some of the sheets into the dryer.' She looked at Bronwen and changed the subject. 'Bronwen, it's a pity we don't have room for a clothes line, isn't it? The washing is so much fresher coming from the clothes line.'

'Mmm,' Bronwen responded. 'After all these years I can still remember the lovely smell when my mother used to bring the sheets in. Never mind, though, it's easier getting it out of the drier, especially when it rains, and you don't have to gallop down the back garden to bring the washing in before it's soaked.'

Geraint laughed. 'Always too late. I remember Eleanor got soaked as well as the washing.'

For the first time in months Bronwen's breakfast table was a happy one. Stella's first steps to bringing Mary out of the depression following her unforgettable, horrible experience seemed to be making waves. Bronwen sensed the difference and the smile of her beautiful nature returned.

Though Mary's mood all too often dropped into despair, there was usually someone around to pick it up.

Bronwen had no thought of her seventieth birthday being of any more importance than any other of her birthdays. Stella and Geraint arranged a surprise party, dragging Mary into the arrangements.

Stella sent Mary, in a taxi, up to The Sunshine Mount Nursing Home to deliver the invitation cards and to let those invited to keep it quiet because the party was to be a surprise.

Stella had asked Bronwen to visit one of the neighbours who had been ill, so she didn't know of Mary's mission.

'Shall I come with you, Mary,' Geraint asked. 'I'd like to see some of the old folk.' He was inclined to forget that he was one of those old folks.

219

'Yes please, Mr Lloyd-Davies. I'll feel safer with you.'

The concept of Geraint Lloyd-Davies fighting off any villains made Stella smile.

Mary came back feeling pleased with herself. She always enjoyed going to The Home. The carers made her welcome; they liked hearing about the new clothes she'd bought and where she'd been. No one questioned her about what the gossip-mongers had said about her terrible ordeal with the kidnappers, or what they had read in the local paper. The story had become old hat, but the matron had warned them not to mention it.

The residents who remembered her were pleased to see her. One of them was innocently tactless and asked Mary what happened to the villains who "attacked" her. Mary's happy smile soured.

'Gone to jail, Cyril,' Megan the carer answered as she pushed Mary forward to avoid more questions.

'They all should be hung up by their balls,' Mary heard Cyril say as she walked away.

She was pleased with herself. She was able to tell Stella all what was said before Bronwen appeared.

Mary's attitude to the rest of the world improved. She was able to help Stella and Geraint with the preparation of Bronwen's birthday party. She was better when people pushed her instead of showing sympathy. However, the nightmares continued. They occurred less frequently as time passed but they persisted in haunting her sleep.

Bronwen's birthday party was a success. An army of caterers took plates and dishes from the back of their van, carried them to the prepared tables and arranged them to look they're most enticing.

'A feast fit for a king,' Geraint said as guests arrived. They had been asked to come promptly and quietly some time before five o'clock.

Bronwen had been enticed into her next-door neighbours until five minutes to five. She wondered why they were so insistent on her seeing their new lounge chairs. She'd seen them before. It was difficult keeping her there until the given time. She thought their attitude strange until she went through her own front door.

Directly inside, Geraint sat on a chair with the biggest bouquet of flowers he could handle, before he held them out to Bronwen.

'Happy seventieth birthday, my lovely lady.' He shouted to let everyone in the house know she had arrived.

'Oh, Geraint, how lovely. Thank you, thank you. I'll go and put them in vases straight away. I don't think I have enough vases. I've never seen such a lovely bunch of flowers.'

The lounge was packed with friends and neighbours. For so many people to be crushed together it was surprising that the silence was kept until she entered the room.

The big bunch of flowers hid her view. She saw nothing but heard a loud, roof-raising chorus of, 'Happy Birthday to You'.

Greetings reached her from every inch of the room and there were flowers everywhere.

'All these flowers; the place looks like a cemetery on Palm Sunday. And all the best people in the world must be here.'

Stella embraced her. She, too, had tears in her eyes. A lump in her throat stopped her from putting her greeting into words.

'Thank you, my lovely,' she said. 'I expect this was you're doing.'

'A bit,' she replied. 'It was a team effort. Come and see your birthday cake.'

It was on a small table beside the big one which was laden with food.

'Oh, my goodness,' Bronwen repeated. 'It must have cost a fortune.'

'Well it was your fortune that paid for it,' Geraint said.

His remark amused everyone. The room rang with laughter and the party began. Smartly dressed waitresses of the catering company, baring tightly packed trays of champagne, entered the room from the kitchen. They mingled skilfully among the guests with fluted glasses of bubbly.

Everyone held up their glasses. 'To Bronwen,' was chorused.

The guests spread themselves into the next room, the big kitchen and the wide hall so everyone had more elbow space.

The party was expected to go on until around nine o'clock but at ten o'clock there were many guests still there. At half-past ten, when Bronwen was so tired she began to droop, she clicked off the brake of her wheelchair, turned towards her room, thanked everyone there for coming, and bid them goodnight.

Geraint had made himself scarce before nine o'clock. Bronwen knew and smiled to herself. She knew him well, as he did her.

Eventually, after a happy birthday, the rooms became silent. Everyone, including the catering staff, Bronwen's cleaners and partners, Bethan and her mother had gone, leaving Stella, Kevin and Mary. The rooms looked as if giant hands had shaken them. Since the moving in to 22, Queen Street, everywhere had been immaculate.

The three, with hands on hips, looked dolefully about them.

'Well,' Kevin said, looking at Stella, 'where do we start?'

'I should have started by hiring an army of cleaners,' Stella huffed. 'Bronwen has told me to get anything we want at any time no matter what the cost. I'm just not used to having so much money at my disposal.'

'I don't feel very well,' Mary moaned, 'I'm going to bed.'

'Oh, no you're not.' Stella grabbed the back of her dress, 'you can start by gathering up the dishes and taking them into the kitchen. The sooner we start the sooner we'll get finished.'

They were surrounded by flowers; most of them out of water. Stella bunched them together in bowls. 'We'll put them in vases tomorrow.'

'I'll start emptying the ash trays and gathering the debris,' Kevin volunteered. 'And I'll put the furniture back as it was.'

'That's it,' Stella stretched up and kissed Kevin's chin. 'What would we do without you?' Kevin looked pleased as Stella went on, 'I'll stack the dishwasher and clear away what's about the kitchen. Some of it can be left until morning; Bethan will be in.'

The hands of the clock in the hall approached midnight by the time the rooms were to Stella's satisfaction.

'That'll do until the morning,' Stella huffed again when the three were slumped in easy chairs. 'I think we've done well, and the party was a big success.'

Breakfast was at ten o'clock the following morning. Stella had attended to Bronwen's early morning toileting before taking cups of tea to her and Geraint. She insisted they lay on for a couple of hours, but she needn't have insisted. They agreed willingly. She took Mary and Kevin cups of tea, too. They remained on the bedside tables, untouched, until lunchtime, when Bethan collected the cups.

Kevin, of course, had stayed the night in the guest room.

There was plenty to talk about across the breakfast table. Bronwen repeated her gratitude. Everyone's kindness amazed her.

The talk was about how people had changed since she last saw them, how some had grown, some had got fat and some looked older.

'Of course, they looked older if you hadn't seen them for ten years,' Stella said. She leant across the table towards Bronwen and said in a hush that everyone heard, 'Did you see my brother, Colin, having a whale of a time?'

'No more than everyone else,' Bronwen replied, looking quizzical. 'Why should I have?'

'Well, he was with Matron Phillips all the time. I saw her smiling and even laughing. I don't remember ever seeing Matron Phillips laughing. They went out together. My brother took her to The Angel Hotel afterwards and there was a twinkle in his eyes.'

'How do you know that?' Kevin asked.

'Because he told me when I saw them out. Matron Phillips looked lovely, didn't she?'

'Yes, she did,' Bronwen smiled. 'She always does. It would be nice if she and Colin got to know each other more and grab a little extra happiness.'

'Perhaps they'll get married and have babies as well,' Mary said, waving a slice of toast at Stella's face.'

'As well as who?' Geraint asked. He somehow guessed what was coming.

There was a pause before Bronwen spoke. 'As well as who?' she asked Mary.

Mary dropped her toast and looked sheepishly at Stella. She had broken her promise. 'Stella. I'm sorry. I didn't mean to.'

'Never mind Mary, I'm fed up with this secret business and Bronwen's birthday has come and gone now.'

Kevin looked across at Bronwen. 'It's just that I've asked Stella to marry me and she's agreed, but we wanted to keep it quiet until after your birthday.'

Mary continued to look directly at Stella expecting to hear some scathing words. She was wrong.

'It's alright, Mary, love. 'You've done well to keep it quiet until now.'

She took Kevin's hand across the table. 'Yes, we're officially engaged now.'

'But I haven't bought the ring yet,' Kevin put in quickly. 'We're engaged, and we will be married in April. I hope that's all right with you.' His glance went from Geraint to Bronwen.

'Well, it's about blooming time.' Geraint got up from his chair and shook Kevin's hand.

'Come here,' Bronwen held out her arms to Stella. She walked to the other side of the table to be embraced. 'I was going to tell you today, anyway, Bronwen, with your birthday being over. But our dear Mary has stolen my thunder.'

'Kevin, you must take her to Cardiff this week,' Bronwen ordered, 'and buy her the finest engagement ring you set your eyes on. Geraint, you see that he has plenty of money in his account.'

'No need for that, Bronwen,' Kevin shook his head. 'Thank you, you've already given me too much.'

However, he did as he was told. Stella arranged for Dora from The Sunshine Mount, who knew Bronwen's needs, to stay the day. She knew Dora would be glad of the opportunity to earn a little extra money. Stella didn't think Bethan and Mary were capable on their own to look after Bronwen and Geraint.

Stella and Kevin had a happy day in the city. They came home with Stella flashing a diamond and sapphire engagement ring, leaving Kevin with little left in his bank account.

If Kevin had had his way, the marriage would have taken place the following week and leave immediately on honeymoon. For Stella, that was impossible. Who would look after Bronwen and Geraint? Geraint was easy enough; he was able to walk and his health, since the operation, was good. However, Bronwen's care was more complicated. She was unable to walk and was conscious of her paralysed legs. She didn't like to be seen undressed or be bathed by any stranger.

Stella shared the problem with Matron Phillips.

'I'll take your place,' she said. 'I'm well overdue for holidays, I have no domestic commitments now the boys are in university and I'd like the change. I know Bronwen wouldn't mind me looking after the two of them. I can arrange for our deputy matron to take my place.'

Stella felt stunned. Nothing could have been easier. 'Matron, are you sure? You know how conscious she is about anyone seeing her legs. She'd be most grateful to you.'

'Well, she shouldn't be. I owe her a great deal. Did you know she has financed my sons at university? It would have been financially impossible for me. I'll be glad to do some little thing to show my gratitude.'

'I must be honest,' Stella replied. 'I did know what Bronwen did for your boys; we have no secrets from each other.'

'That's that then,' the matron smiled. 'Let me know the exact dates.'

Stella took from her bag a golden embossed envelope containing her wedding invitation and handed it to the matron.

'This is the date of our wedding. It would be convenient if you could join us the day before. There are plenty of rooms.'

'No problems, then. I'm looking forward to it.'

As Stella was about to take her leave, the matron said something which surprised her.

'Stella, would you please call me Helen? It would be best under the circumstances. Colin and I have become good friends.'

Stella grinned. 'It will be hard, Matron, but I'll try. And, yes, Colin has told me.'

Stella and Kevin had a quiet wedding in April. The marriage took place in the local church and the reception in 22, Queen Street.

Stella looked particularly beautiful in a pale blue lace, exquisite wedding gown and Mary, not in velvet as at first decided, but in a deeper blue silk, ankle-length dress.

Professional caterers prepared a wedding feast for just a few more than twenty people. Stella was conscious of the fact that she had been married before and insisted on the wedding being modest.

She and Kevin left the same day for a Caribbean cruise, arranged by Geraint as a wedding present from Bronwen and himself, paid for with Bronwen's money.

Chapter 26
Sadness, Loneliness and Shame

Since the day all the numbers of Bronwen's National Lottery ticket made her a millionaire, the world had changed for her and those dear to her. There had been times when she had cursed having, what was to her, a vast fortune, but overall, she enjoyed it. She did on the happy day she waved Stella and Kevin off on their honeymoon.

It seemed like a dream. She and Lewis often laughed when they talked about what they would do if they were rich. However, they couldn't have been happier than when they had just enough to exist from week to week. It was a rare occasion when there were a few shillings left over to go into Post Office savings. Now, she had more money than she could deal with. Geraint frequently reminded her, that almost as fast as it was spent, the interest on what remained was ample.

When Stella and Kevin were away on their honeymoon, life went on for a while as it normally had done since they all moved into the salubrious Queen Street house. An unforgettable tragedy ruined it.

Helen was an excellent replacement for Stella but Bronwen missed her light banter of managing the home and making everyone feel at ease.

Helen wanted everything to be perfect for Bronwen and Geraint, not to let Stella down. She was used to running a home for thirty-two residents and couldn't stop herself being meticulous in her changed environment.

She was up at dawn and did half a day's work before Bethan came in to find "the family" already at the breakfast table. Mary was conspicuous by her absence. Helen turned a blind eye to the fact that she was allowed to stay abed until mid-morning and contribute little to help with the running of the household. Bronwen made excuses for her.

'Mary stays up at night because she enjoys the late-night films. She makes up her sleep by lying in for a while. She's not completely recovered since…' She couldn't put the horrible experience of the kidnap and rape into words.

Helen made no comment. She didn't mention the fact that Mary drank more than half a bottle of wine as she watched television, and that the early headaches she complained of were hangovers.

Helen decided to leave Mary to her own devices; not even entering her room to help to keep it tidy. She didn't know that Stella made her do it and get out of bed at a reasonable time to help with the morning's tasks.

Helen enjoyed being at 22 Queen Street and would say or do nothing to spoil it for herself. She enjoyed having breakfast with them as she did other meals. With her sons away at university, hers was a lonely widow's existence in her own home.

Being at Bronwen's home was interesting; even exciting. Helen was able to be less formal than she was at The Home. A stream of visitors came: Bronwen's friends, neighbours and the few remaining relatives. Helen kept the kettle boiling and a tray of tea and biscuits always set.

She wished everyone, including Geraint, didn't address her as Matron. She had made it clear that her name was Helen.

Bronwen, as usual made excuses. 'They've always known you as the formidable matron, Helen,' she said with a grin. 'They don't know that under that professional front there's a heart as big as our washing-up bowl.'

'You don't have a washing-up bowl,' Helen smiled warmly.

'You know what I mean. And there is one of our callers who calls you by your lovely name.'

Bronwen referred to Colin. He called on most days to find out if Bronwen, Geraint and Mary wanted to go somewhere—and to see Helen. Kevin had asked him to take his place in cradle-lifting Bronwen off and on her wheelchair when necessary; usually when they went shopping or visiting.

He enjoyed the responsibility, though he wasn't as big and strong as Kevin, nor as young. Bronwen helped him by taking her wheelchair as near to the front door of the house as possible, so that the lifting was just across the pavement, directly onto the back or front seat of the Mercedes. Kevin was able to carry her from the lounge, or her room at the back of the house, without effort. It wasn't so easy for Colin.

Helen always went with them to ensure their safety. She folded and packed the wheelchair and Geraint's mobility scooter into the back of the car as she'd seen Stella doing. Sometimes the wheelchair needed help in town to get over the threshold of shops.

Helen sat in the passenger seat beside Colin and their conversation was that of two people who enjoyed being together. Bronwen sensed more than friendship between them and she was rarely wrong about such matters.

Mary missed Stella. She found Matron nice enough, but she was too fastidious.

Post cards arrived with beautiful pictures of the Caribbean. They ended with love from Stella and Kevin, although it was Stella's handwriting every time.

'Like a real married couple.' Mary sighed after Bronwen read the few lines aloud. 'I wonder if she's pregnant yet.'

Geraint was flabbergasted and looked sharply at Mary, thinking that perhaps she hadn't realised what she'd said.

'Really, Mary, that's a most irregular remark. They've only been married a matter of days.'

Bronwen changed the conversation. 'It looks lovely there, Geraint. I'm having itchy feet. We must go on another trip; and soon. You're always asking me to think of ways of spending money. We'll go somewhere very, very, very expensive.' Her remark made them laugh.

'Do you think all your friends and neighbours will object to you going away, Bronwen?' Helen asked. 'They queue to see you.'

Bronwen smiled. 'Their visits are confined to the afternoons, Helen. They know how busy the mornings are here, and I can't think of anyone who would overstay her welcome; not with you, Matron Phillips, being in charge.'

'Oh dear,' Helen frowned, 'I hope they don't consider me a bully.'

'Not at all,' Bronwen replied, 'you're much too nice for that. One of my old neighbours hasn't called for months and I know it isn't because of you being in charge. She stopped coming when Stella was home.'

'I know who you're referring to,' Geraint interrupted, 'and you mustn't worry about that. It's best she keeps away.'

Bronwen referred to Mabel Curtis, Mickey Curtis's grandmother. She felt hatred for Mickey, but not for Mabel.

'She can't help what a bad lot her grandson is. He's out of her way for a long time now. A long time to her, anyway; she could be dead before he's out of prison. She has no one. Just think how she must be feeling; the loneliness and shame she has to live with. She's lived in this street all her life, she knows everyone, and everyone knows her. But I've been told no one speaks to her any more. She can't come here, I don't want her to, but I feel I must go to see her and take her something. I'm told she hardly ever goes out, not even to Chapel or to do her shopping unless she has to, poor thing.'

Mary stared at her mother with her mouth open, her tongue dropping outside her bottom lip. She seemed to be able to think better that way; understand what was behind her mother's words.

She shouted. 'I couldn't face his gran, Mammy! I couldn't go in that house. I would smell him! I hope he dies in prison and all those who were with him! I don't want to hear you say anything more about the Curtises! I want to forget, forget! I can't pass the house. I don't want to see anything to do with Mickey Curtis!' Mary was beginning to get hysterical. Helen calmed her.

'It's all right, Mary, you don't have to, and we all understand. The memory of what you went through will fade with time, as it will with all of us. But your mother must be allowed to follow her heart.'

'I agree,' Geraint murmured, as if to himself. 'You'll stop having those terrible nightmares, Mary, and your mother will stop blaming herself for what happened to you. She donated the hundred thousand pounds to an organisation which helps the victims of crime, but that hasn't eased her conscience enough. Only time will, and seeing you well, and brave enough to overcome the horror.'

Mary's eyes filled with tears of self-pity which flowed down her clumsily made-up cheeks. Helen didn't help Mary with her make-up as Stella did.

'Go and see her, Mammy. She has nobody to love her as I have. I know it's not her fault.'

'I'll come with you,' Helen volunteered. 'I'll just stay in the background. It's a good thing I'm here because I'm sure Stella wouldn't want you to go into that house on your own.' Helen had heard, in detail, how Stella and Kevin squeezed the information out of Mickey of where Mary was being held for ransom.

'No,' Bronwen replied. 'I'll go on my own. I won't need help except to get through Mabel's front door and I know she'll give my wheelchair a nudge.'

'Don't go today, Bronwen,' Geraint advised. 'We're all too emotional. Go in a couple of days.'

'Poor Mabel could be dead by then,' Bronwen replied.

She was right.

When Bronwen knocked on Mabel's front door two days later, she didn't appear smiling to welcome Bronwen as she always had. She knocked again before putting the basket of groceries she'd brought onto the doorstep. She freed her hands to turn the knob and open the door. It didn't budge.

She rapped the knocker again and would have called through the letterbox had she been able to reach it by bending over from her wheelchair.

She guessed Mabel was too ashamed to face anyone so wasn't answering the door to anyone. That thought made Bronwen determined not to go away until she saw her.

She turned the knob again and gave the door a harder push. The flaking wood of the doorjamb near her hand began to crumble.

226

On a third hard push the door became ajar but its bottom was stuck to the floor.

A teenage courting happened to pass by. The youth, deciding to demonstrate his kindness and strength to his pretty girlfriend, asked Bronwen if they could help her. They were strangers to Queen Street. Bronwen guessed they were visiting because she didn't recognise their faces.

'Yes please,' Bronwen replied. 'I can't get my chair in until the door is wide open, and it's got stuck at the bottom. Would you mind giving it a kick? You're young and strong; it will open for you.'

The couple gave no thought to the possibility that Bronwen was breaking in; not a cripple in a wheelchair.

'Get back a bit, then, the young man beckoned. 'I don't want to push you over in the attempt.'

He gave the door a push with a strong shoulder before kicking in the bottom of the door. It burst open with a crash against the passage wall.

'There you go,' he said. 'Do you want help to get over the step?'

'If you wouldn't mind,' Bronwen smiled her gratitude, 'but I don't want to hold you up.'

The girlfriend stepped forward and manoeuvred the wheelchair into the passage.

'Thank you, my lovely. That was very nice of you both.'

Bronwen was amazed that the noise hadn't attracted Mabel to the door. Even if she'd been asleep, she couldn't have failed to hear the rumpus.

Bronwen closed the front door before making her way to the middle room. Mabel was nowhere to be seen and Bronwen shivered with a morbid expectancy. She knew Mabel hadn't gone out; something was wrong.

'Mabel,' she called. 'Mabel, where are you. It's Bronwen. I want to see you.'

No response.

Bronwen wondered what to do. To remain and snoop around would be trespassing and an intrusion into Mabel's privacy. She should have turned and left the house, but she couldn't. The more the seconds ticked by the more something inside kept her there.

She looked about the kitchen, which was the all-purpose room; it had an unused atmosphere about it. It was uncannily neat. The kettle and pots on the hobs gleamed like new. The fire-grate was cleaned out and set for rekindling, a pristine white cloth was on the table, but not set for a meal. The covers of the fireside chairs were freshly laundered, and the cushions plumped with no signs of being used.

Bronwen went to the foot of the stairs and called out Mabel's name several times. She felt a strong urge to go upstairs.

'Blast these legs,' she snapped to herself. 'Blast the wheelchair.'

Hot with frustration she went back into the kitchen and wondered what to do. It seemed as if Mabel had gone away with no intention of returning.

She decided to take a look in the scullery before leaving the house to ask Geraint what she should do. Though she guessed what his response would be.

'Leave well alone, Bronwen. It's none of our business and being Mickey Curtis's grandmother makes it a tricky business.'

The door between the kitchen and the scullery was closed. Normally, it was always open. Bronwen pushed it open with a gadget she kept on her wheelchair for such purposes and wheeled herself through.

What she saw haunted her for the rest of her life. Mabel was hanging by the neck from a stout rope she had hitched over a heavy beam which supported the scullery structure. The rickety, kitchen chair she had used to stand on had been kicked over by the last movements of her small feet. They were still, blue, almost black. Her slippers had dropped onto the floor.

Bronwen gulped. She couldn't scream; she couldn't move. 'Dear God, what have we done?'

She spontaneously glanced up at Mabel's face. It was blue, her eyes bulged, and her tongue sagged from her mouth. It took some seconds for Bronwen's brain to move. What could she do? Nothing, nothing.

With trembling fingers, she fumbled through her jacket pockets, took out her mobile phone and made to dial her home number. She misdialled twice. For the third attempt she had to pause and tell herself to pull herself together.

Helen answered. The menu on the house phone told her it was Bronwen.

Bronwen, it's me, Helen. Do you want me to come down to give you a heave over the step?'

Bronwen was a long time responding; her eyes were on Mabel's hanging body and words were sticking in her throat.

'Come down now. Come now. Geraint to come. Not, not Mary.'

It wasn't difficult for Helen to sense something was very wrong. She fled from the house without putting on a coat and called out to Geraint as she darted for the front door.

'Mr Lloyd-Davies! Come down to Mrs Curtis now. Mary, you stay here and watch the house.'

Helen ran down the street, past the six houses, as fast as her legs could carry her. She entered the house and made straight for the scullery.

As Bronwen had, she gasped, and almost collapsed at the horrible sight of Mabel's hanging body.

'Oh, dear God,' she screamed, put a hand to her mouth and dashed to the scullery sink to vomit.

On recovering she wiped her mouth with a blue-checked tea towel that was near the sink and snatched Bronwen's phone out of her hand which was stiff on her lap. She dialled the emergency number, explained that someone was dead. She stammered Mabel's name and address.

The whaling of the emergency ambulance approaching Mabel's house brought many people of Queen Street to their doorsteps. They wondered what could have happened. Mickey was still in jail, so it could have nothing to do with him. Poor Mabel, they thought. She must be very ill and would be taken to the hospital.

Many of the neighbours loitered in front of their houses to see Mabel being carried out on a stretcher, followed by Bronwen in her wheelchair with Helen and Mr Lloyd-Davies behind. He'd arrived just before the ambulance, having staggered down on his Zimmer frame.

'The Bronwen Dew's lot,' more than one neighbour sneered. 'Trust them to be about when there's trouble.' Forgotten were the thousands of pounds Bronwen had donated to get essential repairs done to many of the houses in the street and the thousands she had donated to help the poor and unemployed of the town.

Mabel hadn't been a scholar, but she learned to read and write and was able enough to leave a well-written suicide note. Bronwen knew she would have put much thought into writing her last letter.

"To whoever will find me.
I am sorry for the wicked way I am ending my life. I no longer want to live. I am tired, lonely and depressed. I am ashamed for being unable to bring up my grandson to be a good man. He was not all bad. I saw goodness in him. No one else did and I am too

ashamed to face anyone for what he did to Mary Dew, whose mother, dear Bronwen, has always been my friend.
    Mabel May Curtis."

Helen was the first to spot the note on the kitchen table. She handed it to Bronwen to read before the ambulance came. The paramedics might not take it, but she knew the police who arrived at the house shortly afterwards would. Bronwen sobbed as if her heart would break.

She, Helen and Geraint returned home, passing neighbours without acknowledging those who were standing on their doorsteps. The faces looked down in sadness; some feeling guilty for ignoring Mabel, instead of helping her through her terrible ordeal.

By the time Stella and Kevin arrived home from their Caribbean honeymoon, Mabel had been buried and people were still in mourning. On entering number 22, Queen Street, all were there to welcome the happy couple home, but an invisible mist of misery marred the atmosphere.

'What's happened here?' Stella asked, as Kevin moved their suitcases out of the hallway. 'It's as if someone's died.'

'Someone has,' Helen said. Bronwen was too tearful to respond.

'Who?' Kevin asked as he entered the room. He looked at Colin who had come to welcome them back.

'Sit down, both of you.' Geraint beckoned Stella and Kevin. 'Perhaps Matron would make tea for us and we'll tell you what has happened.'

'Yes, I will.' Helen was relieved to leave the room and be occupied preparing something that might help to cheer the air.

Bronwen was in tears. Her state of mind was as bad as when Mary was kidnapped, but the grieving was different. When Mary was missing, Bronwen's anxiety affected her thinking. This time was different; she wept continuously. It looked to Stella as if she'd been weeping for days. As, indeed, she had, except when the doctor administered something to make her sleep and stood over her as to took it, to ensure she did.

Her grey eyes were red-rimmed and puffy; she had no make-up on, or if she had it had been wiped away with her tears. Strands of her normally immaculately groomed hair wisped over her face. She usually looked years younger than her seventy years, but she didn't just then.

Stella knelt beside her wheelchair and embraced her with dread in her. 'Bronwen, why are you so heart-broken?'

'Because it's all my fault,' Bronwen softly cried, wiping away fresh tears to look into Stella's wondering expression. 'Geraint will tell you in a minute. It's lovely to have you back. You look prettier than ever.'

Stella's cream-colour complexion had become a rich, dark tan making her teeth appear whiter, and her big, brown eyes glow with health and beauty. Kevin too, was deeply tanned and his fair hair had been bleached to the colour of ripe corn.

Kevin looked at the faces about him as he spoke. 'We lapped up the hot sunshine every day. We had a wonderful time, but it wouldn't have been had I known something bad had happened here.'

Geraint began to explain what had happened. 'Mabel Curtis is dead,' he said, looking firstly at Stella before glancing up at Kevin. He was standing behind Bronwen's chair.

'And something tells me her passing wasn't straight forward,' he said as he took a chair beside Colin.

Helen came into the room carrying a tray for tea. It looked heavy. Colin rose to help her clear a space on the low table between the big settee and the fireplace.

'Colin, would you bring the two plates of biscuits from the kitchen table?' Helen asked. 'I'll pour the tea for everyone.'

'Helen has been an absolute treasure, Stella,' Bronwen attempted a smile at Helen as she put milk into the cups. 'And a tower of strength since I found Mabel.'

'Don't talk about it, Bronwen, my dear,' Geraint put a hand on her arm. 'Let me tell them.'

Whilst waiting for everyone to be given a cup of tea Mary relieved the silence. 'Stella, you both look stunning,' she said. 'Did you take photos? It looked a lovely place in your postcards.'

'Yes, love, we did. I'll show you when the time is right.'

Geraint related the events of Bronwen going to Mabel's house, having to break in and finding her in the scullery. He explained how she took her own life in words that he hoped took the sting out of the terrible tragedy. He explained the way Helen handled the situation by calling the emergency ambulance and police. It was then in their hands. He tried to soften the horror of the scene which had shocked Bronwen.

Bronwen sobbed silently as she listened. 'And it's all my fault,' she repeated.

Stella sprang to her side, knelt and put her arms about her. 'Why is it your fault? She was unhappy and ashamed; she wanted to die.'

'If I hadn't won all that money, Mary wouldn't have been taken by Mickey and those others. I shouldn't have taken it. Mickey wouldn't have hurt Mary and things would be as they used to be.'

'If you hadn't won all that money and been so generous, we wouldn't be living the marvellous lives that we are. Think of all the happiness you've spread.'

'Stella is right,' Helen interrupted. 'You're a lovely woman; goodness shines from you. Mabel was depressed, and her grandson has wasted his life. Taking Mary wasn't the only bad criminal act, but for Mabel, it was the last straw. She's at peace now.'

Stella remained on her knees beside Bronwen. She, too, began to weep. Kevin leant over her and brought her to her feet. Bronwen look up at him as he spoke.

'We're all here together, Bronwen, like a family. I know you won't forget the terrible ordeal of finding Mabel, but the memory is bound to fade. We'll help you to forget.'

His hand was near her. She took it into hers. 'Thank you, Kevin. I think I'm beginning to see light.'

Mary interrupted. The loudness of her voice took them all by surprise. 'If anyone's to blame, it's me,' she said, pointing to herself. 'I should have had more sense than to go into that car park when that Rambo called me. I didn't even know him. But you all know how stupid I am. I've been told often enough.'

There was a stillness as they stared at her. Her profoundness stirred some guilt because what she said was correct; there were times when Mary's backwardness caused frustration.

'No, no, my lovely. You mustn't think that.' Bronwen stopped crying. Her self-pity turned to Mary. 'You were innocent. Why shouldn't you have followed that man? You thought he was being nice, as you think of everyone. I don't want you to change.'

'But she has changed,' Helen interrupted. 'Thanks to Stella's help and your support, she's changed from a fat women into a smart lady. Her clothes are beautiful; clothes she wouldn't be able to afford if it weren't for your wealth.' She looked at Mary. 'Of course, Mabel Curtis's death wasn't your fault or anyone's fault. Let's all try to put it to the back of our minds and pass on.'

'Well said, Matron,' Geraint responded. 'It's time you wiped your tears away, Bronwen, and let us see you smiling again, for God's sake. It's getting me down, and I know it is the rest of us.

'I know Mabel's death was terrible for you, but it's over. I've had enough of it; self-pity, guilt, remorse. Why? There's no need for it. We are in God's pocket, thanks to you, and we should show our appreciation by living each day accordingly. Stella and Kevin are home from their honeymoon. Let's celebrate. There are a few bottles of champagne left over from the wedding. Matron knows where they are; let's pop a few, shall we? It's past six o'clock. The sun is over the yardarm.

'Let's then face tomorrow and every other day with the same joy as you have provided with your unexpected fortune. If you like, we can begin talking about the next trip you mentioned you'd like to make. And there would be nothing more exciting for me than to plan it.'

Stella sprung from her knees. 'I'll get them.' She was referring to the bottles of champagne. 'We'll all have a nice tipple before we eat. I'll send Kevin to the chippies; no cooking tonight.'

Helen followed Stella to help her. She had been sitting close to Colin. Stella noticed, when Geraint was giving his sermon, Colin reach out his hand to hold hers. Their eyes met, and she smiled.

Helen took two trays and began setting them with glasses whilst Stella brought the champagne.

'I'll give Colin a shout to open the bottles,' Helen said. 'A man can do it better than we can.'

Stella gave Helen a sidelong glance. 'You and my brother seem to be hitting it off very nicely?' It was a question, but Helen grinned and didn't commit herself. She went to the door between the two rooms and called him. 'Colin, Stella nor I can open these bottles.'

'Right-o,' he called back. 'I'll try do it, but I'm no expert with champagne, either.'

The milieu cheered. The evening was pleasant. The happy atmosphere of 22 Queen Street began to return.

Bronwen drank champagne and shed no more tears. However, the strain of the past week remained in her eyes for many days.

Chapter 27
Making Plans

Matron Helen Phillips' two weeks' holiday at twenty-two Queen Street was over. She had dedicated herself to the care of Bronwen and Geraint. She had worked hard and enjoyed every day. She should have felt as if she needed a rest before returning to her demanding position at The Sunshine Mount Nursing Home, but she didn't. Through Bronwen she had met Colin; her life changed.

Stella helped Helen to pack her personal belongings. Her wardrobe was scanty, and the contents of her underwear drawer were clean and sensible; nothing that could be considered glamorous. She had only one suitcase and a small grip containing toiletries and make-up.

'Very dull and uninteresting compared with your clothes, aren't they Stella?' Helen felt dowdy. 'Would you come shopping with me one day? Bronwen has been over-generous, as you would guess, and I would really like to brighten myself up a bit.'

'You always look smart,' Stella commented, 'your clothes are classic, but I understand what you mean. And would I like to come shopping with you to help you to choose some glamorous things? I certainly would. Since Bronwen had all the numbers up, I've learned how to spend without having to ask myself if I can afford it. We'll go to Cardiff. You say when.'

'In a couple of weeks, then. I have to get back into my stride at The Home.'

Mary carried Helen's cases from Stella's room at the back of the house into the hallway.

'Why don't you stay, Helen,' she suggested. 'There's plenty of room upstairs.'

'Thank you, Mary. I've loved it here, but my real place is with my residents at The Home. I must go and say farewell to Bronwen and Geraint.'

'I can't begin to tell you how grateful I am for your wonderful care, Helen. You've become one of the family.' Bronwen was glad to have Stella back but she was sad to see Helen leave. Their relationship had strengthened during the past two weeks.

'Can we call on you again when Stella has to go somewhere? Though, I can't see her going anywhere again without us. And we'll be going on a trip before long. You can come with us if you can get away.'

'I don't think so,' Helen tutted. 'Not until I've retired, anyway. And that won't be for some time.'

Kevin and Colin were on a renovation job in the town. Kevin left the site to have lunch at Queen Street and to drive Helen's car to the front of the house. Its engine had been turned over once by Colin. Being an old model, the battery was apt to run down. Helen was pleased and surprised to see Colin stride into the house behind Kevin.

'Came to see you off,' Colin said. 'It feels as if you're going miles and miles away, not just to the other end of town. I'll be in touch, and if you have any trouble with your car or the roof of your house falls in, you will let me know, won't you?'

'Thank you, I will.' Helen got into her car and drove off. Everyone from the house, including Bronwen in her wheelchair, stood at the front of the house to wave her away.

That evening, Bronwen and Geraint were alone together in the lounge. Stella, Kevin, Mary and Bethan had gone to The Colliers' Arms for a change of company and to leave the two older people alone.

'I'm glad we're on our own, Geraint,' Bronwen said. She had an expression on her face which Geraint recognised. She had been planning something which would surprise him.

'Oh dear,' he replied, 'something ominous has been hatching in that mind of yours and I feel it's about another trip.'

Bronwen chuckled. 'You know me too well, Geraint. I have been thinking and thinking a lot because what I'm about to suggest is no small matter.'

'Well, what is it, girl? I'll take a deep breath then you can tell me.' He made a pretence of taking a deep breath.

'I want to get away from here as soon as you can arrange things.'

After Geraint's deep breath he coughed and spluttered. 'My goodness, you have been thinking hard. I thought this was ideal for you.'

'It is, and it's been grand here, but things have changed. Stella and Kevin are now married and need their own space. Yet, I feel safer when she is close by in case these legs of mine need help, as they increasingly seem to. I'm not getting any younger and neither are you. I want you to have a carer close to you, too.

'Our existence here must be odd to those around us and we are known to everyone within a radius of twenty miles, at least. I'd like to escape that for a long time.

'I want to get away from unpleasant memories, such as what happened to Mary and Mabel Curtis. Everyone knows what happened to Mary and they must think about it every time they see her. We must get away for a time.'

She paused to allow Geraint to speak, though he looked dumbfounded. As she spoke, he had shaken his head and nodded it. Sometimes he nodded instead of shaking.

'Well,' he spoke slowly. 'If that's what you want, I'll see that you get it.'

'First, we go on our long trip. I don't want the others to know how I feel about our home here because when we come back, we'll live here for a while, as we have done. If I still think we are still living a strange life, we must think of a more permanent move. Not too far from here but out in the country somewhere where we will have no close neighbours.'

'I think you're absolutely right. I'm blooming fed up with visitors, though I wouldn't have told you. But it's imperative that we keep this to ourselves until we are back from our trip. How about if we called a meeting tomorrow to talk about going on this long trip? A wonderful trip that will do us all good, especially you and Mary. Kevin and Stella have just come back from a trip, so I'll give it a week or two before I book. I'll get this strip sorted out in no time when I know what I must do. But we don't even know where we're going yet.'

'Right,' Bronwen spoke as if everything had already been accomplished. 'We'll go in early September; back in plenty of time for Christmas. It can be done. Firstly, we'll get them all here at the same time. We'll find out where they would like to go. I don't want anything said about a move until we are back here after a good, long trip.'

Geraint's eyes remained wide with surprise. He found it difficult to take in what they had just discussed.

'Bronwen, I don't know about you, but I'm going to have a large whisky and blow to it not mixing well with the medication.'

'I'll have a bigger one,' Bronwen nodded. 'But make it a gin and tonic. Go easy on the tonic.'

The sleeping arrangements had been changed in the house. Stella had moved into one of the bedrooms upstairs which she shared with Kevin. She wasn't too happy about not being near Bronwen, but she couldn't let Kevin know how she felt. Bethan had agreed to live in and take the room which was adjoining Bronwen's room. It had been Stella's, and that which Helen had recently vacated.

Bethan was gentle and kind, but Stella was afraid that when Bronwen needed help during the night, Bethan wouldn't hear her. Without being called, Stella was always aware when Bronwen needed assistance. She knew Bronwen would have struggled rather than awaken her and she would be the same with Bethan.

Stella was in a dilemma. It was expected that she shared Kevin's bed and she enjoyed that. Being married to him felt right; she had love in her heart for him that must have been there a long time, but she had been afraid to let it rule her. Now she was afraid of not being near Bronwen for whom she had cared for over ten years. Bronwen was used to having Stella to rely on. Stella felt she was faced with an unsolvable problem.

Bronwen, however, understood the way of Stella's thoughts. Bronwen always knew a day would come when she would have to share her. She wished she could rely on Mary more, but that had been tried and abysmally failed. Mary had escaped from a downward trend of life by her mother winning millions of pounds. Her appearance, lifestyle and way of thinking had improved beyond expectations but Bronwen couldn't expect miracles. Mary was intellectually disadvantaged and would always need her mother's support rather than the other way about. These were times when Bronwen cursed all her selected numbers of the lottery coming up but there were times when she thanked God for his generosity. Mary would live comfortably for the rest of her life as long as she had someone to guide and advise her.

The day after Bronwen had expressed her plans to Geraint for moving residence and confirmed her idea of taking a trip in September, he began planning. He gave instructions for all members of the household, whatever they were doing, to be home at seven o'clock that evening.

He telephoned Colin and asked him if he could make himself available to come to the house at that time. Bronwen had suggested to Geraint that he ask Colin to keep an eye on 22, Queen Street while they were away. That evening would be good time to put it to him.

Geraint called Colin. 'A little later will do if you can't make it at that time, Colin. We'll wait for you. I realise how busy you are but it's business, Bronwen, and I wish to talk to you about.'

'I've arranged to meet Helen when she comes of duty this evening,' Colin said. It sounds important Mr Lloyd-Davies. I'll be at the house at seven and I'll ask her to drive down. Will that be all right?'

'Yes,' Geraint agreed. 'As I said, we'll wait for you. We would like to see Helen. She's almost one of us now.'

Helen had forgotten to give back her front door key, so she let herself in. She arrived at 22, Queen Street at half past eight to find everyone, not sitting in the lounge sipping drinks, as she expected, but all around the dining table.

'My goodness,' she said, sensing a strained atmosphere, 'is this a meeting of the United Nations. Have you decided to attack or surrender?'

Her remark amused everyone. They realised how it must have appeared and a few chuckles lightened the air. Colin got an extra chair and nudged Kevin's bulk further alone the table to make room for her.

'Mary, go and get Matron a sherry, please,' Bronwen asked. Mary looked astonished that she should be trusted to pour the correct amount of sherry in the correct glass, but she arose from her chair and did as her mother asked.

Geraint opened the meeting. 'With all the money Bronwen has, she would like to use some of it to travel and see a bit of the world before we are too old and decrepit.'

Mary interrupted by noisily returning to the room. She brought Helen her glass of sherry in a large wine glass, carefully balanced on a tray. The glass was to its brim, almost spilling over. No one commented; they were consumed by thoughts of what Geraint was about to say.

Helen took her drink, looking unsure of whether she should, or ask Mary to change the glass. She chose to take the glass and drink just as much as she wanted.

'Thank you, Mary,' Helen said as Mary went back to her place at the table. She put the tray in front of her looking pleased with herself.

Geraint went on. 'So, we can put our heads together and decide where to go. It will be a longer trip than the Mediterranean cruise; that was just a taster and we liked it.'

The loudest response came from Mary. All eyes turned to her. 'I'm glad it will be for a long time. Get away from here. I wish we didn't have to come home. Get away from everybody and be safe.'

Mary's admission took the words from all others. They stared at her with surprise. No one would have thought Mary would want to get away from the place she was familiar with.

Bronwen and Geraint stared wide eyed with surprise. They both thought Mary would be the last one to agree to moving. Geraint nodded to Bronwen.

'Colin, we wonder if you would keep a watch on this house while we are away. There are vandals at large and I have to say it, we are not liked by many around here. That's all I will say about that because you know what I mean.'

'Of course, Bronwen. I would have done that even if you hadn't asked.'

'Thank you, Colin. I won't expect you to be our watchman for nothing.'

Bronwen didn't give Colin time to object to being paid.

Geraint spoke up. 'Now, where are we going? I want to begin planning this trip tomorrow.'

Bronwen held up her hand, which again silenced everyone. They wondered what was next on the agenda. 'Before we start on that, Geraint, we'll have supper. Helen must be very hungry. She's just come off a long, hard day's duty. Stella and Bethan have made a load of sandwiches, cold meats and cheese. I'm peckish myself.'

As Bronwen spoke Stella left the table and made her way to the kitchen. Mary and Bethan followed. Kevin asked everyone what they wanted to drink. He and Colin chose beer, the others, except Helen, chose soft drinks.

Helen asked for water. She had drunk more of the sherry than she'd intended. 'I'm half way to being drunk,' she giggled, 'I've kept alert because the chat has been so exciting. I didn't want to miss a word.'

'I'd better drive you home, then,' Colin said. 'I'll just have this one pint.'

Helen smiled. She looked pleased.

As they ate, the conversation remained on Geraint's second point; the trip to see a bit of the world. Where should they go? Caribbean was off the list because Stella and Kevin had recently been there.

'Anyway,' Stella said, 'I think it would be too hot for Bronwen and Mr Lloyd-Davies. They'll want to sightsee. Where Kevin and I were is a place for lounging in hot sunshine.'

235

Kevin leant forward in his chair. He had something to say that no one else had thought of. 'We must consider luggage and how much we can fit into the Merc. If we'll be travelling by air, we can take only take two cases each; one biggish one and one smaller. We don't want the palaver we had when we went on the cruise.'

'That's not enough,' Mary pouted.

'We'll have to make it enough,' Stella looked hard at Mary. 'We can buy things as we go from place to place and do bits of laundry. We'll have to if we're going for a more than a couple of weeks.'

'That is, if I can book such rooms,' Geraint broke in. 'We have to decide where we're going so that I can start the arranging. The earlier we book the more likely we are to have what we need. Can this table be clear now so we can get on?'

The girls leapt from their chairs and made for the kitchen, each carrying a large tray. The table was soon clear of the debris of the meal.

'When do you intend to go?' Colin asked.

'Early September.' Bronwen surprised everyone.

'As soon as that?' Kevin's question was to Bronwen but looked at Colin. He was partially committed to him. Colin had become reliant on Kevin in his business but Bronwen, also, needed him. She wouldn't be capable of taking a difficult journey without Kevin to lift and carry her.

'It's all right, Kevin. You made it clear to me that your first duty was to Bronwen. I'll honour that. I'll soon get someone who wants a job until you come back.'

'Thank you, Colin,' Bronwen nodded. 'I'd suggest we go next week but I know that reservations have to be planned and available. But to tell you honestly, I can't wait to get away from this street for a while.'

'One last small point,' Colin changed the subject as he looked at Helen, 'Can I say you and I will keep an eye on this while they're away? I've already agreed to do that myself, but I'd appreciate you in on this in case I'm not around.' 'Oh, yes, indeed,' she replied. 'I have a key. I can pop in on my way to work or afterwards, depending on my shifts. But one question hasn't been answered; where are you going?'

'Thank you, Helen,' Geraint nodded. 'Back to that now. What part of the world would you like to see, Bronwen?'

'It's not only where I want to go; it's where all of you want to go.' The truth was, Bronwen didn't know; she hadn't made up her mind, apart from the fact that she wanted to go away from Queen Street for a while and as soon as possible.

Suggestions and objections were called out across the table.

'Australia, the country of the future.'

'Too far.'

'Germany and Switzerland.'

'Too close. If we're going, we might as well go further.'

'Greece or Spain.'

'Everybody goes there.'

'Morocco or Tunisia.'

'Poor sanitation.'

'Israel—no, not safe yet.'

'Shut up, for God's sake!' Stella shouted.

Helen and Colin were creased with laughter. 'I'm glad I'm not coming with you,' Colin choked, 'I wouldn't know where I was.'

'Yes,' Bronwen frowned. 'There's only England, Scotland and Ireland left. We can go there anytime. We're all sounding ridiculous. The only person who hasn't suggested anywhere is Geraint and he's the organiser. Let him decide.'

'No, Bronwen. You're the one who should decide,' Geraint argued. 'You're paying.'

Bronwen was amused. 'My knowledge of the world is nothing. After all your reading and the time you spend looking at the holiday resorts on your computer, I expect you to choose. Now tell us where you would like to go?' Bronwen was persuasive and Geraint felt that she, truly, expected him to choose where they should go.

'Well, there is a place I would like to see before I meet my maker, and that is America. New York, for example, looks a magnificent city on the Internet and there's so much to see there. What a thrill it would be to walk up Broadway and Time Square, to go up the Empire State Building and stay at the finest hotels in the world.'

Geraint had entered a world of his own. 'To see New York would be an ambition achieved. But that's only one city. America is a massive continent.'

'We could visit Ellis Island.' Kevin's suggestion brought Geraint back to reality. 'It's a famous museum now.'

'And there's The White House in Washington and the Pentagon,' Geraint added.

'I'd like to see Hollywood,' Bronwen added. 'I've read that there are film-sets we could visit, and they are the same as we see in the films.'

'It would take a year to see all of America. I would like to make a plan of a tour, so we could see as many of its wonders as possible in, say, three months or so.'

'And there are the best shops in the world in New York. All the rich and famous go there,' Stella sounded exciting, looking at Mary, 'They say it could take a week to look around Macies and there are dozens of others.'

'Stella, we'd have a lovely time,' Mary, too, became excited. 'And we could go to Disney Land, couldn't we, Mr Lloyd-Davies?'

'That's not in New York, but we could go to Florida and other places. I could plan a tour of America if you would all agree. It will be restricted to a small tour; America is a big place.'

'You could see the Grand Canyon and go up as far as Niagara Falls,' Colin interrupted. He, now, sounded as if he would like to travel with them.

'That sounds wonderful,' Helen interrupted. 'Go to America, Bronwen. You could sometimes go from place to place by air. You wouldn't always have to travel long distances by road.'

'And it would all cost a small fortune,' Geraint said. 'It would make a dent in your winnings, Bronwen.'

'Good,' Bronwen replied. 'Shall we go to America, then?' she asked, looking at the eager-eyed faces around her. Everyone agreed.

'Right, I'll start planning tomorrow,' Geraint rubbed his hands with glee. 'This is going to be a real tester. But I'll say now, first stop will be New York. We'll fly from London in September, as Bronwen requested.'

Bronwen felt her house happier than it had been for a while. Recent bad experiences were forgotten, at least for the time being, and life was moving on.

Helen and Colin were the first to leave the room.

'I'll take you home, Helen. You are too much in your cups to drive.' They bid everyone a good night. 'And don't worry about this house. It will still be here when you come back.'

'I'll start on my project tonight, not tomorrow,' Geraint said as he rose from his chair at the table. He was anxious to get to his computer.

He had lost sleep over Bronwen's sudden brainstorming of a few days before. After that evening's discussions, his concerns dissipated. He would have no trouble dropping off that night.

He had settled in nicely to 22, Queen Street. He felt secure and was more comfortable with Bronwen than anyone. He knew the feelings he had for Bronwen were reciprocated. Everyone loved her, though their relationship was different. In Geraint's eyes Bronwen could do no wrong.

Recently, however, he had found her constant stream of callers to the house getting on his nerves. He also sensed the burden of listening to everyone's troubles was getting too much for her, but she would never admit to that. Those problems she could solve by giving money were easy but there were others which were emotionally disturbing.

It would be especially good to move away from that house just six doorways down the street, where Mabel Curtis had lived.

On fine days Bronwen used to enjoy taking her mobility scooter up and down the street. The neighbours got used to seeing her and, quite often, would invite her into their homes for coffee or tea, dependant on the time of day.

'I'd like to, my lovely, but this scooter doesn't jump, unfortunately,' was the usual excuse.

'Sorry, Bron, I forgot you can't get over the doorstep.'

They would chat outside the houses and sometimes she was kept too long for comfort. Geraint would go to the front doorstep and call out to her to come home.

After the death of Mabel, she stopped going down the street; she couldn't face passing that house. She limited her outing to going up the street, which wasn't as pleasant. At the top end were a few shops; a mini-mart, a chemist and the post office. The bottom of the street opened onto a patch of green common ground which allowed a view across the valley. Lewis often took her there and she had sweet memories of it.

For Bronwen, moving wouldn't erase the terrible sight from her memory of Mabel hanging by her neck from the scullery rafter, but it would help.

Mary, moving away from a neighbourhood where a terrible thing happened to her, wouldn't obliterate it from her mind, but might help enough to stop the nightmares. Being a millionaire would do nothing to obliterate that. But then, she thought, had she not become rich it wouldn't have happened.

It had been said that Mary brought the trouble on herself, and now five people were in jail because of her backwardness. There were some who blamed her for Mabel Curtis's death. Mary didn't know of the spiteful gossip but Bronwen did.

It was said the Dews seemed to think they could get away with murder because they were rich. Bronwen wasn't like that before all her numbers came up in the lottery. One or two people who called on her had no qualms about letting her know what was being said.

Directly after the discussion to decide future plans, Geraint went to his room. He felt tired but not troubled.

'Yes,' he said to himself, 'moving from here is the right thing to do.'

He set about undressing to get into his pyjamas before Stella did her nightly check on him. She always served him with a warm drink to help his medication go down. He was in bed and almost asleep before she knocked on his door. She had to rouse him.

'Sorry, Mr Lloyd-Davies, but you must take your medication. Your mind is too full of the Big Apple tonight.'

'Yes, you're right; it is. And I would have forgotten about my pills. My old brain is in decline, I'm afraid.'

'Nothing wrong with your brain,' Stella replied. 'I'd swap with you any day if I could, but your brain hasn't declined enough to allow a daft thing like that.'

She helped him take his medication. 'I don't think you need your night sedation, do you?' His lids were heavy with fatigue; he shook his head. Geraint fell asleep with sights of New York dominating his thoughts.

Chapter 28
New York, New York

The days following the evening of the gathering around the dining table at 22, Queen Street, the home held a different milieu. An undercurrent of excitement spiked the atmosphere.

Everyone continued their everyday routine, except Geraint. He worked on his computer every hour he wasn't sleeping or eating. Bronwen objected.

'Geraint, you're working too hard. It's a holiday you're planning, not working out if we have enough military force to invade China. Please, love, ease off a bit.'

'But Bronwen, I'm enjoying every minute. As soon as I sit at that computer and bring up a map of America, three hours pass like three minutes. I want it all to be done and dusted long before the middle of August. The sooner I know where we are going the sooner I can make the bookings for hotels, trains, air flight or whatever will be the most effective. You know, the phone alone cost a year's pay, let alone the travel.'

'Tut-tut,' Bronwen frowned. 'We'll have to ask for a bank loan, will we?'

'You've said that often enough and the answer is, no. I'll stop before you reach that.'

They laughed together at their own jokes.

'Anyway,' Geraint went on, 'our flight to New York is booked; first class of course, and I've made arrangement for our mobile scooters and your wheelchair to be attended to. I must say, travelling first class makes things easy. People seem to fall over themselves to be helpful.'

'Yes, I know, but I feel so guilty being taken to the front of the queues and through the security checks. I see all those people, standing, waiting, some with small children and I feel like shouting out to them that I haven't always been rich.'

'We all feel like that,' Geraint replied. 'You are just not used to having money. If you had been born rich, you'd pass those less fortunate than us without a second thought.'

'Anyway, talking about being rich, we are booked into the Marriott, a most high-class hotel. It will be our base for four nights, with the possibility of it being more. I didn't like the attitude of the person I spoke to at first; he sounded as if he thought we were the hoi polloi. He said he'd have to check his vacancies and would get back to me. I told him he better had, or I would speak to someone with some authority. He soon changed his tune when I told him I wanted two, maybe three, of his best apartment suites. I gave him your credit card number; I hope that's all right, Bronwen.'

Bronwen gave Geraint a quick look. 'We are the hoi polloi. Mustn't get above ourselves.'

She was right. He ignored her remark and went on.

'Today, I will speak to Mr Clapworthy and tell him we need more credit cards; at least two more for you and two for me—just in case we spend more than expected. We can't risk our credit running out.'

'My word, you're a clever man, Geraint Lloyd-Davies. It seems, the older you get the cleverer you get. Nothing of this would be possible without you.' Bronwen's flattery pleased him.

'Rubbish,' he said. 'Anyway, I'm not so clever. To plan this tour of America, I've had to ask a representative from an air travel agent in Cardiff to call on me this week to give advice on the route we should take. There will be a fee for his visit, I hope you don't mind? He's coming from a travel agent's in Cardiff.'

'You can have someone from Timbuktu, if you like, Geraint. We'll ask him to stay for tea.'

The following Wednesday, Mr Julian Shears, a smart, bearded, uniformed American Airways representative, carrying an impressive briefcase came to see Geraint.

On finding 22, Queen Street, Julian Shears wondered how people, living in such a humble, terraced home, could afford the trip for which he was called to help. His mind changed when inside the palatial house and sharing Bronwen's teatime. All members of the household were there to entertain him.

Geraint ate little; he was anxious about taking the officer to his room to have the benefit of his skill to plan a tour of North America which would include all the most interesting sights.

Geraint ascended the stairs on the stair-lift with Mr Shears treading close behind him. He had forgotten his briefcase; Mary lifted it from beside the chair he had been sitting on. She went upstairs and handed it to him. She blushed a brighter pink when he thanked her.

He followed Geraint to his room where he had laid out a small-scale map of North America. Mr Shears opened his briefcase and withdrew a notepad and a pile of brochures.

Two hours' later he and Geraint withdrew from the bed-sit-cum study smiling and nodding heads. They both looked bleary-eyed and were apologising to each other for the exercise taking so long. However, the tour was satisfactorily planned, and a number of hotels had already been contacted. Geraint was well satisfied with the meeting. He was finding the task complicated, but he didn't let anyone know.

Everyone wished Mr Shears a safe journey back to Cardiff.

'I take it you have our address to send your fee note, Mr Shears. We look forward to hearing from you,' Bronwen said.

'Thank you, Mrs Dew, I do. And Mr Lloyd-Davies has my company's number, my mobile number and my home number should you wish to contact me. I've done this many times before but never for myself, unfortunately. I'm sure you'll all have a wonderful time; I envy you.'

'Be careful, Mr Shears, or Bronwen will be roping you in to coming with us,' Stella smiled a beguiling smile. She was aware of Kevin's frown of jealousy and enjoyed it.

'My wife and daughters would have something to say about that,' he smiled. 'But one day, perhaps, I'll win the National Lottery and we'll do what you're about to do.'

He was unaware that one of the people he was looking at had had all the numbers up one evening in 1998. No one enlightened him.

That evening talks of the trip continued. Bronwen took the lead.

'I wouldn't want to move away before Christmas in spite of what I said the other night of being anxious to get away from this street. I couldn't have been thinking straight. There are friends and neighbours who I want to see at Christmas, irrespective of the bad things that have happened. Anyway, we're taking a long trip and should be away for three months or more, won't we, Geraint? We'll be away from the street for a while.'

'Yes, we will.' Geraint spoke slowly as if he were working out dates in his mind. 'I know what States we'll be going to now and the routes, but more hotel and flight reservations have to be made.'

Bronwen decided she had everything she would need; the same clothes as she had taken on the Mediterranean cruise.

Stella and Mary couldn't agree with that. 'Buy some new things. You've worn your favourite suits a lot. We'd like to see you in something different.'

'Yes, Mammy, buy some new clothes. You'll be saying next that you can't afford them.'

'It's not that I can't afford them, but I just can't buy for the sake of buying. I'm not used to it, yet. I'll never be a big spender.'

'Go out with the girls and practise, then,' Geraint insisted. 'It seems they've got used to it, especially you, Mary.'

'There won't be many formal evenings as there were on the liner, mind,' Geraint warned. 'The dress will be mostly casual.'

'Well, I'll get a couple of trouser-suits like you wear, Bronwen,' Stella said. 'Something that will do for all occasions.'

'I don't care what any of you buy,' Kevin emphasised from behind a Home and Garden magazine. 'Each of us can only have two cases; one big one and one smaller one with bits and pieces. I don't want the pantomime I had when we went on that cruise.'

Stella responded. 'Yes, my lovely, you've already warned us twenty times.'

Mary dared to point out. 'Anyway, one case is enough for a man but not a woman.' Her remark brought on a few chuckles.

Geraint wasn't amused. 'Well nothing is going wrong this time, I'll tell you that for sure. I'll have planned everything down to the last minute. So, I expect you all to stick to the rules.'

'And don't forget,' Kevin went on, 'as I've reminded you already, we're going by air this time and there's a limit on the weight of your cases.'

'Not travelling first class, though,' Mary had a doubtful expression across her brow. She wondered how much she had better shed from her suitcases.

Geraint spent many hours of every day in his room. He was a busy man having total responsibility of the trip to America. Every booking or reservation he made he checked and double-checked and would check again before the departure day.

Bronwen continued to be concerned about it becoming too much for him, but he seemed to thrive on the responsibility. The bigger the challenge the more he applied himself. She decided not to interfere; he'd have a rest from the account books and his computer when they went away.

She was excited about all that was going on in her life. It was beyond her wildest dreams. She felt important; at the helm of a big project. Yet Stella and Mary won the argument about her buying new clothes. Stella was in charge of that.

They went on a number of shopping sprees and she bought a few elegant suits. She still spent more on others than she did herself. She bought Geraint some casual wear. Short sleeve check shirts, cotton slacks, sandals and underwear. He didn't know how to dress, other than if he were going to an office—then a pinstriped suit, a long sleeved, stiff-cuffed shirt, and always a tie. When on the cruise, he had asked advice from Kevin. When at home, he always asked Stella. Geraint's dress sense became a joke, but they couldn't hurt him.

Sometimes Helen went on the shopping sprees. She had a dress sense which Stella called "quiet". She always looked immaculate, but she admitted to Bronwen that her wardrobe needed sprucing up. She said she feared ending up like an overdressed tart.

Her outlook had changed since knowing the "Dew family" and having lived at their magnificent home for a few weeks. She felt she had become part of them by having met Colin. She had more to devote herself to, other than work, her home and her sons.

When they were home during the university long summer breaks, they noticed a change in her. They guessed it was because of Colin Pritchard; they were pleased.

They both could drive and shared a car. It helped when Stella told Helen that when they were all away in America, she would be pleased if she used her Volvo. It was safer being used and left on the verge opposite 22 for three months or more.

Helen was sad when the big day for their departure arrived. She'd arranged an off-duty day to help with the last-minute preparations and to wave them off.

Stacking the car with all the suitcases and two mobility scooters entertained many of the neighbours. Bronwen's wheelchair still had to be fitted into the back of the Mercedes but that would be the last to go on because she would need it. The chair had sophisticated mechanisms; designed for sitting or reclining. People had become used to seeing Kevin carry Bronwen from her chair into the car and, at first, they considered it strange.

Kisses and hugs over, farewells and good lucks wished, Bronwen's wheelchair in the back of the Mercedes and her sitting by the impatient Geraint. Helen's face was at Bronwen's window. Her remark, 'Don't worry about the house. Colin and I will look after it,' washed away the last threads of regrets Bronwen had for leaving.

Kevin switched on the engine and off they went.

'Thank the Lord for that,' Geraint said. 'Anyone would think we were making our way into the jaws of death.'

It was a Thursday in September. The roads were reasonably quiet, it being a weekday, but an early autumn mist layered the main road to London. It didn't matter; everyone was happy and excited about going aboard a jumbo jet.

'I just can't believe it,' Stella remarked. 'This time tomorrow we'll be in New York. It's a miracle and all because Bronwen is a millionaire and she wants to give it all away. I'm glad one of them is me.'

'I agree, Stella, but Bronwen's fortune can't buy back time, so we old folk will have to stop at a road-side place to answer some calls of nature.' Geraint voice reached her over the sound of the purr of the engine. He went on, 'I'll call the airport on my mobile to find out if our flight is running on schedule. I expect it is, but it won't hurt to check.'

When they were about half way to Heathrow Airport, Kevin stopped at a roadside service station.

'Good,' Mary said, 'we can all do with a stretch of legs.'

'I'll move them in the ladies loo,' Bronwen responded as Stella unfolded her wheelchair. Kevin gently lifted her out of the car and lowered her onto it.

'It's close on twelve o'clock,' Stella decided, 'After we've all been to the toilet perhaps we ought to take some lunch here.'

That was agreed and as they all sat around enjoying their choice of items from the menu, Bronwen's mobile phone rang. It startled her.

'Whoever is calling me.' She looked puzzled. She found using the mobile phone complicated and used it only when she had to.

She picked it up and called out, 'Hello!' The reply was a loud buzzing which blotted out a distance voice. 'Hello!' she repeated a little louder. 'I can't hear you.' She listened to blipping and buzzing. 'It's someone calling the wrong number. I think I heard someone telling someone to turn back. Well, that means nothing to me.'

'Switch off, Bronwen,' Geraint advised. 'I don't know of anyone who knows your mobile number. You're right; it must have been someone dialling a wrong number. I'll call the airport, now, to find out if our flight is on time.'

They forgot about the wrong number and began chatting amongst themselves about the items above the service counters. 'Too expensive, though.'

To allow everyone to carry on chatting instead of listening to him calling, Geraint moved onto the next table which was unoccupied.

He was telephoning for, what seemed, a long time. He had, in fact, failed to get through. He eventually went back to his seat at their table.

'Can't understand it,' he said, 'all the lines are engaged each time I've called. There must be a hold up of some sort. All the lines to London seemed to be jammed. Something must have happened. Nothing that can't be put right, though, I'll be bound.'

'Never mind,' Bronwen said. 'Even if the flight is delayed, we'll be taken to the first-class lounge. I've been told it's very grand. We'll have high tea there, I expect.'

Kevin teased Mary. 'High tea is when you have to stand on the table to eat, Mary.'

She believed him. 'I can't eat standing on a table, Mammy,' she whined. 'Stella will have to hand it to me.' The others laughed.

'Right, then,' Kevin got up from his chair, stretched his broad shoulders and yawned. 'Let's be off then.'

Stella took his hand. 'You yawned, Kevin. I hope you're not too tired to drive, because I can never drive through the traffic near the airport.'

'No, love, I'm all right. We're more than half way there.'

They were all seated comfortably in the car, feeling totally safe in Kevin's hands.

The river of traffic had increased.

'Strange, this isn't a rush hour,' Kevin said. 'Yet the traffic has increased in the last hour. And look at that traffic going back to Wales. The hold-up is miles long. I wonder why.'

'Well, I don't. Here we go, everybody!' Bronwen called out. 'New York, here we come!'

But they didn't get there. When Geraint had that feeling that something was wrong, his intuition was correct. Something horrible; beyond imagination had happened and that would never be forgotten. The world recognised a rule of hatred and terror.

The day was Thursday, September 11th 2001. New York would never be the same again. The evil destruction by al-Qaeda extremists made the world shudder.

Chapter 29
A Tragic End

Driving to Heathrow was delayed but Kevin was, eventually, able to steer to a stop against the curb outside the departure lounge. It took longer than expected.

'We're later than scheduled,' Geraint remarked. 'Something is seriously wrong.'

Panic surrounded them. Hundreds of people were rushing hither and thither, crowding the area. There were shouts and screams, increasing the pandemonium of fear from people who were desperate to get to New York.

An unusual number of policemen were scattered within the crowd and in areas surrounding it. Some carried fierce-looking revolver guns. Mary spotted them and became frightened.

'Uh,' she gasped. 'I've seen them on the telly.'

Stella embraced her. 'They're only pretend guns, love.' She didn't sound convincing.

A smartly-dressed woman was heard shouting at a uniformed man who was barring her from entering the departure concourse. 'My son is getting married on Saturday. I must get to the Waldoff Istoria today.'

'Go home, Madam. You won't get to New York today.' The officer was trying to calm her before striding across to where Kevin had parked the car and was standing by its boot, prepared to open it.

'Don't do that, sir!' he shouted. 'Move out of here, immediately.'

'I will when I know where to go.' Kevin tried to show calm but felt far from it. 'Where is the parking lot? We are the Mrs Bronwen Dew party. First class. We've paid to be attended to from here.'

The man looked at the impressive car and loaded roof-rack. He spotted the New York labels on one of the cases.

'You must move from here, sir. Go home. All flights to New York are cancelled until further notice. If you don't move, the police will come and move you.'

Kevin was dumbstruck. He couldn't move. In the few minutes since he stopped where he had, he became blocked in.

'How!' he shouted, pointing to the car in front and behind.

'You'll have to wait now.' The officer was flustered. The puce facial colour indicated his frustration. He ran towards a policeman who was armed with a gun. Kevin couldn't hear what the officer said to the policeman, but he guessed. The policeman called two others. They strode to the front of the line of cars and began ordering their drivers to move on.

In the Dews' car, no one spoke. Bronwen's voice broke the ominous silence. 'My God, Geraint. Is it always like this?'

'Not as far as I know,' he answered as he stared with disbelief at the bustling crowd.

He had planned for the car to arrive near the spot where Kevin had managed to stop, outside the departure lounge. He had arranged for porters to be there to unload the car, take the luggage to be weighed and security checked. In the meantime, Bronwen and her party should be taken to the first-class lounge until they were called to board their plane.

That did not happen.

Geraint risked getting out of the car and managed to get near enough to a uniformed staff-member. 'What's happened, Officer? Is it Armageddon?'

The officer's high-coloured, stressed appearance became blank. He didn't know of Armageddon. 'Aye, mate. There's been bombing in New York. That's all I know for sure. It's bad and there are no flights from here to New York until God knows when. You must move from here, now, and get yourselves home. For all we know, London will be next.'

Geraint went forward, through the automatic doors into the building, much to Kevin's annoyance. As he got into the driving seat he complained. 'He's gone in there. What if the way becomes clear and I'm told to move on?'

'He won't be long, Kevin.' Bronwen spoke as if she'd sent Geraint in. 'He's gone to get more information. New York bombed? It must be exaggerated.'

Stella added, with frustration, 'He's gone without his Zimmer. I hope he doesn't fall.'

Bronwen was right. Geraint soon returned, shaking his head and muttering. 'Dear God. What next?' He didn't speak in his usual clear tone.

'Geraint! What were you told?' Bronwen sat with bated breath.

'The World Trade Centre in New York and its surrounding buildings have been destroyed. It looks bad. And it's correct; no flights to and from New York until, God knows when. We must go home, Kevin.'

Geraint dropped his head into his hands in a way which indicated that he was badly shaken.

'Geraint, what is it?' Bronwen said. 'It's not your fault that things have to change. Our trip is on hold, and that's that.'

'There is a God,' Geraint whined. 'Can't you see, Bronwen, if I had booked our flight just one day earlier, we would have been involved in this most wicked warfare. We would have been right there, in the thick of it. We could have been injured, killed. Thank God, thank God.'

Bronwen, Mary and Stella cringed at the thought.

The cars in front had been moved on. Kevin could waste no time in moving away; a uniformed man was slapping a threatening palm on the bonnet.

'That's right,' Stella said. 'You did exactly right, Mr Lloyd-Davies. When we get out of this place of Hell, you must close your eyes and try to rest. You did exactly right.'

It was hours before the airport was an acceptable distance behind them. The traffic was deadlock. Kevin was steered into the wrong lane several times. Eventually, Geraint's sharp, ageing, bespectacled eyes saw a sign indicating the main highway to Wales. At least, they were on the road to Wales; the way home.

The roads to and from London were becoming increasingly congested. Geraint and Kevin decided it would be wise to take a minor road back. It was considered that when travelling through the countryside they were more likely to come across an inn, or other such suitable place, to stop for the night. But they were disappointed.

It was late evening and a mist hindered whatever light remained. They were tired and emotionally disturbed, due to the radical change in expected events. Their homeward journey continued in the capable hands of the stalwart Kevin.

Under the circumstances they weren't surprised to find the minor road busier than it usually was. Travellers to and from the London Airports had the same thought in mind as had Kevin and Geraint—there would be less traffic. There might have been, but Kevin was heard several times to curse the driver of a large Range Rover being too close behind him.

'If I have to make an emergency stop, that idiot behind us will end up on Bronwen's wheelchair.'

She was reclining on it at the time. 'I blooming well hope not, Kevin. I don't know him.' She meant it to be funny, attempting to cheer the atmosphere.

Stella attempted a giggle. 'Come on, all of us. Let's brighten up. We have a lovely home to go back to. And we'll be happy there until Mr Lloyd-Davies' holiday plan will go ahead.'

Those were her last words. She 'Screamed!' Fate cruelly intervened!

Destiny struck!

When driving around the bend of a narrow stretch of the road which was darkened black by overhanging trees, Kevin dipped his headlight for an oncoming lorry. In the dense shade he didn't see a monstrous tractor, illegally parked at the roadside. It had broken down earlier, in the light of day.

Why hadn't it been towed away? There were no danger or warning signs. Kevin drove into it at speed. The front of the car shattered as metal intermingled with metal. The Land Rover behind crashed into the back of the Mercedes, also at a high speed.

The oncoming lorry, in its attempt to stop, skidded into the side of the shattered Mercedes. Sharp slices of metal intermingled with those seated inside it.

Police cars and emergency ambulances arrived on a scene of horror. Stella and Kevin, on the front seat of the once-magnificent vehicle, were killed.

Geraint died of his injuries in the ambulance on its way to the nearest hospital. Bronwen and Mary survived, but were severely injured.

After many weeks of being treated and nursed in an Oxfordshire hospital they were taken by ambulance to the Sunshine Mount Nursing Home at Pendarren.

Mary was helped out of the ambulance by a carer. She was new to the home but knew of Bronwen and Mary through hearsay.

'Hello, Mary,' the carer greeted. 'Glad to be back, I expect,' Mary nodded.

She limped to the entrance on crutches. Her legs had been badly injured. She wore a bright-coloured bobble hat which was precariously place on her head to disguise the unsightly appearance of her head injury. Her shoulder length hair had been cut, and part of her head had been shaved to facilitate treatment and healing of the traumatic surgical wound. She relied on the incongruous bobble hat to hide her head and to detract from the part-healed face wounds.

Bronwen's deformed legs had been crushed between two heavy parts of car and tractor debris. They sustained multi-fractures which had been

beyond correction and necessitated amputation. She also received chest and facial injuries.

Bronwen was pushed into Willow Lounge on a dilapidated wheelchair. Her own, versatile, hi-tech electric chair had been ruined in the car crash. Her dentures, also, were destroyed in the car crash. Spittle dribbled from the side of her mouth.

The residents had been looking forward to welcoming her and Mary back. When they saw Bronwen, there were gasps and murmurs of pity and disbelief. They wouldn't have recognised her. She wasn't the beautiful, proud, upright lady they knew and expected, but a crouched, bedraggled, unkempt lady in a stained, well-worn overcoat. Her once long, shining hair was un-groomed with loose strands straggling down her face. She made no effort to push them back when looking at Tilley Tittle-tattle who was sitting in the same chair as when she last spoke to Bronwen. With sadness she looked down at the bear treads of the wheelchair. Bronwen had had deformed legs but always wore pretty shoes. Bronwen's gaze was already on the bare treads.

'Never mind, Bronwen,' Tilley remarked. 'You didn't like them legs anyway. It's good you are alive. And you don't have to worry about how your Mary will cope when you are gone. They say there's plenty of your winnings left.'

Bronwen slowly raised her head and nodded. Tilley was known for expressing herself in words that offend.

Bronwen wasn't offended. There was no emotion. Water continued to flow under Pendarren Bridge, even after Bronwen occupied Martha Tate's bed.

Please try to ignore errors.
They are not mine